Matchless Margaret

BOOK FOUR
THE HAPGOODS OF BRAMLEIGH

CHRISTINA DUDLEY

Copyright © 2021 by Christina Dudley

All rights reserved.

No portion of this book may be reproduced in any form without written permission from the publisher or author, except as permitted by U.S. copyright law.

ISBN: 978-1-963408-03-4

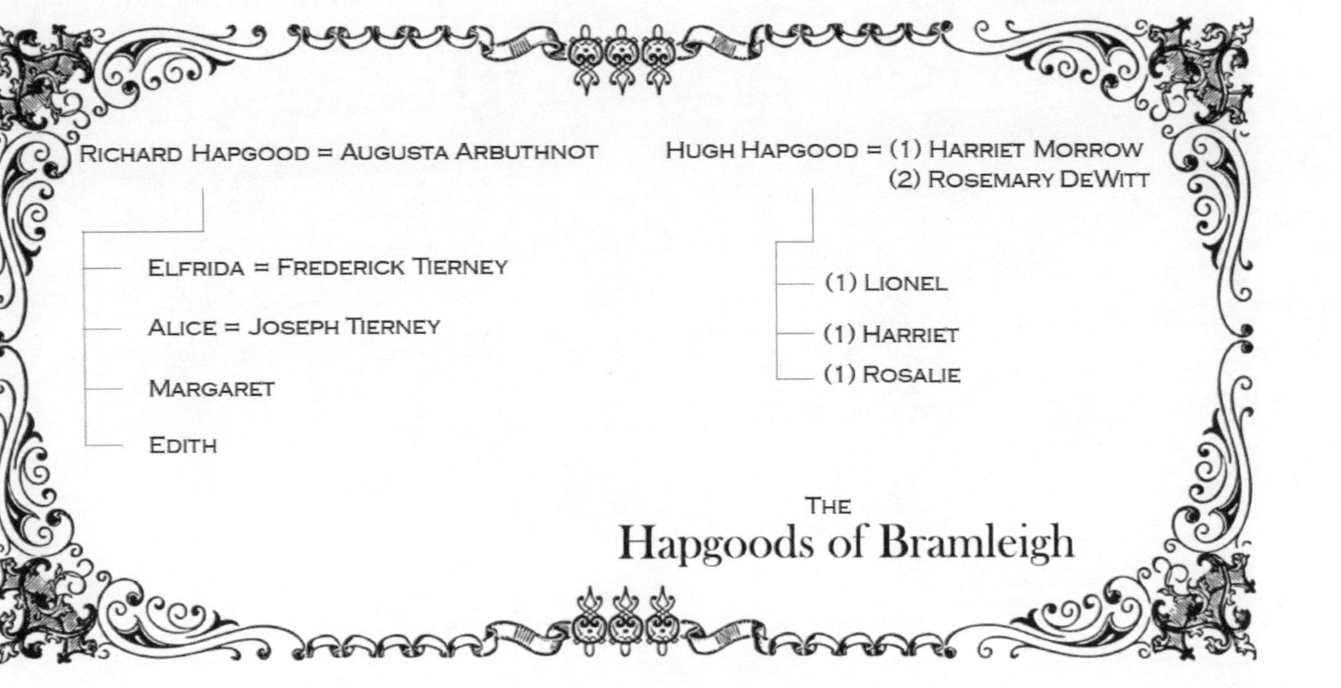

The
Hapgoods of Bramleigh

PROLOGUE

'Tis time to right all Mistakes.
—George Farquhar, *The Recruiting Officer* (1706)

Finding himself once more on *terra firma*, Dashiell Waite crutched laboriously through the dock gate, both to make way for removal of more infirm soldiers and to ride out the rolling waves his mind continued to imagine.

Lord.

What might have been—should have been—a fortnight's voyage from Lisbon to Portsmouth had stretched over the Bay of Biscay's choppy autumn waters to three weeks, reminding him once again why he had committed to His Majesty's Peninsular Army rather than the Royal Navy. Three long weeks of seasickness, which kept him green and grim to varying degrees. And yet Waite considered himself altogether fortunate. Fortunate to count still two legs to his person, however poorly the lamed one served him. Fortunate to have survived the weeks in makeshift hospital in Salamanca, where the infection nearly took him. Fortunate as well to endure the additional weeks of retreat into Portugal, a retreat characterized by limited supplies, wretched weather, and occasional skirmishes. Against all odds, he found himself on English soil again, after two years' absence.

When the ground beneath him ceased to heave, he gripped his crutches again to make his slow way through the dockyard, past hurrying sailors and observant loafers in deep discussion, past piles of timbers and a vessel in the stocks. His man would follow with the trunks, but Dashiell refused to be driven to the Wheel and Compass. No, he would make his own way, halting though it might be. After so long, it was a pleasure to direct himself, and to do so by his own efforts.

Some hours later found him in the inn's smaller parlor by the fire, tankard of ale in hand and injured leg supported by a second chair. Dashiell had only just got rid of the chatty landlord, after the man pumped him dry of news from the Peninsula, and by surly looks he managed to turn away any others who thought to approach. The country might be interminably at war, but he intended, if only for this one evening, to enjoy some peace. Setting the tankard gingerly upon the rickety table, he reached into his waistcoat for Charmaine's letter.

Its contents were already well known to him. He had read the missive several times daily since it reached him in the field hospital, to the amusement of his fellow casualties, who lay nearby and took to bantering him when he unfolded its perfumed pages.

But this was no love letter.

At least, Dashiell didn't read and re-read it for his cousin's bare two lines of affection, if affection it could be called. Charmaine Blakely was a cool-headed young lady, and, if Dashiell nearly losing a limb at Salamanca could not draw effusions from her, the contents she shared with him certainly would not.

My dear Dashiell,

We were very glad to hear that your recuperation continues apace and that you are past the greatest danger. Mama also rejoices because, as you are aware, she was never in favor of you "playing soldier," and she thanks Providence that you have been spared to return home and take up your responsibilities. She and Papa trust you will be recovered enough by spring to be married, and I find myself content with the idea.

We anticipate your return for more reasons than these, however. It pains me to say that friends in town tell us your mother has formed a new and most regrettable attachment to one Mr. Alwyn Arbuthnot, a bluff spendthrift with an ill reputation. It seems that, if not for the reluctant support given by his provincial brother-in-law, Mr. Richard Hapgood of Bramleigh, Somerset, this Mr. Arbuthnot would never be able to afford to live in town and make himself agreeable to the unwary. You know how we worried when your mother, only recently widowed then, seemed in danger of falling into the clutches of that fortune hunter Mr. Sneke! With you so far away on the Peninsula and refusing even to ask leave of Sir Edward Pakenham, all seemed lost. It was only the grace of God, says Father, that Mr. Sneke was arrested for debt and your mother forced to give him up. But what would such a deliverance avail her, cousin, if she only escaped the fat to fall into the fire? If she were now to fall prey to this Mr. Arbuthnot?

My father and mother urge you to make haste for England, as soon as your convalescence permits. They say you must take Mrs. Waite in hand and remind her of her duties to Family and to you, her son. Papa says we cannot be always running up to town to watch over her and asks how you and I will afford to marry, if your late father's wealth be diverted into so undeserving a channel?

And such a connection Mr. Arbuthnot would be! We hear the man's brother is no better, having fathered a child out of wedlock with a serving maid some years ago, and there are further scandals attached to the Hapgood relations as well—something about elopements and impersonations and I know not what. It is too dreadful to consider.

*Do come, Dashiell, and set all to rights. We depend on
you.*

Your own Charmaine.

It was, for Charmaine, a far franker letter than she usually wrote, which he took to be a measure of her desperation. If Dashiell had not raced back to England when his mother was being wooed by the impoverished Mr. Sneke, it had not been (as Charmaine accused him) because he feared asking Sir Edward's leave. It was because he failed to decipher his betrothed's hints and allusions. He failed to read between the lines. He had had no idea how serious things were, nor how resentful the Blakelys would become, when his seeming indifference left them to deal with the matter (or not deal with it, as it happened).

Dashiell had since decided that, if any man wanted to learn whether he and the woman of his choice understood each other well, he had only to remove himself from her and reduce their interactions to the written word. In their two years apart, he found Charmaine revealed little of herself on paper. Her brief letters rehearsed her rather unvarying activities: the small circle of people she saw, their repetitious conversations, which dances she had partners for, what she wore, what she purchased, whose appearance or conduct she found lacking. Any feelings for him that welled up would merit, perhaps, a half-sentence, and any criticisms of him she wanted to express or things she wanted to urge upon him were (as in this letter), attributed safely to her parents.

Had it always been thus?

His own attempts to share more of himself through his letters had been politely ignored. Once he had written of a dream he had, where he had been on a galloping horse, Charmaine riding pillion behind him. He felt her hands slipping from where they gripped his waist, but the more he urged her to hold tight, the more they slackened. "What do you suppose it meant, my dear?" he wrote. "I hope it only expressed fears that you might slip from me. We are apart, but that need not prevent us being open with each other." The usual weeks passed before his letter reached her and the usual additional weeks before her reply came to hand. When it did, he opened it eagerly, only to find her familiar inventory of topics, and one short allusion to his concern: "I hope you are sleeping better. The weather should be cooler there now."

It did not take many months of this to realize they would grow no closer during their time apart. And she might be content to marry him, but this widening distance had not hastened his return. How had he never remarked that Charmaine rarely came straight out and said what she meant? Did she even understand him, or he her? Did she hold him at arm's length because she was still angry with him for going?

"We will do better when we see each other face to face," Dashiell told himself. And, speaking of faces, Charmaine was gifted with a lovely one, one that Dashiell's miniature of her could not do justice to.

His intended's family might accuse him of "playing soldier," but they would have disparaged any venture of his that required leaving them, much less one that involved foreign lands or rough company or danger, and serving in Wellington's Peninsular Army encompassed them all.

He had relished every minute of it.

Lisbon. Bussaco, in the mountains of Portugal. Almeida, Badajoz, Ciudad Rodrigo. These were not merely names on a map printed in the newspaper, read from the comforts of home. These were places he camped, marched, fought. And serving under Sir Edward, brother-in-law to Wellington, had even brought him within the orbit of the great man himself.

No, he had not missed home, these two years. Truth be told, he could barely say he missed Charmaine. She had been fresh from the schoolroom when he went, and schoolroom misses held little interest for a bold young man beginning life.

But all good things must come to an end.

When his wound at Salamanca put him out of commission, nearly his first thought upon regaining consciousness was how happy the Blakelys would be. They would not have wished him actually dead, of course, but anything *short* of death that forced him home and back into the channel of life they ordained for him—well, that could not be otherwise than welcome. Now that the Frenchies had almost blown his leg off, Dashiell Waite would return to England where he belonged. He would take up the duties of Chardis under his uncle Matthew; he would marry his cousin Charmaine, to whom he had been engaged from her cradle; the happy couple would divide their time between Chardis and London; and Dashiell would, he supposed, molder away for the rest of his existence. And before these enticements became reality, he must apparently save the Waite fortune from rogues like this Alwyn Arbuthnot.

Perhaps the interminable voyage from Lisbon had not been interminable enough.

"The landlord says to keep to myself, if I insist on forcing my way into this room," came a voice.

Waite glanced up, a rebuff on his lips, but it was Haworth! Haworth, who had but one arm left to him and who had shared the ordeal of the field hospital.

"Charles!" he cried, struggling up to clap him on the shoulder. "What are you doing here? You sailed a week before me."

"And had even worse luck, I suspect. We arrived but yesterday. I could scarce believe it when I heard the *Merete* was in. What was losing a paltry left arm, compared to those seas, eh? Fortunately, turning green complemented my ginger whiskers."

The man grinned at him, and Dashiell found himself grinning back as he sank once more into his seat. He nodded toward a neighboring armchair. "You'd better take that one. With only the one arm left, you need to cosset it."

"That's right," agreed Haworth. "I'm not offering up any more appendages for Marmont's target practice." He settled with a luxurious groan. "Now if the man will just bring me my chop and ale. It's hard to get his attention when he has to kiss the shoes of high-and-mighties like yourself first. But I see you've eaten and are comfortable now, with time to peruse your beloved's letter for the thousandth time. I'd think you'd grow tired of reading what a handsome dog you are and how she pines for you."

Dashiell gave a mirthless chuckle. "That might get wearisome, I grant, but now that we have left the hungry ears of our fellow soldiers behind, I don't mind telling you the letter has nothing to do with any of that."

"Indeed? What else do plighted lovers discuss? I wouldn't know, sadly. Nor am I likely to, now." He gave his empty sleeve a flip, accompanied by a dramatic sigh.

"My heart bleeds," said Dashiell, taking another sip from his tankard. It so happened Haworth's aunt had purchased his commission, and, in his absence, both the accommodating woman and her son had also seen fit to die. While Haworth lay in danger of his life, the news that he was suddenly the recipient of an estate bringing thousands of pounds per annum did much to speed his recovery, and Dashiell did not doubt the ladies who ignored him heretofore would find his lanky form and ginger coloring more winning now, no matter how many arms he might be lacking.

Interrupting his thoughts, the barmaid tripped in with his companion's food and drink, and Dashiell kept his gaze lowered so he would not have to notice her simper and overwarm manner.

When she had gone, Haworth was grinning again. "I might as well have been invisible. But perhaps she ignored me to spare me embarrassment. That unaffectionate young lady of yours better look to it you aren't stolen from under her nose."

"I'm more likely to be swept up by the press gangs than by a young lady, if I stay here too long," Dashiell countered. "But I don't mean to pass more than the night, in any event." He waved the letter at Haworth. "Miss Blakely writes to share bad news, as it happens. She says my mother is being preyed upon by a fortune hunter, and would I please come home to manage the situation."

Haworth whistled. "I say, Dash. That is indeed bad news. Can anything be done?"

"Possibly. If she hasn't already married the man."

"A good couple months have already passed since that letter was written, however," Haworth pointed out. "If the deed be not done yet, it is about to be, and you had better act fast."

Dashiell shrugged. "If it is too late, there is nothing I can do about it. But I have already decided that—if it be not too late—I will plead my maimed and aching leg and steal my mother away to Bath for the winter. Her pursuer, who they say has barely the funds to maintain a London establishment, will surely not be able to afford a second home. He will therefore be obligated to besiege some other wealthy woman closer at hand."

His listener speared his chop with his fork and gnawed a bite from it, chewing thoughtfully.

"Brilliant, Waite. The very plan," said Haworth after he swallowed. "And Bath! I, too, was considering nursing my wounds there this winter. My sainted aunt's home is but a few miles distant in Bradford. I could easily live in town and run back and forth to settle matters." He attempted another bite, but the chop spun away and flopped back onto the dish.

"For God's sake," said Dashiell. Leaning over, he snatched the plate from Haworth and made quick work sawing up the chop into manageable bites. "Come to Bath by all means, but you will have to hire yourself an attendant of some sort because I have no intention of playing nursemaid."

"Nonsense. You know you love me. But who will look after your own limping self?"

Dashiell's brow rose. "If I cannot lower myself with dignity into the waters, I will have my mother and Charmaine to take pity on me."

"Well, unless your mother boasts the strength of an ox," returned Haworth, chewing, "it will require the both of them, I imagine. Take it from the man who helped carry your stretcher off the field, when I had two arms to my name: you, Dashiell Waite, are no feather."

CHAPTER ONE

Tranquillity [and] Satisfaction,..being the natural Consequences of prudent Management of Ourselves, and our Affairs.
—Joseph Butler, *Analogy of Religion* (1736)

All who knew her agreed: Miss Margaret Hapgood would never marry. The reasons for this conviction varied. It was not that she was without attractions—after passing her coltish years, where she outgrew her sisters and approached the height of her father, she then gained softness and a measure of grace. Though she was no beauty like her eldest sister Elfrida (whom, in truth, few women could hope to match), Margaret had hair the gold-brown of ripe barley and candid hazel eyes which drew the gaze upward, away from her too-wide mouth and too-thin nose.

No, it was not Margaret's appearance that doomed her, went the general opinion. And it was not even the Hapgoods' financial situation. Money matters at Bramleigh had improved in the previous four years, thanks to the successful marriages of Margaret's older sisters and to her parents' health concerns. Margaret's father the squire was a quieter man than formerly, having recently suffered his second "spell," in consequence of which he reluctantly let pass the keeping of the hounds to his neighbor Lord Marlton. And a host of imaginary ailments had kept Margaret's mother abed (and not spending money) for nearly a decade. The Richard Hapgoods of Bramleigh might never be wealthy again, but they had clambered from the pit of penury and had lately even afforded both a drawing master for Margaret's younger sister Edith and an increase in wages for Bramleigh's three overworked servants.

Was it then Miss Margaret's own personality which stood in her way? Those familiar with her owned that she was too plainspoken, and—worse—too quick to speak those bald thoughts.

"We lose nothing by asking her outright if she would like ever to marry," Elfrida observed to her sister Alice, as she stitched away at little Freddie's long clothes. "She would be sure to answer truthfully."

Alice swung the clip of the brass microscope outward and removed the slide of lace-fly wing she had been inspecting. "I did ask her in my last letter, Elfie. You remember—she was angry because Cousin Hetty said she ought to marry Mr. Norman DeWitt, since no one ever knew what he was thinking because he never spoke, and everyone always knew what Margaret was thinking because she spoke it whether it ought to be said aloud or not."

Elfrida chuckled at this, her violet eyes mischievous behind their spectacles. "I remember. I don't know why she flew into the boughs about it. Hetty certainly wasn't the first to have that notion. Well, then, how did Margaret reply?"

Alice frowned and placed the slide back in its case. "She didn't, now that I consider it. I have her letter here somewhere—oh, dear—it was such a short one that I believe I used the reverse side to draw upon. Here it is! See there? She says, 'I have forgiven Hetty only because I am far too busy with the care and running of Bramleigh and looking after my father and mother to bother with trifles. She and Lionel have always lived to tease.'"

"A more apt description of Lionel than of Hetty," said Elfrida. "But you are right—she does not answer directly, and that is most unlike our Margaret. What will become of the girl? I suppose she *could* marry Norman DeWitt eventually—although she would probably have to propose to him, rather than the other way 'round. I don't think he would mind her blurts and frankness, or, if he did, he would never tell her so because it would require opening his mouth."

Perhaps it was due to Margaret's usual "blurts and frankness" or to the distance from Buckinghamshire to Somerset that her older sisters failed to perceive she had indeed answered Alice's question. Because the main obstacle to Miss Margaret Hapgood ever abandoning the single state was that she considered herself *indispensable* at Bramleigh. There could be no doubt that, in the past four years, she had grown into her role as mistress, and neither the squire nor his indolent wife interfered with her smooth running of household affairs. Not that either parent spent much time under their third daughter's eye or thumb. The squire was still given to wandering out of doors, trailed by his remaining hound Caractacus, who, with advancing age, now kept tamely enough by his master's side. And Mrs. Hapgood, of course, was content to rule the smaller domain of her bedchamber.

No, it was left to the larger community to shake their heads over the situation, and among the anxious were the heir to Bramleigh, Mr. Hugh Hapgood, and his wife Rosemary, who lived in the nearby village of Patterton.

"I feel I am to blame," Rosemary admitted to her husband, as they returned from a supper at Bramleigh one autumn evening. A supper in which Margaret monitored her father's pork consumption and reduced the would-be footman Hal to scarlet-faced mortification when he knocked over a glass in serving the soup. "It was I, after all, who taught her household management. With our girls and Edith in lessons with their governess, and Margaret left to shift for herself, I felt I could not leave her helpless—"

As no one was about, they were holding hands, and Hugh gave her arm a swing. "You to blame, my dear? I never once recall you telling *me* I'd 'eaten quite enough' or 'wouldn't Mr. Lewis be disappointed to find I'd gained a stone instead of lost one, as he recommended.'" Her husband's imitation of Margaret's reproaches made Rosemary laugh because she could not picture such a growl emerging from the young lady.

"Nor have you ever frozen the children with an icy glare when they were clumsy or made our servants wish themselves sunk into the earth like poor Hal," Hugh continued. "No, my love. You taught Margaret useful skills, but the manner in which she *wields* them as weapons is entirely her own contrivance. And what would have become of them all, had you left her in total ignorance of how to manage the household?"

"I imagine Mrs. Hapgood would have been forced to put aside her ailments and rise to the occasion," answered Rosemary. "The squire, perhaps, might have attempted to fill the gap, but I don't suppose he knows a tea chest from a tablecloth."

"Precisely. And you are optimistic in thinking Richard could ever compel Augusta to do her duty. He has never managed to make her do anything she didn't want to, after all."

Rosemary carried his hand to her face and pressed her cheek against the back of it. "It's because you Hapgood men are too kind, too apt to indulge your wives."

"If your brothers Roscoe and Norman were anything like Augusta's Alec and Alwyn, you would find me tyrant enough," Hugh countered, but his eyes were smiling. "At least, I hope you would. How long has Richard subsidized the brothers' house in town? And Alec's cast-off woman and her child? And both men's idleness, which leads to all manner of mischief?"

"Too long," she sighed. "It is too bad, and Mr. Lewis says we must all be careful to keep the squire calm, now that he has had two of his episodes. And surely, if Margaret were to marry and be carried off who-knows-where, Bramleigh would the sooner be brought to wrack and ruin. But I grieve, nevertheless, that she is so eager to carry a burden not intended for her."

Here her husband halted and, tugging on her hand, drew Rosemary to him. "And you, dear love, are not intended to add Margaret and my cousins to your own burden. The girl is barely twenty. She has plenty of time to discover whether ruling Bramleigh be her highest ambition, especially if her subjects ever begin to revolt, which I suspect they might."

"Years slip by more quickly than you think," she answered dryly, remembering her own twenties passing in a twinkling. "And, should something happen to the squire in that time, I would be happier knowing she would always have her own establishment."

"You refer, of course," rumbled Hugh, "to when I inherit Bramleigh and eject forcibly whichever of the Richard Hapgoods remain."

Rosemary laughed again. "I know you will be kind and just, but you will be master all the same."

"And as master you imagine I will not assist my cousin's wife and daughters in finding a new dwelling? A cozy cottage, such as we now enjoy?"

"I am certain you will." She squeezed his arm as they set in motion again. "You comfort me. Very well: let Margaret marry or not marry, as she wishes. And who can say? Perhaps she would enjoy reigning over a cozy cottage as much as she does Bramleigh."

"More, I should say," Hugh returned. "For then she need never fear, as her father does, that her parasitic uncles will descend like locusts and eat them out of house and home. No, Rosemary. Have no fear for Margaret. Rather, it is Alec and Alwyn Arbuthnot who must dread the blankness of a future without the squire's support."

Completely unaware of being an object of conversation and concern, Margaret saw to the shutting up of the house for the night. The prayers had been read by her father from a passage she marked, the kitchen had been inspected for cleanliness and the tasks for the next day discussed, and Hal had been counseled one more time on what was expected of him when he waited at table.

"I was pleased you did not simply march in and *dump* the food upon the table, as you are wont to do when we have no guests," she told him, ignoring his sullen expression, "and I think—apart from upsetting Mrs. Hugh Hapgood's glass—you have improved marvelously, considering you prefer tasks out of doors and not in company. I do not expect we will ever do much entertaining, but, with a little more practice and earnest effort, Hal, I feel you might not be ashamed to serve even those not related to us."

"Miss," was his only response. He dragged his foot along the flagstone floor to avoid her gaze until, with a pursing of her lips, she dismissed him.

Taking up her candle, Margaret gave the kitchen a last glance before marching up the back stairs. Snoring reverberated from her father's chamber, and no light peeped from under her mother's door, but she could see Edith had not yet retired. With a crisp knock Margaret announced herself and poked her head into her little sister's bedroom.

"Still awake? I suppose you think candles are ten a penny. And you know you shouldn't draw in dim light. Do you want to end in wearing spectacles like Elfie?"

"I am fifteen. Elfie's eyesight was already poor by my age," replied Edith, but she laid aside her sketch.

Leaping on the bed with an undignified bounce, Margaret reached for it. "Why, it's us! I don't remember sitting for you."

"You didn't. But I have enough sketches of you to copy one. See? This was from when Elfie and Alice were visiting. You were holding little Freddie, but I've made him into a flower basket. And for Hetty I just used one of the thousand drawings I have of her. In this one she looked the least cross."

"Hmm," said Margaret, studying her hair in the composition. "Very nice. But who is it for? Your private collection? I don't suppose Papa wants a picture with Hetty in it, and I don't suppose Cousin Hugh requested a picture of *us*."

Margaret couldn't be certain, but she thought a ripple of embarrassment washed over her sister's face. "Lionel asked for it."

"Lionel!"

"To take with him to Oxford in October," Edith said shortly. "I still have to add Rosie, of course. I'll put her *here*, on the other side of Hetty."

Margaret frowned. "I'm not certain I like the idea of us hanging on a wall in his room, for all those other young men to see."

"We won't be. He said he would—keep it in his trunk, where only he could take it out and look at it."

"Oh. I *suppose* that would be permissible, then. My! I can't say I understand. If girls were allowed to go away to university, I should never ask for a picture of Lionel and Hetty and Rosie to sigh over."

"Who said there would be any sighing?" demanded Edith, snatching the sketch from her sister and rolling it up. "Besides, if you were ever to leave us, Margaret, I would more likely draw you a picture of Bramleigh, with Button and Dorcas and Hal and the family standing outside, looking eager to do your bidding. Whenever you felt low or homesick, you might gaze upon it and remember the joys of ordering us about."

"You!" cried Margaret, giving her a shove that nearly rolled the smaller Edith from the bed. But she was not entirely displeased. In truth, Margaret adored ordering others about. "I suppose you think Bramleigh could run itself! Everyone ought to be grateful I've proved so capable. Besides, the servants can't complain. The very definition of a servant is you must do what your mistress tells you."

"Even if she tells you in an onerous fashion?" Edith protested. "Which you most certainly do. And nowhere do I recall the definition of a 'sister' including any vow of obedience."

"That's because you should have looked under 'younger sister,'" retorted Margaret.

For the longest time, the age gap between them, along with Edith's smallness and docile nature, kept down any rebellion, but even Edith could show signs of resenting Margaret's authority. Signs such as struggling to her knees, taking hold of a pillow, and swinging it at Margaret's head. It hit her sister's face squarely with a satisfying *whoof*, sending hairpins and feathers flying, and Margaret emerged sputtering with surprise and indignation.

"Why—you little—!"

"You shouldn't have pushed me!"

"I only did so because you deserved it. *Entirely.*"

"No, you deserved it," insisted Edith. "And not only for nearly tumbling me from the bed. You've become a perfect termagant, Margaret, and I imagine if I gave each member of the family and every servant at Bramleigh a pillow, they would all delight to hit you in the face with it."

"Oh? And where would everyone be without me, I should like to know?"

"Here. But happier. Because you've grown insufferable."

"Nonsense. You would all be in despair. Have you forgotten what confusion reigned after Elfie and Alice married? Button would serve us the same meal three days running. Dorcas broke things and forgot things and neglected things. Hal was always napping, if he could even be found. Neither Papa nor Mama could be troubled with household management, and, if not for Mrs. Hugh Hapgood's kindness and my own aptitude—"

"Yes, yes," sighed her sister at the twice-told tale. "So you have said. If you have nothing new to contribute, I think I'll go to sleep now. Remember, Margaret, candles are not ten a penny." Leaning over, she blew out her light and wriggled under her coverlet, shutting her eyes tightly.

Margaret gave an offended sniff, but then she shrugged. Some people could not bear the truth.

Twenty minutes later, when her hair was brushed and braided, her prayers run through, and a mental list of what must be accomplished the next day composed, she climbed into her own bed and put out the candle.

Her last thought, before she fell into a contented sleep, was that she must ask her papa to show her the rent books because she was certain he was not as scrupulous in their maintenance as he ought to be. As she herself would be, that is. Why, think—if they were able now to afford Edie's drawing master, what else might they afford, if only better records were kept?

Chapter Two

Eagre feeding foode doth choke the feeder.
—Shakespeare, *Richard II* (1597)

Margaret's happy plans for expanding her sovereignty were rudely interrupted by Death.

Not her own death, to be sure, but that of her uncle Mr. Alec Arbuthnot. On the very same night, some 150 miles to the east, Alec Arbuthnot made an after-hour visit to the kitchen of the London townhouse he shared with his brother Alwyn.

One of the footmen had been laid low by the grippe, which meant the man's portion of the evening meal went unclaimed, and it was the thought of this roasted half rabbit that drew Alec down the stairs to his doom. He was a roundish man, from his round, bald head to his expanding circumference, to which these midnight raids on the cook's stores added.

Under a cloth lay the innocent remnant. Seizing it, and forgetting altogether how many little, brittle, ticklish bones rabbits have, Alec crammed a generous portion in his mouth, chewed, attempted to swallow, felt a hunk of bone-laced meat lodge crosswise in his gorge, staggered around for a few truly awful moments, and was discovered the following morning by the scullery maid.

The special messenger arrived at Bramleigh with a letter addressed to Mrs. Hapgood, and Margaret, after scrambling for a coin to pay him off, dashed upstairs with Edith at her heels.

Mrs. Hapgood, to no one's surprise, fainted dead away at the mere mention of a special messenger, so Margaret felt no qualms in opening the letter herself, reading it aloud while Edie fanned and patted their mother to revive her.

My dear Augusta,
You must bear up, dear sister, for I have a painful communication to make to you, and I fear for the blow I deliver here to your affectionate heart. Our brother Alec is lost to us! He was discovered within this hour, collapsed and stone cold on the flagstones in the kitchen, a rabbit hindquarter in his hand. We can only pray his suffering was brief.

This event could not have come at a worse time, for I am sorry to say Alec had accumulated some debts that he intended to repay by holding to the strictest econo-my. Now the creditors will descend, and, I fear, with-

out a sizeable donation from your husband Richard, I may not be able to retain the town-house. At such times as these, Family is the only comfort, Augusta. Do write immediately, enclosing a letter of credit from the squire, if possible. I would come in person to make this request, but I am overwhelmed with grief and the death arrangements.

Your loving, remaining brother,
Alwyn Arbuthnot

Margaret came near to fainting herself, at this bundle of news, and Edie abandoned attempts to resuscitate their mother to come and read over her sister's shoulder. When each had done so twice through, they stared at each other, horror-stricken. While Uncle Alec had never been a great favorite, they knew Mrs. Hapgood would take the news of her brother's passing very ill, and, as for their father and the demand for a letter of credit—!

"What will we tell Mama?" whispered Edith, tugging Margaret into the passage. "Oh, dear. Oh, dear."

"We will have to tell her the truth," Margaret whispered back, pulling the door to behind her. "We must! But perhaps I—will begin by saying Uncle Alec is taken ill. Yes. And then, maybe in another day or two, we can say he has died."

"But our uncle Alwyn is expecting a response 'immediately'!"

"Yes, yes." Margaret wrung her hands. "Very well. We will say he is taken ill, and then—perhaps by this evening?—we will announce he has died. She always keeps to her room anyway, so she would never know whether another letter arrived or not."

Forgetting that she had resented her older sister's authority, Edith looked to her now in their extremity, and they found themselves clutching each other. "It will be very bad, Margaret. Mama is so terribly fond of both her brothers."

"Don't I know it? But it will only be more screaming and fainting and dithering, after all, and she has done that always. It's just a matter of degrees. No—no, Edith—it's Papa who will be the greater trouble."

"Do you suppose?" asked Edith. "I cannot think Papa will be heartbroken to lose Uncle Alec."

"Of course he won't be! I think he dislikes Uncle Alec even more than Uncle Alwyn, ever since Uncle Alec got that Seven Dials innkeeper's daughter with child. No, I mean Papa will be beside himself with rage when he hears Uncle Alwyn wants a letter of credit!"

Edith's grip on Margaret's upper arms tightened so that Margaret thought her hands would go numb. "Yes, you're right. But Mr. Lewis said Papa is to be kept calm at all times, lest he have another episode—a *fatal* episode this time."

"I know—and this will *kill* him," fretted Margaret. Her own face was rather scarlet. "Those worthless uncles! What utter nonsense, Uncle Alwyn saying Uncle Alec meant to keep strict economies! Neither one of them knows the meaning of economy! Elfrida has been saying for years now that they must be made to stand on their own feet, but nobody listened—"

"Could we ask Elfie if her Frederick would write a letter of credit?" suggested Edith.

Margaret bit her lip, thinking, but then she shook her head. "We haven't time for all that. And I'm certain Elfie would refuse even to ask her husband because she so disapproves of our uncles. No. No. I must come up with a solution myself. Today. *Now.*"

Edith held her breath, her brown eyes searching her sister's hazel ones. Margaret shook herself loose from Edie's grasp, that she might pace back and forth, carefully avoiding the third floorboard, which creaked. Her mother would likely come to shortly, so there was no time to be lost.

"Papa must write to Uncle Alwyn and say there is no money to give him, which is no more than the truth—"

"I might give up my lessons with Mr. Eldridge," proposed Edith dismally.

"Never! Why should you have to lose your drawing master because our uncles could not live within their income?" Margaret snapped. "And I suspect Uncle Alec's debts amount to far more than the allowance Papa makes Mr. Eldridge. No—more drastic measures are called for. Uncle Alwyn must break the lease of the town-house. He must sell what furnishings he may to pay the creditors, and he must—he must come live at Bramleigh."

Edith's eyes grew round as guineas. "Live at Bramleigh! I don't know but Papa might rather give him a letter of credit."

Sighing, Margaret had to concede this. The squire and her uncle permanently under one roof would be insupportable to either man. But it was equally unthinkable to Margaret that, after the struggles to restore the family finances, they should permit her Arbuthnot uncles to sink them again, possibly for all time.

"Well, he cannot remain in London," she said again. "Town is far too expensive. Perhaps if he were to choose somewhere else? Cousin Hugh might suggest something in Crawley."

This was as far as Margaret got with her plans before they heard their mother's moans through the door, and they were compelled to rejoin her.

Even announcing her brother Alec's supposed illness brought on the swoons and shrieks and laments Margaret predicted. For all her tendency to drama, Augusta Hapgood truly adored her brothers, and she regretted she had no stronger means to express her concern than the ones rather threadbare from everyday use. But sincerity lent her swoons, shrieks and laments volume and endurance, and this performance led regrettably to the premature end of Margaret's patience. Had she not been so worried about the situation as a whole, she might have kept her temper and held to her original timeline, not announcing Alec's death until after supper. As it was, after a mere two hours of provocation, Margaret escaped the room to fetch her mother some tea, and, when she returned, she said bluntly that another messenger was come, and Alec Arbuthnot was no more.

"Margaret!" cried Edith with a frown. Not that Margaret could hear her over her mother's prolonged shriek, but she could read her sister's lips.

So violent was Mrs. Hapgood's response that it drew even the squire, who had returned from his daily ride and was feeding Caractacus tidbits from the sideboard. The doctor Mr. Lewis had told the squire countless times that he was to maintain serenity in his speech and movements, that his heart not be overtaxed, but Mr. Lewis had known Richard Hapgood long enough to know he only gave the prescription for form's sake, and the squire's fate must be left to heaven.

"What's this, girls? Augusta?" he demanded, bursting into his wife's chamber after having stomped up the stairs. His ruddy face was ruddier than usual, and beads of sweat dotted his brow.

"Oh, Richard!" cried his wife. "My beloved Alec! My beloved Alec is no more!"

Such an astonishing announcement required some minutes of repetition and hysterics and incredulous questions and doleful answers before it could be understood. But once it was, both girls turned away, that they need not witness the relief and delight flash across their father's face before he pasted on an expression of appropriate gravity. Dragging Mrs. Hapgood's wheel-chair across the floor, he took a heavy seat in it and reached to grasp her fluttering hand while Margaret proposed a course of action.

"Don't you think Uncle Alwyn had better give up the house in town, Papa?" she prodded. "He does not say how much debt Uncle Alec left, and I imagine Uncle Alwyn has debt of his own, so if they were to give up the house and sell the furnishings, the amount might possibly be covered. Or perhaps enough funds could be raised in that way to put off the creditors for now."

The squire was nodding, but when he raised his gaze to hers, she realized he was still dazed and only half comprehending. "You don't mean to say, Margaret, that you think your uncle must live at *Bramleigh*?" he croaked.

"Of course not, Papa," she assured him hastily. "I know that would make none of us happy."

"What do you mean? It would make *me* happy!" wailed Mrs. Hapgood. "My grief! I cannot bear it. To lose Alec, and then not have Alwyn beside me? Oh! Oh! My heart races and I feel that pressure upon my chest. Edith, darling, send Hal for Mr. Lewis at once."

"Where should he live, then?" asked the squire, ignoring his wife and looking much reassured. Nor did Edith obey her mother straightaway because, if matters were to be settled on the instant, she did not want to miss it.

"He must come to Bramleigh, or I will surely go into a precipitous decline," insisted Mrs. Hapgood, sitting up in annoyance. "You remember that one winter, Richard, when you had all given me up for lost? That all began with such a pressure as I feel now."

"He had better not come here, however," Margaret replied, taking her mother's other hand. "You know Mr. Lewis said Papa must not have excitement or mental disturbance—and you must admit, Mama, our uncles usually manage to upset Papa."

"Alas! Alec will never upset your papa ever, ever again!" sobbed Mrs. Hapgood.

Perhaps. But the fact of his passing might achieve the same end, Margaret thought. The squire swabbed his forehead with his handkerchief and did indeed appear on the verge of a spell, and she felt for the first time that having the family look to her for absolutely everything did have its drawbacks in a crisis.

"Well, then." She lay her mother's hand back on the coverlet, that she might pace as she had in the passage. "Let me see…Uncle Alwyn must give up the town-house and sell the furnishings. That much is agreed upon. It would not be good for Papa's health for Uncle Alec to live at Bramleigh, and it would not be good for Mama's health to be separated from him at present, grief-stricken as she is."

"That's right," said both the squire and Mrs. Hapgood in unison, their eyes on their capable daughter.

"So," Margaret continued, tapping the air with a thoughtful finger, "Uncle Alwyn must have some small establishment of his own, only not so dear a one as the town-house, because he must be able to pay for it with whatever remains after the debts, or, if nothing remains after the debts, with whatever small allowance Papa can continue to pay out."

Here the squire grumbled at the reminder of how his brothers-in-law had always sucked the lifeblood from him with their demands, and Mrs. Hapgood burst into fresh tears, hiccupping, "My Alec will never need an allowance again! And Alwyn—so dashing and gay—to be buried alive in some country lodging! He will surely pine away, and if I lose them both, I will not be long behind them."

"I had thought your cousin Hugh might suggest some place in Crawley, Papa, only that might be too near London to keep Uncle Alwyn from temptation," said Margaret. "It must be someplace modest, in any event. You had better write to Uncle Alwyn these plans, and say you will continue his allowance on these terms, if that sounds amenable to you."

Another grunt from her father, but Mrs. Hapgood sat up even straighter. "Richard—why may not Alwyn add Alec's allowance to his own? Alec has no more need of it, and it will all come to the same thing. That way his new establishment need not be so very small and retired and mean!"

"Why I am paying grown men an allowance, as if they were sons of mine and it was owed to them—" began the squire.

"Because they are our flesh and blood!" cried his wife.

"It must needs be, for now, Papa," Margaret resumed hastily, "because whatever home he finds must be large enough to admit Mama paying him a visit, as a comfort to her." (Here Mrs. Hapgood ripped her hand away from her husband to clap for joy.)

"And I think—yes—it had better be somewhere where there is some small social life because—well—in the longer term, Uncle Alwyn must find other means of support."

"Other means?" echoed her father. "What other means?"

"I mean to say a *wife*, Papa. He must find a wife with a tidy little fortune and live off her. It is past time, I daresay."

"He will have no trouble with that," breathed Mrs. Hapgood. "Alwyn has ever been irresistible to ladies."

"They've resisted him well enough to this point," her daughter retorted. "Either their eyes are opened before he can secure them, or he himself cries off. Whatever the cause, neither of those things must happen again. He must marry the next lady of sufficient means who will have him."

"Where will he find this lady, if he could not find one in London?" was her father's next question. "He had better not live near us because we have no one in the county, now that Miss Birdlow is married to her cousin."

Margaret and Edith exchanged a glance, knowing their uncle had had no more chance of marrying a viscount's daughter than he had of flying to the moon. "Indeed," agreed Margaret, "so somewhere else."

"Taunton?" suggested Edith.

"Taunton! Whom should he ever meet there?" scoffed Mrs. Hapgood.

"Clifton, then?"

The squire scowled. "It's a pretty pass we've come to, if we must be connected with widows of slave-traders."

"Richard! Who said anything about slave-traders?"

"Who do you think has the funds to build those elegant houses in Clifton, Augusta?"

"Well, if the houses are so elegant, I don't suppose you would permit him to live there in the first place."

While her family bickered, Margaret seated herself at the desk by the window and gathered pen and paper. She could draft a letter and have the squire copy it in his own hand. He would have to decide anyway what to do about the requested letter of credit. Shaking the ink bottle to make certain its contents had not dried out and frowning at the pen, which would want mending soon, she took a deep breath and began to write.

CHAPTER THREE

The good old rule…the simple plan,
That they should take, who have the power,
And they should keep who can.
—Wordsworth, *Rob Roy's Grave* (1803)

Alwyn Arbuthnot chose Bath.

"Bath!" roared the squire, even as Mr. Lewis counted the pulse at his wrist and scolded, "Richard, Richard. Calm yourself."

"Bath! And not a word of, 'Thank you, brother, for continuing to support my most unworthy self'? Nor the least attempt to choose a humbler location, out of shame for his dependence? No! No, Lewis, he chooses Bath—Lansdown Place, he suggests, as if I owe him any more than a stall in Cheap Street!—and he has the gall to say it is for Augusta's comfort! Suppose I decide not to send my wife to him for the winter, after all? Would he also like his own carriage? How else may I add to his comfort and subtract from my own? If there remains anything, he will demand it of me. Nay—assume it already his!"

"There, there," returned the doctor mildly. "I was not aware Augusta's presence was so material to your well-being, after all this time. A change of air and the solace of her remaining brother would not be amiss at present, and you have already promised her. Beyond her usual litany of ailments, she does seem downcast, Richard."

"Well, then, why may she not comfort herself in Bridgwater or Minehead, as well as Bath? Alwyn might take a lodging there at half the cost, as we proposed."

"But Papa," broke in Margaret, sweeping into the room with Edith, both laden with bundles of clothing and mourning trimmings, "would not Bath better suit our purposes? I am sure there are more potential wives for him in Bath than Bridgwater."

"Nonsense. In Bridgwater he can marry some brickmaker's daughter."

"But how will he *meet* her?" Margaret insisted. "If Uncle Alwyn must find a wife in a new place where he knows no one, it would be helpful if the place offered opportunities to meet others. In Bath he can wheel Mama around and even take her to a concert, if he can persuade her."

"But suppose the ladies imagine it is his wife he is wheeling about?" Edith pointed out, looking up from the black ribbon she was weaving through a sleeve.

Margaret frowned. "He will just have to be loud about it every-where he goes. 'My sister Augusta' and such. Be sure to tell him so, Papa."

"It is not decided yet!" bellowed her father, striking the mantel-piece in emphasis. "I understood that, in addition to finding a wife, he must now practice economy. How will he save me any money, if I must now support both him and my own wife in Bath?" He turned on Mr. Lewis and jabbed an accusing finger at him. "You remember, Lewis? You have not forgotten how Augusta nearly drove us into the poorhouse with her love of shopping? Frills and furbelows for herself and frills and furbelows for the house! Have I now given up care of the hounds, just so Augusta may run wild on Milsom Street?"

"Papa, Papa," urged his daughters, while Mr. Lewis scolded, "Richard, if you die of apoplexy this very afternoon, Augusta and the girls will be far worse off than if you lose some money in Bath this winter."

"And how," seethed the squire, ignoring them, "does he propose to push my wife's chair up and down the town, if he lives as high as Lansdown Place? If he thinks I will pay for him constantly hiring sedan chairs for her, he is gravely mistaken. No, he had better live lower down." By which his listeners understood that he was already beginning to resign himself.

"Perhaps Queen Square?" suggested the doctor. "Or Green Park Buildings? Though Augusta may object to the damp, so near the river. I hear Mr. and Mrs. Geoffrey Wynstanley stayed in Frances

Square during their wedding journey. Near to Sydney Gardens, I believe."

"And we must all consider convenience," grumbled the squire, "however expensive it may be."

"For one winter," Mr. Lewis said.

"One winter is the thin end of the wedge."

"I hope not," admitted the doctor. "I hope one winter is but one, short, finite winter."

"Yes, Papa," agreed Margaret. She held up two lengths of black ribbon and set the narrower one aside. "Precisely. It will cost more than you hoped, but we can still try to rein him in. Tell Uncle Alwyn he may only take a lease for the winter, in such part of town as you approve. And, come spring, if he has not found other means to support himself, he must remove to a smaller, cheaper place in Bridgwater or Minehead or somewhere. Will that not do? When he understands that there will be limits in future, he will surely make the most of this opportunity."

The squire's fury leaked from him as she spoke, as if his ship of self had taken a cannonball to the hull, and he sank into the nearest chair.

"What is it, Papa?" breathed Edith, laying down her sewing to draw close to him. "Do you feel unwell?"

"No, no—stop that, Lewis!" He flung off the doctor's hand. "No. It is only that...well...the man has had every opportunity all these years. Both of them have. It is obvious that, short of another rabbit bone delivering me of Alwyn, I will never be free of his useless carcass hanging around my neck. And then, when I go down to the grave—well, girls, then you may all take up residence in the poorhouse together. Bath or Bridgwater, here or Hades, it will make no matter in the end."

This uncharacteristic display of moroseness shocked his daughters far more than his rage. Margaret gasped and knelt by the arm of the chair, and Edith felt a lump grow in her throat.

"Stop it, Papa," urged Margaret. "You must bear up. It will not come to that. I tell you, perhaps Uncle Alwyn will realize the danger he puts us in and choose to *act*."

"Act," snorted her father. "All my eye and Betty Martin. No. You will all have to throw yourself on Hugh's mercy or the charity of your sisters' husbands."

"Then it won't be so very, very bad," sniffled Edith, "for they are all so kind."

He turned a gimlet eye upon his youngest. "So you think now. Everyone is kind until they are forced to provide a life maintenance to a host of unwanted dependents."

The girls exchanged dismayed looks. Could it be true? That Hugh and Rosemary would tire of them? That Elfie and Alice would eventually shake their heads and wish their sisters at perdition?

"Perhaps," Edith ventured, "I may support Margaret and me with my painting one day."

The squire only grunted and lay his head back, shutting his eyes.

"How generous of you, poppet," Margaret said, squeezing her sister's hand. But even more comforting to Edith was the sight of Margaret rallying. "Papa, you must write to Uncle Alwyn very firmly about our plan," Margaret commanded. "One winter only, and no

Lansdown Place. He might complain that these are hard lines, but you must remain resolute. You must insist! Elfrida says you are ever too indulgent of Mama and her brothers, but that must cease now, for the sake of your health. If you like, I will look over your letter to make sure you are decided enough and that there is no possibility of misunderstanding. Or, if you prefer, I will write this one, too, and you may copy it in your own hand."

At that, her father's eyes popped open. His mouth worked, and he sat forward, giving more grunts and huffs. He raised a stubby forefinger to point at her. "That—so—you—it—"

"Gracious, Richard," cried Mr. Lewis. "Stand back, girls! He is having a fit."

Had Mrs. Hapgood been present, she would have screeched and collapsed at this warning, and, for a terrible moment, Margaret felt the temptation herself. Was their doom to fall upon them so soon, even at this very moment? But the sight of Edith's pale face steadied her, and her chin rose. She must be strong, if only for her sister. "Let us pray for Papa, Edie," she uttered, tugging Edith down beside her.

Before the girls could do more than assume a prayerful attitude, however, the squire found his voice and barked, "Get away from me, Lewis! I'm no more having a fit than you are! Girls! Get up! This is no deathbed scene, damn it all. I only mean to say that I have just now formed my own plan."

"Your *own* plan, Papa?" echoed Margaret doubtfully. But she obeyed and rose, relief plain on her face.

"Yes. What—you think you are the only one in this house with ideas? Yes, I have a plan. I will *not* write to Alwyn and tell him this, that, and the other, so on and so forth, which he will ignore, as he always does, after he shakes out the letter to see if I have enclosed that damned letter of credit *this* time. No. *You* will write to him, Margaret—you're never at a loss for words—and *you* will tell him he may only have a house in Bath for the winter at such-and-such a rate and in such-and-such a neighborhood. And you will say that he may only have your mother's company, after all, if he will submit to having *your* company as well."

She stared at him. "*My* company, Papa?"

"Yes—what—your ears not work? I say *your* company, girl. You've had plenty of practice at Bramleigh telling us all what to do and getting us all marching to your tune. It's time you put those tendencies of yours to better use. You must go to Bath this winter with your mother, Margaret, and make sure she does not spend us into the workhouse. And you must choose an appropriate match for your uncle and do all in your power to ensure he carries it off. Failing that, you must help him remove to some shabby lodging in Bridgwater or Backwater, for all I care, for the rest of his days." He fell back in the chair again, exhausted by his own vehemence. "What say you? Will you do it, Margaret?"

"Bath," marveled Edith, who had only been as far as Taunton. "Bath! Papa, what if Margaret herself were to find a husband?"

"All to the better, as long as she doesn't choose someone as useless as your uncle." The squire stabbed his finger at Margaret again. "And any flirting on your part comes second to your responsibilities there."

"'Flirting!'" repeated Margaret indignantly. "When have I ever been guilty of flirting? I have only been to two balls in my life and hardly had anyone unmarried to stand up with, apart from our cousin Lionel."

But her excitement showed. She had few memories, after all, in which she was not overshadowed by her other sisters' greater glory. Even Edith had more of a fuss made over her because she was the baby and because she could draw. But to go to Bath for an entire winter! Even with the responsibility for her unruly uncle and invalid mother, it would be an adventure like no other.

"And put away that mourning!" her father bellowed. "There will be no black ribbons on any of you, be damned to him! We can't have you showing up at the Assembly Rooms looking like frights. You'll be hundreds of miles from anyone who ever heard the name Alec Arbuthnot."

"I wouldn't know how to flirt," Margaret went on, her tone grown rueful. She tossed her sewing aside. "Or how to catch a husband. I always seem to say what comes into my mind, and Lionel tells me he would run the other direction if he met another young lady like me. It is just as well. Uncle Alwyn and Mama will be all I can manage. And what if I cannot even do that much?"

"Then off he goes to wherever £150 per annum will keep a roof over his head and food in his mouth. I'll sign no more bills for him!" huffed the squire. "And he'll call himself fortunate, for when I've pitched over the perch, I doubt Hugh or your sister's husbands will do half as much. Nay, if he has any brain in that brushed and pomaded head of his, he will snatch at this last chance."

"But Papa," Margaret felt obliged to point out, "it will cost you even more if you send me to Bath as well."

"Nonsense. If you do as I ask, you will save me money in the end. And you will carry your mother's pin money for her, so she cannot burn through it in a day."

Edith was drumming her heels and waving little excited fists. "Bath, Margaret! I am eaten with envy! Do you suppose you will visit the auction rooms to see the art?"

"I can't imagine we would. We don't want them purchasing any paintings, you know."

"Oh, too bad! But you will surely go everywhere else that is exciting and fashionable, or how will Uncle Alwyn meet his bride? You must write to me all about it, Margaret."

"Of course I will," promised her sister, "but first, it seems, Papa and I must write to Uncle Alwyn."

Chapter Four

**I am going to the Bath, with more opinion of...
the change of air, than of the waters.
—Horace Walpole, Letter to H. Mann (1759)**

Before the coach bumped and jostled down the Wells Road into Bath, the exhausted Margaret was certain that, upon arrival, she might require as much nursing and tending as her invalid mother. But then she caught her first glimpse of the town, expanding row upon row up the hillsides, ivory gold in the pale sunlight, and she felt a rush of renewed vigor.

"Mama, do look!" she urged in a low voice. "I see the tower of the Abbey."

From her corner of the coach, Mrs. Hapgood groaned. "I dare not open my eyes—the light—I am certain my head is splitting."

"Only think, though—in a few minutes you will see Uncle Alwyn! He will take us this very afternoon, I hope, to see our lodgings, though the lease does not begin until tomorrow. We may at least look at the outside, may we not? And determine how long a walk it is from everywhere else? Henrietta Street, he writes, is across the Avon on the Bathwick side."

"I will not walk anywhere," declared Mrs. Hapgood.

"I mean to say I will wheel you, Mama."

"Nor will I be wheeled! I must lie down. We will sit quietly in our room with the comfort of my brother's company."

"Oh, Mama!" Margaret could not help saying, despite the presence of the other passengers. One of them was a matron who occupied nearly the entire facing seat, her tiny husband pinned in his corner and half covered by her skirts. This woman eyed Margaret dourly, but Margaret thought she spied sympathy in the tiny husband's eyes. He surprised her by piping up, "Absolutely essential to enter one's name and address in the Pump Room guest book when one arrives, else no one will know where to find you."

His wife frowned him back to silence, but Margaret felt her eagerness grow. If it was *de rigueur* to announce one's arrival in the guest book, surely her uncle would accompany her, if her mother would not! Uncle Alwyn would want all of Bath to learn of his arrival.

In no time at all they were making their way up Stall Street, Margaret straining to peer out, before the coach clattered to a halt outside the White Hart.

As the footman assisted her down and the two of them supported Mrs. Hapgood, Margaret continued to look about her. All was bustle—the vehicles in the streets, the horses snorting and stamping, the coachmen calling and handing down baggage. There were passersby in stylish cloaks and trimmed bonnets and frock coats, and there were invalids in Bath chairs with their attendants. Oh, could she ever see enough?

The matron heaved herself down the steps of the coach with her pendant husband and set off toward the Pump Room, and Margaret thought she would scream with impatience, that she could not follow. Biting her lips, she suppressed this undutiful feeling and led her mother through the door of the inn. It would never do to lose sight of why she found herself in Bath in the first place.

With the passing of an hour, the Hapgoods were settled in their small back room, and Mrs. Hapgood lay abed, the coverlet tucked beneath her chin and her eyes shut. "Where can Alwyn be?" she moaned. "He assured us he would arrive on the 10th, and here it is the 11th. Suppose something has happened to him, and I will be deprived of both my beloved brothers?"

"I am sure he is only delayed, Mama," Margaret replied. "You know he can never keep to definite times and places." She turned from the window, her eyes brightening. "But I could step across to the Pump Room and look over the guest book to see if he has come. He might have, you know, but decided to venture to Henrietta Street to see about the lodgings!"

Her mother's eyes screwed shut more tightly. "You cannot go alone to the Pump Room, Margaret. It would not be proper."

"Oh, Mama! I could throw a stone at it from here—what could possibly happen to me? I would just trot over and glance at the book and write our names and address in, and hurry back. I will be so quick no one will even notice me or think whether it is proper or not for me to be there."

Mrs. Hapgood yawned. "We will be here for a few months, dear. There is no need to go careering about. Why don't you write to your father and tell him we are safe in Bath and he need not worry."

Margaret sighed. If she knew her father, he was not worried in the slightest and probably felt like a schoolboy on holiday. But she left the window to sit at the deal table and begin a letter to Edith. Scratching away for some time, she had just described the large matron and her tiny spouse when the sound of gentle snores reached her ears. Then she straightened up quickly enough! *Asleep?*

Her heart beginning to pound, she rose quietly and crept to where her mother lay, mouth slightly open. *Asleep!*

She would only be gone five minutes at the most, Margaret assured herself, slipping her cloak from the hook. And, if the guest book yielded no information, she would find the innkeeper again and ask if he had any news of Uncle Alwyn since their arrival. Should Mrs. Hapgood awaken in her absence, she could at least be placated with new information.

In the short hour she had been imprisoned with her mother, Margaret found time enough to consider her initial response to the marvels of Bath and knew it would not serve. No, indeed—it would never do, to appear the country bumpkin she was! After all, no one else alighting from the coach gawped and gulped and looked every direction at once. If anyone had noticed her, they must have known at once that she spent her life buried in the provinces. No—she must adopt the confident air of lofty unconcern that marked the refined young lady.

Her sisters would have laughed at Margaret affecting a polished air, but, for the first time in her life, not a single sister was with her, and she must learn for herself.

Her hair smoothed and her cloak gathered about her, she made her way outside. With the departure of the day's coaches, the street and innyard were free of horse traffic, but there still flowed a stream of people and Bath chairs, and, after only the slightest hesitation, Margaret plunged in among them.

She took care this time not to look about, only lifting her chin, eyes half-closed in what she hoped was a world-weary fashion, as she crossed Stall Street and headed for the Abbey.

It might have been because she was so intent on pretending to know precisely where she was going that she did not actually look where she was going, and the next thing she knew, her booted foot hooked something as she passed under the colonnade, and she found herself stumbling into one of the columns, which gave her head a friendly knock.

Through the stars wheeling in her vision, Margaret heard several things simultaneously: a clatter of wooden crutches on cobbles, a great deal of cursing, and another voice saying, "Oh, me—I meant to catch you before you blundered into that post, but I've only got the one arm, you see."

It was another moment before Margaret *could* see, but, when her vision cleared, she rather wished her blindness had been perma-nent. Before her were two gentlemen, a one-armed, ginger-haired one standing over the other, who was sprawled on the pavement, scrabbling after the crutch she had inadvertently kicked away. It was the sprawled man who cursed (though under his breath now), and the ginger one who babbled at her in continued apology while restoring the crutches to his friend.

"Oh, dear," whispered Margaret, taking in the one-armed man's empty, pinned sleeve and the other's ferocious scowl (which, remarkably enough, did not detract from the handsomeness of his face). She wondered what the latter's disablement was—he appeared to have all four limbs to him, but then there were the crutches...It must be gout. Or lumbago?

"Are you quite all right?" asked the ginger-haired man again. "You'll have a nasty bump on your forehead, I'm afraid." With his remaining arm he heaved the other to his feet and gave him a clap on the back. His friend, though he still bent slightly, favoring one leg, was some inches taller than she, and she was a tall girl.

"It is nothing," she answered, averting her eyes from their infirmities. Not that it was any easier to look at their faces. The one-armed man was pleasant enough, with his mild eyes and sincere smile, but the other—! That one was pale beneath the tan of his skin. A lock of dark hair drooped over his brow, like an arrow directing Margaret's gaze to his narrow grey eyes. His lips pressed together, and deep lines flanked them. She gulped. He might be handsome, but he was definitely also annoyed and apparently in some pain. She squeaked again, "I am terribly sorry."

"Nothing to be sorry for," the ginger-haired man assured her. He nudged his friend. "Right, Dash? Can't come to Bath without expecting to be run off our feet by town beauties." He laughed at his little joke.

The other only grunted in response, his lips tightening further. He gave Margaret a curt nod, however, which only increased her embarrassment. She was used to her father, who would have roared at her, instead of swallowing his wrath, and it was the thought of him that made her say to the gentleman, "No, I do apologize, truly. I wasn't paying attention. My father would call me a 'great, lumbering, clumsy lob' if he were here and feel much relief in doing so. Perhaps you ought to try it."

Her candor surprised a grin from her victim, but it was so fleeting that later she thought she must have imagined it. But his expression did soften, and he touched the brim of his beaver hat and bid her good afternoon. Turning adroitly now on his crutches (accompanied by another wince that she could not help but notice), he continued on his way. The ginger-haired man frowned and blurted, "I say, Dash," but finding the other did not turn, he gave Margaret a regretful shrug and followed.

"Heavens," she muttered. So much for an unobtrusive visit to the Pump Room. Now she would enter with a bump on her forehead big as a rhinoceros horn! At least the gentleman she injured was headed away up the town. If they had also been going to the Pump Room Margaret knew she would have retreated instantly to the inn. And so much as well for passing herself off as a refined young lady—'great, lumbering, clumsy lob' indeed! Would she never learn to think before she spoke?

Sighing, Margaret proceeded through the colonnade into the churchyard, watching her step this time lest she fell another crippled resident.

Her first entrance into the Pump Room was enough to banish these thoughts, however, and she was glad of her cloak, which allowed her all unseen to pinch herself with excitement. An orchestra played in the gallery at one end of the grand space over the buzz of the crowd. In such a parade of elegant attire and such a din of meetings and greetings, Mrs. Hapgood need not have worried that her daughter would attract notice. Her unremarkable cloak and plain chip bonnet were invisible enough. But Margaret didn't mind, and she forgot altogether her vow merely to scribble in the guest book and be gone. She took a full ten minutes to pace the length of the room, watching others from beneath lowered lashes. She saw where a grizzled woman served out cups of the famous water to the firm and infirm, young and old, alike. She inspected the statue of Beau Nash in its alcove. She even counted the ladies without male companions to guess at the number of potential matches for her uncle and was happy to find more ladies than gentlemen.

But at last she remembered herself and returned to the book, running her gaze down the entries. There was no "Alwyn Arbuthnot" on the open page or the few preceding, but one line did give her pause: "Mr. Dashiell Waite and Mrs. Humphrey Waite, London." *Dashiell Waite.* Could this be the "Dash" she had so heedlessly knocked down? No woman had accompanied him, but she saw no other claimants to the name. The register listed their address in Bath as 4 Princes Street. The entry directly below read, "Mr.

Charles Haworth, Bradford-on-Avon, Wiltshire," which would not have interested her, except that he also listed Princes Street as his address in Bath—10 Princes Street, in his case. Surely then this Charles Haworth was the ginger-haired, one-armed man who was so much more gallant than his companion? She wondered if she would encounter them again, and, if she did, if anyone might make an introduction. Not that Mr. Waite would be eager to add a maladroit young lady to his acquaintances. Alas! She would like the opportunity to make a better impression.

Carefully, Margaret wrote, "Mrs. Richard Hapgood and Miss Margaret Hapgood, Bramleigh, Somerset," followed by their new address of 12 Henrietta Street. It would not surprise her if her uncle had completely forgotten his sister was due to arrive in Bath, but surely, if he were here already, he would wander into the Pump Room with the rest of the fashionable crowd this afternoon and all would be rendered clear.

In the event, no such *éclaircissement* was necessary because Margaret returned to discover her uncle at her mother's bedside. She was pleased to see that the loss of his brother had left him largely unmarked. His hair was still dark, his demeanor cheerful, and his clothing well turned-out. Perhaps the plan to marry him off would not be hopeless, in spite of his past failures to capture the prize.

"There, there, Augusta," Alwyn was saying, patting her shoulder and offering his handkerchief. "I miss Alec too."

"He was such a g-good bro-brother!" sobbed Mrs. Hapgood, blowing her nose. "Always so thoughtful and loving! I treasured his letters and visits. And he would have come more often, had my husband not taken such an unreasonable dislike to him!"

Her father's dislike being not very mysterious to the rest of the family, Margaret only rolled her eyes and shut the door quietly. Her uncle sprang up to embrace her. "Maggie, how you've grown! How well you look. Only, you must try some of my cold cream—those spots of youth are so vexing, and you have quite the eruption upon your fair brow."

"It's not an eruption," she grumbled. "It's a bump. I ran into a column in the colonnade."

"Margaret, how clumsy of you," chided her mother. "I'm sure you have only yourself to blame, though, because I told you not to go out alone."

"I didn't run into the column because I was *alone*," Margaret protested. "I ran into the column because I tripped over some man's crutches."

"Worse and worse," said her uncle.

"Oh, dear. What became of the poor cripple?" Mrs. Hapgood asked. "I hope you gave him a penny."

"He wasn't that sort of cripple, Mama. I suppose he must have been a sailor or a soldier and got some injury because he was with his friend who had only one arm—"

"This wretched war!" interposed Mrs. Hapgood dramatically.

"—And, when I tripped on his crutch, it flew out from under him, and he collapsed on the ground. His friend had to help him up, and the crutched man was quite cross about it."

"Can't say as I blame him," her uncle remarked. "As if lameness in the service of King and Country were not enough, without great clodhopping girls kicking away one's supports."

Margaret's brow knit, but she let this pass. If she were to manage her uncle and mother successfully, it would be well to allow them their small victories.

"Never mind all that," she said briskly. "I am sure the gentleman suffered no lasting harm." A memory of his tightened lips flitted through her mind, but she put the thought from her. "I am glad you have found us, Uncle, and that Mama will have the comfort of your company. And you hers. It must have been trying for you, the arrangements for Uncle Alec and shutting up the London house and finding lodgings here." At the least it had been trying for Margaret and her father to dictate these activities from afar.

"It was an experience I hope never to repeat," was his reply.

"I must say, Uncle Alwyn," Margaret began again, "after my little accident in the colonnade, I made it to the Pump Room and was pleased to see we will be in such stylish company. Such elegance I saw there, and so many lovely ladies. I am certain you will be quite popular."

"Alwyn is popular wherever he goes," Mrs. Hapgood beamed, patting her brother's hand. "I will be proud to have him at my side."

"Indeed," agreed Margaret. "But, of course, he will not always be at your side, Mama. Sometimes you will have to put up with my company instead, because remember Uncle Alwyn must exert himself to find a wife."

"Oh, yes," Alwyn said, rising to look out the smeared window. He tugged at his cravat. "I did mean to write to Richard about this."

"About what?" asked Margaret sharply.

Her uncle plucked at his sleeves and straightened his waistcoat before replying. "Well, about that particular task."

"Uncle—what can you mean? You had a half-dozen opportunities to mention anything you wanted, in all the letters that went back and forth. Do you have some misgivings about seeking a wife?"

She saw his cheek work, before he could master himself. "Well, only one misgiving, Maggie. To be plain: I have already given my heart to someone."

She stared. "Have you?" When he didn't answer, she added, "Is—she rich? You know she must be rich, of course, for your future comfort."

"Eliza is quite wealthy."

Margaret sagged in relief. "Oh, good. Why did you not say so? Papa would have been pleased to learn of it. Well, then."

"Oh, Alwyn!" cried his sister. "Who is this Eliza? Tell me you have not chosen some barmaid like Alec did—though at least he had the sense not to marry her."

"She is no barmaid. Whoever heard of a wealthy barmaid, Augusta? No, she is quite a respectable, wealthy widow near in age to me."

"Better and better, Uncle Alwyn! Have you—already proposed to her, then? In London? But—if you had, and she had accepted, surely you would have told us and spared everyone this upheaval."

He cleared his throat. "It so happens I was on the point of proposing when my courtship encountered some obstacles. Or, more particularly, *one* obstacle. In the person of her son. I have not met the lad, but he returned most inconveniently from abroad, told his mother he objected greatly to her marrying such a man as I (and thus depriving him of his inheritance), and whisked her away from town before you could say Jack Robinson. The poor darling sent me a tearful farewell note saying she would always hold a place for me in her heart, but she could not possibly cross her only beloved son."

"It's an outrage!" declared Mrs. Hapgood, slapping the bed in her indignation. Her brother tsk-tsked and returned to sit beside her.

"But Uncle Alwyn, if she has indeed given you up and her son has snatched her away, don't you think you had better give her up as well?" faltered Margaret. "Because—surely you cannot refuse to consider any other ladies you meet while we are here." *We only have a few short months!* she wanted to add.

He shook his head slowly and provokingly. "I am sorry, Maggie, but I fear Eliza is the only one for me."

"But—there have always been plenty of other ones, have not there?" Margaret pointed out, flushing as red as the bump on her head. "And you have managed to be parted from every last one of them with no harm done!"

He sighed once more and gazed mistily at the bed curtains. "Not this one."

Margaret could scarcely credit what she was hearing, and small blame to her. How could it possibly be, that this ridiculous uncle, whose countless romantic scrapes and imbroglios had formed the backdrop to her growing-up years, should now consider himself devoted to the one woman unavailable to him, when so much depended on him choosing someone—anyone—! "But you will never see her again!" Margaret persisted. "Will you? Where has her son taken her?"

"I do not know, though she once mentioned having family in Hampshire."

Margaret felt a faintness that had nothing to do with the blow to the head she had received. Could he truly mean what he said? If he did, he most certainly ought to have said so before! What would become of all their well-laid plans? One thing was certain: she must not tell her father, or the storm that would follow would surely bring on the Fatal Episode.

Digging her nails into her palms, she sank into the chair by the writing table. She must keep her head. She had known her uncle all her life, and surely this fancy would pass as all the others had. Perhaps he always went through a spell of considering the woman indispensable. Indispensable until she was dispensed with, that was. The best strategy would be to let him forget her naturally, by filling his days and thoughts with new people and new scenes and new activities. Yes. Not that any alternative presented itself.

She waited to speak until she could sound offhand. "I am sorry to hear you have been parted, Uncle. I would have liked to meet her. Perhaps one day your paths might cross again? In the meantime, we will try to keep you occupied while we are in Bath."

He sighed. "Thank you, Maggie. I am at your service. And yours, Augusta."

"Very well," Margaret smiled, feeling her spirits lift a little. "Then perhaps you and I might go now to see the lodgings in Henrietta Street? And Mama may join us if she feels refreshed."

It was only when they were passing Argyle Buildings, pushing Mrs. Hapgood's chair before them, that Margaret thought to ask, "Uncle, dear, what is the surname of your lost lady? Perhaps I may be able to find out more about her family."

He turned from admiring a shop window to beam at her. "What a capital idea! If it can be done, Maggie, you will do it. So capable. Sadly, I do not know her maiden name, but Eliza's married name was Waite."

"W-Waite?" croaked Margaret. Surely not. *Surely* not.

"Waite. Are you growing hoarse, my dear? It must be this cool air. Yes. Her name was Waite. Mrs. Humphrey Waite."

CHAPTER FIVE

Ile racke thee with old Crampes,
Fill all thy bones with Aches, make thee rore.
—Shakespeare, *The Tempest* (a.1616)

Wrestling himself into the armchair nearest the fire, Dashiell Waite slung his crutches to the floor with an oath and shut his eyes.

"Such language!" came his mother's voice, as she swept into the room, smiling and nodding at Haworth. She was a tall, handsome woman with a kind face and her son's coloring, though his two years in the field under relentless sun had left his countenance more lined than hers. "How tired you look, my dear. Was the King's Bath not soothing?"

"It was delightful."

Seeing her doubtful expression, Haworth added, "The waters were blissfully hot. I think they will do Dash and me a great deal of good this winter."

"Hmm. They do indeed seem to have had a restorative effect upon you, Charles, but I cannot say my son looks improved."

"Don't fuss, Mother," Dashiell muttered. "I was well enough when I emerged from the bath. This is only a twinge."

"From a little tumble he happened to take afterward," explained Haworth.

"Tumble!" cried Mrs. Waite, coming to examine Dashiell more closely, as if she expected a hidden wound to burst forth.

Dashiell scowled at his friend. "'Tumble!' Nonsense. I did not trip over my own crutch. Some ridiculous young girl kicked it away and sent me sprawling in the colonnade."

"How horrid, to treat an infirm man so!" his mother gasped. "I hope her parents rebuked her."

"I am *not* infirm," he insisted. "I simply have an injured limb. Nor did any parents rebuke the creature because she was by herself, I believe."

"A child by herself?"

"Madam," interjected Haworth again, unable to let the misapprehension continue, "this was no child who crossed our path—she was a young lady. A rather pretty one. And she did not kick Dashiell's crutch with malice aforethought, as it were. I am certain it was an accident."

"In any event, she was a great, lumbering, clumsy lob," Dashiell said, his grin reappearing. "She said so herself."

"Oh," said his mother, looking from one to the other uncertainly. But she smiled then, to see her son smiling. "Well, then. For the sake of your injury, I hope you will not encounter the pretty young lady again, if she is so frightfully awkward. You must be careful, dear, with your crutches. I worry already about the slippery cobbles. Perhaps you should call a chair, rather than walk."

"I am afraid I cannot oblige you," he answered dryly. "For the best way to ensure that I never make a complete recovery would be to coddle this blasted weakened limb. No—I would rather risk encountering every last clumsy young lady in Bath than call a chair, if I can help it."

"Very well, dear. Don't take on so." She sat opposite him and leaned to pat his uninjured knee. "Forgive me for fussing over you. You have been gone so long and were in such danger that I cannot resist the pleasure of fretting myself *in person*."

He covered her hand with his own and squeezed it. "And you must forgive me for plaguing you for my own entertainment. Have no fear. We will get along, Mother."

Seeing Mrs. Waite's eyes fill with tears, Haworth excused himself, mumbling something about being expected home. And though his own lodging nearby held no one beyond his valet and was only ever visited by the landlady with food and linens, neither of the Waites prevented him going.

"It was so difficult to have you so far away, Dashiell," began his mother, when they were alone. "And to know that any news of the war and any letters I had from you were weeks in reaching me! I could not help but think that, even as I read your assurances, you might have been wounded since you wrote, or—worse than wounded—and I would not know! How I feared for you, and how I missed your father at those times—I missed someone with whom to share my burden."

He sighed and squeezed her hand again. "I know. I am sorry for it. But here I am now, despite your fears, and, unlike poor Haworth, all in one piece."

She frowned at his jest. "Darling, how can you be so nonchalant about his terrible loss?"

"Again, you must pardon me. Soldiers' humor. Haworth is wont to make light of it himself, and I believe his newfound means will render his de-limbing altogether negligible in the world's eyes. But I mean to say you need no longer fret over me, and I am sorry you had to bear your burden alone. I hoped you would find your brother's family some comfort in my absence."

"They were...some." Her tone was grudging. "But you know your uncle never leaves Chardis very long. I suspect your aunt Celia and Charmaine would have liked to stay in town with me, if my brother allowed, but as it was..."

As it was, as Dashiell well knew from Charmaine's letters, his mother had been left too often to her own devices.

"And, for my final apology," he added teasingly (if somewhat disingenuously), "I am sorry my condition required you to leave town. If I am tripped by no more young ladies, perhaps we need stay here only a few months."

"Oh, Dashiell, you know I would rather be with you than any- where else," she assured him, but her lip trembled a little. "You mustn't suppose otherwise. And I am so pleased the Blakelys will join us shortly and stay a while—at least your aunt and Charmaine will. I will not be lonely now. Besides which, there is so much to amuse in Bath! One does get tired of making the same rounds in town and seeing the same people—at least one gets tired of *most* of the people."

Her voice trailed off, but he had no difficulty following her thoughts. And as he had always been a man who believed in taking a bull by the horns, he did so now. "I suspect you are remembering your particular friend now, Mother. That Mr. Alwyn Arbuthnot."

Blushing like a girl, she turned her face away and arranged the skirts of her blue wool gown. "I—wish you might have met him, Dashiell. He was a very kind gentleman. And had rather an air about him—like your father."

"Perhaps one day I will." He waited for her to meet his gaze again, but when she did not, he steeled himself and asked, "Did he want to marry you, madam?"

"Oh!" Mrs. Waite sprung from her seat, her hands folded over her middle. "I cannot say. I...suppose so. He sometimes hinted—"

"And what would you have said, had he asked?" pressed Dashiell, inexorably.

She faced him with a kind of despair. She loved her son all to pieces, naturally—had missed him ceaselessly in his absence—but he was so direct in his manner—he had always been, since he was a little boy—that sometimes she was helpless before him.

"I—do not know. I would not have been able to give him any answer, even had he proposed, until I heard from you."

"Would my uncle Matthew have approved of the match?"

Once more she sank into the chair opposite him, quieting the movement of her hands with an effort. "He—oh—I suppose Matthew would not have approved. You know what a conservative, stolid man your uncle is! My brother has no imagination, no sense of adventure or even desire of it!"

"That I do know," replied her son, his tone wry. He felt a surprising stab of sympathy for his mother. Had she, too, felt herself chafing under her dull brother's authority? "Uncle Matthew is a *rock*. With all the benefits and drawbacks thereto."

"Yes. Precisely. He can be depended on in all circumstances, but he cannot be moved. He cannot be softened. And, like all rocks, he is singularly devoid of fancy. He finds it a weakness."

Her son regarded her. She had always been a tender, fanciful woman, and it could not be denied that the entire Blakely family considered both characteristics weaknesses. Their impatience with his mother's nature must indeed have chafed.

And would he, Dashiell, now replace that authority with his own heavy hand? If he sometimes resented the Blakelys' desire to direct the course of his life, should it be so startling to find that his mother also suffered? Also suffered and also resented? And she, being a woman, could not run away to join His Majesty's Peninsular Army, as Dashiell had.

Perhaps her flirtation with this Alwyn Arbuthnot had been the equivalent of his own bid for freedom. If it was, he understood. But they all had duties and responsibilities. Dashiell's wound had forced him to return to his own sooner than he would have wished, and his return signaled also the end of his mother's relative autonomy. He might sympathize with her longing to do as she pleased, but that did not mean he should let her throw herself away in a foolish match.

After another minute he compromised with himself: his mother should not marry this Alwyn Arbuthnot person, but, if she found someone more suitable, he would not stand in her way. She would be as free as Dashiell could let her be, within the parameters of prudence and wisdom. He would not require her to lay her fortune, undiminished, at the Blakelys' feet. His uncle's family had enough of their own to be getting on with.

That is, there was no need for both of the Waites to sacrifice themselves.

Grimacing slightly, he sat forward and used his arms to bend his weak leg at the knee. Then he took both her hands in his and his narrow grey eyes found her softer ones. "See here, Mama." (When she heard this gentle address, her mouth opened in pleased surprise.) "Perhaps my uncle Matthew had his reasons for opposing any marriage to Mr. Arbuthnot, some of the reasons bad and some excusable, from his perspective. But what your brother thinks no longer pertains. He is head of the Blakely family, and I, for what it is worth and for however long it lasts, am head of the Waites. And I say we will enjoy ourselves this winter and have what adventure and pleasure this little spa affords."

"Oh, Dashiell!" She embraced him, and he tolerated it, though it put additional weight on his pained leg. Nor did he object when she draped on the arm of his chair and fumbled for her handkerchief. "Oh, Dashiell—while we are being confidential—I should not say this, but are you certain you want my brother not only as your uncle, but also as your father-in-law?"

His head reared back in surprise—were his feelings so obvious? But in reply he only grunted.

"You *still* intend on marrying Charmaine, do you not?" she pressed.

"We are engaged," was his bland answer.

She bit her lip, as if she would keep further words back.

"What is it, madam? You clearly have more to say. Is it about Charmaine?"

"Well—I cannot help but feel one reason she and her mother come to Bath is to spy upon us! It's all very well for you to talk of adventure and pleasure, but they will report back to Matthew, you can depend upon it."

He laughed. "Good heavens! What foul misdeeds do you envision, that you fear Aunt Celia and Charmaine's disapproval?"

"Perhaps I am being foolish, but I am certain they come not only to watch over me, but also to ensure you do not escape Charmaine!"

His look was measuring. "What makes you think I want to escape Charmaine?"

"You were engaged very young," she replied slowly, choosing her words with care. "She is a beautiful young lady and a wealthy one, and she is my own niece, but, as she has grown, I find I know her less and less. She has not...invited me into her confidence." When he remained silent, his gaze withdrawn from hers, Mrs. Waite's shoulders drooped. She had come to think her son would not have stayed away so very long or even have gone in the first place, had he been more eager to marry his cousin. But, if he were now determined to do so, she would not jeopardize her relationship with him by crossing either one of them. No, indeed. Whatever Dashiell chose, she would support him.

This decision made, she swallowed her doubts and put the best face upon the situation. "Never mind. I am sure all will be well. With us under the same roof, we will all come to know and love each other better with each passing day."

"Or all come to hate each other."

"Dashiell!"

But he was done being serious. "Come. While my aunt and Charmaine are under our roof, as you say, they must do things the Waite way. And I say we will have pleasure and adventure (of the innocent variety), as much as our hearts desire. We will attend the theatre and concerts and subscribe to the circulating library and Sydney Gardens, and I know not what else, and they may write to Uncle Matthew whatever they please. I am not leg-shackled yet, and, before this winter is through, madam, you will rejoice that neither are you."

CHAPTER SIX

The womman fleth and he poursuieth.
— John Gower, *Confession Amantis* (1393)

"**Y**ou mean to say she is here?"

"I *think* she is here," Margaret hedged. She was sitting with an embroidery hoop in her lap in their new drawing room, beside her mother, who was tucked up near the fire. Margaret's uncle stood at the window, staring into the street as if he might spy his lady love at any moment. Because the lodging came simply furnished and because Margaret had refused their entreaties to make sundry purchases to beautify it and render it more comfortable, their removal to Henrietta Street was the work of an afternoon. Their baggage was brought from the White Hart; the cook, serving maid, and footman attached to the lease were interviewed and found lacking but inevitable; and the family once again made the walk over, pushing Mrs. Hapgood's chair while Alwyn bowed and nodded agreeably to passersby.

It was easy enough for Margaret to delay sharing her information (although she avoided looking too closely at their fellow Bath dwellers, lest she see the crippled man and his one-armed friend again), but once their removal was accomplished, she decided it would be better for Alwyn to be forewarned, rather than taken by surprise.

"You see, I saw that name—Mrs. Humphrey Waite—in the Pump Room guest book yesterday," she explained. "If it is indeed the one you know, she and a Mr. Dashiell Waite are staying in Princes Street. She cannot be his wife, of course, or she would be Mrs. Dashiell Waite. And it would be odd if she were his sister-in-law because then she would have her husband Mr. Humphrey Waite with her, would she not?"

But her uncle wasn't attending. He was murmuring, "Eliza! Eliza, it is you! I will storm Princes Street immediately!"

"You will do no such thing!" cried Margaret, jumping up. "Suppose you were to march over there and knock on the door? If this son of hers opposes the match as you say, he will never admit you, and then he will indeed whisk her away where you will never find her!"

"He will not mind when he meets Alwyn," spoke up Mrs. Hapgood. "He has only to know my brother, to love him."

"Nonsense," Margaret replied shortly. But she did come to pat her uncle's sleeve, to soften this speech. "Forgive me, Uncle Alwyn, but meeting you will not suddenly transform you into a wealthy gentleman of spotless reputation. And perhaps even those qualifications would not be enough to overcome his opposition." She thought with an inward shiver of Mr. Dashiell Waite's narrowed eyes and the pained line of his mouth. "Perhaps this son of hers would prefer his mother not to remarry at all. He may like to have her about to nurse him."

"Are you saying I should abandon her to such martyrdom?" demanded Alwyn, shaking off his niece's hand and pressing a fist to his chest. "Never! Let him hire a nurse."

"I mean nothing so dramatic, sir. I am only saying that we must be clever about this, if we wish you to succeed."

"Clever?" he echoed, stopping short. "Yes, begad, you are right. We must be clever." He pulled on his moustache as he absorbed this, no clever plans springing immediately to mind. But the pensive expression on Margaret's face reassured him, and he glowed with admiration. "Ah-ha. Yes. We will outwit this obstinate, selfish son, or my name isn't Alwyn Arbuthnot. 'Clever'?—ho, ho, yes indeed. Look at our Margaret. She will manage it, as she does everything. Gadzooks, what a girl! Augusta, how came we to have such clever girls in our family?"

Mrs. Hapgood beamed at them, and Margaret swelled with importance. Never mind that Dashiell Waite did not appear someone easily got the better of—if anyone could do it, surely she could? Why, she had been unofficial head of household for four years now, and everyone depended on her. She had already expected to matchmake for her uncle and had not quailed at the thought. Having their options reduced to just one particular woman made things more difficult, but not impossible. The woman's son would certainly pose a problem, but the woman's own feelings (if her uncle did not mistake or exaggerate) were certainly in their favor. Eyeing her uncle appraisingly, she thought that, with a little tutoring, it might be done.

She held up a finger and had the delight of them instantly falling silent. "Firstly, Uncle Alwyn, we must be prepared to encounter your lady and her son. There are only so many places and activities in Bath. It may be a week, or it may be as long as a fortnight, but our paths will cross, and we must be prepared."

"A fortnight?" protested Alwyn. "I do not believe I can wait a fortnight."

"I said it *may* be. Likely it will be shorter. In any event, when you see Mrs. Humphrey Waite you must behave as you would with any other acquaintance. That is, you must not exclaim, or run at her, or try to clasp her hand, or whisper tender things, or any such."

Mystified, he stared at her. "But what will I do, then, if not any of those things? I thought we wanted her to marry me."

"We do," said Margaret patiently. "But we must not arouse her son's fears, or he might abscond with her. Therefore it must appear that you have given her up."

"But—that would wound her! And she might decide to give me up in return!"

"If you haven't forgotten, Uncle Alwyn, she already did give you up—remember the tear-stained letter she wrote you? She is willing to sacrifice herself to her son's guidance. This is why we must tread carefully. We must renew her feelings for you and make them strong enough to withstand opposition. It is not forever. It is only until we can allay his suspicions. If he sees you are not trying to elope with his mother, and that you treat her no differently than any other lady of your acquaintance, he will relax his guard, and you will have your chance."

"Very well, very well. But what chance will I have, if I only see her by lucky accidents once a fortnight?"

"No, no, Uncle Alwyn. You will see her more than that. We will discover some of their plans, and our own will be made to coincide, don't you see? And then you will appear in the best light, as a good brother and a good uncle, and the son might come to think you an acceptable match for his mother."

The good brother came to sit beside his sister, who rubbed his sleeve. "And how will we discover their plans, Maggie, if I am not to seek her out or show Eliza any special attention?"

His niece frowned. How indeed? If any Hapgood or Arbuthnot appeared unnaturally curious about the Waites, it would unravel their scheme. "I—will have to work that part out."

"Perhaps you could flirt with the son, Margaret," Mrs. Hapgood suggested.

Margaret shuddered. The man might be crippled, but he was handsome all the same, and she had kicked his crutch away! "Why does everyone always propose that I flirt? I'm sure I've done nothing to justify it. You must put it from your minds. Never mind the *how* for now. I daresay, if they are prominent people, their whereabouts will be no mystery. We will cross that bridge when we come to it."

It took neither a fortnight nor even a week for their paths to cross again, however, for it was only a few days later the metaphorical bridge to be crossed presented itself, and the metaphorical bridge turned out to be the literal Pulteney Bridge. Margaret and family were returning from a stroll to Union Street, and the Waites and Charles Haworth must have been returning from Sydney Gardens because—all at once—there they were, fifty-odd feet away, coming toward them!

Margaret saw them first: a man swinging on crutches, accompanied by another with a pinned sleeve and a tall woman, graceful and elegantly dressed.

She choked back a gasp. If they had not actually been *on* the bridge, walled in on either side by the shops, and if it would not have been painfully obvious, she would have spun her mother's chair around and fled. As it was, she only had time to hiss, "Uncle! I believe it is they!"

"Who?"

"They! Your lady and her son. You must show no undue excitement!" She was hardly one to give advice because her own face was aflame. She would have lowered her gaze and hid beneath her bonnet brim, if she were not afraid of missing what passed. But when she flashed a glance at her uncle, his calm amazed her. His seeming perfect indifference! Could there indeed be two Mrs. Humphrey Waites in the world, and the one drawing near was nobody to him?

But no. From the corner of her eye Margaret saw the elegant lady stop short—hesitate. If Mr. Waite had not that very moment caught the tip of his crutch in a gap in the stones, from which he jerked it free, annoyed, all might have been lost. As it was, his mother recovered quickly, throwing her own mantle of dignity over her countenance, and Margaret was left to marvel that her elders should be so expert in disguising their feelings.

If the two people most intimately concerned could be trusted not to arouse suspicion, that left her free to venture the tiniest peek at Mr. Waite, just to see if he truly were as handsome as she remembered. She had no desire, of course, to thrust herself forward, to force upon him any acknowledgement of the gawky girl she was certain he was glad to forget. Unfortunately, her tiny peep coincided with Mr. Haworth raising his arm to point out something in one of the shop windows, and, as Mr. Waite followed the movement, his gaze crossed Margaret's and—briefly—held. It then flicked to the still-pink bump on her forehead, as if for confirmation. His lip curled, and he looked away.

Margaret found her heart hammering as if the man had chased her up a hill.

The two parties might have passed without further incident but for Charles Haworth's keen interest in any pretty young ladies who entered his orbit. He noted Margaret's neat figure (the day was mild enough that she wore her pelisse of peach sarsenet, rather than her wool cloak) and took care to look full in her face when they were near enough. He, too, recognized her at once, but he had not the self-possession of his friend.

"I say!" he cried, halting and executing a little bow. "Good afternoon, our young lady of the column." Smacking his own brow with his remaining hand, he added, "Or, of the colonnade, rather. I did not mean to refer to—" his eyes touched involuntarily on her injury, and he reddened.

"To my clumsiness?" Margaret supplied, chagrinned, as she bobbed a curtsy.

The parties had no alternative but to check their progress, though both Alwyn and Mrs. Waite hung back, feigning indifference. Haworth chuckled at her bald remark, his discomfiture fading. "Well, if you were clumsy the other day, I was clumsy just now, so we are both quits." He bowed in turn to Mrs. Hapgood and to Alwyn Arbuthnot. "Madam. Sir." They inclined graciously but made no move to introduce themselves, leaving Haworth uncertain again. He turned to his friend. "Dash, you recall this young lady from a couple days ago?"

Margaret could not miss the twist of Mr. Waite's mouth now as he held one of his crutches away from his body to make his own bow—perhaps a fraction too precisely—and replied, "To be sure. Such a first impression is not easily forgotten." But his face was wiped of its mockery when he straightened again and addressed Mrs. Hapgood. "We have no master of ceremonies on this bridge to introduce us properly, madam, but I am Dashiell Waite, this lady is my mother Mrs. Humphrey Waite, and this is our dear friend Mr. Charles Haworth. Haworth and I had the good fortune to run into your daughter outside the Pump Room recently."

"Or *I* into you, rather," muttered Margaret.

She wondered if Mr. Waite would seize his mother and flee straight away upon learning their identities. Well, if he did, Margaret would have the rest of the season to help her uncle forget the woman.

Perhaps the sight of Mr. Waite's crutches and Mr. Haworth's empty sleeve marked them as fellows in infirmity, for Mrs. Hapgood lifted her hand from the armrest of her chair to flutter fingers at them and say in her breathless voice, "Mr. Waite. Mrs. Waite. Mr. Haworth. Delighted, I am sure. I am Mrs. Richard Hapgood of Bramleigh, Somerset, and this is my brother Mr. Alwyn Arbuthnot and my daughter Miss Margaret Hapgood."

The effect was electric—at least upon Mr. Haworth and Mr. Waite. Haworth emitted a miniature shriek that he hastily modified into a spasm of hiccups, while the latter's eyes widened for an instant, before his brows flew together and he took a half-step, as if to block his mother from view.

It was Mrs. Waite who spoke then, her voice calm and neutral. "How do you do. I believe Mr. Arbuthnot and I have met before. At the Sherillton rout, was it not?"

"It must be so," Alwyn agreed, her equal in composure, "for all London was there, it seemed, fighting their way up the staircase."

"I am sure that staircase was no more crowded than Gay Street this morning, however."

"Nor any steeper, I suppose."

Mr. Waite was recovering, though his words were clipped. "What brings you to Bath, Mr. Arbuthnot?"

Alwyn pretended not to hear the hostility behind the question. He placed a hand on Mrs. Hapgood's shoulder. "Why, I accompany my dear sister, who has not been as well as we would hope. Her husband could not be spared, so Margaret and I have her care this winter."

"The best of brothers," Mrs. Hapgood smiled up at him, and Margaret managed a murmur of agreement.

"But I hope *you* find yourself in health, Mrs. Waite," Alwyn continued.

"Perfect health, Mr. Arbuthnot. It is not mine which brings us to Bath. Rather, we are here because my son and Mr. Haworth are recovering from severe injuries they sustained on the Peninsula, where they served under Wellington—"

"Madam," Mr. Waite interjected, through clenched teeth, ignoring the polite chorus of admiration and concern from the other party. Margaret could not determine if he was anxious to get away or simply embarrassed by his mother's pride in him. Whatever it was, Mrs. Waite did not take it amiss, only holding up her hands in deprecation.

"I regret to say we must cut short these greetings," Mr. Waite said. "We are expected."

"My sister-in-law and her daughter Charmaine arrive shortly," his mother explained, "and you cannot blame a young man for being anxious to see his betrothed again."

"Charmaine," repeated Mrs. Hapgood. "What a rare and lovely name."

"My niece Miss Blakely is a rare and lovely young lady."

"Madam." He smiled at his mother, but the hint was clear.

More bows and nods and curtsies followed, Margaret conscious of a prick of disappointment. A betrothed? And a rare and lovely one? If the man had been in Portugal with the Marquess of Wellington, how had he found time to engage himself?

She did not dare look at Mr. Waite again, but Mr. Haworth's puppyish parting grin drew a reluctant smile from her, and Dashiell experienced his own prick of annoyance. That was all he needed—Haworth taking up with the only people in Bath who ought to be avoided, if not fled from altogether. The young lady was comely enough, to be sure, but what did it matter? And what mattered it that Dashiell's own thoughts had strayed her direction more than once since she sent him sprawling in the colonnade? Charmaine and he would soon be reunited. And, even if that were not the case, now that he knew Miss Hapgood's identity and her unfortunate connections, he would think of her no more. And neither ought Haworth.

He would have to have a word.

And so the first meeting was got over.

CHAPTER SEVEN

They can disappoint with a smile,
or ruin even with a compliment.
— *A New & Impartial Collection of Interesting Letters
from the Public Papers* (1757)

"I think we had better leave Bath."

"Only yesterday you told me we should enjoy ourselves as much as we might."

"Only yesterday I did not know Alwyn Arbuthnot followed you here."

Mother and son confronted each other within the entry of their home on Princes Street, their voices low.

"He hasn't 'followed me,' Dashiell! How could he? I never said where I was going—I promise you," his mother insisted. Her lip trembled. "And you saw how he behaved. He has accepted that we cannot be together, and I have no intention of making a spectacle of myself. Moreover, I resent you treating me as if you were the parent and I the child."

Her son regarded her, a gleam of respect lighting his eye. "I apologize if I gave you that impression. It is out of both affection and duty that I would warn you against any person of doubtful reputation, Mama, as I hope you would warn me. And I have no fear you would make a 'spectacle' of yourself. However, Arbuthnot might look to the main chance, if you have so serendipitously reappeared. If this is indeed serendipity."

Mrs. Waite threw up her hands in exasperation. "Oh, Dashiell. I assure you: the man is neither so cunning nor so deep that you should suspect him of scheming. He is a simple man, for better or worse. If he says he is in Bath because his sister is unwell, then I believe him. And if he could see me again and remain so easy, so unruffled, all danger is past." Only a keen ear could have detected any wistfulness in this last speech, but all of Dashiell Waite's senses were nothing, if not keen.

"Besides," she continued, "as you pointed out immediately upon your return to England, he is a supposed reprobate and fortune hunter. Even if he had pursued me to Bath, I am nearly fifty years old, and here he will soon find himself distracted by new faces, some of them as wealthy as I and many far younger."

"Come, come," he rejoined, attempting to tease her back to cheerfulness, "if you want me to say you could pass for a tripping young maid of twenty-nine—thirty at the uppermost—you will find me willing enough."

"What foolery," she replied, but her mouth twitched, and he found himself smiling in return. "Does that mean we will stay, Dashiell?"

He sighed, his momentary lightness flagging. "It need not be decided today. We could hardly flee right off, in any case." He flicked his watch open, even as the longcase clock in the passage began to strike.

"Charmaine and Aunt Celia," he said. "They will arrive at any moment."

If anything, she was even lovelier than he remembered. Her thick hair and lashes darker, as were her clear green eyes. Her mouth was a perfect rosebud, except when it parted to reveal even, white teeth. Her delicate hands fluttered as she spoke, rings glinting in the candlelight. Charles Haworth followed the light and movement like a doomed moth, laughing at Charmaine's lightest jest and chewing his lip in unconscious agitation. Dashiell, on the other hand, appeared entirely serene, his countenance betraying nothing.

And what did he feel, seeing her again after two years' separation, when their emotional distance had come to mirror the geographical?

He loved her still, of course. After a fashion. Out of sheer habit, he supposed, their engagement being of such long standing. As he was some years older, his earliest memory of her was when he was playing with a ball, and his three-year-old cousin threw herself, howling, to the floor, crying, "Want it! Mine! Ball! Want it!" Dashiell's father had frowned at him to relinquish the toy, and he complied, more amused than annoyed, but not without muttering under his breath, "Horrid little beast."

On looking back, he thought little Charmaine might have expressed herself unpleasantly, but at least she was forthright about it. As she grew older, she learned to mask her feelings and desires, as people do, but she still expected him to anticipate the unspoken and to respond appropriately. Take this evening, for example. He greeted her with a welcoming smile, told her he was glad to see her again, and pressed the hand she offered. He asked after the Blakelys' journey and listened attentively to her chatter. He thanked her for the letters she wrote while he was away and said again how happy he was to have them in Bath. And yet, as they all sat at supper, he knew she was not pleased with him. She sat at his left hand, with Haworth on her other side, but she turned more often toward poor Haworth, leaving Dashiell either to contemplate the ivory curve of the back of her neck or to make conversation with his aunt.

"How delightful to find you will be our neighbor while we are in Bath," Charmaine was saying to Haworth as the soup was removed.

"Yes—yes, delightful," agreed Haworth. "That is—mutual feeling—"

"Dashiell did not mention you had formed so close a friendship while in hospital. No, no—do not misunderstand me! The fault lies with him. He is not one to share his innermost thoughts on paper."

"Forgive me," Dashiell said, not without noting the injustice of her accusation. "I did try to keep hospital details to a minimum. Not bore you with bandages, as it were."

"Hmm..." She smiled, turning again to Haworth. "What did you write to *your* sweetheart, Mr. Haworth? Did you confine yourself to meditations upon Portugal, the movement of armies and what Wellington said about thus-and-such?"

Flushing scarlet, Haworth stumbled, "Oh! No sweetheart worth writing—that is—no sweetheart and nothing to write. I mean—dash it!—Wellington is a fine man."

"Well, whoever your correspondents were, Mr. Haworth, I'm certain they must have trembled for your injuries."

"Heh." He gave his empty sleeve a shake. "Just the one—injury, you know. Just one injury. And nobody to mind. They—er—they were all—dead themselves, I'm afraid." This statement was met with a gasp from Charmaine and her mother, leaving Haworth to glow an even deeper scarlet and signal in desperation for more fish.

As the footman sprung forward, the lid of the dish clattering noisily, Mrs. Waite took pity on her son's friend and interposed. "Poor Charles had the misfortune of losing his only remaining family, his aunt and cousin, while he himself lay in danger."

"Oh, dear!" breathed Charmaine, her green eyes widening with entrancing dismay. "Forgive me for raising such a painful subject!"

"Lost an arm but gained a coat of arms, eh, Haworth?" Dashiell grinned, drawing a shocked look from his aunt and a shake of the head from his mother.

Haworth snickered. "Some find my dis-arming disarming." Charmaine looked from one to the other of the gentleman, trying to muster an answering smile.

"You must bear with their soldiers' humor," Mrs. Waite explained. "The two of them are not fit for decent society."

Mrs. Blakely set down her fork. "Speaking of decent society, Eliza, I believe there has been some falling off in refinement since I was last in Bath. Charmaine and I stopped in the Pump Room to enter our names, and I recognized not a single personage in the guest book. Such a collection of nondescript Misters and Misses' I never saw before! I daresay the good and great have decamped for Brighton."

"It may be," answered her sister-in-law. "I have never been to Brighton. But it matters little to me if the fashionable set has followed the Prince there. Dashiell and I thought he would benefit most from the waters here, so here we will remain." She colored then, remembering suddenly how it was not at all certain, after all, that they should remain there. "At least, for the present," she added lamely.

Haworth, released by the general conversation from the paralyzing spell of Charmaine's attention, found his tongue again. "And they may be nondescript, as you say, madam, but we have met some charming people already."

Had Dashiell not been seated so far away, he would have kicked Haworth under the table. As it was, he could only cough elaborately into his napkin. His aunt ignored this and asked, "Indeed? What sort of charming people?"

"Oh, a clumsy but winsome young lady, her chair-bound, invalid mother, and her uncle, Mr.—er—" Realization dawned belatedly on Haworth here as well, and his eyes goggled and he emitted several strangled gulps before taking refuge in his own counterfeit coughing spell.

"Gracious!" said Mrs. Blakely, "there must be too much vinegar in the sauce."

"It seemed mild enough to me," her daughter answered. Looking to her betrothed, she found his countenance blank, so she turned again to Haworth. "You were saying? What were the names of the clumsy but winsome young lady and her family? We should dearly like to be introduced to pleasant company."

"Er—" the combination of Charmaine's beautiful green eyes and the Pandora's box he had opened threatened to finish Haworth off altogether. "Er—what *were* their names? Dash it—pardon me—I mean to say, *blast*—er—pardon again—soldier's language—unforgiveable. We only met them once or twice. Or, the girl twice, the rest once. Er—"

Charmaine laughed at his perplexity, and, in his panic, Haworth plunged into outright falsehood, seizing upon the first similar name that came to mind. "It was—Amberforth! Mr.—Miss Alex—that is, Alice—Amberforth and family. Brother Alex and so on. Yes."

"Amberforth?" cooed Charmaine. The green eyes slid back to Dashiell. "Dashiell, was there not an Alex Amberforth in your letters? An ensign from Hertfordshire who died at Almeida? You never mentioned that he rose from the dead and has come to Bath."

You never mentioned that you actually read my letters, thought Dashiell.

Aloud he said, "Haworth mistakes himself. Amberforth is indeed no more. The man we met this afternoon in company with the clumsy young lady was called Arbuthnot. Alwyn Arbuthnot."

It was the Blakelys' turn to color and choke. Mrs. Waite hastily gestured for the footman to go, even knowing the man would press himself to the other side of the door.

"Dashiell!" quavered his aunt. "You cannot mean that man is here!" She glanced at her sister-in-law and lowered her voice, as if Mrs. Waite would then not be able to hear her, from the foot of the table. "You cannot mean he has pursued—that he—"

"He has not pursued anyone, Celia," Mrs. Waite interrupted. "And you need not hesitate to name what you are thinking. I know very well how you and Matthew feel. There is nothing between Mr. Arbuthnot and myself. Now. He has only come to Bath to care for his sister, the woman in the chair Mr. Haworth referred to, and—Charles, do forgive us for venting private matters in this fashion—his presence has nothing to do with me, I assure you!"

Mrs. Blakely drew herself up, outrage vying with her desire to preserve decorum. "So you say, Eliza. And you may even believe as much. But—this is insupportable! He, here? I must write to Matthew—he will have much to say on the subject." In the absence of her oracular husband, however, she looked to her nephew. "Dashiell, what will you do about this?"

His eyes gleamed. "Do, madam?"

"Surely you—we—must remove from Bath?" she suggested. "It would not do to remain for the winter, would it, with that man about?"

"My mother has promised not to elope with him, Aunt," was his dry reply.

Here Mrs. Blakely's fingertips rose to her brow. "I should hope not! But can he be trusted not to try to persuade her?"

"My dear Celia, please do not speak as if I were not in the room."

"Oh, Eliza!" Mrs. Blakely's hand fluttered back to the table. "Forgive me. Oh, my. The man's reputation...!" She looked to her daughter for assistance and was relieved to observe that Charmaine was quite of her opinion. It was obvious in the set of her lips and the faint line that marred the smoothness of her forehead. If Charmaine agreed the situation was impossible, that would settle the matter. All the Blakelys yielded to Charmaine. She had only to hint at her wishes for others to comply. She would manage this dreadful state of affairs.

"What a shame," Charmaine said now, favoring Dashiell with an appealing smile. "We did so look forward to our time here. Such a welcome change from our little world at Chardis."

There was a pause. Haworth suspected he was not the only one holding his breath. He thought regretfully of his own lease at 10 Princes Street and the months stretching ahead alone, if the others packed up and went away.

For Dashiell's part, he realized it was indeed easier to understand her when they were face to face. At least, in this case. He knew the Blakelys disapproved any match between his mother and Mr. Arbuthnot, so it followed naturally that they expected Dashiell to do all in his power to prevent one. Including break his new lease in Bath and flee somewhere—anywhere—out of danger. Without saying so, Charmaine was testing her hold on him: would he know what she wanted? And, if he did, to what lengths would he go to please her?

He rolled the stem of his wineglass between his fingertips. And why should he not please her? Even if his mother promised not to make a fool of herself with Arbuthnot, and even if Arbuthnot were no longer preying on Dashiell's mother, the season would still hold its awkward moments. Perhaps even its painful ones, for Mrs. Waite.

And, after all, there were other spas in England, to which they might repair. It was easy enough to go. Some money would be lost, but there was money enough. The Blakelys and even Haworth could be convinced to exchange Bath for Cheltenham or Tunbridge Wells. Why not go, then?

And yet.

Something in him resisted surrendering so speedily to Charmaine's unspoken demand. If they were to be married, would this not set a regrettable precedent? Should she not even be made to put her request into words, that he might have the opportunity to qualify it?

She should, he decided.

All this inner debate was the work of a moment, and then he said, "Have you changed your mind about staying Charmaine? I thought you and my aunt intended to spend at least a month with us."

The appealing smile vanished. Then returned, pinned on again with determination. "And so we do, Dashiell. After so long apart, we should like to see more of you, and how Mama loves the theatre! But, naturally, if you and my aunt Eliza are not in Bath, we will not be either."

"Not in Bath?" He affected mild surprise. "Whyever should we not be in Bath?"

The smile wavered again, and when Charmaine replied, Dashiell imagined her little white teeth must be gritted. "Why, you heard Mama, Dashiell! She does not think it appropriate to remain here, if the unfortunate Mr. Arbuthnot also stays in Bath."

"Ah, yes. But what do you say, Charmaine? I had thought you also enjoyed the theatre and would be pleased to shop in Milsom Street."

"Oh! Perhaps. But I am easily pleased. You need not worry about me. It may worry Mama but—but—well, Mama's wishes are not everything, of course. Naturally, we will do whatever you decide."

"*You* have no preference then?"

Her eyes glinted at him, and Dashiell was startled by a memory of one French soldier with eyes like that who charged him at Fuentes de Oñora, sword drawn and mouth open in a scream Dashiell couldn't hear.

"I have said. Whatever you decide," Charmaine repeated icily. "I would have thought it obvious that—well—in any event, my wishes must come second. And if you choose to go against Mama's advice...you will have your reasons. I am sure your choice will be for the best of all involved."

Not precisely like the French soldier, then, Dashiell amended. If that man had Charmaine's resolve, Dashiell probably would not have escaped Fuentes de Oñora alive.

This was all too much for Mrs. Waite. She had not endured her son's peril in battle only to see him felled by Charmaine for her sake. "Dashiell, darling, you need not worry about me. I will gladly go where you choose."

"I rejoice to hear it, madam." He picked up his glass now, giving its contents a swirl and affecting a ruminative expression. Then he set it down again. "Aunt, I thank you for sharing your opinions with us, and I appreciate your concern. But, upon reflection, and as Charmaine has no preference either way—" (a sharp intake of breath from her at this) "—I am for remaining in Bath. I trust my presence will be enough to deter Mr. Arbuthnot from further interference. Now, may we call in the next course?"

CHAPTER EIGHT

I should blush...to be ore-heard.
—Shakespeare, *Love's Labor's Lost* (1598)

When the clock struck ten, Margaret could wait no longer and burst into her mother's chamber. "Mama, will you be rising soon? Tilly has dressed my hair, and I can send her to you."

Mrs. Hapgood yawned and stretched. "Is Alwyn up already?"

"Not yet," admitted her daughter, "but I believe I heard him stirring."

"Then why do you wake me? You mustn't keep such country hours, Margaret. We are in town now. Why don't you go away and write to Edith?"

"I've already written Edith about yesterday, and nothing has yet happened today worth mentioning!"

"And what will happen today, dear?"

"That's what I want to talk about."

Mrs. Hapgood showed her first signs of interest and rose on one elbow, her nightcap askew. "Might we go shopping, Margaret? There are so many, many new shops since I was last here. Your father did give us some pin money."

"Yes, well, perhaps another day. We have a far more important commission, you know, and we must make progress toward that first."

With a sigh, her mother fell back against the pillows and shut her eyes again.

Undaunted, Margaret skipped over to perch upon the bed, holding out a sheet of notepaper. "See, Mama, I have been thinking things over. I have made a list of two columns. In the first: activities in Bath we may participate in at the least expense. And in the second: places where we are most likely to encounter the Waites." She waited, but Mrs. Hapgood made no response.

"I have not put shopping on the list," Margaret went on, "because things can be so very expensive, but I have put 'window-gazing.' Window-gazing in Milsom Street and Union Street and Bond Street and Orange Grove and Margaret Buildings..."

"May we not *buy* anything at all?" demanded her mother crossly.

"Knock, knock." Alwyn stood in the doorway stifling a yawn, but at least he was dressed. "I say, the food in the breakfast room is stone cold."

"It was warm enough at nine," said Margaret.

"But who was awake to eat at nine?" he puzzled.

"I was awake at *eight*."

"I told you, Margaret, that it wouldn't do," her mother chided. "You had better tell that cook—what is her name? Flink? Flitch?"

"Flint."

"Flint, then. You had better tell Flint we expect breakfast at ten or half-eleven."

"Never mind," said Alwyn. "Margaret can eat as early as she pleases, Augusta, and you and I can breakfast in Sydney Gardens. I believe those are served at eleven."

"You cannot breakfast every day in Sydney Gardens because we cannot afford it," his niece reminded him. "We must practice economy. I will tell Flint ten o'clock, as a compromise." Eager to move on to weightier matters, she sprang up and pulled a chair close to the bed for him. "Do come look, Uncle Alwyn. As I was telling Mama, I made a list of two columns, in order to match our activities with those most likely to throw you together with Mrs. Waite."

Obligingly, Alwyn plucked it from her fingers and read, "Walking: walking in town, walking up Beechen Cliff, walking in Sydney Gardens—lots of walking, in short. Window-gazing: window-gazing in Milsom Street and Union Street and Bond Street and—"

"And see in the second column?" she interrupted. "Given her son's infirmity, it is in walking and window-gazing that we have the best chance of meeting Mrs. Waite without her son."

"But it was in walking that we met with *all* the Waites," Mrs. Hapgood pointed out.

"Yes," Margaret conceded, "but I believe he can't do that sort of thing every day, with his injury. I persist in thinking it less likely he will accompany her, especially if we choose the more difficult walks:

Beechen Cliff, or up to the Circus and the Royal Crescent. It would be very taxing on his leg."

"Please do not refer to a gentleman's 'leg,' Margaret. At least in company. And I do not know that I am any more able to join you on arduous walks than Mr. Waite is. You and Alwyn had better go without me, for I will not make the attempt and you would never be able to push my chair."

"Eliza did say she was in Gay Street and how steep she found it," Alwyn remembered, his eyes lighting up. He stood hastily and straightened his cravat. "Maggie, let us set out at once! We will walk all over town until we see her. We will not venture up Princes Street, but perhaps we may go as near as Queen's Square."

"Wait, Uncle Alwyn! I hate to say it, but I think you had better stay with Mama today and not show yourself."

Deflating like a soufflé, he asked, "Why ever not?"

"Because we must lull her son Mr. Waite, remember? And lull Mrs. Waite, for that matter. You managed it so beautifully yesterday that we must not bungle it now by being overhasty! The next meeting must appear entirely by chance. Therefore, I thought I might go abroad on my own today—I could buy our Sydney Gardens subscription."

"But Margaret," protested her mother, sitting up and dropping all pretense of resting, "I've already told you, you cannot traipse all over Bath by yourself. We are not at Bramleigh anymore."

"Couldn't I take Tilly with me? We might stop at the market and purchase you some sweets (you said yourself that Flint's pastries were abominable), and then go as far as the library I saw in Bath Street when we were at the White Hart."

"We-e-e-ell..." Mrs. Hapgood wavered. The cook's treacle tart the night before had indeed been equal parts sticky and uneatable.

"Do see if they have that novel about Wolfstein," urged her uncle, resigning himself. "Whoever lived here before left only books of sermons and some poetry. If they do not, Marshall's on Milsom Street will."

"And I may pop into the Pump Room," Margaret added. "To see if there is news of the Waites. For all we know, they may already be leaving Bath."

"They can't leave right off," observed her mother, "for their visitors have only arrived."

"Yes." To her vexation, she felt herself blush. "Mr. Waite's intended and her mother."

"Well, go, go, then." Mrs. Hapgood waved her off. "I suppose you mean to keep us imprisoned all winter. Alwyn and I will look after each other. Only try not to draw attention to yourself, my dear."

Tilly met Margaret's request to accompany her with placid acceptance. She was a doughy girl with dull eyes, given to silence that Margaret hoped was not resentful, but it was either endure the girl's company or stay home. Armed with a basket, Tilly slouched along, compelling Margaret to restrain her own strides on this beautiful crisp day, lest it not be obvious to onlookers that she was abroad with her maid.

Mrs. Hapgood might disagree, but Margaret thought the delights of window-gazing amidst the shopping arcades of Bath very nearly as enjoyable as making purchases, for how should one ever choose? There were haberdashers and mercers, stationers and shoemakers, drapers and glovers, lacemakers and confectioners, watchmakers and toymakers and jewelers. Colorful and elegant displays filled each bow window, and Margaret's pace slackened until Tilly had no difficulty keeping up. When her mother and uncle were with her, Margaret dared not linger anywhere to admire, and the perpetual strain of reining them in precluded any enjoyment of her own. But today she might look without fear, and, as a result, she felt generous toward them, selecting items from the stalls of foods in the Guildhall and from the costermongers' barrows.

The circulating library was modest but well-stocked. Because of its location near the baths, the patrons were mostly elderly and infirm, but she didn't mind. Marshall's would certainly cost more, patronized as it was by the elite.

Looking over the catalogue, she saw no "Wolfstein," but the clerk informed her it was actually entitled *St. Irvyne* and retrieved it for her. She paid him the quarterly fee of six shillings, choosing a newish book called *Sense and Sensibility* for their second selection. Reading aloud to each other in the evenings would be another inexpensive pastime.

Tilly said nothing as her basket grew heavier, but Margaret felt guilty nonetheless. Another sign of how provincial she was, she supposed. A more worldly girl would not dwell on the servants' discomfort, but at Bramleigh they were so dependent on their three that unhappiness could not be ignored. She would skip the Pump

Room, she decided, to spare Tilly, and proceed directly to Sydney Gardens.

To be honest with herself, she was also glad to avoid the Pump Room because she would rather not encounter Mr. Waite. "Though why should I fear seeing him?" she wondered, as they re-crossed Pulteney Bridge. "He does not own Bath. I have as much right as anyone to go where I please. Yes, I may hope his mother will marry Uncle Alwyn, but I cannot make her do it. I only scheme to give her opportunities to meet him. So there, Mr. Waite! I will not fear your surly looks, even if you be at Sydney Gardens today."

Her burst of defiance proved unnecessary, however, for there was no sign of him when they reached the Sydney Hotel. Margaret read over the subscription prices, murmuring, "I had better do three months." (Tilly set down her basket and rubbed her lower back.) "Three months for three people. There is a discount that way. Too bad the subscription to the Ride costs twice as much—Uncle Alwyn would like that. But that would not even include hiring a horse."

Tilly saying nothing to this either, Margaret stepped aside to fish in her reticule for coins. And it was while she was sorting through her pennies and half-crowns that other voices carried to her.

"I should have liked to visit that new shop in Orange Grove your aunt Eliza mentioned. I do not see why we had to rush over here."

"Because I wanted the walk to be as long as possible and as fast as we might, so *he* wouldn't come, Mama. You heard how my aunt said to him that she thought he pressed too far yesterday and made his limp worse."

Their voices moderated as they drew nearer, and Margaret hazarded a peek. She saw a lovely young woman with dark hair and green eyes and a frame as small as Edith's, elegantly attired in russet wool. Her mother was somewhat taller and graying, but she had the same small mouth and clear eyes, though those clear eyes regarded her daughter with a troubled expression.

"I'm sure he sensed your displeasure, my love."

The young lady gave a light laugh. "Are you? How are you certain, since he did not beg my pardon or change his mind? I knew from his letters he would be an indifferent wooer, but he has failed to meet even those low expectations."

"He was very glad to see you again," her mother said humbly.

"He *said* he was. I care not a snap for his words. If he were glad to see me, he would have made a greater effort to please, since I made it abundantly clear I did not agree with him. He takes me for granted, Mama, and I won't stand for it."

Margaret paused in her coin-scrabbling, amazed. Here was a different sort of confidence! Imagine being so beautiful and self-assured, dismissing an unsatisfactory "wooer" with that imperious air! This girl would pay her fees with guineas, Margaret was certain; nor would she waste time hoping the servants were content.

"Do you mean to drag us out of the house and up and down hill our entire stay, then, to punish and avoid him?" the young lady's mother persisted.

"No. Rest easy, Mama. For one thing, I do not intend on sacrificing our visit to the theatre on Thursday, for you know I have been longing to see *The Foundling of the Forest*. But if he has not made amends by then, I will save my smiles for his friend."

"You cannot mean that, Charmaine!"

A sudden shower of clinking and jingling distracted them, and they turned to see a confused young woman and her ponderous maid chasing a score of coins in various directions. Or, at least, the young woman chased them, while the maid simply stomped on those that came nearest her and bent to retrieve them.

Recalled to themselves, not another word was spoken. Mrs. Blakely took hold of her daughter's elbow and steered her within.

It took Margaret several minutes to recapture every last farthing, and even then she hesitated to follow the ladies inside right away.

So that was Mr. Waite's betrothed! She must be, with that name! Charmaine Blakely was indeed rare and lovely. And, judging by her words, more than a match for such a man. They made a handsome couple.

Margaret sighed. Of course his chosen one would be beautiful and elegant and confident and cultured—Margaret had never even heard of *The Foundling of the Forest*, much less been "longing to see it." And it went without saying that the words "great, lumbering, clumsy lob" would never in a thousand years issue from such a charming mouth.

She wondered what Mr. Waite could have done to displease his beloved so. How could he, moreover, prove an "indifferent wooer" to one so charming? She did not doubt that, if Miss Blakely directed her smiles toward the more susceptible Mr. Haworth, that gentlemen would be knocked down like nine-pins.

There were no answers to be had outside Sydney Hotel, however, and Tilly had taken up her basket once more and was shifting it from arm to arm to remind Margaret that some of them had burdens to carry. Nodding, Margaret gathered her courage and entered the building. To her relief, the Blakelys were nowhere to be seen, and she could buy her subscriptions in peace.

"Home now?" prodded the taciturn maid.

"We may stop briefly there and leave the purchases," replied Margaret, determined to ignore the girl's hint, "but then we must cross the bridge again and return to town. I have one more errand which I forgot till now."

Pulling tight the strings of her reticule and tucking it in her pocket, she said simply, "I must buy tickets for the theatre Thursday evening."

CHAPTER NINE

**Your charms will shine bright enough, lady,
to dazzle a soldier's eye.
—William Dimond, *The Foundling of the Forest* (1809)**

"'Tis she, L'Eclair, 'tis she, the only she, the peerless, priceless Geraldine," declaimed Florian, the back of his hand pressed to his brow.

Margaret could not help herself: without lifting her head, she turned her gaze the barest fraction from the stage to peek across once more at Charmaine Blakely's box. For all the splendor of the Theatre Royal, from its garlanded and pilastered façade on Beauford Square to its Casali-painted ceiling panels, lyre-shaped balconies, and blazing chandeliers within—for all the excitement of sitting in a box and seeing her first play thus, Margaret found she could not give more than half her attention to it. She was too drawn by the party opposite.

Her own family had arrived unfashionably early, over Alwyn's protests. Margaret had insisted. "We must wheel you all the way to the Theatre, Mama, and find someplace to put your chair during the show and assist you to your seat. Only imagine trying to do all that if the house is already full and there is nothing for everyone to watch but us!" Mrs. Hapgood and her brother did not argue long. If Margaret's tight fist had unclenched enough to buy theatre tickets, they would do better to let her have her way.

She was looking her best in a russet-brown silk gown (a gift from Elfie and Frederick), her hair painstakingly wound in curls on the iron by Tilly. Smoothing her skirts she murmured, "Remember, Uncle Alwyn, you must continue perfectly indifferent to Mrs. Waite if she comes. You might even use your quizzing glass to inspect some other lady, if the Waites chance to be seated where they may observe us."

As it happened, they were seated in the best possible place to observe them, occupying the box directly opposite. Margaret had nearly despaired of them by the time they arrived, however, for by then the house was long filled, the curtain risen, and Longueville halfway through haranguing Bertrand to keep his solemn oath.

"Oh, thank heavens!" she whispered, catching sight of a flash of green. It was Charmaine Blakely entering the box in a breathtaking gown of changeable taffeta. Her appearance drew the eyes of the audience away from the actors, so Margaret felt safe to stare, though her own attention soon flitted to the rest of the party. Why should

Mr. Haworth hand the young lady to her seat? Was it because she was still displeased with Mr. Waite? Oh, of course. Mr. Waite could not manage it with his crutches. He did not look sore about it, though. No—his face wore its customary handsome, surly expression. The effort of climbing the staircase with his injured leg had cost him—that wayward lock of dark hair had come loose again—but he looked nothing short of beautiful in his evening dress. Was ever a man so good-looking?

Margaret blushed at the thought, grateful that no one would notice.

As Dashiell took his seat beside Charmaine, he pretended to examine the program until the house had its fill of scrutinizing them, though he had spied Alwyn Arbuthnot as soon as he entered the box. "Blackguard," he muttered. "This cannot be chance." Beneath lowered lids he watched the man glance over, nod (presumably at Mrs. Waite), and then return his regard to the stage. Dashiell would have turned then, to observe his mother's response, but he found his eyes wandering to Miss Hapgood instead. The young lady was dressed most becomingly in a shade that complemented her pretty hair, and color had risen in her cheeks. If the bump on her forehead remained, it was invisible at this distance. She was gazing frankly at their box, and he wondered what she was thinking. Did she know of her uncle's history with Dashiell's mother?

Without pausing to wonder why he did so, he lifted his head and looked directly at her.

Margaret inhaled sharply and felt her face flame, but the man's gaze transfixed her, and she could not tear her eyes away. The space between them seemed to shrink, and the actors' voices faded to a hum. In her distress, she bumbled and dropped her fan, and when she bent to retrieve it, she was tempted to huddle behind the velvet-padded wall of the balcony. *He knew!* screamed her guilty conscience. *He knew she was scheming to capture his family fortune, and he wanted her to* know *he knew.* Why else should he stare thus? And surely it was guilt that made her feel almost dizzy. She should not be trying to fool this young man who had done her no wrong and who had served his country honorably. She should not be trying to swindle him of his inheritance. For once, Margaret envied her mother's tendency to swoon in pressing circumstances; it would be lovely to escape consciousness, if it would not make her even more conspicuous to Mr. Waite.

She would ignore him. Them. Not look over there anymore. She would watch the play. Watch Rosabelle the servant swishing her skirts, singing for her soldier boy to come.

"Who is the pretty young lady who catches your eye?" Charmaine asked.

"Is she pretty?" he replied, not the least embarrassed to be caught.

"Both pretty and novel," she answered. "But then, are not new faces always more attractive than those long familiar?"

He gave her a long look. The proper reply, he knew, would be to assure her that she outshone every woman present. Perhaps she did, but he felt no inclination to say so. On the contrary, the set of her mouth and her lowered lashes irked him. But Charmaine had gone an entire day and a half without saying more to him than what necessity demanded, and he deemed it unwise to widen the breach.

Therefore he smiled at her and put a finger to his own lips, indicating that they should be quiet and attend the play. When he drew his finger away, he touched it briefly to the back of her gloved hand.

Satisfied, she let the matter drop.

He settled back in his chair, letting his face fall into shadow. They were all playing their games, he supposed. He sensed, from his mother's utter stillness beside him, that she was not indifferent to Alwyn Arbuthnot across the theatre. But what were that man's feelings on the matter? Arbuthnot lounged between his sister and his niece, occasionally leaning in one direction or the other to say a word or to attend one. At one point he raised his quizzing glass and inspected a buxom young woman in the lower seats. Was Dashiell's mother right in declaring him to be a simple man? If it were true, he no longer posed a danger. His quarry had proven elusive, and he had given up the chase. If it were not true—well, time would tell.

Onstage, the hero's valet L'Eclair wooed the heroine's maid Rosabelle, jesting with her, catching her and kissing her. Mrs. Blakely gave an uncomfortable titter, and Charmaine whispered to Haworth, "Mama is fearful I will be corrupted by seeing such shameless behavior," to which Haworth responded with another collection of choked sentiments. Dashiell hardly noticed the interchange, his attention drawn again to the box opposite.

"Saluting is one of the first lessons in a soldier's trade," proclaimed L'Eclair, gluing his lips to Rosabelle's. Miss Hapgood shifted uneasily and cast her uncle and mother a helpless glance. Arbuthnot didn't notice, as he was enjoying the scene himself, and Mrs. Hapgood had fallen into a doze. The stage kissing went on and on, interspersed with further repartee, and Dashiell watched Miss Hapgood's alarm giving way to fascination. Her lips parted; her hand rose falteringly to touch her throat, and she swallowed. Her head turned the merest fraction toward the Waites' box, and Dashiell found he was holding his breath. *Come. Look at me.*

But then the tiresome actors burst once more into song, rousing Mrs. Hapgood with a start and her daughter from her trance. Miss Hapgood gave herself a little shake, her hand dropping back to her lap.

Dashiell frowned in annoyance. And in annoyance at his annoyance. Whether or not this Miss Hapgood were as innocent as she appeared hardly mattered. The Waites must be on their guard against the entire family. Haworth was safe now—Charmaine's beauty had taken care of that—so why should Dashiell need reminding? It would be too absurd to warn his mother off the uncle, only to take a misguided interest in the niece. Not, of course, that he was at liberty to take any interest, misguided or otherwise. Engaged men had no business taking interest in other women, period.

A thought streaked through him then, unbidden: *Charmaine might marry Haworth instead.* But he quashed this disloyal idea. Besides—even if she came to prefer Haworth (the thought of which, of course, ought to fill Dashiell with jealous fury), that would not render Miss Hapgood one jot more appropriate. Pretty or not pretty; innocent or scheming; candid or devious—he must think of her no more.

But no sooner did the curtain fall on the end of the second act, than Dashiell said to Charmaine, "My dear, you asked me when the play began who the young lady was who drew my attention. I would like to introduce her party to you because they are, in fact, the infamous Mr. Arbuthnot, his sister, and his niece. Shall we visit their box?"

Not only Charmaine's eyes grew wide. Dashiell thought Haworth would tumble from his chair. Mrs. Blakely looked daggers, and Mrs. Waite paled.

"An enemy is often more fearful in imagination than reality, wouldn't you say, Haworth?"

Thus appealed to, Haworth was torn between agreement and a desire to please Miss Blakely. He strove for playfulness, pointing at his empty sleeve. "I would say both sorts hold their perils."

"Touché. Nevertheless…" Taking a crutch under his arm, with the other he drew back the curtain and gestured for the ladies to precede him from the box.

For a moment he thought Charmaine would refuse. She nearly did. "I should not like to miss any of the third act."

"Nor should I," he agreed amiably. "We will merely make our introductions and return before the curtain rises again. If you would prefer to remain here, however, with your permission, I will merely point you out from across the theatre."

"I will not put you to the trouble." With set lips and a glance at her mother, Charmaine led the women out.

Both relieved and disappointed, Margaret saw the Waite party leave their box, and she could not say which feeling was uppermost.

Alwyn sighed. "Well, Maggie, they have gone, and not much was accomplished, though I followed your instructions to the letter. I am sure it stabbed Eliza to the heart to see me leering at that minx through my glass."

"I am sorry for that, Uncle." She felt like sighing herself, her zeal for their plan having flagged in the few days they had so far devoted to it. Margaret was discovering the difference between plotting to entrap and actually putting such a plan into action.

But they could not abandon their course now. More than ever she must lift the burden of her uncle from her father's bowed neck, especially after the additional outlay of sending her with Alwyn and Mrs. Hapgood to Bath. Edith's letter, received just that morning, remarked on the squire's improved spirits. "Margaret will set it right!" he had crowed.

Mrs. Hapgood yawned, patting her mouth. "How delightful to be at a play again, and such an exciting one! I do believe Florian will turn out to be Eugenia's lost child. Yet even if I have guessed the ending, it is so well done I would not want to miss a minute."

Margaret remembered Miss Blakely's supposed longing to see *The Foundling of the Forest* and could only suppose she felt otherwise. Perhaps that young lady found it dull to guess the ending.

A muffled knock interrupted them, but when they only looked blankly at each other, it was followed by the door opening and Charles Haworth putting his head through.

"Good evening, Miss Hapgood. Mrs. Hapgood. Mr. Arbuthnot. What a pleasure to see you again. Forgive me for intruding. As Mrs. Waite mentioned when we met the other day, we have friends who have joined our party. Will you allow us to introduce them to your acquaintance?"

The surprise was so complete that it was a moment before they could give their assurances, rising from their seats, and then Haworth opened the door fully to admit the Waite party. The box seemed much smaller when eight people filled it, though Mr. Waite remained leaning in the doorway.

Haworth performed the introductions, managing admirably until it came to presenting Miss Blakely. Then he had the misfortune of stepping back, that the rest might see her diminutive person, and treading upon her foot, which threw him into agonies of remorse and embarrassment. "Oh, dear! I—do forgive me, Miss Blakely—unforgiveable—I—apologies—er—may I present—this young lady is Miss Blakely."

"Now Charmaine will be maimed in the foot, to match your missing arm and my defective limb," said Mr. Waite dryly. "If not for my aunt and mother, our new acquaintances might think our party altogether lame."

"On the contrary. I am perfectly well," Charmaine said, favoring her betrothed with a chilly smile.

"How are you enjoying the play?" Mrs. Waite asked Mrs. Hapgood, when a little silence had fallen over the company. She had taken care to stand nearer the Hapgood ladies than Alwyn Arbuthnot, who stood like a polite block behind his niece.

"Delightful," breathed Mrs. Hapgood. "But long. I seldom keep late hours anymore."

"Do please sit down again, madam, if you are fatigued," Mrs. Waite urged her. "We will not stay long."

Mrs. Hapgood dropped with a happy sigh back into her seat, and there was another pause. Under ordinary circumstances, Charles Haworth and Alwyn Arbuthnot would have papered over the awkwardness with their easy chatter, but Haworth was still mortified from crushing Miss Blakely's slipper, and Alwyn did not want to risk breaking any of Margaret's rules. Mrs. Blakely clung to a disapproving silence, as did Charmaine, who bore additional resentment against Dashiell for calling her "lame," even in jest.

Far from appearing abashed by her displeasure, however, he continued to lean in the doorway, and an objective observer might have thought he was enjoying the ticklish situation.

That left Margaret to blurt, "Mama has made her predictions for how the story will end, but we will not spoil your own enjoyment of the play, in case she is correct."

"Has it spoiled yours, Miss Hapgood?" asked Mr. Waite.

"Nothing could spoil my enjoyment of it," she answered, flustered by this address. "I have never been in a theatre before—and have only ever seen two other plays in my life. Both of them were Shakespeare and performed by traveling companies at the Taunton Fair."

Charmaine stared at such an admission of provinciality, but Mrs. Waite smiled at her. "Mr. Dimond's work benefits from a fine company and fine setting. Shakespeare needs no such dressing up."

"Perhaps not, but I like the dressing up all the same."

More innocuous remarks followed on the quality of the production and the elegance of the setting, and then Charmaine surprised everyone by speaking up. "My mama here is an old-fashioned sort," she said, favoring Margaret with a friendlier smile than the one she directed at Dashiell. (She meant it to punish him: if he chose to displease her by forcing this acquaintance on her, she would displease him in return by embracing it.) "Which means she thinks there is far too much kissing and lovemaking in this play."

"Charmaine!" her mother reproached her.

"There *is* a lot," Margaret agreed, returning the smile. "I was embarrassed at first, but I confess I rather began to like it."

Then it was Mrs. Hapgood's turn to look heavenward for aid, though Alwyn couldn't repress a chuckle.

"Do you find Florian or L'Eclair handsomer?" Charmaine pressed.

"Oh—I suppose L'Eclair. Because his hair is so dark." No sooner were the words spoken than Margaret blushed furiously, afraid the dark-haired Mr. Waite would see right through her and know it was his own appearance she preferred.

Her words led her mother's thoughts in a different direction, however. "My own husband is a fair man, Mrs. Waite," Mrs. Hapgood began, "but fair men tend to ruddiness, you know. Not like my dear brothers—Alwyn here—so dark and handsome, as was my other brother Alec, whom we lost recently..."

"Not that Uncle Alec was so dark in his later years!" interjected Margaret, panicking. "He was quite, quite bald by the time he died." The last thing they needed was for the Waites to think Mrs. Hapgood was trying push Alwyn Arbuthnot on anyone!

Margaret's tactlessness led to another loud silence, but fortunately the theatre manager appeared then onstage to indicate the audience should return to their seats. Mrs. Waite turned again to Mrs. Hapgood. "We are sorry to hear of your bereavement." A nod toward Alwyn included him in this condolence. "I lost my dear husband some years past, and I know how difficult it is. Let me say again what a pleasure to meet you all, and I hope we will see you again soon."

"Very soon," added Charmaine. She looked at Margaret. "Do you ride? Mama and I purchased our ride subscription at the Gardens just yesterday."

Margaret, who had not been on so much as a pony from the time she was ten and who well remembered the price of Ride subscriptions, was forced to answer, "I'm afraid not."

"Oh! Well, then, would you join me for a walk in the Gardens? We might venture into the labyrinth."

To Margaret's credit, the excitement she felt was for the thought of making a friend her age, and only secondly did it occur to her that this would also further the Hapgood aims. She nodded eagerly. "Yes, please! I should like that very much."

"Tomorrow, then? Perhaps at eleven? We might even try their breakfast at that hour."

"Oh." Margaret's face fell a little. She had not budgeted for many treats, and the evening's theatre tickets had consumed a week's worth.

Charmaine, however, was very good at understanding the unspoken, and she said quickly, "Or never mind, this time. Perhaps the others may breakfast, if they come. Everyone must amuse himself. But for us, we will venture into the labyrinth. Mama and I were too timid to attempt it yesterday, lest it actually take us hours to find our way out! Please say yes."

"Yes!" agreed Margaret. "At eleven. We live very near the Gardens."

"Then we will meet you just before the entrance."

The Waite party took its leave, Mr. Waite allowing them all to pass out before he took up his crutches again. He cast Margaret one last glance, and, if either could have known it, their thoughts were much the same: what would come of this evening's work?

Chapter Ten

**The heart commands the head, to fight its
unjust quarrel, and say it is its own.
—Edward Young, *The Centaur Not Fabulous* (1755)**

After some discussion, Margaret decided her mother and uncle
could accompany her to the Gardens the following day.

"Miss Blakely did say 'we,'" she pointed out, "which means she
will have at least her mother with her, so why may not you and Mama
also go for a walk?"

The next morning proved frosty, however, and only by persever-
ance did Margaret have her family to the Sydney Hotel before eleven.
They waited with their backs to Pulteney Street, admiring features
of the building, so their anxiety would not be obvious.

"What will your mama and I do, if only Miss Blakely and her
mother come?" asked Alwyn.

"Perhaps walk at a distance behind us? You might invite Mrs. Blakely to join you, but I do not suppose she will accept."

"Considering the evil eye she gave me at the theatre last night, I don't suppose she will."

"Nevertheless, an invitation is only good manners. I suspect Mr. Waite is not the only obstacle to you winning Mrs. Waite, Uncle."

"Good morning!" called a cool voice, and they turned to see Charmaine Blakely approaching, her mother and Mrs. Waite some little ways behind her. Her trim green cloak with black piping and matching reticule made Margaret feel dowdy, and whatever eagerness she displayed the night before was nowhere in evidence.

At least Mrs. Blakely's restrained greeting was to be expected, and the presence of Mrs. Waite a pleasant surprise. "Good morning," said that lady. "What a fine day, though chilly."

"We will warm up soon enough if we walk quickly," Charmaine said. "I hope you are a good walker, Miss Hapgood."

"I fear I may disappoint you," Margaret confessed. "I am used to accompanying my mother, and one does not go very fast wheeling a chair."

"You go ahead and keep up with Miss Blakely, and leave Alwyn to push me," Mrs. Hapgood suggested. "We will keep to the wider gravel paths, lest my chair be in the way."

Mrs. Blakely frowned. "Then Eliza and I will follow the girls. I do not know that they should go into the labyrinth unaccompanied. And we had better purchase a map, so that we do not get lost."

"Oh, Mama," sighed her daughter. "What is the fun of a labyrinth if one does not get lost? They told us that the entire thing was only a half-mile long."

"And they also told us it sometimes takes people as long as six hours to traverse!" Mrs. Blakely protested.

Charmaine ignored this. She turned to Margaret. "You aren't frightened, are you? That we will be the only girls ever to lose their way in Sydney Gardens and never be seen again?"

"I think I have a good sense of direction," Margaret replied honestly.

"See?" Charmaine demanded of her mother. "We will not be lost. And Mama, I would prefer if you and Aunt Eliza kept your distance. If we need rescuing, we will scream. Or I will scream. Miss Hapgood has a good sense of direction, and I can scream very loudly, if I choose."

"Celia, shall we let the girls have their fun?" Mrs. Waite interposed. "If they take too long, you and I can purchase the plan and go in search of them."

Mrs. Blakely wrestled with this. "Well, perhaps. What would you say to an hour, Charmaine?"

"An hour and a half."

"Oh, my dear. An hour and a quarter?"

Mother and daughter bargained like merchants, and Mrs. Blakely gave way, of course. "Very well. An hour and a half."

Alwyn leaped in to say mildly, "Mrs. Blakely, Mrs. Waite, you are welcome to join my sister and me on our stroll."

Mrs. Waite looked to her sister-in-law, and, after a long moment, Mrs. Blakely grudgingly accepted. "Charmaine, we will see you in an hour and a half. Under the orchestra."

"Very well." Charmaine seized Margaret's arm and hustled her away. Once they were free of the others, she released her, and Margaret discovered it took every inch of her longer stride to keep up with the smaller young lady's admirable pace. Margaret would have liked to look about her but could only spare glances at the orchestra sawing away, its elevated platform flanked by a semicircle of sheltered tables. The frost had not deterred the crowds, and the girls were soon surrounded by families and couples and friends arm in arm, darting children with their scolding maids, and scores of doddering invalids.

Miss Blakely showed no interest in any of these and grew crosser by the second. When Margaret was detained by several children chasing each other around her, her companion huffed in irritation.

"Dear me," said Margaret, trying to detach the children's hands from her cloak. "You had better choose another base to run around. We are in something of a hurry." There were so many of them shrieking and calling and jostling that no one attended her straight off, and she bit her lip in dismay and threw Miss Blakely an apologetic look.

In doing so, she chanced to spot a wiry lad stealing up rather closely behind Miss Blakely, his hand outstretched and a glint of something in it.

"Oh, no you don't!" cried Margaret, springing forward and dragging along whichever children were still clinging to her. Bumping Miss Blakely aside, she grabbed at the youth's wrist and shook it until the tiny pair of scissors he held clattered to the gravel.

"I didn't mean nothin'!" the boy protested, as the other children scattered. When the tug he gave failed to break Margaret's grip, he opened his mouth wide and bit down on her gloved hand. She yelped, more from surprise than pain, and, with another jerk, he wrenched free and fled.

"Gracious!" exclaimed Miss Blakely, when she had recovered her balance and made sense of the situation. "One would think we were in Seven Dials, with such scamps about!" Her cross look was gone, and she was now regarding Margaret with something like admiration. "You astonish me, Miss Hapgood. How quickly you acted, to save my purse from that naughty little thief!"

"I think it was *thieves* in the plural," replied Margaret. She was panting with excitement. Bending down, she retrieved the scissors and held them up for inspection. "I believe the younger children provided the distraction so the boy could cut your purse."

"Are you injured?"

"No." Margaret removed her glove to be certain and then said again, "No. At least, the skin is not broken."

"We will certainly report them! To think we have paid a subscription fee only to be accosted on the very grounds! Do you suppose we should do it right away?"

Margaret considered this. "Well—only if you think it cannot wait. But if we did it now, it would take much of our time, and we could not venture far into the labyrinth, Miss Blakely."

"You're right. We will do it before we leave, and waste Mama's time, rather than our own. And won't you call me Charmaine?" Whatever ill will she had been harboring toward Margaret or Margaret's family that morning, Margaret's rescue of her purse banished it. She threaded her arm through the taller girl's. "And mayn't I call you Margaret?"

Margaret did not know how far to trust her companion's change of mood, but she appreciated it all the same, and she willingly agreed to Charmaine's suggestions. Arm in arm they proceeded to the entrance of the labyrinth and, smiling at each other, ventured in.

"If we see anyone holding a map, we must go in precisely the opposite direction," said Charmaine, "that we may get good and lost."

Margaret couldn't help but laugh. "Are you always this contrary?"

"Who says I am contrary?"

"Your mother might," she answered boldly. And in her head she added, *and so might your betrothed*.

As if the same thought had crossed her own mind, Charmaine said, "I'm not a bit contrary, but if people *will* persist in being unreasonable or uncooperative—!" The first passage they chose ended in a wall of shrubbery, and they retreated. "And I suppose I was difficult with Mama, but she can be so fussy and anxious sometimes, it makes me want to scream. Are you never impatient with your mother?"

Margaret remembered how Mrs. Hapgood had exasperated her into announcing Alec Arbuthnot's death prematurely and laughed again. "You are right. It doesn't count, being contrary with one's mother."

"And I am always ladylike with Mr. Waite," continued Charmaine. "I suppose you know we are engaged?" Her tone was more matter-of-fact than boastful. "I never contradict him when he is wrong. Not directly. A lady ought not. Though he ought to *under-stand* when he is wrong, without being told."

"Is—he often wrong?" asked Margaret.

"Very often! He is the most maddening man, to tell the truth. But he is my cousin and I have known him all my life, and we are to be married, so that is that." Dropping Margaret's arm, Charmaine kicked at one of the pebbles in the path and dragged her hand through the hedge, snapping off a leaf or two. "For one thing, he treats me like a fond uncle—and not even a very fond one!"

"Perhaps because you have known each other, and known each other as cousins, all your life," Margaret suggested.

Her new friend scowled. "Of course not! Look at the play last night: Florian and Geraldine were cousins, and they were quite enchanted with each other."

"But they did not know they were cousins until the end of the play."

"Nevertheless, they grew up together—Florian was just a child when he was found in the forest. Never mind—it doesn't matter. Dashiell is hopelessly stolid and prosaic. Not loverlike at all."

Margaret, all too aware of how that man's merest look made her insides gallop like runaway horses, had no answer to this, but Charmaine needed no further prompting.

"If he loved me, for instance, he would never have joined His Majesty's army two years ago. He came and 'asked my permission' (so he would say), but I was so angry that he would want to do something so *unnecessary* and *stupid*—!" She kicked at the gravel again and peered down a passage to her left.

"You mean he joined the army after you begged him not to?" asked Margaret.

Charmaine stopped short. "Begged him? Of course I didn't beg him. Didn't I just say I was always ladylike with him? I merely told him he must do what he liked and then treated him very coldly thereafter, by which he must have known I was displeased, and he went anyhow. Ooh! How furious I was! I did not answer his first *four* letters to punish him." Just the memory of her vengeance made a smile overspread her features. But then her latest turn spiraled into another blocked passage, and they were forced to turn back.

"And now look," Charmaine said, frowning again. "He went and got himself injured. It brought him home, I grant you, but am I to have a husband who can never dance? I *adore* dancing. And I do not intend to deny myself dancing simply because he went and got himself blown up. It is too bad his friend Mr. Haworth is missing an arm. I don't suppose he will dance either, and it would serve Dashiell right to see me courted by other men."

"Even if he may not dance with you, Mr. Waite must have seen that Mr. Haworth finds you very pretty," said Margaret, grasping at a straw in this whirlwind. None of her sisters or acquaintance ever talked like this.

Charmaine surprised her by bursting out in a tinkling laugh. "Isn't Mr. Haworth funny? He cannot string two words together around me. He gulps like a fish and bungles everything. I suppose his embarrassment will pass—one cannot remain long incapacitated by someone one will see every day, but, oh! how I wish Dashiell were even the tiniest bit as *bouleversé* by me as Mr. Haworth. It is no fun at all to have a betrothed so—imperturbable. If he is like this now, what will he be like after ten years?"

Their next turning brought them to a little gazebo of sorts, where a number of people were consulting their maps. The girls turned their backs on them.

"My two older sisters have been married for four years now," Margaret offered, "and their husbands remain quite fond of them. To be sure, they were excessively fond of them to begin with. My eldest sister Elfrida and her husband actually *eloped*." (The conditions of Alice's marriage had been even more scandalous, but Margaret decided there was only so much she dared tell such a new friend.)

To her surprise, Charmaine only grimaced at her. "It so happens, Margaret, I have heard of your sisters' adventures. Or misadventures, one might say. *And* of your uncles'."

"You have?" Margaret felt her heart sink.

"Indeed. Why do you think Mama is so disapproving?"

"I—well, I—"

"Your uncle Mr. Arbuthnot is not a very eligible *parti*, I'm afraid."

This was indisputable, but Margaret resented it all the same. "He is a very kind and amusing man," she said stoutly. "And handsome for his age and a good brother and uncle."

Charmaine raised her perfectly arched brows. "I am sure he is."

"You say that as if you would like to contradict me!" Margaret fired up. "I tell you he is. Whatever you may have heard. And my sisters are now very respectable gentlewomen in Buckinghamshire."

"You would know best about that," was her friend's infuriating reply.

Margaret's hands drew into fists, and she didn't even notice the twinge in the one the boy thief had bitten. "Well, if we Hapgoods and Arbuthnots are so objectionable, why did you invite me to walk with you today?"

"To make Dashiell angry," said Charmaine simply. "Oh, come now. You are turning red as a cockscomb."

Undeterred by this personal remark, Margaret was determined to know the worst. "And why would it make Mr. Waite angry if you were friendly to me?"

"Because we none of us want his mother to marry your uncle, Margaret, even if he is kind and amusing."

It was no worse than she suspected, and yet Margaret swelled with indignation. Not accustomed to hiding her feelings, she only managed to choke, "None of you need fear—if he once—admired—Mrs. Waite—he will trouble her no more!"

"How angry you are," Charmaine observed. "When you have calmed down you will see that I have not said anything without justification, even if my honesty repels you. I was cross this morning because I felt Dashiell should not have put me in the position of having to defend the family from fortune hunters, but when you saved me from the little gang of thieves I decided I rather like you. As long as your uncle knows he may not marry Mrs. Waite, I do not see why we may not be friends after all. I should like to know someone in Bath my own age and sex."

Afraid she would blurt out something to dash her uncle's hopes forever, Margaret could only shake her head and blink back tears of wrath. "Fortune hunters"! The smug little creature! To speak of Margaret's family thus and think they could still be friends!

She must get away from her as soon as possible, or her heedless tongue would be her family's undoing. "I must—I will meet you again at the exit of the maze," Margaret gasped. "You have given me much to think about. Please—excuse me. You must please excuse me."

And, without waiting for Charmaine's reply, she hurried away.

Chapter Eleven

The giddy and the thoughtless vulgar may spend an hour with pleasure in these gardens, but the man of taste and discernment will enjoy it.
—Nathaniel Spencer, *The Complete English Traveller* (1772)

Charmaine was right in thinking Margaret would see the truth in her words after she calmed down.

Perhaps an hour later, Margaret stood at the center of the labyrinth, blindly watching a stocky couple on one of the Merlin's Swings. The lady screeched with pretended dismay while her companion huffed and puffed, pumping his legs and arms to keep the suspended board in motion.

"I ought to be thankful, I suppose," she told herself, "that she was so candid with me. It seems to be more than she will do for

Mr. Waite. How it hurts, though, to be called 'fortune hunters'! As if I wanted any fortune for myself! I only want to save Papa. But I suppose she didn't say anything worse about Uncle Alwyn than Elfie or Papa ever did, even if they have more right to say it. And I suppose Alice and Elfie did scandalize everyone in Somerset when they got married, so it's small wonder if whispers of it reached London." If people gossiped about her family, her own behavior today would only add to it. Miss Blakely would surely tell her mother how Margaret had abandoned her in the maze and why. For this reason, Margaret waited here, hoping to intercept Charmaine and make peace, as the ticket taker for the swings assured her the maze had no other exit.

She wondered if she should admit defeat. How could Uncle Alwyn hope to prevail against so many opponents? Mr. Waite. Mrs. Blakely. Charmaine. Presumably the absent Mr. Blakely. Perhaps even Mrs. Waite herself, who might not be indifferent to him, but neither was she encouraging. If Margaret could only convince Alwyn to set his sights elsewhere, perhaps they all could be friends—she could be friends—with the Waites and Blakelys. Perhaps she could be trusted and liked for herself.

Two young bucks, who had been whooping and drawing attention to themselves when they were on their swing, now descended to saunter around the grove. In circling past her, one of them favored her with a bold stare.

Margaret looked pointedly away and pretended not to see him.

He nudged his companion, and they slowed to stop directly in front of her.

"Care to take a turn on the swing?" asked the one who had stared. He had a lopsided grin and an overly familiar tone. "My treat."

"No, thank you," she answered, not meeting his eye.

"Pretty girl, alone by herself," he persisted.

She said nothing.

"She's waiting for another gent," crowed the bold young man's friend. He was shorter than she and had a projecting tooth.

"Aw, come on, then," said the first. "He shouldn't have let you wait by yourself."

"Nor did he," lied Margaret roundly. "My friends—all of them—will be along shortly. I simply walk faster than they do."

"You've been standing here the whole time we were on the swing," the first one persevered.

Horrid man! She turned away from him and shielded her eyes with her hand as if she expected to see her party appear at any moment. In fact, Margaret would be grateful beyond measure if Charmaine would come at last—two girls would have an easier time than one, dismissing impertinent attentions.

Her unwelcome swains followed the direction of her gaze. "I think she's making it up," said the short one.

"That's right," his friend agreed. "I don't see any gent."

"That's because I'm standing over here," came a new voice behind them.

The threesome turned—Margaret as startled as the other two—to find a tall man with dark hair and narrow grey eyes leaning on his crutches, studying them.

"Mr. Waite!" squeaked Margaret.

"I'm sorry to have been so long," he said mildly.

The buck who first accosted her frowned, even as he and his companion retreated. "You might have said you walked faster than your friends because they were crippled!" he accused her, as if this were all her fault.

"Oh, they aren't all crippled," was Mr. Waite's pleasant reply. "Just me." When the men were gone, he continued in the same bland tone, "What happened to Charmaine? My aunt said you were walking together."

Margaret bit her lip, her relief at being rescued ebbing. "We—er—had a little argument, I am ashamed to say, and I needed a few minutes of solitude to reflect. I should not have left her, however. It's been quite a time, and I did think she would be along by now. I would not like her to be subject to such insolence! First the thie—" she broke off abruptly, not wanting to mention the gang of children. Who knew if she and Charmaine would ever be allowed to wander by themselves again?

Smoothing the front of her cloak, she changed tacks. "How did—you come to be in the maze?"

He held up one of the six-penny plans sold at the entrance, his eyes gleaming. "My aunt was in something of a pother that you and Charmaine had not yet returned, so I volunteered to fetch you."

"Oh, dear. I am sorry for your troubles. Especially with your leg—" she broke off once more, remembering too late that her mother told her it was indelicate to refer to gentlemen's limbs.

He grinned. "Haworth and I spent a more soothing morning than you, I suspect: hot baths, hot tea, a good champing by the masser.

Afterward I felt a new man." He waved one of his crutches. "Soon I may even be able to discard these altogether for a cane."

"That is very good news for you," she smiled, forgetting her embarrassment and glad he did not press her about the thieves or her argument with Charmaine. "But you must want to rest. If you give me the map and show me which way you came, I will choose a separate path, find Miss Blakely, and return with her."

But he tucked the map in his pocket and indicated a bench nearby. "A few moments more, and I will accompany you myself, Miss Hapgood. I don't suppose you want to risk being fatigued by strange young men again."

She did not, to be honest.

It was very odd to sit beside him, watching the people on the swings. She could not think of anything to say, as most subjects seemed taboo: their families, Charmaine, his infirmities.

"Is your hand troubling you, Miss Hapgood?"

Unconsciously Margaret had been touching and trying to flex it. She folded both hands in her lap. "It is nothing."

"Might I see?" he asked. "I saw a great many nothings in Spain and Portugal. Some of them worse than others."

"I assure you, Mr. Waite, it is nothing of that nature."

"Not a cannonball, then, or a musket shot? I am relieved to hear it."

When he went on watching her expectantly, Margaret saw no alternative but to draw off her glove. To her dismay, the little thief, while he had drawn no blood, had left a semicircle of red marks behind, and the skin was swelling and bluish with bruising.

After a hesitation, Mr. Waite gingerly took her hand by the wrist and fingertips to inspect it more closely, and Margaret prayed he did not notice the shiver that rippled through her.

"You are right in saying this is no common battlefield wound," he agreed, "for these look very much like teeth marks."

"D-do they? How—peculiar."

One eyebrow arched. "Peculiar indeed. Miss Hapgood, if you will not satisfy my curiosity, I must deduce that *these*"—he traced the marks lightly with his own fingertip—"were given you by my own beloved Charmaine."

"By Miss Blakely!" cried Margaret, snatching her hand back and beginning to work her glove back on, though it made her wince. "Ridiculous. Of course Miss Blakely did not bite me. If you must know, a little gang of children surrounded us when we entered the Gardens. Several of them provided a distraction, while one—the biter—attempted to cut Miss Blakely's purse. When I—warned him off—he bit me."

Amazement and amusement swept his handsome features. "You 'warned' one off, and he flew at you to bite you?"

"Well, no," admitted Margaret. "I had hold of his wrist, and, in his panic, I suppose, he saw no alternative way to break free."

He chuckled silently. "Great heavens. I figuratively doff my hat to you. Perhaps I should let you search for Charmaine by yourself; you have no need of my feeble protection."

Instead of smiling, she turned to him earnestly. "Mr. Waite, Charmaine and I decided we would not report what happened to us straight away because we wanted to take our walk. It is so hard sometimes to be a young lady, you understand. If our mothers thought thieves and bothersome young men would be hounding us, they might not permit us to go about on our own in future. And the danger is really not so great, for two young ladies together."

"If they can stay together," he said, still looking amused. "Are you promising you would never again quarrel with Charmaine? I find it nigh impossible myself."

"Of course I cannot promise, but I have learnt a lesson today and would do my very best to avoid quarreling hereafter. Mr. Waite—I only ask that you would not mention my hand, please. Or those young men. I am not asking you to keep a secret, exactly, but only not to—*volunteer* the subjects."

He bowed in acknowledgement. "Very well. But, if I had not come along, those young men—"

"Yes," she interrupted, rising to her feet. "Yes, I am very glad you did come along and am grateful for your assistance. Please do not think I am not. But as I explained, two young ladies together are safe enough."

"Especially if one of the young ladies is you, it appears." Out of politeness, when Margaret stood, Mr. Waite too began to struggle to his feet, and she resisted the urge to offer help.

"We had better find Charmaine, hadn't we?" she prompted. "Or I can, if you need more rest. Suppose, like me, she finds herself harried by someone because she is alone—she is such a tiny thing."

"That is true." There was a note in his voice Margaret would almost have called reluctance, except that it couldn't be. He arranged his crutches under his arms. "A woman of your character and stature is better suited to fend off ruffians than she."

That gave her a pang. He meant she was *hulking* and unladylike compared to Miss Blakely, she supposed.

Shaking out the map, Mr. Waite traced a finger along it, much as he had traced the teeth marks on Margaret's hand. "You see there is only one correct route from the entrance, but it wanders into every corner of the maze. I did peer into other allées as I went, but there are so many I could easily have missed her."

"Oh, dear. She might be anywhere. Perhaps if we called out as we went? I wish there were more of us to search. How is it that Mr. Haworth did not accompany you?"

"Hm. I'm afraid I set him another task."

"Do look, Mr. Waite," said Margaret, scrutinizing the plan. "What if, at each of these forks, you were to wait at the joining, and I would quickly run down either path? Each time, I would venture down the blind alley first, to rule it out. Then we could move to the next joining, and so forth, until we discovered her?"

"A masterful plan, Miss Hapgood. One you arrived at with dispatch and expressed clearly. It is our country's loss that, not only do we balk at allowing young ladies to wander Bath by themselves, but we also discourage them from purchasing army commissions, for you would make a very good general. After you, please."

She was glad the brim of her bonnet hid her face because she could not help dimpling at his praise. It *was* praise, was it not? Though perhaps not many young women liked to be told they would make good generals. Mr. Waite did not seem disgusted with her, however.

Glancing at him, she replied, "I am happy to follow, as well. If you have a bett—if you have another idea, rather, for finding Miss Blakely."

"None whatsoever. I am a soldier, you know—or I was—and am used to following orders. A confident commanding officer inspires confidence in his troops. Lead the way, Miss Hapgood."

If Margaret had come to feel remorse for losing her temper, Charmaine did not appear to suffer similar regrets. When Margaret finally came upon her, on the far side of the maze, sitting calmly in one of the gazebos, Charmaine merely greeted her with, "Well? Have you dismounted from your high horse?"

This question so renewed Margaret's annoyance that she ignored it. "How long have you been sitting here, Charmaine? I was waiting for you at the exit, and you never came."

Charmaine rose, shrugging. "I haven't your vaunted sense of direction, and I supposed you or Mama would come eventually in search. Speaking of whom, where is Mama? I suppose she is beside herself and will lock me up in Princes Street for a day or two."

"She was indeed concerned, but it was Mr. Waite who offered to search for you. He is at the nearest turning. And I have asked him not to mention the little thieves who bothered us, lest it add to anyone's worry."

Charmaine looked at her sharply. "And how should Dashiell even know there were any thieves, seeing as I have not suffered the loss of my reticule? There was no need at all to speak of it. I would not have taken you for a blabber."

"Nor am I!" declared Margaret. "He happened to notice I was rubbing my bitten hand and asked for an explanation." It was well that she had promised not to quarrel with Charmaine again because she found herself once more on the verge. All she knew was that, if Edith had handed her a pillow, Margaret would have delighted to hit Miss Blakely in the face with it.

"You might have put him off, at least, Margaret," persisted Charmaine.

"He caught me unawares. And, as I suffered my little injury looking out for you, I wish you would not chide me for it."

Charmaine's merry laugh rang out. "There, there. How easily you become cross. You cannot expect me not to be a little short with you, when I have waited so long."

But Margaret's moods could not revolve so rapidly as her new friend's, and a grumble lingered in her voice when she answered, "We better rejoin Mr. Waite, in any case. I am sorry he has had to walk so much on his crutches."

"Whose fault is that but his own? No, I will not feel badly over things for which I was not responsible. Come."

She took Margaret's arm as they set off and whispered, "I will reward him, however, for showing a little interest in me, even if it was Mama who made him do it."

They proceeded up the allée, and when she caught sight of him around the hedge wall, Charmaine beamed, releasing Margaret and stretching out her hand. "Dashiell, you came to find me! I thought I should be lost forever."

"Ah," he smiled at the sight of them, balancing his crutches that he might squeeze the hand she offered. "'If a man have an hundred sheep, and one of them be gone astray, doth he not leave the ninety and nine, and goeth into the mountains, and seeketh that which is gone astray?' Or, at least, does he not send Miss Hapgood to do the seeking?"

"Hm." Charmaine's smile remained, but she did not seem overly pleased to be compared to a sheep, even a precious one. "Naughty Margaret, if she told you I was the one who strayed, when it was actually the other way 'round."

"No, no," he replied. "Miss Hapgood was the soul of honesty and admitted as much. Perhaps you would have preferred the story of the hired hand who deserts his sheep? Alas. I wish I were a more literary man, but my first attempt has fallen flat."

"Perhaps," suggested Margaret, "you might leave off the Bible and say how glad you are the Sydney Gardens labyrinth hides no minotaur, like its namesake in Crete."

"I might," he answered readily. "But, as you were the one to guide me through, Miss Hapgood, does that make you Ariadne?"

Margaret had an uncomfortable memory that Ariadne assisted Theseus out of love for him, and she had no response. Fortunately, Charmaine thrust herself back into the conversation. "Well, if there were a ferocious beast in the heart of this maze, Dashiell, I would rejoice that you might slay him."

"Thank you. Though Miss Hapgood has already proven an able defender, and I would lay money on her in future—if you can manage not to provoke her into abandoning you again."

The last thing Margaret needed, she thought, was for Mr. Waite to turn Charmaine against her. And it made her sigh to be reminded that he thought her heroic and unladylike. But she said nothing, keeping her head lowered and pretending to study the map as they walked.

On pretense of leaning down to brush a clump of dirt from his crutch, Mr. Waite stole a glance at her.

There followed not another objectionable comment. Instead, he turned his attention to Charmaine, complimenting her appearance, hoping she had not been harassed while she waited for rescue, asking her opinion of the Gardens in general and the labyrinth in particular. Flooded with attention, she blossomed, her charming laugh tinkling out repeatedly. When they rejoined their parties below the orchestra platform, Mrs. Blakely had not the heart to reprimand her happy daughter, and she too was pleased by Mr. Waite's attentions to Charmaine. Mr. Haworth confounded himself, attempting to express relief that the young ladies had been found, and the parties were soon going their separate ways. Another meeting was anticipated—Margaret heard something about shopping and another something about a concert, with no clear idea of who was expected at what or when they were happening. Charmaine embraced her as if they had spent their time in uninterrupted delight. As for Mr. Waite, he hardly looked her way as he bid them good-bye.

And then it was just the Hapgoods and Alwyn again, passing out of the gateway and returning leisurely along Pulteney Street, Margaret wanting nothing more than to take a nap or—inexplicably—have a good cry. She could hardly determine which.

Chapter Twelve

**Each succeeding day inured Wolfstein more…to the idea
of depriving his fellow-creatures of their possessions.
—Percy Bysshe Shelley, *St. Irvyne* (1811)**

No sooner did Wolfstein join the banditti than Margaret looked up from her reading. Her mother was dozing nearest the fire, Elfrida's latest letter slipping from her hand, but even Uncle Alwyn did not appear to be attending.

"Uncle Alwyn," she began, shutting the volume, "tell me again how it went with you and Mama, while Miss Blakely and I were in the labyrinth."

He started. "Oh! Well. Quite well. The time sped by. We discussed the play at length. We walked to the canal bridge and then circled back and sat at one of the tables to hear the music and watch the passersby. You would have been pleased with me, Maggie, for I directed most of my conversation to Mrs. Blakely, though she only replied with the barest civility. Eliza said little—she talked more with your mama—but I had the joy of hearing her voice and, I hope, she mine."

"Yes, I am glad it was a pleasant time. However, if Mrs. Blakely was barely civil, it is because, as I guessed, it is not only Mr. Waite who objects to your designs on his mother—"

"Designs!" he uttered. "I protest the word 'designs'! My intentions toward Eliza are entirely honorable."

"I speak from their perspective, Uncle. As I was saying, it is not only Mr. Waite who objects. I'm afraid all the Blakelys do as well. Miss Blakely told me so while we were walking. I was vexed, I admit, but then I decided that, apart from her manner, I was not justified in being so, because she only spoke the truth, if baldly."

Unlike his niece, Alwyn Arbuthnot was too long accustomed to gossip and opposition to mind a little more. "Ah, well, I thought as much. Happily, Eliza is no girl of eighteen. She is a woman and must make up her own mind, whatever her family thinks. Did you ask Miss Blakely if they intend to remain in Bath?"

"I didn't, but Charmaine made no mention of leaving. But you are not hearing me. I mean to say that she called you—called *all of us*—fortune hunters!"

This, too, left him unruffled. Lying back in his chair, he crossed his ankles. "If I were only interested in Eliza's fortune—and, I confess, there have been ladies I pursued who had little else to recommend them—Miss Blakely would be justified in calling me that. But in this instance, Maggie, while I might not marry Eliza if she 'had not a penny,' as stage players are wont to say, I certainly would do so, even if she were considerably poorer. Even if we had to live in humble lodgings in Bridgwater, as your father would like me to. Therefore, in calling me a fortune hunter, Miss Blakely mistakes herself. But in calling *you* one, perhaps, she is not far off the mark."

For the second time that day she found herself sputtering with outrage. "Me? A fortune hunter?" She flung down *St. Irvyne*. "What care I for Mrs. Waite's fortune? I only want you to marry someone—*anyone*—who can support you in a modest fashion because Papa must be kept calm, and your money problems distress him mightily!"

Mrs. Hapgood blinked awake. "Oh, my. Did Wolfstein leap to his death? What did I miss?"

"You missed Uncle Alwyn calling me a fortune hunter while repudiating the name for himself," her daughter snapped.

"Well, my dear, I'm not sure I see the harm in it," her mother said, to Margaret's increased indignation. "Your papa certainly sets great store by money, so it's no wonder his girls do too."

"Richard should not worry so much. These things have a way of working out in the end," Alwyn added helpfully.

Margaret groaned. The Arbuthnot side of the family had ever been hopeless with financial matters, and if things had a way of working out, it was only because the Hapgoods ensured they did, at the cost of much sacrifice and hand-wringing.

Retrieving the book from the floor, she took a deep breath. And then another, for good measure. "Mama, Uncle Alwyn, the thing is, I feel badly that we are trying to deprive Mrs. Waite of her money."

"But I'm not trying to deprive her of her money," said Alwyn. "I mean to share it with her."

"To deprive her son, then," Margaret amended. "Deprive Mr. Waite of his inheritance, a good man, who—"

"Stuff and nonsense, Margaret," her mother protested. "Mr. Waite will still have his inheritance, when my brother and Mrs. Waite have died."

A considerably diminished inheritance, Margaret thought, if any remained at all. "But supposing Mr. Waite is not able to marry Miss Blakely, for want of income?"

They pooh-poohed this and said much to the effect that a young man ought to stand on his own two feet (never mind that Alwyn Arbuthnot never had, to Margaret's knowledge). Presently she gave up, only telling herself that her prior machinations had given Uncle Alwyn his opportunity, and he must sink or swim now as he saw fit. This must be her compromise. She would do no more to assist him.

No sooner did she decide this than doubts assailed her. For what, oh what, would become of them all if he failed? If he failed, and, at long last, brought down the Hapgoods with the Arbuthnots? And how could he not fail, when so many were arrayed against him? Could she really leave this to him, when so much was at stake? Should she not form some secondary plan?

When Alwyn suggested they attend the concert in the Upper Rooms on Wednesday, where they might again see the Waite party, she acquiesced. Let them have their doom, then, that much more quickly. At least she would then have much of the remaining time to remedy matters, if remedies were possible.

"But," she added, holding up *St. Irvyne*, "if we are to buy tickets for the concert, we must sit at home evenings until then to economize. Therefore, let us take up Wolfstein's adventures again."

"Very well. Do start over, though," Mrs. Hapgood proposed, "where Wolfstein sank into insensibility, because I fear I did too."

Doubting her mother would last any longer this time, Margaret obeyed. "'Chapter One,'" she read. "'Red thunder-clouds, borne on the wings of the midnight whirlwind, floated, at fits, athwart the crimson-coloured orbit of the moon...'"

Not far off in Princes Street, Dashiell, Haworth, Charmaine, and Mrs. Blakely sat at cards, while Mrs. Waite worked at her sewing. Dashiell had suggested casino, suspecting Mrs. Blakely would have no head for more strategic games and that Haworth would be too distracted by Charmaine to play well. He was right on both counts, but perhaps they were all somewhat distracted that evening.

They had thus far avoided discussion of the Hapgoods and Alwyn Arbuthnot after leaving Sydney Gardens, confining themselves to generalities. Charmaine had been pure sunshine, bestowing smiles and laughter all around, wheedling her mother back into good humor, rallying Haworth to more blushes and confusion, and occasionally brushing Dashiell's arm or hand in seeming unconsciousness. Her good mood buoyed the entire party, and Dashiell wondered if he was the only one immune to the enchantment. It was not that he did not appreciate her high spirits—a happy Charmaine being far preferable to an unhappy one—it was that they did not banish the memory of her earlier behavior. The glitter of her eyes and hard set of her mouth. For such a beautiful girl, she could look rather deadly. In her face was none of the frankness and transparency of, say, a Miss Margaret Hapgood.

Miss Margaret Hapgood.

When he penetrated to the center of the labyrinth, he was surprised how swiftly he spotted her, standing by herself, her gaze fixed on the Merlin's Swings. He had been looking for two young women together, after all. But something about this particular young woman's stillness drew his eye. She was deep in thought, and he found himself stilled as well, trying to read the emotions flitting across her face. A troubled mixture of hurt, indignation, embarrassment.

He did not know how long he watched her, but he was roused when two young men obstructed his view, the first stopping actually to address Miss Hapgood. Without realizing it, Dashiell swung into motion, hardly feeling his leg injury, though whether that were due to the morning's ministrations or his focus he could not now say.

The first damsel rescued, as it were, Dashiell should then have been anxious to find the absent Charmaine, yet he found himself lingering.

Miss Hapgood was, he discovered, an odd blend of frankness and reticence, and the remorse she expressed for arguing with Charmaine caught him off guard. He could not picture Charmaine doing anything similar, for Charmaine drew a veil over things she deemed unpleasant, leading the other parties to suppose she had forgiven and forgotten. Only later did they realize she forgot nothing.

Therefore, Miss Hapgood's shamefaced admission that she lost her temper with Charmaine cheered Dashiell unexpectedly, and he surprised himself in turn by speaking of the treatment of his injury, a topic he usually avoided. Candor evoked candor, it seemed.

And, when she smiled to hear he was improving, something curious awoke in him.

She had a very nice smile, Miss Hapgood. Her teeth were not flawlessly straight like Charmaine's—and she might even be accused of having the slightest gap between her two front ones—but it was a disarming smile, simply because it was spontaneous. It was honest. She did not smile to allure him; she smiled because she was genuinely glad for him. And he, paradoxically, found that alluring.

More surprises followed. To learn the two young ladies had been set upon by child thieves? And that Miss Hapgood not only preserved Charmaine's purse but also suffered being bitten?

He knew women of mettle, certainly—there had been a few soldiers' wives, camp followers of Wellington's army, whose devotion and courage he admired—but they were different creatures altogether. Sturdy, plain, a little grim.

Not that Miss Hapgood was *delicate*. She was tall and glowed with health, and she had certainly kicked his crutch a fair distance when they met. It was that, as with all women of their class, he could more easily picture her sewing or playing a pianoforte, than seizing young criminals and shaking them.

And there was nothing brawny about the hand he took in his own. Which he ought not to have done, only it somehow happened.

She—

"Dashiell, it is your turn," Charmaine interrupted his musings. Her voice was light, but her smile did not reach her eyes.

"Pardon me. Wool-gathering." He placed his nine on the table to pair with the seven and the two.

"That was the second time I said your name. What had you so deep in the thicket, pray?"

Dashiell waited until Mrs. Blakely captured the knave before responding. "I was thinking of the labyrinth in Sydney Gardens."

"Oh, yes," said Mrs. Blakely. From the note in her voice, she had been anxious to raise the subject. "My dear Charmaine, what would have happened, if Dashiell had not found you?"

Charmaine took a long breath and shot her betrothed a warning look which he interpreted perfectly: he was to say nothing about the two girls separating or about thieves or anything of that nature. "But he did find me," she answered, laying two cards down before her queen. "Rather easily. Was that what you were thinking, Dashiell?"

"Something along those lines."

Another few minutes passed before Mrs. Blakely went once more unto the breach. "My dear," she said again, "I hope you do not plan on being great friends with this Miss Hapgood."

"And why is that, Mama?"

Mrs. Blakely darted an apologetic glance at her sister-in-law, but Mrs. Waite did not look up from her sewing. "It will give *that man* ideas," she whispered.

"Say Mr. Arbuthnot, Celia," Mrs. Waite said steadily, taking another stitch.

"Mr. Arbuthnot, then," conceded Mrs. Blakely at normal volume. "He was very polite and harmless this morning, but there is no guarantee he will always be so."

"He will indeed always be so," Mrs. Waite continued in the same tone. "It is his nature. I tell you again, there is nothing to fear, either from him or from me."

"Oh, Eliza," her sister-in-law said placatingly, "I mean to say—that is—is it *wise* to—"

"Have no fear, Mama," Charmaine interrupted. "And, Aunt Eliza, I hope you will forgive me, but I thought it prudent to warn Miss Hapgood, for her uncle's sake, that we might all understand each other."

"Warn her?" asked her aunt coolly. "Of what? I do not see what she has to do with the matter."

Charmaine shuffled the deck of cards and began to deal them again. "My dear aunt, I just supposed that her family spoke plainly among themselves, as we do. And, knowing how both Dashiell and my father would prefer Mr. Arbuthnot not to—trouble you, I let Miss Hapgood understand our position."

Mrs. Waite's lips thinned, and Mrs. Blakely leapt in again. "Do you mean, Charmaine, that you gave Miss Hapgood to understand we Blakelys and Waites were not in favor of such a match?"

"I—hinted at your disapproval, Mama, yes."

There was a pause while her listeners absorbed this. Then Mrs. Waite ventured, "And—how did Miss Hapgood respond?"

"I suspect I did not phrase it tactfully enough—no, Mr. Haworth, do not defend me. I assure you, I *can* be too frank at times. And this must have been one of those times, for she took umbrage at first. I was mortified that I had offended her—you see, I try to get on with people—"

"All that is affable!" burst out Haworth.

"—Thank you. And I think she did at last come to see our point of view." She threw her betrothed an arch look. "As Dashiell said, an enemy is often more fearful in imagination than reality. Now that I have made things clear, there is nothing to fear from Miss Hapgood, and I would very much like to be friends with her. Friends and *not* enemies."

"Are there not other friends you might make in Bath, who do not come with such encumbrances?" her mother asked.

"If my taste ran to octogenarians," laughed Charmaine. "But seriously, Mama, would you mind Miss Hapgood if she didn't have her uncle? Because I rather like her. She is pretty and amusing. Would you not agree, Dashiell?"

He considered his cards before replying. "You have spent more time with the young lady, but she seems pleasant enough and pleasant-looking enough."

"Bah!" cried Charmaine, with a flutter of her lashes. "I would despair if I heard myself so spoken of!"

"Th-thankfully, no danger—you would—highest praise—" bluttered Haworth.

"Do *you* find her pretty, Mr. Haworth?" she turned on him next. "Or just 'pleasant-looking enough'?"

Thus cornered, Haworth sputtered and equivocated until Dashiell rescued him. "He means to say, I'm sure, that he found her pretty enough until he saw you."

"Indeed, yes," agreed Haworth with relief. "Thank you."

She laughed merrily once more. "My, how smoothly you work together, you two. Mr. Haworth provides the sentiment and Dashiell the delivery."

Haworth turned scarlet, but Dashiell only half-smiled. If Charmaine expected him to insist that he too shared the sentiment, she was disappointed. But the next instant she made to tease Mr. Haworth again. "La! Mr. Haworth, I suppose you mean to break every heart in Bath this winter?"

"I-I?"

"Y-you," she mocked, waving her hand of cards at him. "For you know it is no use flattering me, engaged as I am to Dashiell here. Therefore you must be planning to practice on me before you unleash your powers on other ladies."

Naturally, Haworth could muster no intelligible defense to this, and she was left to maraud at will. "Indeed—young, old, pretty, hideous, rich, poor. They will all be yours. You are master of your own fate. You may choose whom you will."

Not only was Haworth unable to reply, but her speech had the effect of silencing Dashiell as well.

Of course he knew already that, unlike Haworth, he was not "master of his own fate"; he could not choose whomever he willed. Though, even if he *could,* most men considered great wealth and a beautiful bride a welcome doom, after all.

No. It must be what Charmaine said at the theatre: novelty had its lure. Miss Margaret Hapgood, with her open countenance and her candor, was novel. Why should he not "like" her, as Charmaine did, and for the same reasons?

He was an engaged man, as Miss Hapgood knew, but that did not preclude the two of them being friends. Inasmuch as single young men and women could be friends. In fact, his engagement was what made his interest in her so thoroughly safe! So thoroughly harmless. Because it never could be anything more than liking. Than friendship, if they succeeded in becoming friends.

Dashiell told himself such things, as play continued, Haworth clearing the four center cards in a sweep. And, despite being a keen, clear-sighted young man, it must be admitted that he actually made the mistake of believing them.

Chapter Thirteen

Let us have the length of all the rein;
In shoppings, auctions, jauntings, or quadrille,
Leave us to spend, and lose whate'er we will.
— *The London Magazine* (1767)

Charmaine's note came as Margaret was finishing breakfast.

"Mama," she said, "what do you suppose? Miss Blakely invites me to go shopping with her today. May I?"

Mrs. Hapgood set down her toast, her mouth falling open. "Shopping? Did she say whether Mrs. Blakely will accompany her? I should like to shop as well, Margaret, but you have said we may only window-gaze."

"And so we may. Even if I go with Charmaine, I will only window-gaze, you may be certain. And she does not mention her mama, only that I am to write back and say where and when I will meet her, if it is agreeable."

"Well!" declared her mother. "Alwyn and I will certainly accompany you until you meet Miss Blakely. Then we will leave you girls alone and go a-window-gazing ourselves. You don't want to have Tilly slumping after you, do you?"

"Not especially," Margaret admitted. "But suppose Charmaine does bring her mother?"

Alwyn folded his napkin and lay it down. "Then it will be Sydney Gardens all over again. We will invite her to join us, and she may say yea or nay."

"And Mrs. Waite may be with her," Mrs. Hapgood pointed out. But Margaret guessed from the way her uncle consulted the looking glass over the sideboard that this had already occurred to him.

It was none of her business now, she reminded herself. Like a pendulum, she swung between wishing he would succeed and wishing he would fail. She would fret over wronging the Waites, and then she would fret over the peril to her father and possible ruination of her own family.

In spite of this, Margaret was still a young lady on her first visit to Bath, and her heart leapt at the thought of wandering all the glittering shops with a new friend. She need not borrow trouble. Little could happen in one day.

An hour later Charmaine sailed up to her outside the Pump Room in another smart wool cloak, this one cardinal red, and, putting her arm through Margaret's she whispered, "This time I've tucked my money away!" Curtseying to the others she added in a louder voice, "Mama and my aunt Eliza will be here shortly! They wanted to accompany Dashiell and Mr. Haworth as far as the King's Bath, so I bolted." And again, *sotto voce* to Margaret: "Who wants to see every cripple and valetudinarian in Bath clustered together? I will be so glad when Dashiell no longer needs crutches, though I suppose nothing can ever be done to grow back Mr. Haworth's arm."

As soon as Mrs. Blakely and Mrs. Waite hove into view, Charmaine hustled Margaret away toward the colonnade and Union Street, giggling with mischief.

"This is where I first met Mr. Waite and Mr. Haworth," Margaret said breathlessly.

"Yes, I heard about that. At least your bump has mended. You do not look so much the unicorn."

Margaret shook her head ruefully. Friendship with Charmaine would always require a certain level of forbearance, it seemed, but she would not quarrel again if she could help it. And she would enjoy the freedom it provided.

The day passed in a delightful blur as they made their way up Bond Street's parallel islands of shops to Milsom. The shopkeepers were busy with Miss Blakely, who had no hesitation in asking them to unroll bolts of silk or to fetch her the lace she saw in the window or the trinket that caught her eye.

For her part, Margaret played a game with herself: in each shop she would imagine the one, solitary thing she would buy, if she had the money. And how difficult it was to choose! At the jeweler, would she select the topaz cross or the handsome herringbone chain? At the milliner, would she refurbish her bonnet with the velvet ribbon or the feathers, both dyed rich chestnut? Which fragrance most tempted her at the perfumer? Which illustration would she choose for Edith at the print-shop—the view of Bath from the Bristol Road or the fireworks at Sydney Gardens? The toy shop was a cave of wonders, and Margaret wanted the lot of it for Freddie, but, if she could only have one item, it had better be the brightly-painted jumping-jack. At the end of Milsom, Marshall's library did prove grander than the one in Bath Street Margaret patronized, but she was not above airily recommending *St. Irvyne*: "Shelley's prose is somewhat high-flying, but my uncle and I find it thrilling!"

"You haven't bought a thing!" complained Charmaine, as they ended at a draper's, where Margaret was admiring a striped wool for her father that would hide dog hairs. "Dashiell will surely remark when all my parcels are delivered, and I will not be able to counter that he should see how many were sent to Henrietta Street!"

"Shall he mind that you have spent so much?" Margaret asked, when they emerged once more in the street.

"He will raise his eyebrow in that dreadful way of his or make some little comment, but it's not his business to mind. It isn't his money. Yet. It's Papa's! And Papa cannot complain because he keeps me positively *buried* in Hampshire, so how am I to know what is *à la mode* until I escape? And then how can Papa expect me to stay dowdy once I know better? I must have a new pelisse, I have decided. In the cold I cannot always go about in cloaks. As short as I am, a cloak makes me entirely shapeless."

Margaret knew there was nothing in her own wardrobe, present or future, to compare with Charmaine's, so she replied, "My sister

Elfrida writes that she has a new violet-blue redingote with frog fastenings. She saw the picture in Ackermann's."

"I think I know the very one," said Charmaine, her steps slowing as they descended Milsom, heading for Molland's. "Is Elfrida the eloping sister?"

Biting the inside of her lip at this description of the most beautiful and admired Hapgood, Margaret managed to say, "Four years ago, yes. Elfie and Frederick eloped. It did make a stir at the time, but now they are quite the most respecta—"

"Respectable people," Charmaine interrupted. "Yes, so you said. How many sisters and brothers have you?"

"We are four sisters, and the only brothers I have are my brothers-in-law. Elfie's Frederick and Alice's husband Joseph. Frederick and Joseph are brothers themselves, so if Alice has any children, Elfie and Alice's children will be double cousins!"

They were at the door of Molland's, and the girls were distracted for a time by the delectable offerings on display. When they had each ordered a tea and a pastry (Margaret permitted herself this reward for good behavior), they found seats at the window.

What heaven to be cozy indoors with food and drink! Margaret was glad it did not rain and she could watch the parade of shoppers and invalids and servants. The interest and novelty of the afternoon had driven her family's problems from her mind, but now she had leisure to remember them and wonder how her uncle was getting on with Mrs. Waite and Mrs. Blakely or if, indeed, they had merely greeted each other and gone their separate ways.

Evidently Charmaine's thoughts followed the same course because she began abruptly, "Did you tell your uncle he had better give up wooing Dashiell's mother?"

Margaret's shoulders sagged. "Yes, I did, so you needn't hound me about it."

"Do you call one question 'hounding?" Charmaine scoffed. "Well? What did he say?"

"That, in effect, everyone must look out for himself."

Charmaine made a face. "Not precisely reassuring. Very well, then. And you? Do you want your uncle to marry her?"

What answer could she make to this? Being Margaret, she made an honest one. "I would not mind it for his sake. He is a kind and amusing gentleman and she a kind and respectable lady."

"And he is gentlemen of limited means and she a rich lady."

With deliberation, Margaret took a sip of her tea before answering. "I cannot think of any person who would mind if their beloved family member chose a partner of comfortable means. Don't family members always wish each other happy and comfortable?"

"Hmm." Charmaine frowned. "I am not so certain of that. Dashiell, for instance, does not seem particularly concerned whether I am happy and comfortable." She gave a luxurious sigh and propped her chin on her hand. "Never mind your impoverished uncle. I'm bored of him. What I would really, really like, would be to dance and flirt my way through Bath this winter! I would have a hundred suitors, and Dashiell might be one of them, if he liked, but not if he was always going to be a cross old bear. You see, I don't want to be tolerated and humored! I want to be adored. Aren't you lucky? *You* aren't already engaged. *You* may dance and flirt and find a husband while you are here."

"I—don't want to find a husband, and I don't know how to flirt." She could not prevent a blush. For while it was still true that she didn't know how to flirt, the thought of a husband was no longer unimaginable. That is, if he were anything like Mr. Waite.

"Don't know how to flirt?" exclaimed Charmaine. "Why, I'll teach you. It's the most delightful thing in the world. I was having the loveliest time, before Dashiell returned." She smiled over this happy memory before suddenly clapping her hands together. "I've got it! It's perfect—I will tell my family I am helping you catch a husband, and the two of us will dance and flirt to our hearts' content. This way we can go to assemblies! What fun we'll have. I may have forbidden Mr. Arbuthnot to marry my aunt Eliza, but I will make up for it by helping you catch a rich husband."

"But—"

"Oh, come. You will enjoy it. You're pretty enough, and flirting is so easy. All the gentlemen will fall at your feet, like so many birds shot through."

"Will they?" Margaret breathed, quite unable to envision it.

"They will. I don't mean to say they will all propose—they aren't all so witless as to offer for a portionless girl, but they will like you very much and *wish* they could, all the same. You have only to smile and cast down your eyes and make them feel important and witty and handsome, as if you hang on their every word, and it is done!"

Margaret suspected Charmaine's vivid beauty had much to do with her success; nor was she certain, in any case, that she wanted a collection of such dupes about her. Even if one of them offered for her, despite her poverty, could such a simpleton make a good husband?

"Charmaine, if it is so easy, why do you say Mr. Waite treats you like a fond uncle? Why does he not tumble at your feet as well?"

"Oh, that stupid Dashiell," grumbled Charmaine, scowling. "For one thing, I do not flirt with him. It is impossible to flirt with someone you have known your entire life and who has always treated you as a superior older brother treats an amusing and annoying younger sister. For another, gentlemen who actually *are* important and witty and handsome aren't as flattered when young ladies treat them as such. But never mind Dashiell. I don't want to think about him."

A draft that scattered the crumbs on their now-empty dishes heralded the entrance of a lean gentleman with silvering hair and a woolen scarf wrapped twice around his throat who blinked and looked about him. When the two pretty young ladies caught his eye, he gave a little smile and nod.

Having no idea who he was, Margaret returned her gaze to the window, but Charmaine favored him with a longer look.

"Sir Dodkins!" another man called. "How are you, this fine day? We have escaped rain thus far."

"Yes, indeed. I am well. Yourself?" answered the gentleman.

Margaret smothered a yelp when Charmaine pinched the hand the little thief had bitten. "What did you do that for?"

"This is your first lesson," she answered, smirking at Margaret for the pain she had caused her. "We will leave now. Watch me with this Sir Dodkins and learn."

"We cannot speak to him," Margaret protested in a whisper. "We have not been introduced. And he is old!"

"I'm not going to speak to him, and you don't have to marry this one. Come!" Grasping Margaret by the elbow, she rose. With her handkerchief she wiped her fingers before pulling her gloves back on, but she did not replace the wisp of fabric in her pocket.

With wondrous naturalness, Charmaine made her way toward the shop entrance by a circuitous route that wound past Sir Dodkins and his acquaintance, Margaret trailing after her. As she went, her handkerchief slipped from her grasp and fluttered down.

But Sir Dodkins did not see it!

Margaret had only one instant to consider—should she retrieve Charmaine's handkerchief or walk on? Walk on, surely. She could not stop to bumble around among the tables.

Without slowing, she made to sweep past, only to be jerked to a halt when a heavyset lady shifted her chair and pinned the edge of Margaret's cloak to the floor! Charmaine was nearly to the door as Margaret tugged once, twice—"Pardon me, madam," she murmured, lightly touching the woman's forearm.

The woman recoiled as if Margaret had done her a mischief and fixed her beadily.

"I am so sorry, madam. It appears your chair—"

"Yes, I am using this chair," the woman replied, turning away from her again, affronted, only to find herself being bowed to by a lean older gentleman with silvering hair.

"I beg your pardon, madam," he said. "If you would allow me the liberty..." Without waiting for her to respond, he fixed his gloved hands on either side of her chair and shifted it slightly, freeing Margaret.

Margaret smiled her shy gratitude. "Thank you, sir."

He bowed again. "Sir Dodkins Hargate, at your service." And, with a nod at the seated woman, "And yours." A cough then overtook him, and he took refuge in his woolen scarf.

Margaret bobbed a curtsey and hastened to rejoin her friend.

"Little fool! Whyever did you scurry away like that?" Charmaine chided when they were in the street again.

"What else could I have done? I could not have spoken to him, after all. And, since he did not see you drop your handkerchief, I could not observe how you might have handled the situation."

Shaking her head, Charmaine sighed. "Alas, I did not make allowances for how age might have affected his eyesight. Though he must be in Bath for that cough. Catarrh, most likely. In any event, next time I will drop a large, red tablecloth."

"Will there be a next time?" asked Margaret.

"Of course, there will. 'Sir Dodkins Hargate'—the man is either a knight or a baronet, Margaret, so we will surely see and hear of him again. Fancy, if your first conquest is a knight or a baronet! Where is that library of yours in Bath Street? Let us look him up in Debrett's."

Charmaine guessed the spelling of Hargate correctly, and putting their heads together they read:

Hargate of Hargate Hall.

Dodkins Hargate, 3rd baronet, born June 1, 1752, married July 18, 1781, Marcia, daughter of Rufus Wandworth, Esq. of Ridley Park, in the county of Dorset, by which lady (who died 1794) he has a still-born son, December 4, 1782; Marcia, born August 12, 1787 (died 1809), married October 14, 1808, Walter, son and heir of Walter Chambers, Esq. of Pennington, in the county of Dorset.

"A widower," said Charmaine triumphantly. "And a childless one."

"An ancient widower whose daughter was even older than I," said Margaret. "I had rather choose someone else to practice on, if you please."

Her friend clapped shut the book. "What does it matter, if it only be for practice? And Sir Dodkins liked you. I could tell by the look in his eye. No, he will do very well to swell the ranks of your suitors. The more the merrier, you know. Ah, what fun we will have! I only wish my pleasure were not limited to the vicarious."

Margaret could not help frowning at her. "I hope Mr. Waite may never hear you say such things, Charmaine. He might fear you did not care for him."

"Let him fear. I will love him in precisely the amount he loves me, so he had better look to himself." Her green eyes glowed with what Margaret was coming to recognize as danger.

Margaret only shook her head again. Charmaine might envy her for being free to flirt with antique, catarrhal widowers, but Margaret knew better than to say that a hundred such were not worth one single, solitary Mr. Waite.

Chapter Fourteen

...Well dressed, well bred,
Well equipaged, is ticket good enough,
To pass us readily through every door.
—William Cowper, *The Task* (1785)

Some days later, when the Hapgoods and Alwyn Arbuthnot arrived at the Upper Rooms for the promised concert, they were not speaking to each other. Or, to be precise, Margaret and Mrs. Hapgood were not speaking to each other, and Alwyn was lying low.

The bone of contention made its appearance when the family dressed that evening. Margaret, fresh from Tilly's sullen best efforts, caught a flash of something on her mother's gown as Alwyn helped her with her cloak.

"Mama—is that jewelry you have on this evening?"

Mrs. Hapgood clutched her cloak to her and turned her back, while Alwyn rushed to the door ahead of the footman. "Come, my girls, we mustn't be late!" But, in hurrying past his niece, she spied an unusual gleam from the folds of his cravat.

"Stop!" cried Margaret, holding up a peremptory hand. "At once. Everyone, stop."

"Now, Margaret," began her mother in a wheedling voice.

But it was too late. Margaret marched over and disentangled the woolen folds from Mrs. Hapgood's hands, drawing back the cloak to reveal a glimmering brooch in the shape of a rosette, with small, sparkling stones encircling a larger green one.

"Where did this come from?" Margaret gasped. "I've never seen it before!"

"It's only paste!" declared Mrs. Hapgood, slapping her hand away.

"Paste or not, where did it come from?"

When her mother did not answer, Margaret rounded on her uncle, only to discover him holding a hand suspiciously to his cravat. He gave her a sheepish smile. "Now, my dear girl..."

"Don't you 'dear girl' me, Uncle Alwyn! Are you hiding something? And what do you know of this brooch?"

With a sigh, as if to deprecate her unreasonableness, Alwyn lowered his arm. Sure enough, a gold pin punctuated with tiny stones nestled in his cravat. "Paste as well," he assured her.

If not for her immaculate curls and gown, Margaret would have sunk onto the stairs and put her head in her hands. As it was, she almost wailed, "But where did they come from, and what did they cost?"

Alwyn patted her arm as if she were a distraught child. "My dear g—er, Maggie, rather—it was when we were shopping with Mrs. Blakely and Eliza—"

"You were supposed to be *window-gazing,* not shopping!" she broke in, remembering every last item she had *imagined* buying while she accompanied Charmaine, only to permit herself a half-shilling biscuit and tea in the end.

"But the two of them bought a great deal," Mrs. Hapgood reasoned with her. "Fabric and jewels and gewgaws and I know not what else! What Alwyn and I purchased was nothing at all, in comparison. We showed such restraint."

"But I only gave you each five shillings," Margaret persisted. "These cannot have cost ten shillings, even if they are paste!"

Mrs. Hapgood tapped her lower lip thoughtfully with a gloved finger. "Hmm...actually, I cannot recall what they cost. Alwyn, do you remember?"

"As a matter of fact, I don't. You see, Maggie, they extended us credit. So we needn't fuss over it now. Ten to one it'll be a couple months before they send around the bill, and who knows what may happen between now and then? Come now. Hadn't we better go? You wanted to be so early when we went to the play, yet here we stand, dithering over a few pounds here or there."

"A few *pounds!*" screeched Margaret.

"What would you have?" demanded Mrs. Hapgood, losing patience. "We could not buy nothing! We could not appear utterly penniless before Mrs. Blakely and Mrs. Waite."

"But we nearly *are* penniless," Margaret retorted, "and they already know it, don't you remember? That's why nobody wants anybody to marry Uncle Alwyn. So what shame is there in economy? See here: there is nothing we can do about this tonight, but tomorrow I will visit this jeweler because these items must be returned."

Both Mrs. Hapgood and Alwyn protested at length. How could she be so unreasonable? Did she really think they could be all winter in Bath and spend nothing? These pieces were beautiful, and the shopkeeper was so gracious and told them what a bargain they were making! They would die of shame if Margaret returned them!

But Margaret could not and would not yield. Tempers and voices rose, to the interest and enjoyment of the servants, and neither side gave ground. If the tickets to the concert had not already been purchased, Margaret would have cancelled the evening's activities at once, but, as with so many things, she thought bitterly, it was too late.

It was a silent walk, apart from their boots on the pavement and the creak of Mrs. Hapgood's chair, and even her first entrance into the Octagon Room could not distract Margaret. Was ever a family so hopeless? Did she really once take pride in thinking she could manage them? That she could succeed where everyone else failed? The more fool she. What if the shop would not take back the jewelry?

Because they were so late, the room was full, and Margaret was too preoccupied to notice the Waites and Blakelys stationed by one of the fires. She saw her uncle straighten, however, thrusting out his chest and making his bows in various directions, while Mrs. Hapgood graciously bestowed nods from her chair. Their ornaments sparkled nicely in such a setting, and the two of them threw off their earlier moods with an ease Margaret could not fathom.

Evidently the afternoon of shopping had cemented something between the two parties because it was the Waites and Blakelys who approached them, inviting them to sit together for the concert. Or, at least, Charmaine and Mr. Haworth invited them. Mrs. Blakely only pursed her lips; Mrs. Waite smiled but hung back; and Mr. Waite did no more than make them a distant bow.

"How glum you look," Charmaine told her, when they passed into the concert room and were seated at the end of a row, as far as possible from their mothers. The musicians were tuning their instruments, so they could speak without being heard. "Are you not excited to be here? I hoped we would see your beloved, but we are unfortunate."

"My beloved?" echoed Margaret, surprised from her gloom.

Charmaine giggled. "Of course I mean Sir Dodkins. Your first conquest. He who rescued you from the Terrible Weight pinning you to the floor."

"Oh, him," Margaret muttered. "What nonsense. Do stop."

"Oh, la! Young ladies who do not appreciate their swains risk losing them to more enterprising peers."

"You are welcome to him." Mischief of her own prompted Margaret to add, "Perhaps you should appreciate your own swain properly, lest someone else snatch him up."

Charmaine flicked her fan open to its widest and waved it. "They can't," she said simply. "Dashiell is an honorable man, and he would sooner serve Napoleon than break his engagement to me, however much I make him suffer! Do not change the subject. I am being serious. I told Mama how we met Sir Dodkins, and she said the Hargate family is a respectable one, and a longstanding and wealthy one. And Dorset neighbors your Somerset. In fact, the only drawback I can think of is that you would be Margaret, Lady Hargate. Margaret Hargate. It nearly rhymes, but at least it isn't Margaret Hargaret."

To Margaret's great relief, the concert began, so Charmaine must leave off. It seemed this friendship would be a costly one. Costly to her peace of mind and costly in that her mother and uncle would want to maintain the pointless charade that they, too, had money.

For his part, Dashiell observed Charmaine and Miss Hapgood with mixed feelings. It was evident that, whatever Charmaine was saying, Miss Hapgood disliked it. Could Charmaine not see that she was troubled tonight? Dashiell saw it in a glance. Her face was downcast, as when he had first seen her in Sydney Gardens. What could it mean?

With an effort he turned his attention to the music, a performance of Gluck's "*Che farò senza Euridice.*" The piece was a favorite of his mother's, and Dashiell saw she was listening with a smile, her eyes dreamy and her fingertips tapping as if she were at the pianoforte.

"*Euridice, o Dio, risponde*," sang the tenor, his hands clasped to his chest in appeal.

Dashiell saw Alwyn Arbuthnot settle back in his seat, on the far side of Mrs. Hapgood's wheeled chair, glancing toward Dashiell's mother as he did so. As if she felt this, her head turned a degree.

Nothing was said—it was the smallest gesture—and yet Dashiell knew.

Despite all her assurances and her outward calm, his mother still cared for this man.

And the man knew it and was biding his time.

"I must purchase that sheet music at once!" Charmaine declared during the interval.

"The—er—Euridice or the 'L—Love sits'—the Handel?" Haworth gulped.

"'Love in her eyes sits playing,' to be sure, you droll man. 'Love sits' indeed!"

Her laughter only rendered Haworth more tongue-tied, but he managed to stammer out how delighted he would be to hear her play.

"Hearing Charmaine perform is one of her father's and my chief pleasures," Mrs. Blakely declared. "Do you play, Miss Margaret?"

Caught off guard, Margaret replied, "I'm sure not as well as Charmaine."

"Fiddlestick," said Mrs. Hapgood, determined to boast in her turn. "Margaret plays the best of all my four daughters."

As the other Hapgood girls had limited repertoires indeed, this was technically true but hardly anything to crow about.

"Did you prefer the Gluck or the Handel, Miss Hapgood?" Mr. Waite spoke up. He was standing behind Mr. Haworth, and something was different about him.

"Your crutches!" Margaret exclaimed. "What has happened to them, Mr. Waite?"

A smile broke over his lined face. "I have graduated, you see. To this cane." He gave the item a flourish.

"That is splendid, sir!"

"Too bad he still cannot dance," said Charmaine. "Which means the two gentlemen I would most like to partner me are both *hors de combat*. But I will not let it stop me. Dashiell, Mama—I insist we attend the next assembly. When we were in the Octagon Room, I peeked into the ballroom and we simply must go. It has been an age, and you cannot expect me never to dance again."

"If I could—would give anything—still, pleasure to watch—" bumbled Haworth.

"See? Even Mr. Haworth would be satisfied just to watch Margaret and me dance," Charmaine insisted. "Dashiell, say we may go."

"If you like, and if Miss Hapgood and her family like."

At his words, Margaret's gloom swamped her again. Subscription fees to the assembly rooms, on top of everything! But Alwyn was already expressing his approbation, and the deed was done. Now it just remained for her to juggle the budget and find the money, as ever. She would very much like to attend an assembly and would have been filled with happy anticipation, if not for the anxiety of the paste jewelry. The pounds' worth of paste jewelry. How could she enjoy herself and write to Edith all about it, if in the same letter she must confess the purchase of the paste jewelry?

The conversation moved on—Mr. Haworth and Alwyn trying to think of any dances Mr. Haworth could participate in—ones which would involve no "arming left" or "hands across" or "take hands and circle." Whenever one made a suggestion, Charmaine was quick to run through the figures in her mind and, more often than not, find something to make it impossible.

"You never did say whether you preferred the Gluck or the Handel, Miss Hapgood," Mr. Waite spoke again, when there was a pause.

"Oh! The Gluck, I suppose. They are both lovely."

"Then I will buy *both* pieces," pronounced Charmaine, "and Margaret and I will hold a recital for you all."

The idea may have delighted a proficient like Charmaine, but it filled Margaret with horror. "Please excuse me from my share of it. I'm sure I would far rather hear you play both pieces, Charmaine."

"Don't be modest, Maggie," Alwyn urged her, seemingly suffering the same delusion as Mrs. Hapgood, that Margaret's performance could equal Charmaine's.

"Yes," agreed Charmaine, poking her. "Don't be modest, Maggie. Shall we say, a week from today, in Princes Street? Ten days?"

"No!" Margaret protested, alarm making her forget her manners. "We already heard professionals this evening—why should we hear the same works performed by rank amateurs?"

"It would give us great pleasure," murmured Mrs. Waite. This remark was seconded with decided head-nodding from Mr. Haworth and a polite smile from Mrs. Blakely.

This was dreadful. But, apart from outright refusal, Margaret could see no escape. She made one last effort. "My sight-reading is abysmal, and we have no instrument in Henrietta Street on which I may practice, but, if you are determined to suffer, far be it from me to deny you."

"You may practice on our instrument," Charmaine said. "Mayn't she, Dashiell? Whenever she likes."

He hesitated. "To be sure."

That infinitesimal pause made Margaret want to sink into the earth. Of course he didn't want her in his house! He didn't want any single one of her family in his house! Why must Charmaine be so obstinate, and why must everyone give way to her?

"And you must come for supper beforehand, Mrs. Hapgood, Mr. Arbuthnot," he added after another moment.

"Mama hates to eat from home," Margaret lied desperately, wanting to spare Mr. Waite. "But we thank you. Her tender health requires a particular diet."

"I'm sure it requires nothing of the kind," Mrs. Hapgood protested. Having not eaten in company in years, she could think of nothing more delightful, and only think of the opportunity it would afford Alwyn! How thick of Margaret.

"It's settled then," said Charmaine. "You will name the day, and you may ask our chef to prepare whatever you like, Mrs. Hapgood. Ah! We must take our seats again, but how glad I am that Margaret and I have two things now to look forward to: dancing and performing."

If there was a second half of the concert, Margaret did not hear a note of it, such a whirl her mind was in. She could not decide which would be worse: to invade Princes Street where she was not wanted, or to avoid Princes Street altogether and then perform a piece she had never once played. On one point her thinking was clear—if she was to name the day, she would put it off as long as she possibly could.

CHAPTER FIFTEEN

**Yea, and elsewhere, so far as my coin would stretch, and
where it would not I have used my credit.
—Shakespeare, *Henry IV, Part I* (c.1597)**

"I'm sorry, miss, but we cannot take back items after they have been worn," the jeweler explained. He was a small, soft person with a round face, but there was nothing soft about the look in his eyes.

"But they were only worn once, for a few hours," Margaret pleaded, wishing she had not mentioned the wearing at all. She held them out for his inspection. "You see no damage was done to them, and, as you were so kind as to give them on credit, will you not take them back now, with our thanks?"

"What business would I be in, if I merely lent things out, for no payment at all?" he argued. "I am not in the habit of renting my merchandise."

"I understand, but I am asking if you might make an exception, sir. I assure you I would tell no one of it, so you needn't fear others taking advantage."

"As *you* are trying to take advantage?"

She felt her hands gather in fists. Did he not guess what it cost her, to make such a humiliating request? Taking a long breath, she said, "Sir. I do not mean to take advantage of you. And if you were so kind as to assist us in this matter, I would be certain to tell everyone what a good jeweler you are and what fine items you stock. Won't you please consider it?"

With finality, he held up his hands and backed away from the counter. "I am very sorry, miss, but I too have financial pressures and responsibilities. Please enjoy your purchases, and we thank you for your custom." With that, he scurried into the back room.

Reluctantly, she replaced the ornaments in her reticule and tucked it in her cloak. She wished she had asked him how much they cost or when the bill would be sent, but she would know soon enough, she supposed. In the meantime, little could be done except to practice even stricter economy.

"That is too bad, my dear," Mrs. Hapgood sighed, not altogether convincingly, when Margaret presented her once more with the brooch. "I did tell you that it would be a fruitless errand."

"Yes, you did."

"If you fear we will not be able to pay the bill when it comes, why not simply ask your father? I'm sure he did not expect us to survive on the ha'pennies you have been doling out."

Some while later, she sat in the morning room, re-reading Edith's last letter, in which her youngest sister had much to say about their father's health: "He has caught a cold, and Mr. Lewis says it is a mercy because it has forced him to lie abed for several days, but it has been rather wearing for me because it gives Papa far too much time to think about Uncle Alwyn. His earlier optimism is fading, and now he asks repeatedly whether I have received news of any progress. I try to soothe him and set his thoughts on less trying subjects, but you can imagine with what success."

Reading this passage, Margaret knew she could not write now of this new extravagance and add to little Edith's burden. Her own shoulders must bear it. Nor could she ask her oldest sister Elfrida for advice or even for a small loan, for a letter from Elfrida also lay at hand. In it was much about little Freddie's frightening bout with the croup (now thankfully passed), followed by other news which stayed Margaret's pen:

> *Frederick and I rejoice to hear you are at last seeing*
> *more of the world. We thought briefly of paying a visit*
> *to Bath ourselves, but all plans of that nature must*
> *give way this winter because I am expecting again, and*
> *Alice thinks she may be as well! You know how difficult*
> *it was for her when she lost the other one, and how*
> *Mama scolded her and said it was because she was "too*

much out of doors, wading in creeks and scrambling up trees." Whether or not it was true, Alice felt guilty, so please say nothing to Mama yet. At any rate, her Joseph is cossetting her, and Alice complains he will not let her do anything, by which she means any of her usual tomboy activities...

No. However much Margaret might like to be relieved of her worries, she wanted still more to be made thrice an aunt. She would not trouble her older sisters with ill tidings either.

Margaret shut her correspondence in the drawer and took out her budget, grieving over all the items listed as "debits," which would soon outweigh the one "credit" of Squire Hapgood's initial outlay! To these she must add £1-8s for subscriptions to the balls in the Upper Rooms. Thankfully, Mrs. Hapgood demurred, saying, "I have no desire to sit in my chair in a hot room late at night twice a week. Alwyn will accompany you, Margaret, and you can tell me about them later."

Tapping her pen on the desk, she wondered if she should make an estimate for the jewelry. Uncle Alwyn had hinted that they cost several pounds. That could mean anything—three? five? ten? Please, God, let it not be ten!

In any case, Uncle Alwyn said it would be a couple months before the jeweler sent his bill. In the meantime, they must continue to scrimp where they could.

In the budget she scrawled a note of interrogation far down the debit column, to be filled in later. They had indeed scrimped the last two days, Margaret forbidding them from venturing farther than Sydney Gardens and church, and when Tilly presented her with Flint's menu for the week, Margaret drew a line through every meat dish, ignoring all protests. She had not even risked a visit to Princes Street to try out the new music, for fear of leaving her relations unsupervised.

Charmaine's invitation to shop for ball finery was likewise refused, though Margaret did so with a pang. And something of her regret must have made itself known in her note because a knock interrupted her solitude, and the footman Hudgins appeared. "Parcel for you, Miss."

"A parcel?" Eagerly, Margaret took the small box tied with string, slipping the card out first.

M—

To show I bear no grudge for you being such a bore, I am sending you this trinket to wear tonight, and, indeed, any night, for as long as we are friends. I cannot remember where I got it, but I think it will suit you. In return, you must let me call at Henrietta Street tomorrow, that we might discuss the ball at length!

—C

"The lovely thing!" breathed Margaret, holding up a necklace of seed pearls and pale pink chalcedony. How too, too thoughtful of Charmaine! Such a donation was worth bearing a thousand of her provoking remarks. It would be perfect with Elfie's ivory sarsenet that Margaret had made over, and she would wind a pink ribbon through her hair to match.

Graver thoughts driven away, she hurried upstairs to dress.

At Alwyn's insistence, it was past eight o'clock before they made their way into the ballroom.

The lumpish Tilly had exerted her best efforts: Margaret's gown was clean and pressed and her hair dressed and ribboned becomingly, but it was Margaret's own eagerness which made her hazel eyes sparkle and her cheeks glow.

Streaming with light, the Upper Rooms milled with people in their finery. Margaret clutched her uncle's arm, trying not to hop with excitement. The Octagon Room was fuller than it had been for the concert, and a bowl in the tea-room rang with the sixpences paid for refreshment. There were people on the staircases, in the passages, lining the walls in the tiers of benches, moving through the quadrille figures. In addition to Bath's usual crowd of the aging and decrepit, Margaret saw young ladies, scheming mamas, groups of young men puffed up and ready to be admired. Striding to and fro, bowing here and addressing a word there, holding court, was the elegant Master of Ceremonies Mr. King, to whom Margaret was too awed to speak a word when he drew near in welcome.

"Ah, so this is Miss Margaret Hapgood," Mr. King beamed. "Mr. Arbuthnot, you will be glad to hear I was already requested to make an introduction, if your niece should appear."

"My gladness will depend on who made the request," replied Alwyn loftily.

"You will not object, surely, to a baronet? It is Sir Dodkins Hargate of Dorset. A respectable widower of large fortune. Shall I call him over?"

Alwyn raised an eyebrow at his niece. "No objection at all, Mr. King." But when the Master of Ceremonies glided away, Alwyn dropped his condescending manner. "Baronet? How came this baronet to know of you? You never mentioned any."

"Uncle!" bleated Margaret. "Of course I don't know him, to speak of. Charmaine and I saw him at Molland's last week. He's a hundred years old, if he's a day, and he has a dreadful cough. It never occurred to me to mention such a person."

"That's as may be, Maggie, but you heard King: the man's a baronet and rich. If he wants to dance with you, it won't harm you, and it may very well help you. The social world operates on credit. Having no rank or fortune of your own, you must rely on the baronets of the world to vouch for you."

Silenced, Margaret surrendered to her fate, but in the time it took Mr. King to fetch Sir Dodkins, she glanced about for the Waite party.

"They are not here yet," said Alwyn, reading her mind. "I told you we were early."

Too soon Mr. King was returning with Sir Dodkins in tow. The baronet was coughing into his handkerchief, but he stowed it before reaching them.

"Mr. Arbuthnot, Miss Hapgood—Sir Dodkins Hargate."

"Miss—Miss Hapgood," the effort to suppress a cough made the baronet's voice veer wildly. "Would you do me the honor of dancing the next with me?"

"Yes, thank you, sir." She could not think of anything to say after that, and Sir Dodkins was coughing again, but Alwyn mercifully smoothed their way, beginning to chat on all manner of Bath subjects.

"We have spent much time in the Gardens, as we live so near," Alwyn wound up, "and have explored every inch, I expect."

Sir Dodkins made Margaret another bow, and she was happy to see his gray hair still covered the crown of his head. "Have you even ventured into the labyrinth, Miss Hapgood?"

"Yes, once. With my friend Miss Blakely."

He smiled, and she noted he also still had a full set of teeth. "Ah. Was Miss Blakely the young lady with you at Molland's?"

His remembering Charmaine cheered Margaret up. Perhaps he was merely passing his time with her, and the person he really wanted to meet was Charmaine? He would be disappointed to learn she was already engaged, but at least Charmaine would enjoy his disappointment.

And then Sir Dodkins was leading her to the floor. The number of couples had grown, and Margaret was alarmed to see it might take a half hour to work everyone through the figures.

For the first minutes, Margaret was spared making conversation, as the exertion of crossing the large ballroom brought on the baronet's cough again. But after he fought this down he asked, "Is this your first time in Bath, Miss Hapgood?"

"Yes. I have come with my mother and uncle, for the sake of my mother's health."

"I hope she is not too poorly," he said on the next pass. "As you can see, I have a touch of catarrh—" as if to prove his point, his words came out in a burst as he tried to suppress another paroxysm. Apart from these sporadic doublings-over, as fits took him, he moved limberly enough.

"She is well—for her," answered Margaret. "I think the novelty does as much as anything to cure her, for she has yet to take the waters."

"I need not ask if Bath agrees with your health, Miss Hapgood, for you are blooming."

"Thank you." She mustered a weak smile, which then blossomed into genuine delight when she saw the Waite party appear at last in the doorway. Every male eye might fly to Charmaine, again wearing her changeable silk taffeta, her dark hair dressed and curled and wreathed with roses, but Margaret picked Mr. Waite out first. Tall and upright, leaning casually on his cane, his evening dress immaculate—Sir Dodkins could no more compare to him than a withered stump to a virile oak.

Mr. Waite's gaze traveled the long ballroom slowly as Mr. King rushed to welcome them, and though Margaret and Sir Dodkins were some ways down the line of dancers, he saw her and inclined his head in acknowledgement. Margaret felt a flutter of she-couldn't-say-what.

Mercy.

She must absolutely stop thinking about that man. For a thousand reasons she must. Stop thinking of his handsome dark face, stop thinking of his grey eyes that so disconcerted her, stop thinking of his fine person. Stop thinking of the day they sat together by the Merlin's Swings, when he ran his finger along her hand. She was sure he didn't dwell on it as she did.

"Have you other family, Miss Hapgood?" Sir Dodkins interrupted this reverie when they crossed hands for the promenade.

"Er—two older sisters, married. One younger sister and my father, at home in Somerset. One nephew." She did not mean to sound so cursory, but, of course, her mind had been elsewhere. Then, flustered, she asked, "And you? Have you other family here in Bath or at home?"

No sooner were the words out of her mouth than she remembered with a plummeting sensation that, no, he had no other family—his family was dead, of course, all dead—wife, son, and daughter! Had she not read as much and discussed it, with Charmaine? Oh, heavens. But perhaps he had a few remaining cousins, dear to him? A sibling?

To her dismay, his face darkened with sadness, as if someone had snapped closed the shutters on it. *Margaret, Margaret*, she berated herself, *this will never do!* Although she had no interest in him as a potential suitor, that did not mean she meant to wound him. For the thousandth time she reminded herself always, always to think before she spoke. Only see what a little distraction did to her! Margaret did not need her sisters or Charmaine beside her to point out that no other girl the baronet partnered this evening would extinguish him thus; mindful of the honor he did them, they would all have consulted their Debrett's and remembered what they read.

To her relief, another attack of coughs required him to bury his face in his handkerchief. Margaret sighed remorsefully, but, in averting her gaze from Sir Dodkins, she saw the Waite party still engaged with Mr. King, who appeared to be making introduction after introduction. There was much bobbing and bowing and curtseying. Charmaine said something that made her admirers roar with laughter, and even Mr. Waite's lip curled in amusement, and envy swamped Margaret. Social credit or no social credit, would this dance never end?

"Sadly, I have lost my wife and both my children," Sir Dodkins answered her at last (unwittingly twisting the figurative knife in Margaret as he did so). "My daughter Marcia when she was not much older than you, I suspect."

"I am so very sorry," was her inadequate reply. But her sincerity was plain, and he nodded.

Finally, after more endless loud silence between the partners, the dance eventually did end, and Sir Dodkins bowed over her hand and muttered something that was swallowed up in yet one more cough. Just when she thought she could put disaster behind her and join her friends, however, here was Mr. King again with some young puppy who requested Margaret for the next, and she was whirled away again, hard put to hide her vexation.

At least Charmaine and another young man joined the set, and Margaret saw Uncle Alwyn bowing to Mrs. Waite.

"You—dance well," the puppy addressed her when they went round in circle. Margaret already could not remember his name, but he had round, dark puppy eyes and was panting with the exercise.

"Thank you."

"Is it your first time in Bath?"

"Yes."

"Do you like to ride? I just recently purchased the finest horse in three counties."

Sensing her salvation in this comment, Margaret waited for the next steps to bring them together. "The finest horse, you say? Do tell!"

Miraculously, the puppy's description of his new horse and the marvelous bargain he struck in acquiring him consumed fifteen entire minutes. Margaret had only to hear the next installment, smile, and nod whenever they came together, and the rest of the time she was free to look about her. Charmaine and her partner appeared to be enjoying their dance—or, at least, Charmaine appeared to be enjoying it. The young man looked like a hooked fish that had been slammed against the bucket to stun it. Uncle Alwyn and Mrs. Waite smiled at each other as they danced. Not in an obvious manner, but their contentment was plain.

She told herself she was not looking for Mr. Waite, but she was conscious of disappointment nonetheless when she didn't see him. Perhaps, because he could not dance, Mr. King forced him to make a fourth in a hand of cards? If he was trapped in the card room, Margaret might not see him again at all this evening. But, no, there was Mr. Haworth, who by the same token would have also been forced to play cards. He stood woebegone as he watched Charmaine's partner, who, if he was not much to look at, did at least have two arms to him. And there again was Sir Dodkins, being talked at by a middle-aged woman in a tall, feathered turban. When the baronet caught Margaret's eye, he looked pensive and did not return her faltering smile. Oh, dear. She would have to tell her uncle that her dance with Sir Dodkins might have done more harm than good.

"—the Ride?" asked the young puppy.

Margaret had no idea what he had been saying, so she uttered, "Indeed! How splendid. And pray, what color did you say your horse is?"

"A—bay," he said, puzzled. (He had, after all, already referred to its coat several times.) "A bright bay."

"Splendid," she said again, glad to hear the orchestra play the closing strains.

"It's nine o'clock. Will you have your tea with me, Miss Hapgood?"

Seeing Charmaine being led off toward the tea-room by her own partner, Margaret submitted to this, bracing herself for more ceaseless horse talk.

He led her through the Octagon Room into the tea-room, and in neither place did she see Mr. Waite, whom she was *not* looking for. Tossing a shilling in the glass bowl, the puppy gestured her toward two vacant chairs at the end of the farthest table. Perhaps he hoped the location would provide a measure of privacy or quiet, as the room swelled with the din of conversation and chairs scraping back and forth and waiters rushing in every direction. The disadvantage of their distant seats became clear after some minutes, however, when the puppy's chatter trailed off and he began to frown in impatience.

"I say, I thought the waiter would bring our refreshments next. He has come this way several times but will not meet my eye. No, no, this is insupportable!" he complained, over her demurral. "If you will excuse me, Miss Hapgood, I will catch one of them and make sure you get your tea!"

Margaret had no objection to the young man taking himself off, and she sat, more pleased than otherwise, humming. She only wished her chair did not face the wall, that she might look about her less obviously. Perhaps, if she did not see Mr. Waite at the ball again, she would tell Charmaine that, yes, she would like to come to Princes Street to practice on the pianoforte. After all, if she must perform, she might as well not butcher the piece.

But she was too honest a girl to deceive herself long.

What you really seek, Margaret Hapgood, is an excuse to see Mr. Waite. Your friend's intended husband. Out of all the gentlemen in Bath, why should your thoughts tend his direction? You hardly know the man beyond his appearance and one solitary conversation! He has, I grant you, a very nice appearance, but what matters that? If he knew—if anyone knew your thoughts, how aghast they would be! How repelled!

But another inner voice piped up in Margaret's defense, observing that Charmaine did not seem to love her intended, nor even to *want* to love him. If such were Charmaine's feelings (or lack of feelings), did she really deserve him?

These thoughts were both fruitless and unwise, however, and Margaret hastened to silence them. Charmaine might or might not love or deserve Mr. Waite, but neither did she deserve Margaret's disloyalty, especially when she so kindly shared her jewelry with her.

The memory of the necklace spurred Margaret to greater vehemence. This ill-advised *tendre* for Mr. Waite must be rooted out! Confessed to no one and completely done away with. Thank God no one suspected! No harm was yet done. No one knew that, if she were permitted, she might love him. No, no—she meant *like* him. *Margaret, see here. You must—*

But before she could tell herself what, precisely, she must do, her self-inflicted sermon was cut short, as a teacup materialized before her.

Looking up, she saw its bearer was none other than the man she had just been vowing to cut from her heart.

He gave her a slow smile.

"Good evening, Miss Hapgood," said Mr. Waite.

CHAPTER SIXTEEN

Surely...a man of common penetration may see to the bottom of a woman's heart.
—Samuel Richardson, *Sir Charles Grandison* (1753)

"Thank you," said Margaret, her heart starting to thump. The teacup rattled against the saucer, but she managed to take hold of it without spilling.

And then, just as he had in the labyrinth, Mr. Waite carefully lowered himself into the chair beside her, angling it toward hers and resting his cane against the table.

"Oh!" began Margaret, thinking of the absent puppy who would return at any time.

"Yes?"

"Er—nothing."

"How are you enjoying the ball, Miss Hapgood?"

She wanted to say it was a hundred times better now, but she managed to stuff this down.

"I like it very much."

"You have already made some conquests, I see."

He did?

She smiled shyly. "You sound like Charmaine. I am sure the two gentlemen I danced with were only occupying themselves until they could partner her."

"Ah, and now you fish for compliments."

"No, indeed," cried Margaret, stricken. "I am sorry it sounded that way, I assure you—"

To her surprise, his lined face crinkled up in a chuckle and he gave her a friendly grin. "How easy you are to joke, Miss Hapgood. Perhaps because you are so frank and sincere yourself, you assume the same of others."

Frank and sincere? She thanked heaven for his blindness. Otherwise he might guess her inappropriate feelings for him, or how she originally hoped to foist her spendthrift uncle on Mrs. Waite. (Her inappropriate feelings weighed more heavily at the moment.) It must be her imagination that made her feel as if he could see through her.

Her guilt reminded her of more guilt. "Mr. Waite, I do welcome this opportunity to tell you that you needn't host our family for supper or a recital—"

"Why not?"

"Oh—because—it would be an intrusion."

"I have already issued the invitation."

"Yes. Thank you. But you did not have much choice in the matter."

"Of course I did. Please do not trouble yourself, Miss Hapgood. Unless, of course, you dread coming and would like to be excused."

She did dread coming, but not from any excess of politeness. She dreaded being underfoot and a nuisance to him. She dreaded playing poorly and suffering by comparison. She dreaded him thinking she was trying to throw her uncle at his mother.

"Charmaine did say you could name the day," he reminded her. "Have you chosen one?"

"Er—no. Not yet." It occurred to her that he might just wish to be done with it. "Perhaps in another week or two?"

"When you wish. Charmaine will be able to answer for our engagements."

Manners dictated he put a good face on it and that she stop arguing the matter, so she let the subject drop and took another sip of her tea.

"You must be getting along better with her," he began after another moment.

"Yes, I think so, as I grow used to her. Has she said as much, or is it so plain?"

"It is a guess of mine," he answered, "because you are wearing something that belongs to her."

Margaret's hand flew to her throat. But before she could explain, here came the puppy again, bearing two teacups, his brow furrowing as he drew near.

"I see I am anticipated," the puppy said sternly.

"You must not blame Miss Hapgood," drawled Mr. Waite. "I am a friend of the family, and when I saw the open seat beside her, I availed myself of it." He indicated his cane. "With my crippled leg I find I must take frequent rests."

"Oh. Yes, of course, I suppose."

Margaret set down the teacup Mr. Waite had brought her and reached for one of the puppy's. "The tea is so weak, I am happy to drink two cups."

The forestalled young man shifted from foot to foot, studying Mr. Waite. "Perhaps if you have rested long enough, sir..."

"Mm. I'm afraid not. Quite achy this evening."

"Very well, then." Reluctantly, he made them each a bow. "I will leave you now, Miss Hapgood. Sir."

When he was out of earshot, she turned on her companion. "Is your injury really giving you pain?"

"It has its uses," was his reply. "Would you rather sit and drink your tea with that young man? I can call him back."

"Do not trouble yourself," she answered, though he had made no move to rise. "I do feel badly, though. He paid sixpence for this cup."

"When a gentleman brings a lady tea, he must do so as a gift, not as an exchange of favors. But to return to my subject: I see the tea was not the only gift you received tonight. How came you by that necklace?"

"It is Charmaine's. She lent it to me, which was very generous of her. Not to keep, of course, and I will give it back whenever she likes," Margaret babbled. "I was hoping to thank her, but I have not yet had the opportunity. Perhaps if I return to the ballroom now—"

"I have never seen her wear the necklace," said Mr. Waite.

"No? Well, I do assure you it is hers. She sent it with a note this afternoon. I suspect she does not wear it often because she said she could not even remember where it came from."

He chuckled again, but silently this time. "Ah, 'beshrew that heart that makes my heart to groan.' I gave it to her, of course. Before I left for the Peninsula."

"Oh, dear. Oh, my." Margaret's fingers flew to the necklace again. "I am sorry, Mr. Waite. I did not mean to—that is—I—will return it instantly. I am certain she would never have loaned it to me, had she realized..."

"Are you? So certain?"

She opened her mouth to insist but then clapped it shut again, remembering how Charmaine had been so angry with her suitor for leaving, that she refused to answer his early letters. No, as a matter of fact, Margaret was not at all so certain. What if it was not just generosity that motivated Charmaine to lend her the piece? What if she also intended Mr. Waite to see the necklace and to see how little she valued it?

Miserably, Margaret slid her chair back and rose. She did not want to be in the middle of Charmaine's and Mr. Waite's curious relationship. She did not want to play any part in Charmaine torturing her betrothed; nor did she especially want to hear Mr. Waite saying Charmaine made his "heart to groan."

"I will return it, at any rate," she said stiffly, "and remind her of its origin."

Mr. Waite was laboring to his feet as well, as etiquette dictated, but he held out a hand to arrest her that almost, but did not quite, reach her. "Come, Miss Hapgood. I did not intend to make you uncomfortable. Never mind where the bauble came from or how it came to be around your neck, rather than hers. There is no denying Charmaine has an eye for such things, for I daresay the pink of the stones suits your coloring far better than hers." His mischievous grin flashed again. "Please. Have mercy on a poor cripple and give me another few minutes before I escort you back to the ballroom. You might finish your tea, at least."

She had no choice but to resume her seat, although she could not think why he should want to sit longer with her. Did he have his own motives of revenge? Did he hope Charmaine would see them together and feel her own heart groaning as well?

Five minutes, she decided. She would allow herself to sit for five more minutes.

They seemed in danger of spending the allotted time in silence, however, with both of them watching the tea-room comings and goings. Margaret cast about in her mind for something to say and was on the point of blurting the vapid "Is this your first time in Bath?" when Mr. Waite said, "It is selfish of me to detain you. I am sure you would rather be dancing. Do you love it as much as Charmaine does?"

"I do love dancing," said Margaret. "It's the partners who are rather trying."

When he laughed at this, she added, "I only mean I am unused to dancing with strangers, and it is hard to make conversation. This is only my third ball, you know."

"I didn't know, actually." He was grinning, his face crinkling up again in that attractive way. "Are balls not frequent affairs where you come from?"

"Not frequent at all!" she assured him. "I have mostly danced with my sisters and the occasional dancing master. Bramleigh—my home—is quite buried in the country, and there is nobody beside Viscount Marlton ever to host a ball."

"And you always know your partners at Lord Marlton's balls?"

"I'm related to most of them. Don't laugh! I've known all of them my entire life. Let me see...this summer I danced with my father's cousin Hugh, who must be forty, if he's a day, and who is married to our former neighbor Rosemary. And I danced with my cousin Lionel twice, Hugh's son, who is sixteen and now gone away to Oxford to study. And I danced with Mr. Roscoe DeWitt, who is the brother of Rosemary—he is married to another neighbor. And then Mr. Norman DeWitt, Rosemary's other brother—"

"Married to still another neighbor?" guessed Mr. Waite.

"No, not married. But he doesn't speak."

"Doesn't speak? Is he mute?"

"For all intents and purposes. I believe, during the two dances, which lasted perhaps forty minutes, taken together, Mr. Norman DeWitt only said, 'Warm in here, hey?'"

"A reliable old stand-by, and one I've used myself. And how did you respond?"

"I said, 'Yes, very,' and that was the end." Realizing she was doing all the talking, she gave him a shy look. "But what of you? Do you miss dancing much?"

He paused, his grin fading, and she feared she had asked too personal a question. Then he said simply, "There are times I wish I could. But overall—in general—I don't miss it too much. Perhaps I didn't like making all that conversation either. I would have liked some sisters to partner me. Not all young ladies are as easy to talk to as yourself, Miss Hapgood."

It was Margaret's turn to laugh. "I wish my family could hear you! I have a reputation among them, I'm afraid, for an unguarded tongue. Which is a nice way of saying I am too often heedless and tactless. Sisters may be nice to practice dancing with, but they can also be one's most ruthless critics." Of course, by that standard, Charmaine Blakely might already qualify as an honorary sister, Margaret thought. He would not know that, however, since Charmaine thought it unladylike to speak baldly to him.

Margaret tried another tack. "If you have no sisters, have you brothers?"

He shook his head regretfully. "I had both a brother and a sister, both older, twins, in fact. But they died when I was very young. I have no memory of them, but sometimes I think my mother is still sad about their loss."

At this, his companion turned scarlet and a moan escaped her. She shut her eyes, as if to block something out.

"Miss Hapgood, are you all right?"

"No—I mean, yes, I am all right. I am sorry for Mrs. Waite's sadness. It wasn't that. It just reminded me of the most recent heedless and tactless thing I said." She turned distraught eyes on him. "I asked Sir Dodkins while we were dancing if he had any family!"

Mr. Waite's mouth twitched. "Why, you pitiless creature."

"It was pitiless!" Margaret insisted. "Because he hasn't any! His wife and son and daughter are all dead! If you could have seen how all the light went out of his eyes, Mr. Waite—and it was not that I didn't know they were all gone. I did, because Charmaine and I looked him up in Debrett's. It's just that I forgot, in the moment, and in my desire to be saying something, anything."

"Is there a copy of Debrett's in the Octagon Room? It wouldn't surprise me."

"No, no, it was the other day. He came into Molland's and helped me get my cloak unstuck and Charmaine was teasing me that a 'Sir' would be quite a feather in my cap, so we went to look him up, to discover whether he were a knight or a baronet, you see, and he is a baronet whose family is *entirely dead*."

"Gracious," said Mr. Waite. "I suppose the battlefield is not the only place where carnage can be found."

But the memory of Sir Dodkins' grief was too fresh in Margaret's mind for her to smile at this jest. In fact, she thought Mr. Waite quite insensitive to be making fun, and her reproachful look said as much.

He held up his hands in surrender. "You are right. I am being callous. Rather heedless and tactless myself. My mother tells me (and Haworth, for that matter), that our limbs were not the only casualty of war. She says our soldiers' humor is rough and unconscionable."

Margaret's brow cleared. "Ah...I did not think of that. You must have seen some very...disturbing things. Forgive me, Mr. Waite—I've been callous too, forgetting about...your background. To experience what you did, and then to come home—our concerns must seem trivial, in comparison."

"No, not trivial. By any means. And certainly not poor Sir Dodkins' tragedies," he added with undoubted sincerity. "That was cruel of me. And, as for other concerns, thinking about things that are not so—vital—has its relief and pleasure."

His eyes darkened, and she wondered what memories lay behind them. One could hardly ask. No matter what he said, how silly he must think her, fretting over hurt feelings and balls and baubles!

But, when he looked at her again, she saw no contempt there. "Sir Dodkins may find it difficult to talk about his lost family, but you need not assume he holds it against you. It does not take much time in your company to realize you are innocent of any malice."

"I hope you are right." But her smile returned. He made her feel better.

Seeing her mood lift, the naughty glint returned to his eye. "Of course, to resume my callous line of thinking, it is not always a wretched thing, to be without family."

"No?"

"No. For, without family, there is no one to oppose one's own inclinations and choices. Sir Dodkins, for one, may do whatever he pleases."

Warily, she considered this. She had butted heads with her own family often enough in recent days. But Mr. Waite could not be referring to that. Could he be alluding to his own family's efforts to thwart the match between Alwyn Arbuthnot and his mother?

There was no time to settle this matter to her satisfaction, however, for entering the tea-room at that very moment were the selfsame Alwyn Arbuthnot and Mrs. Waite, she with her hand resting lightly on his sleeve.

Margaret froze, flooded by guilt, though surely she could not be blamed for Mrs. Waite dancing with her uncle and accepting his offer of a cup of tea. When Alwyn laughed at something Mrs. Waite said and tossed a shilling in the glass bowl, Margaret's self-reproach gave way to exasperation. Honestly—where had he come by that shilling? She had not supplied him with any ready money, and why must she be the only one fretting over every last farthing?

She glanced at Mr. Waite and found him also staring at the couple, his narrow eyes narrowed even further. Margaret thought that, if such a look were directed at her, it would slice her in half.

Mrs. Waite must have felt the same because she abruptly dropped Alwyn's arm. She murmured something, and then the two of them approached.

"Ah, Dashiell," Mrs. Waite said, "I thought you must be in the card room. Miss Hapgood."

"Madam." Margaret was on her feet and bobbed a curtsey.

"I came in here for refreshment and saw Miss Hapgood sitting by herself," her son explained, rising slowly. His leg had stiffened, and he fumbled for his cane, grimacing.

"Maggie, were you wanting for partners?" Alwyn asked. "You mustn't be bashful, girl. I could have made King hop to it and find you others."

"Thank you, Uncle Alwyn," said Margaret, mortified.

"It so happens Miss Hapgood had a partner who was fetching tea for her," Mr. Waite interposed, "but I spied the empty seat and collapsed in it, leaving him nowhere to go but away."

"Ah." Alwyn digested this information. "Well, don't be discouraged, Mags. We will find you another. One that won't be so easily chased off. Come have a cup of tea with Mrs. Waite and me."

"I've already had two cups, thank you."

"Mr. Arbuthnot, why do you not take your niece back to the ballroom, and I will sit with my son and have my tea?" suggested Mrs. Waite.

He looked on the point of objecting, but reading her steady gaze aright, he shrugged and extended an elbow for Margaret. "Right you are."

When the farewells were dispensed with, Alwyn and Margaret made their way back to the ballroom, he whistling to himself and apparently pleased with the world.

"You don't sound like someone who has been looked daggers at," she said, half amused.

"Perhaps I am whistling through all the dagger holes," he answered, accompanying this with a playful prod of his own.

"Did you have a nice dance with Mrs. Waite?"

"Yes, indeed. I think we understand each other," he said blithely. "She would have me, if she could. If I could only win the son over, all would be well."

"Indeed? And how do you propose to do that?"

He made a face, squinting up at the chandelier. "Don't know yet."

"Perhaps you ought simply to abscond with her," Margaret suggested. "You and Mrs. Waite dash for Gretna Green, and Mama and I will steal back to Bramleigh."

"Don't think I didn't hint at it, Maggie. But there she's like stone. Her only child, she says. To run off with me would be to lose him forever. He looks a fierce, surly sort, who would as soon strike you with his cane as speak to you, but I suppose there's no accounting for a mother's feelings. Nature and such, you know."

Margaret made a sound of agreement, glad to be spared a more intelligible reply because Charmaine whirled past just then, waving at her as she wove in hey with her set.

"We must get you out there," declared Alwyn, darting glances around for Mr. King. "Why should Miss Blakely have all the partners, when she already has her future mapped for her? Not that I begrudge her the popularity—after all, the girl may one day be my daughter-in-law."

Chapter Seventeen

**Odsbodlikins..you have a..strange sort of a Taste.
—Henry Fielding, *Don Quixote in England* (1734)**

True to her word, Charmaine called the day after the ball, the footman admitting her to the morning room in Henrietta Street.

"Wasn't it delightful?" Charmaine cried, after they embraced and greeted each other. "How utterly stupid that the balls end so early. I could have danced for hours more, I assure you. Private balls are much to be preferred, in that respect."

"At least there are two balls every week, and we will have other opportunities," said Margaret, which made Charmaine roll her eyes.

"Don't be so practical! I swear, if I had but one more hour last night with that Mr. Peabody, he would have offered for me and killed

Dashiell! As it was, he could only grind his teeth and give my beloved murderous looks."

"Then it is fortunate the ball did not last another hour," rejoined Margaret dryly. "And how can you call Mr. Waite your beloved, when you look so gleeful about Mr. Peabody wanting to murder him?"

"Because I crave excitement, and I have three thousand exciting things to tell you, but first you may tell me what exciting things happened to you!"

Before she could prevent them, Margaret's thoughts flew to her time with Mr. Waite, and Charmaine pounced. "What? You're blushing. Tell me instantly! With whom have you fallen in love?"

"With no one! I have fallen in love with no one."

"Well, I won't press you on that. I see we must come at it slowly. Tell me first who you danced with."

"I don't remember all their names—"

"Spoken like a true belle!" mocked Charmaine. "Then you must describe them, and I will supply the names."

Which she proceeded to do. The young man who bought Margaret tea was Mr. Longshanks ("For who could forget *that* dreadful name?"). The freckled man was the murderous Mr. Peabody. The man with the nasal voice was Mr. Fosse. The one with the very large feet ("who must have crushed your toes as mercilessly as he did mine") was Mr. Trumbull. And so on.

"And of course I needn't remind you of Sir Dodkins' name, for, if you say you danced with him before I came, that means you danced twice with him altogether."

"I could not help it. He asked."

Charmaine laughed. "Goose! I didn't suppose *you* asked *him*." But she forbore to rally Margaret further and instead described her own would-be swains, as well as which she would choose, were she not already engaged, and which she thought would make Dashiell most jealous.

"I do not know about making Mr. Waite jealous," Margaret said, slipping back to the desk to retrieve the pearl-and-chalcedony necklace, "but you certainly caught his attention by lending me this. He asked me where I got it, and when I told him, he did not look altogether pleased."

Plucking it from Margaret's hands, Charmaine glided to the looking glass over the mantel and held the ornament to her neck. "No, I was right. It doesn't suit me at all. You are for pinks and ivories, and I for more vivid colors." Turning, she gave her friend a curious look. "So he noticed, then, and he minded. How peculiar that he came to tell you of it, rather than me."

"I was sitting in the tea-room, waiting for Mr. Longshanks to return, and Mr. Waite happened in and took the empty seat beside me."

"Is that so?"

Margaret did not like the sound of that.

"And how long did he sit there?"

"Perhaps ten minutes?" Margaret couldn't help the interrogative note in her answer. She suspected it was more. She suspected she was lying.

"It took ten minutes for Longshanks to fetch your tea?"

"No, but Mr. Waite declared himself unable—because of his injury—to relinquish the seat, and so Mr. Longshanks went away."

"Ah," said Charmaine. Her eyes glittered ominously. "My, my, what favor you seem to have found with him."

"I don't know about that."

"Don't you? I think, in the time I have been in Bath and under the same roof, he has not once crossed the room to sit and talk with me—much less for ten minutes!"

"I don't see how it is my fault," Margaret retorted, "if a man comes and sits down where I am already sitting. If you don't like Mr. Waite's behavior, you had better tell him."

"Oh, have no fear. I will make my displeasure plain. Two can play at that game! It's clear he sees how popular I am, and he thinks he can make me jealous in return."

"But how could he make you jealous, if you did not observe him?" Margaret pointed out. She had feared it might be—that her lovely time with Mr. Waite was simply a ploy on his part.

"Who says I didn't? I mean, I saw *you* when Mr. Longshanks escorted you in. I just didn't happen to look over again. And, as for Dashiell, he knew that, even if I did not see him sit down beside you, you would not fail to mention it to me." She tossed the necklace back on the desk. "He was probably delighted to find you alone, since, crippled as he is, he could not dance with you and get at me that way."

Feeling her throat tighten, Margaret said, "Well, did it work? Are you jealous?"

"Not a jot. He will have to do better than that. Perhaps you can ask him to kiss you next time."

"Considering I did not ask him to do *anything*," Margaret gritted her teeth, "I cannot be accused of plotting a 'next time.'"

"Dear me. So insistent. The lady doth protest too much, methinks."

Then and there Margaret might have broken her vow not to argue with Charmaine, only she suddenly found herself wanting to laugh. Because the girl was *impossible*. Provoking, contrary, impossible. Worse than any of Margaret's sisters, and the Hapgood daughters bickered as much as any sisters might.

"It would serve you right if I did ask him to kiss me," Margaret said, altering course. "He's certainly more handsome than Sir Dodkins, and you treat him so ill. You deserve to lose him."

Instead of taking umbrage, Charmaine appeared delighted by this show of spirit. "Do you think so? But it only counts as ill treatment if he actually suffers. Do you think he suffers?"

Margaret thought about this. "I don't know," she answered honestly. "But he did say—about the necklace, you know—'beshrew that heart that makes my heart to groan.'"

Charmaine came to seize her friend's hands, eyes wide with gratification. "Did he really? He said that, that his heart was groaning? Why, that makes me feel quite charitable toward him. Perhaps I will kiss him myself! I kiss you, for telling me." She did so. "You see if I don't help you get a handsome husband, Margaret Hapgood. Or, at least, a rich one."

This must be all Margaret's comfort because the door of the morning room opened at this point to admit Alwyn Arbuthnot.

"La," murmured Charmaine, "the man of the hour." She made him a pretty curtsey. "Mama was rather flustered by you asking her to dance, Mr. Arbuthnot. I cannot recall having seen her dance in ages. I suppose you mean to put all my female relations in a fever."

"You flatter me, young lady," was his mild reply, as he went to lean against the casement of the window facing Henrietta Street. "Maggie, dear, what plans have you for us today? Shall we walk in the Gardens again? Or round and round the Pump Room, if it be too chilly? I suspect it will be, for your dear mother." Margaret was on the point of agreeing to the Pump Room when his posture straightened, and he peered more closely into the street.

"What have we here? A carriage stopping in Henrietta Street?" His quizzing glass was halfway to his eye before it fell from his surprised fingers. "Ods bodkins, it's Sir Dodkins!"

Margaret gaped, but Charmaine shrieked with glee and scurried to peek out from behind Alwyn. "It is! It is, Margaret! Descending from his barouche! He has come to call on you. My, but he wasted no time. What a conquest."

Before she finished speaking, she was beside Margaret again, thrusting an embroidery hoop into her hands and taking up a book herself. "So staid, a barouche," she whispered. "But one cannot hope for phaetons or gigs from such an elderly man."

The sound of the baronet's coughing preceded him, but his handkerchief was put away when Hudgins flung open the door.

"Sir Dodkins Hargate," he proclaimed in an impressively bored tone, as if baronets called every hour of the day.

"Sir Dodkins," said Alwyn, stepping forward, "what a pleasure to see you again. I believe you already know my niece's friend Miss Blakely?"

"Yes, yes." The baronet made his bows to each and waited for the ladies to seat themselves again before choosing the sofa opposite. "I hope you both are well and that you enjoyed the ball last night."

Charmaine only smiled demurely so Margaret was forced to answer. "Indeed. Thank you. And you?"

"Very much so," he answered. "More than I have enjoyed anything for some weeks." An odd wheezing sound followed this remark, and Margaret supposed he was suppressing another fit.

She did not want to ask why he enjoyed it so much, not only because she feared he was complimenting her, but also because she was afraid of aggravating the tickle in his throat. But she would like to show him she could make harmless conversation, after her regrettable efforts at the ball. Or would it be better all around if he continued to think her gauche? As a result of her confusion, she said nothing at all.

As he always did, Alwyn obligingly filled up the empty space with fluent small talk, including observations on how well the ballroom looked, the number in attendance, the quality of the music and the dancing, and so on, all of which the baronet nodded and agreed to.

"My sister Augusta, Miss Margaret's mother, don't you know, is most regretful that her health does not permit her to attend," Alwyn wound up. "We are glad, Sir Dodkins, that you are not likewise constrained."

Margaret rather admired this clever way of pumping Sir Dodkins for more information on his troublesome health, and she looked up from her embroidery.

"It is a touch of catarrh, merely," the baronet assured him, giving his chest a thump, as if to demonstrate its fundamental soundness. "Already much improved. I take the water every day, in addition to visiting the baths."

"Splendid," said Alwyn. He looked archly at Margaret, and she knew he was reminding her the water subscription was a guinea per month. Sir Dodkins might be old and he might be ill, but he was certainly not poor.

"Miss Hapgood, Miss Blakely," began the baronet, "as you have so recently arrived in town, have you had the opportunity to ride out or drive? There are marvelous views from nearly every direction."

"Most of our explorations have been on foot, sir," admitted Margaret. "Though Mama and I came in by the Wells Road."

"A fine prospect from the Wells Road," he agreed. "Very near Beechen Cliff. Then perhaps I might suggest other vantage points—Claverton Down or Lansdown Hill, for example. In Bath one must take advantage of fine weather. Might I have the privilege of driving you all today?"

Margaret did not need Charmaine to snap shut her book and raise her eyebrows to know that she was being urged to accept. And there was nothing Margaret would have loved more than to drive in an open barouche and take in the views, whether it was chilly or not, if only such a favor did not involve Sir Dodkins!

"What a kind offer, Sir Dodkins. But I am afraid, were my mother to join us, that would make for five people. Perhaps another time."

"Nonsense, Maggie," interposed her uncle. "Augusta may go in my place. Let me propose it to her. If you will excuse me…"

In an instant he was gone, with Margaret left to hide her dismay. Of course Mama would not go. Mama was not even out of bed yet, most likely! Nor would she be tempted by the idea of riding in the open air in December. No, Mama would refuse, and Sir Dodkins would trundle the rest of them away.

"Which drive do you prefer, Sir Dodkins?" asked Charmaine, politely waiting for another coughing spell to taper off.

"B-both—ahem!—delightful. You young ladies may choose. I am at your service."

Charmaine turned eagerly to Margaret and then was obliged to hide her annoyance when Margaret replied, "Perhaps whichever is shorter."

"Let it be Claverton Down, then," agreed Sir Dodkins. "Then we may stop at Sham Castle."

Charmaine clapped her hands at this, and Margaret managed a wan smile, which faded when her uncle returned and announced, predictably, that Mrs. Hapgood vastly appreciated Sir Dodkins' offer but feared her health did not permit—

"Et cetera, et cetera," muttered Margaret. But, what could not be avoided must be endured, and she did her best to appear cheerful.

It was indeed clear and cold and beautiful that day. The baronet handed in Margaret and Charmaine to the forward-facing seat, adjuring them to tuck their cloaks about them, while he and Alwyn took the rear-facing seat.

Margaret found herself enjoying the outing. The baronet's carriage was well-sprung, his horses matched and handsome, his driver skillful. They followed Pulteney Street to Sydney Place, exclaiming over the vista into the Gardens, before crossing the canal and turning away on Heydon Street to ascend the gradual slope of the Down, leaving the clamor of Bath behind. Her annoyance with Alwyn was soon forgotten, for he largely spared her the trouble of conversing.

"Never been to Dorset myself," he was saying, "for all that it neighbors Somerset."

"Very much like Somerset, inland," Sir Dodkins replied. "Hargate Hall is outside Dorchester. Beautiful, mild climate. Good farming. And along the coast are many bathing areas."

"Some neighbors of ours went to Weymouth and Poole on their wedding trip," spoke up Margaret, remembering. Charmaine elbowed her, and Margaret blushed, thinking that Sir Dodkins, like Charmaine, might think she was hinting at marriage.

The baronet chuckled, bringing on a paroxysm of coughs, but when he recovered he asked, "Indeed? How did they like it? I would not have thought Weymouth and Poole fashionable enough for young people."

"The bride did prefer London," Margaret confessed. "But Constance—Mrs. DeWitt—is a giddy sort. Or was. She has young children now." Remembering once again Sir Dodkins' late family members, she winced.

But he beamed at her. "And what would a calm young lady like yourself prefer?"

She would prefer to be the sort of young lady who kept her mouth shut in the first place, Margaret thought. But too late for that now. She was certain Charmaine would accuse her later of encouraging him.

"I haven't thought much about it," she said, as shortly as she might. Then she pointed off in the distance. "Look there! We are high enough to see the Crescent now."

The abrupt change of subject succeeded, and the remainder of the ascent passed in identifying landmarks. When they descended from the barouche to view the folly, with its pointed arch, circular turrets, and square towers, Margaret pretended not to see the arm Sir Dodkins offered and clung to her uncle. But to compensate for her rudeness she listened attentively to the baronet's monologues on the history of Sham Castle, the Roman ruins in Bath, and various other sights.

Once back in the carriage, he instructed his driver to take a different return route, that his guests might see new views. They set off south, across the face of the Down to Bathwick Hill, before turning northwest to enter town again by the New Widcombe Road. Passing the parade grounds and the new streets and houses being built in Sydney Buildings and Darlington Place, they regained Pulteney Street and were soon home.

"Thank you, sir, for the drive," Margaret told him as he assisted her down, her relief at its conclusion making her sound more fervent than she intended.

He gave her gloved hand the barest squeeze. "It was a pleasure, Miss Hapgood. And may I say, I have not spent so delightful a time since my daughter and I would drive the heathlands near Dorchester?"

He could say it, but she did not particularly want to hear it.

She smiled and nodded, escaping into the house, a triumphant Charmaine at her heels.

"He is yours," the latter hissed, as Alwyn slipped away upstairs. "If you want him, you have only to snap your fingers."

"Well, I don't want him."

"He is titled and wealthy and kindly, and he coughed less than he did even a few days ago," Charmaine went on. "In fact, if he improves at this rate, you must act quickly, or he might retreat to his beloved Dorchester, all unscathed."

"Let him!" cried Margaret. "It makes no difference to me."

Charmaine regarded her as one would an unreasonable child. "Listen to me: I am trying to help you. It is every girl's duty to marry as well as she possibly can."

"Then why don't you marry him yourself?"

"Because *I* am already engaged to a rich man, you ninny. Not to mention, your lover did not even offer to drive me home, so little did he notice me. I will have to call a chair. No, Margaret, you will have to marry your rich and eligible man and leave me to marry mine."

"But you don't even love your rich and eligible man!"

"For pity's sake—we have already discussed this. I love him well enough for the purposes. Besides, that is nothing to the point." Marching across the room, she pulled on the bell rope.

Margaret was red in the face, and she threw herself into a chaise, her back to her friend. "It's easy for you to say, that I should marry such an old man. *Your* rich and eligible man is young and handsome, to boot. Why should I not wish for as much?"

"Because beggars can't be choosers," answered Charmaine. "When you come into an inheritance of ten thousand pounds—nay, even three thousand pounds—you may ask for youth and looks into the bargain."

Whipping around, Margaret glared at her. "You are monstrous."

Not that Charmaine's sentiments weren't familiar enough. Had not her own father expressed the same ideas, all Margaret's life? If she were to write home, announcing her engagement to such a man as Sir Dodkins, she had no doubt her father would rejoice. Her sisters, however...

"My sisters would never approve," said Margaret. "They would know I married him only for money."

Charmaine threw up her hands. "Well, if all four of you are so perverse, I am not surprised."

"In any case," Margaret continued, "I don't intend to marry at present. In fact, I don't intend to be away from Bramleigh much longer. I am essential there."

"Mm-hm." Charmaine didn't bother to hide her skepticism. "If you say so. But before you scurry back to Bramleigh unwed, don't forget our recital. Have you decided when we will hold it? It's most rude of you not to choose a day so that we may plan our menu. Shall we say in a week?"

"A fortnight."

"It has already been nearly a week since the concert, and you said a week or ten days then," pointed out Charmaine.

"Another ten days, then. I haven't practiced, and I can't play as well as you, I am certain."

"Then you must come and practice. Tomorrow or whenever you like. If you come in the later morning, no one is ever about. The Gluck is not very complicated. Now where is that footman of yours?" She gave another tug on the bell-wire, tapping her tiny foot. "I might have called my own chair with less trouble. And, if you will excuse me, I am anxious to return home, that I might torture my rich and eligible, young and handsome betrothed."

CHAPTER EIGHTEEN

Now commeth the man that he was detter unto.
—2 Kings iv.1, *The Coverdale Bible* (1535)

Shortly after Charmaine's departure, Margaret learned the cause of the footman's tardiness.

"It was a creditor, miss," Hudgins said, face stony with disapproval. "At the back door. I tried to send him away, but he would only go when I swore I would place this bill myself in Mr. Arbuthnot's hands."

"Give it to me," she commanded, "and I will deliver it. We are fully acquainted with the matter. That will be all."

No sooner was he gone than Margaret flew to the desk and slid a knife under the seal. As she feared, it was from the jeweler. Horrible man! She supposed it was her very attempt to return the items that brought this demand upon them so soon. Once the jeweler knew they could not pay, he determined to wrest what he could from them before other creditors stepped in.

The second surprise was greater and even more unpleasant.

For the bill from "Chauncey Vale, Master Jeweler" was not for three pounds nor five pounds nor even ten pounds.

It was for fifty.

"Fifty!" gasped Margaret. "Fifty pounds! Why, it may as well be a hundred." Was it possible there was some mistake? Could paste ornaments be so much? No, it was no mistake—listed there were the brooch and the cravat pin, each with "rose-cut glass," "gold sheet" and "gold wire." They were truly paste and they were truly that expensive. This Chauncey Vale took himself seriously.

But where on earth would she find fifty pounds? The fine print detailed the interest charged and its rate of compounding, if the debt were not cleared within thirty days from purchase. Which it would not be, because how could it be? And, after thirty days, Chauncey Vale, Master Jeweler, "reserved the right to pursue debt collection and/or other compensatory measures"! What these involved, Margaret hated to think. Would they be turned out of their lodgings? Hauled before magistrates? Could Alwyn be imprisoned for debt?

Fleetly she considered her options. They would cut every expense possible; never mind that they already had cut most. The jewelry could not be returned, but perhaps they might pawn it? She shrank from the idea, but desperate times... A third possibility would be to let the thirty days pass. The interest was ruinous, but perhaps her family would be in a better position by then to hear bad news. Papa might be able to find the money. Or, if Elfie and Alice continued well, their husbands might be applied to.

"Thirty days, thirty days," Margaret muttered, pacing by this point.

On her tenth circuit to the fireplace and back, she halted in horror. It was not even thirty days! So long a time did not remain to them, for the jewelry had been purchased a few days earlier! Oh oh oh!

She resumed her feverish pacing.

How had she ever supposed she could manage her uncle and her mother, when no one succeeded in managing them before? She had judged her father and elder sisters weak, lacking firmness, and now she had fared no better. Worse, for by her own smugness she had convinced her family that all could be well, if only it were placed in her capable hands. Not only would she have to confess her failure—humiliating enough!—but she must ask them for rescue, with who knew what consequences.

"No."

Without realizing it, she spoke aloud.

"I must find a way. I must. They trust me, and I must live up to that trust. I dare not endanger my father's or my sisters' health with a thunderbolt such as this. I will—I will ask Charmaine for a loan." At the mere thought, she groaned. She did not doubt Charmaine would give her the money, but not without exacting her pound of flesh. But it was only a sacrifice of Margaret's pride, and she owed her family that much.

There was no time to be lost. She would go to Princes Street the very next morning. Charmaine was expecting her at some point, in any case, to practice the pianoforte. Margaret would wait for her moment—for the very instant when Charmaine's mercurial moods reached their peak, and she would strike.

But first she must speak to her mother and uncle. On no condition could this happen again. Not even if she had to lock them in the house, which she very well might.

Tilly accompanied Margaret the next day, and it was plain that Hudgins had not kept the bill-collector's appearance to himself, for the maid was, if possible, even more sullen than usual. She probably wondered if her wages would be paid, but Margaret had neither the energy nor the certainty to reassure her.

No, as they trudged along, Margaret sighed over her fruitless talk with her mother. Mrs. Hapgood had not been the least bit discommoded by the jeweler's bill, only rolling her eyes and saying, "Yes, yes, my dear. I'm certain your father didn't expect us to go three months on the piddly amount he entrusted to you. Certainly he intends to send another installment. If you had not been so miserly in the first place, I am sure Alwyn and I would not have felt the need to indulge ourselves."

"There must be no more shopping, please, Mama," Margaret insisted.

"Oh, go along with you. I don't feel well this morning in any event. Such constant activity is more than I am used to. Alwyn will wheel me in the Gardens later, so you needn't stay to fret us."

The house in Princes Street was not so new and fashionable as those higher up the town, but Margaret suspected it had been chosen for its very lack of elevation and its proximity to the baths. Indeed, when the maid ushered her into the morning room, Margaret was met only by the women, and Charmaine was quick to tell her the gentlemen were gone for their "daily ministrations."

"We hope your family is well," Mrs. Waite said in her sweet voice.

Margaret could not prevent a grimace, but she answered, "Very well, thank you."

"Celia and I plan a long walk this morning, to which we would invite you, but Charmaine declares you intend to practice your music."

"We do," interposed Charmaine, "and as Margaret and I saw tremendous views yesterday from Sir Dodkins' barouche, we will not feel deprived of whatever can be seen from Lansdown Crescent."

"I should like to see Sham Castle," Mrs. Blakely said, laying aside her sewing. "Perhaps Dashiell can rent a carriage and take us, Eliza."

"The folly itself is not so marvelous," said Margaret. "It looks better from a distance."

"Rather like Sir Dodkins himself," Charmaine mocked. "Though Sham Castle has the advantage, in that it doesn't suffer from coughing fits. Come, Margaret. Here is the music." And, taking her by the arm, Charmaine led her away to the drawing room, where the pianoforte stood.

Closing the door behind them, Charmaine leaned against it. "Ah, Mama has been so tiresome! I fear she is suffering from envy of your mother."

Margaret stared. "Envy of Mama? Whatever for?"

"For having a daughter whom a baronet courts, naturally."

"He is not doing any such thing," protested Margaret.

"Don't be coy. Why else would he call and ask you to drive?"

"Well—I don't know that he meant anything so serious." Even as she spoke, a memory of Sir Dodkins squeezing her hand sprung to mind. "I think he views me in a daughterly light," she amended. "He said the drive reminded him of being with his daughter."

"Lord. Don't be stupid, I beg you, or I will end in knocking both you and Mama over the head with a brick. A good sturdy one." Seating herself at the instrument, she launched into a series of rapid scales.

"Charmaine," Margaret said. "Stop a moment."

Charmaine only played more loudly, following the scales with thunderous chords. Margaret huffed in exasperation and brought her hand down on the upper keys. "Charmaine!"

"Yes?" Charmaine asked, folding her hands in her lap demurely.

"Tell me: Why is your mama envious? Does she not want you to marry Mr. Waite?"

"Of course she does. A bird in the hand, and so on. But that does not mean she does not wish the bush full as well. And full of baronets, at that. I suspect it galls her that you, a girl not half as pretty as I, nor a fraction as rich, should be driven around Bath by Sir Dodkins."

But Margaret, like Dashiell, was beginning to suspect Charmaine sometimes attributed opinions to her parents that she herself held. She sank onto the bench beside her friend. "Charmaine, as I told you yesterday, you are welcome to him."

"Thank you, but no," Charmaine returned maddeningly. "My bird is far younger and handsomer and equally wealthy, even if he is not a 'sir.'"

"I know that. There is no need to go over and over the same ground. You may tell your mama she has nothing to envy."

"Would you rather have Dashiell or Sir Dodkins?" demanded Charmaine, turning suddenly to fix her gaze on Margaret.

Margaret felt herself color, but she managed to reply, "Mr. Waite, to be sure. Would not any young woman?"

"Crippled leg and all?"

"Crippled leg and all. And his leg is not so very crippled."

"Hmm." But Charmaine was smiling now, feeling herself once again in the superior position. She rose suddenly and pushed Margaret toward the center of the bench. "Your turn. I am sure you must be quite rusty, and I have a dress-fitting presently."

A dress-fitting? Margaret could not lose this moment to speak, then. They might not be alone again, and she could hardly ask for money in front of others. Running her fingers along the piano keys, it was not only rust that caused her to stumble. How to introduce so thorny a subject?

She cleared her throat. "By the by, Charmaine, when would you like your necklace back?"

"You may keep it, for all I care."

Margaret drew a sharp breath. Perhaps here was an opening! Biting her lip, she frowned at the opening bars of the Gluck piece, considering various approaches in her mind.

"For pity's sake, you can't be that rusty. It is C major."

"Yes, yes." Bungling the opening arpeggios, Margaret kept her eyes on the music. Then she blurted, "If I may keep the necklace, would you mind terribly if I pawned it?"

"What?"

Margaret's hands froze, and she made an effort to relax them on the keys. "I said, would you mind if I pawned your necklace?"

"Of course, I would mind," cried Charmaine, as if Margaret had asked to throw it in the Avon. "If you don't want it, just say so, and I will take it back. I thought you liked it."

"I do like it—very much—but I have some little expenses I need to take care of." Her face felt like it had caught fire, but need drove her to meet her friend's astonished gaze.

"Well, I am sorry for that," declared Charmaine, "though I must say, it is not *de rigueur* to mention such things. No, I forbid you to pawn it, I'm afraid. As a matter of fact, I would like it back now."

"You just said I might keep it."

"I've changed my mind."

Shame choked Margaret, but she had gone too far to draw back. "Then—do you suppose you might make me a small loan, Charmaine? I hate to ask, of course—it's horrible of me—but I would repay you as promptly as I could—"

Charmaine gave an incredulous laugh. "Dear me! I cannot believe the things you say. Asking me for money!" She shook her head in amazement. "I suppose you have your reasons for not asking your family—? Yes. I thought so. Well, Papa only gives me a little pin money, but I daresay you are welcome to it. After all, I wouldn't have much of anything ready to hand, if you had not saved me from the thieves in Sydney Gardens."

Relief surged through her, and Margaret gave a shaky smile. "Oh, thank you, Charmaine. Thank you, thank you. It is too, too kind of you—"

In a twinkling, Charmaine was out of the room, and Margaret only had time to fling a quick prayer of gratitude heavenward before rapid footsteps heralded her friend's return.

"There!" cried Charmaine, tossing her reticule on the piano lid. "Take whatever you require. But it isn't all kindness on my part. I will be sure to think what favor you will do me in return."

"Anything!" promised Margaret. Fumbling with the strings, she unwound them and shook out the purse's contents.

The purse's limited contents.

"Four pounds, fourteen shillings, and five pence," she breathed in dismay.

"Am I not Lady Bountiful?"

"But—how did you afford all those things you bought when we were shopping, Charmaine?"

"I didn't hand over coins, if that is what you mean. I told them to send the bills to Princes Street. Mama has a letter of credit at the bankers, and I leave her to take care of it. Don't tell me you need more than this."

Margaret shook her head slowly, despairingly. "I—I'm afraid I do."

"Why, how much do you need? Or, ought I to say, how much does your uncle need? Tell me the truth, Margaret—this is your uncle's debt you seek to pay."

To this she made no reply, but her silence was answer enough.

"Just so," said the latter briskly. She shrugged. "I haven't any more than this at hand, and I don't suppose Mama does either. How much is it?"

"Fifty pounds," whispered Margaret. "It is fifty pounds."

Even Charmaine blinked at this sum. "Dear me. That is more pin money than Mama gives me in a month, and I would certainly have to explain...I know!" She snapped her fingers, her green eyes alight. "We could forge a bill, and I could present it to Mama."

"No! Never!" Margaret recoiled from this. "Defraud your parents? I would rather beg it in the streets."

"You might have to."

Charmaine hummed to herself for a few moments, drumming her fingers upon the piano lid. Then she prodded the dejected Margaret. "It seems to me there are two possibilities. One: you let your uncle go hang for this (as your family ought perhaps to have done long ago). It is his fault, after all. I don't see why you must deal with the matter. Or, two: you marry Sir Dodkins. If you were Lady Hargate, I don't suppose the baronet would miss fifty pounds here or there. You might support ten such feckless uncles with no harm done."

If it were so easy to support ten such uncles, Margaret thought bitterly, why did the Blakelys and Mr. Waite object even to supporting one?

A discreet knock interrupted them, the footman announcing the dress-maker's arrival.

"Tell her I will be right along," said Charmaine. But she gave Margaret one last nudge. "Think about it. And let me know what you choose. But by no means pawn my necklace."

Margaret did think about it when Charmaine was gone. She thought about it while she ran mechanically through the Gluck piece. Once, twice, thrice. The world might be ending, but she need not add musical humiliation to her other burdens. She thought about it when she rested her head on her arms and wished everyone and everything at perdition. She thought about it until her forehead felt hot with the effort of holding back tears.

Charmaine's analysis left out some complicating factors. In the first place, Margaret could not simply let her uncle "go hang," since the debt belonged to her mother as well. And, even if it did not, Mrs. Hapgood would never agree to any plan that consigned her remaining brother to oblivion.

And, secondly, Margaret had no desire whatsoever to marry Sir Dodkins Hargate, even supposing he wanted to marry her. Would not marrying an old man she did not love be the equivalent, morally, of forging a bill and trying to pass it off on the Blakelys?

"It had better be the pawn shop, then," she said aloud. Pressing her hands to her cheeks, she rose to wander the room. Uncle Alwyn likely had experience with such disreputable places. She would have to accompany him, though. If she sent him alone, he might be tempted to buy something else and dig them in still deeper.

She paused beside the fireplace, gazing wearily at a painting of hunters and hounds. The pack was in full cry, pursued by a ruddy, stocky hunter on a black charger. "Oh, Papa," Margaret addressed this figure (who did, indeed, bear a resemblance to the squire), "how I have failed you."

The figure paid her no attention, however, and, after another minute, Margaret turned away with a sigh. She had better go find Tilly.

But when she slipped into the passage, she saw one more hurdle awaited her: Mr. Waite had returned, and the footman was assisting him to remove his greatcoat. His appearance had its usual effect on her heartbeat and her insides, and she retreated. She could not face him now—she couldn't.

His sharp eyes caught the movement. "Is that Miss Hapgood? You must have come to practice on the pianoforte," he supplied, when she only froze. "Has Charmaine abandoned you?"

"Dress-maker," croaked Margaret.

"Ah, yes." He took up his cane again and approached her. As always, when he came fresh from his treatments, he was hardly limping.

"Miss Hapgood—are you well?"

Avoiding his eyes, she nodded, clearing her throat quietly. "Yes, quite well. Thank you. You—too, I hope. I was just leaving."

"Have the two of you quarreled again?"

"Oh, no!"

"Then what is it?"

To their mutual alarm, Margaret's eyes welled. She had a frantic second of inner debate—could she possibly ask *him* for the money? She hardly knew him, really, and he hardly knew her. And what he did know of her was that she had a spendthrift uncle of whom he disapproved heartily. Why would he give her anything, if he guessed, as Charmaine had, that it was really for Alwyn Arbuthnot?

No—she could not ask him. If asking Charmaine took all her courage and humility, asking Mr. Waite was far beyond her.

She shook her head. She must think up some plausible lie for her state. Quickly. Because what if he questioned Charmaine? Margaret thought she would die of shame if everyone knew. If *he* knew.

"It—was the painting in the drawing room," she choked out. "Of the hunters."

Nonplussed, he reached past her (she shrinking away) to push open the drawing room door. He was warm. Or perhaps the warmth came from her, for she knew she was turning pink.

"The painting above the mantel?" he asked in wonderment.

"Yes," said Margaret, inanely. "It made me homesick."

"Because you...hunt frequently at Bramleigh?"

"Well—my father does. The painting made me miss my father." At this, one tear escaped, and she dabbed it with her sleeve.

"I'm sure he prizes such affection," Mr. Waite murmured. "Are you...certain that is the only source of your distress?"

Remembering with what ease he had worked the story of the Sydney Garden thieves from her, not to mention confessions of her provinciality and lack of dance partners at home, Margaret felt a stab of panic. She must get away from him this instant, or everything would come tumbling out, willy-nilly. Or she might throw herself on his mercy. Or both.

"Yes—indeed. I am not so distressed. I mean, I will not be presently. I must go. After I write home, all will be well. My home-sickness, that is. Thank you for your kindness. And the use of your instrument. Please excuse me. If you would kindly send Tilly to me, I will be waiting for her on the step—"

She was backing away from him throughout this speech, and he did not seek to detain her, though his puzzled expression deepened, not unmixed with a trace of amusement. "On the step? Surely you would be more comfortable waiting in the morning room, Miss Hapgood. There are no pictures of hunters to torment you there."

"No, no! I yearn for fresh air. I will be on the step." And, pretending not to hear him say that it had begun to drizzle, she turned tail and fled.

Chapter Nineteen

It is not he who gives you money, but he who puts you into a way of getting it, that does you a friendship.
—Henry Brooke, *Fool of Quality* (1766)

With their quiet nights at home, the family in Henrietta Street soon finished *St. Irvyne* and began *Sense and Sensibility*, though Alwyn declared the doings of four cast-off women of diminished income "decidedly humdrum," and Mrs. Hapgood interested herself most in Colonel Brandon's alleged rheumatism and descriptions of Willoughby.

For her part, Margaret wished she might escape into the Dashwoods' world. It would be such a comfort if, when Margaret's own father died, some Sir John Middleton would rescue the remaining Hapgood women, offering a charming cottage and lively society. Cousin Hugh might help them find a new home, but he had no potential suitors for Margaret and Edith. "And no one would read this book either," Margaret thought, "if it were only about a mother and her unmarried daughters removing to somewhere shabby and confined, where they passed the rest of their lives growing older, poorer, and more neglected."

Nor were the Dashwood girls saddled with an uncle who acted as a continuing drain on their fortunes. But then, Margaret was vexed with Alwyn because he vetoed outright any visit to the pawnbroker.

"Absolutely not, Margaret," he declared with uncharacteristic vehemence. "A pawn-shop is no place for a young lady."

"But you would be with me, Uncle Alwyn."

"Absolutely, positively not. Enter such a den of thieves? Do you imagine you would hand over the brooch and cravat pin, receive fifty pounds for your pains, and go on your merry way?"

This was exactly what Margaret imagined, and her face fell.

"In the first place, pawnbrokers don't give you half the value of what you bring them, and the interest they charge is ruinous. I speak from experience, unfortunately." Alwyn shuddered, remembering having to approach his brother-in-law some ten years earlier, hat in hand.

"But—if I had no intention of redeeming the items, they would just keep the jewelry and sell it themselves, would they not?" Margaret persisted. "And then I would be under no obligation to repay the loan or the ruinous interest."

"I tell you, Maggie, you would be lucky to get ten pounds for your pains, and we would likely have to go to a Bristol pawnbroker, lest it be shouted all over Bath. Put it entirely from your mind." Giving her a chuck under the chin, he added, "There is always money to be had somewhere. You mustn't mind a little pressure or a few threats. When you have been around as long as I, you will learn not to take things so seriously. Something always turns up—why, look at that dull book you're reading us! Those girls—something always turns up for them. A nice little cottage, nice new friends to take them to London, that ancient colonel who likes the younger sister..."

"But that is *fiction*, Uncle! A *story*." But her arguments only drove him to escape the room.

"Hopeless," Margaret muttered. "He does not realize that Papa is the only fairy godmother we have! And when our funds have dwindled to nothing—or less than nothing—what hope will we have then?"

She renewed her determination that, if her uncle could not succeed quickly with Mrs. Waite, he must make plans elsewhere. Weeks had already slipped past since they arrived. She would observe them closely at the fancy ball this evening and decide if it was hopeless—a welcome distraction from wondering if Charmaine had shared their money woes.

Despite being called a "fancy" ball, the Thursday ball was less formal than those held on Mondays, there being no minuets before the country dancing began. To Margaret's eyes the room seemed equally full, though perhaps fewer spectators occupied the tiered benches encircling the dancing space.

Torn between eagerness and dread she looked for the Waite party, but it was Charmaine who spied her first, springing up beside her while clutching Mr. Peabody's hand. "Margaret, find a partner, for we are forming our square! There is Mr. Longshanks looking this way—smile at him."

No smile was necessary, for the puppy Mr. Longshanks obligingly made his way over and begged for Margaret's hand. At least he bore no grudge over the tea-and-Mr.-Waite incident of the previous ball, and Margaret found herself smiling genuinely at his latest monologue on his beloved horse.

When the dance concluded, he invited both Charmaine and Margaret to watch him ride, and Charmaine murmured that she had not imagined the world held such delights. Then she dismissed their partners with a smile. "Now you must be off, the both of you, for Miss Hapgood and I want to have a chummy talk."

"Come," ordered Charmaine, leading Margaret toward the benches. "And meet no one's gaze, lest they interrupt. Why did you not wear the necklace tonight? It would have gone well with that gown."

"You told me you wanted it back."

"Well, you must make allowances for my being surprised and angry. What have you decided to do?"

But first Margaret wanted to know if Charmaine had kept her confidence. Only when she gained this assurance did she relate how Alwyn forbade any visit to a pawnbroker.

"And would you never dare to go on your own? I would go with you."

Margaret's eyes widened at this proposal. "Thank you, but I think we had better not. Besides, he said they would only give a fraction of the amount I seek."

"And he would know, I imagine," smirked Charmaine. She shrugged. "I suppose you must marry then! I told you so. And it is very good that Mr. Longshanks appears interested, for, if Sir Dodkins be not motivated enough, some competition will spur him on. (An apt metaphor, as Mr. Longshanks thinks of nothing besides his horse.) Which would you prefer? The baronet has the advantage in title and wealth, but Mr. Longshanks is younger and hasn't any cough."

"There must be some other way," Margaret said.

"There isn't. Did you give the matter no consideration?"

"Charmaine, I have thought of little else since the man presented his bill!"

"Then what conclusion have you come to?"

"I haven't come to any. It isn't as easy as you imagine."

Charmaine rolled her eyes in exasperation. "I'm certain I could manage my affairs better than you. Look here, Sir Ods Bodkins and that Mr. Beck are headed this way. Whatever you do, be charming about it."

Being told to be charming instantly made it impossible for Margaret, but she accepted Sir Dodkins' invitation to dance with good grace. She could at least refrain from being carelessly cruel to the man, as Marianne Dashwood was to Colonel Brandon, even if, like Marianne, she could not picture him in a romantic light. Her smile took effort, however, for she saw Mr. Waite and Mr. Haworth speaking together at the far end of the room, Mrs. Blakely beside them. She did not have to guess the subject that engaged them, for Alwyn was leading Mrs. Waite to the floor. Oh, how many problems would be solved if only Mrs. Waite's family might overcome their objections to Alwyn!

But even this all-absorbing problem yielded to Margaret's appreciation for Mr. Waite's appearance. This night he wore a coat of blue so dark as to be nearly black, paired with a dark striped waistcoat and black breeches. Even as she stared, she found herself wishing and wishing as hard as Charmaine did, that he could dance!

"How light you are on your feet, Miss Hapgood," said the baronet, recalling her. She hoped her distraction had not been obvious.

"Thank you, sir. You as well."

"My daughter was very fond of dancing," he replied. "And, before her marriage, not opposed to having her old father partner her."

He managed this entire speech as they went round in circle, and, at his words, an entirely new thought burst like a firework in her head. Why—why—what if—? Could it be that—?

Fortunately, the separation required by the figures prevented her from blurting anything out precipitously, so that, when they came together again, she managed to say with miraculous mildness: "Sir Dodkins, I believe your cough has improved."

His faded cheeks colored with gratification. "Thank you. It has indeed. I have had but few fits in the last couple days. I attribute it to time, taking the waters, and my naturally robust constitution."

Margaret smiled at this, but her busy mind now revolved the revelation which had struck her. That is, if she so reminded Sir Dodkins of his beloved daughter Marcia, could it be at all possible that *he* might be broached in the matter of a loan? Could it be at all possible that his fatherly feelings might extend so far as to help her financially?

Margaret resolved not to consult Charmaine on the matter, for she already guessed it would be most assuredly deemed bad manners. *Not done*. After all, there was probably not any person in the wide world who enjoyed being asked for money—but might the baronet not be willing to overlook such a breach of etiquette, in his growing fondness for her, if his fondness were indeed growing?

And such a plan, at least, would not require any moral compromise on her part because it would not involve deceiving him. It would only require that she humble herself abjectly to make the request. And in return for his generosity—if only he would be generous!—she would play his surrogate daughter with alacrity and good cheer during her whole time in Bath! She would dance with him, drive with him, talk to him, do whatever he proposed, in her gratitude.

Yes!

This could serve.

Her feverish thoughts ran on. If Marianne Dashwood had asked Colonel Brandon to lend her fifty pounds, he would not have hesitated, Margaret was certain. Of course, the colonel was in love with Marianne, not viewing her as a daughter, per se, but—well, the situations were analogous enough, she decided hastily. She would think about that later.

"Do you play cards, Miss Hapgood?" was Sir Dodkins' next question, when they came to the promenade.

"I love cards, sir," she answered truthfully, for all the Hapgood daughters were excellent card-players. She was now nearly vibrating with excitement, and it required all her self-control not to make her request on the spot.

"I thought perhaps I might invite your family and Miss Blakely's family to my home for a private card party, then, if you would like that."

"Oh!" Margaret blushed at the implication that Sir Dodkins would hold it for her sake, but she nodded eagerly. Yes—surely, in an evening spent in his home, she could steal a moment apart with him! "Thank you, sir. We would greatly enjoy that."

"I will speak with your uncle, then. And, if you might introduce me to Miss Blakely's family...?"

Thus it was that Margaret, half shy, half eager, took Sir Dodkins' arm after the dance ended and led him to where Mr. Waite and his family stood. As both Alwyn and Mrs. Waite were moving in the same direction, along with Charmaine and her partner, they all arrived at the same time, but it was Margaret and the baronet who drew everyone's attention.

"Sir Bod—Sir Dodkins, rather!" cried Alwyn. "What a pleasure to see you again. My friends, this is Sir Dodkins Hargate, who recently favored Mags and Miss Blakely and me with a drive up to Sham Castle. You know Miss Blakely, of course, Sir Dodkins. Allow me to introduce her family."

"What a pleasure to meet you all," said the baronet graciously, as they all made their salutes. "I was just telling Miss Hapgood that I would like to host a card party at my home in St. James Square, if you would do me the honor of making up a few tables."

"Maggie and I would be delighted," replied Alwyn, while Charmaine dug her elbow into Margaret's ribs. "Though I cannot speak for my sister. She is not much for cards and prefers to stay in, in the evenings. What do you say to it, Eliza—that is, Mrs. Waite?"

Flushing at his little blunder, Mrs. Waite deferred to her son. "As Dashiell chooses."

"Oh, do say yes, Dashiell," urged Charmaine. "And you need have no fear, Mr. Haworth—I will help you shuffle when it is your turn to do so."

"Heh, heh—so kind—almost worth losing this," Haworth flirted heavily, giving his empty sleeve a toss. Then he too glanced at Mr. Waite for approval.

"We thank you," said Mr. Waite coolly. "You may name the day, Sir Dodkins."

The baronet beamed with pleasure. "Shall we say Wednesday, then?"

That would put it just before the dreaded pianoforte recital Margaret and Charmaine had at last scheduled, but when Mr. Waite surveyed the company there were no objections. Alwyn was content to have two whole evenings with his beloved to look forward to, and Margaret was determined to avoid Mr. Waite's gaze. It was silly, but she was certain that, if she looked him in the eye, he would instantly realize she was up to something, and she did not want to explain or defend herself from someone so astute.

The matter settled, the baronet took his leave, not without asking Margaret for a second dance: "Shall we say the penultimate one, before the Boulanger?"

When he was gone, Mrs. Waite smiled at her. "I believe it is to you we owe the honor of this invitation."

"Undoubtedly," agreed Alwyn. "Our Maggie here is a jewel."

Charmaine gave a dramatic sigh. "He shows every sign of being smitten."

"Not *smitten*," Margaret objected faintly.

"And how well he looks," Charmaine went on, "without that woolen wrapper bundled about his throat to protect from catarrh."

"His health is much improved," Margaret said, irked.

Charmaine laughed at her annoyance. "The healing power of love, I daresay!"

"St. James Square might be a difficult climb for you, Dashiell," his mother observed.

"I will manage it," he responded shortly. "Sir Dodkins is not the only one improved by his time in Bath."

"Never fear, Dashiell," Charmaine purred. "Everyone sees your progress. Could you but dance again, my dear cousin, you would be my *beau* idéal! But, in the meantime, here comes Mr. Sandling to claim my hand. Margaret is not allowed to charm all the eligible gentlemen, you see."

Beside her, Margaret heard poor Mr. Haworth give a little sigh, to watch the fair one glide out of his reach once more, and she felt like sighing herself. As awkward as it was to have Sir Dodkins escort her back to her friends and family, it was more awkward to stand partnerless while Charmaine sailed off.

"I suppose I will shuffle along to the card room," said Mr. Haworth, after a minute. "I told King I would. Coming, Dash?"

"Perhaps. Presently." He nodded in the direction of his mother, who stood very near Alwyn Arbuthnot. Mr. Haworth nodded in answer before casting one last glance at frolicking Charmaine and drooping away.

Instead of eavesdropping on the tête-à-tête engrossing Alwyn and Mrs. Waite, however, Mr. Waite turned to Margaret. "Are you free, then? Has the baronet frightened away your other suitors?"

She tried to match his teasing tone. "All of them, I'm afraid. But you need not converse with me, if you have other plans. I will wait beside my uncle."

"I am perfectly content to converse," he replied. "Unlike Haworth, I made Mr. King no promise to play."

The pleasure his words gave her made her forget to be wary. Was he really content to talk to her? If only she could fascinate him! Or if only he were like Mr. Longshanks, and Margaret could introduce some little subject that would make him go on and on at great length! She could listen to him and watch the other dancers for hours and think herself in heaven.

But he reminded her of the danger soon enough. "How is the homesickness, Miss Hapgood?"

"Homesickness?"

"When I last saw you, you were homesick, and said you missed your father. The painting of the hunters—remember?"

"Oh, *that* homesickness," she said weakly. "It is much better, I thank you."

"You have heard from your family, then?"

"Oh—er, no," she admitted. "No—new letter, I'm afraid. I just...am better. You must pardon me for being moody on occasion."

"With all my heart."

Her eyes met his briefly but then as quickly cut away. Across the room Mr. Fosse of the nasal voice lifted a hand in greeting, but Margaret pretended not to see. Talking to Mr. Waite might be perilous, but she found it too sweet to wish it over.

"Thank you, Mr. Waite. Yes—much more myself tonight."

She realized after she spoke that it was the truth. She felt better. And not only because she was near him, which incurred as much guilt as pleasure, but also because things at last bore a more favorable aspect. A wide smile spread across her face. Yes, she felt optimistic again. The baronet was a kind man. And he was fond of her clearly—only see the evidence of next week's card party! Surely, he would be willing to help her. It would not solve the ultimate problem of what to do with Uncle Alwyn, of course, but at least it would buy them time. Perhaps her uncle was right, and something would turn up in the course of the season. In light of this, she might be excused from putting aside her anxieties for the night and simply enjoying this moment beside Mr. Waite, who was so very agreeable! His conversation and his humor and his company. She might pass the winter playing the fond daughter to Sir Dodkins, but it would be these moments in Mr. Waite's company that she lived for.

That last thought brought color flooding to her cheeks.

Puzzled, Dashiell watched the play of feelings across her face. So, then. Whatever distressed her in Princes Street and possibly on other occasions had relaxed its grip. And whatever it was, and whatever had remedied it, she would not talk about it with him. He wondered uneasily if it could possibly, possibly be, that all Charmaine's teasing had some unthinkable foundation in truth. That Miss Hapgood's spirits rose because she indeed hoped to captivate that elderly baronet? "Hoped to captivate"?—nay—it was already done, judging by appearances.

His knuckles whitened where they gripped the head of his cane.

It was none of his business, of course. *She* was none of his business. And he had no right to feel any particular emotion about her or her choices.

And yet he did.

It was not jealousy that lashed him, to be sure—jealousy would be preposterous. He was an engaged man and, a mere month ago, had not known of this Miss Margaret Hapgood's existence. Not jealousy, then. It was simply *anger,* he decided. Indignation. That so fresh and fine a girl as she should, like all the world, be willing to sell herself like a piece of goods in return for financial security. Such behavior might be commonplace enough—Dashiell was no fool—but somehow he thought one of her honesty and frankness would be above such things. That a young lady who fought off thieves and who smiled spontaneously and who spoke her true feelings more often in an hour than Charmaine Blakely did in a lifetime—should not such a unique young lady require more from life? Require more from a lover and a husband than money and rank?

Would you prefer she be in love with this Sir Dodkins, then? a voice inside his head challenged. *That she choose the man freely, for love, and love alone?*

He would not, as it happened.

If anything, that possibility made him feel worse. Angrier. Something-er.

When Margaret next peeked at Mr. Waite, her happy thoughts fled. For she found he was glaring at her. Favoring her with that narrowed gaze with which he sliced people in half. And she was sliced in half.

She took an unintentional step back. What had just happened? How had they gone from sharing a companionable talk to being at odds? Was he angry that she lied to him the other day? Her fib about homesickness had been stupid, yes, and transparent, but it had not harmed him in any way, so why should he now be offended? And there was no doubt she had somehow, inexplicably, offended him.

"Sir?"

Dashiell blinked slowly. Looked away, struggling to regain control of himself. Good Lord, what was wrong with him?

Perhaps, Margaret thought, that nasty glare was a result of something her uncle and Mrs. Waite had been doing behind her? She remembered with a twinge of guilt that she was supposed to be observing them. Perhaps they were standing too closely together, or Uncle Alwyn had brushed Mrs. Waite's hand. But whatever it was that angered Mr. Waite, he wiped his expression clean now, and she knew it was no use asking. He could hardly tell her, when she was so intimately involved with all parties.

She gave a silent sigh. There would be no hours of standing in pleasant company, then. She must go away and spare Mr. Waite her presence. In the meantime, she smiled vacuously at the dancers, wishing the floor would open and swallow her up or the roof would cave in.

To her immense relief, after another silent minute, she spotted Mr. Trumbull of the large feet approaching. Her imitation smile gave way to a genuine one as he lumbered toward her, for it seemed all at once far preferable to have her feet crushed by accident than her heart crushed on purpose.

CHAPTER TWENTY

Be free with him, and tell him all thy thought.
—Patrick Hannay, *A Happy Husband* (1619)

Two colloquies of note took place before the baronet's card party, the first between Dashiell and Haworth at the King's Bath.

"I say, Dash," began Haworth, after he eased onto the stone bench with a pleasurable sigh, "do you suppose that old baronet means to make up to Miss Blakely?"

"To Charmaine? Don't be thick, Haworth."

"Well, I thought it must be, for you've been a bear ever since he issued his invitation. As I doubt he wants to get to know *us* better, it is either Miss Blakely or Miss Hapgood whom he pursues, in making up this card party."

Dashiell trailed a hand through the hot, mineral-rich water. "It is Miss Hapgood, of course."

Haworth brightened at this, even smiling upon a matron who was working an air bubble from under her brown shift. "Well, then! No harm in that. She will do very well for herself. His age aside, I suppose he has everything to recommend him: title, wealth, property—"

"Both arms," mocked Dashiell.

"True," Haworth conceded, "he has both of his arms."

Dashiell splashed him impatiently. "Lord. I was joking. I am certain, in a young lady's eyes, the baronet's many additional decades outweigh one paltry missing arm."

"You think? Not that I wish to compete with the baronet. I rather wish I did. But I—" He broke off to fiddle with arranging the empty sleeve of his shirt. Then— "I suppose Miss Hapgood is a good sort of girl, even with her objectionable uncle. I wish her very well. Miss Blakely is deuced fond of her. And—if I may venture to say—Arbuthnot does not appear to be *so* wretched an uncle. The family behaves circumspectly enough, and I have even heard Miss Blakely complain they are too thrifty for her taste."

"I suspect praise for these virtues should be placed at Miss Hapgood's feet, rather than her uncle's," Dashiell said dryly.

"Even so, I stand by my opinion. An uncle easily managed by a young niece cannot be so very bad an uncle."

"Are you saying I should let my mother marry him, if she chooses?"

Haworth frowned, rubbing his shoulder. "I don't know either party well, of course, but I suspect your mother rather likes the man."

The two men were silent a few minutes, each occupied with his own thoughts. When Haworth spoke again, it was clear his had veered in a different direction.

"You know, Dash, I was thinking I might run to Bradford for a spell after our supper with Arbuthnot and the Hapgoods. See how matters are getting along. I did not spend much time there before coming to Bath."

"Will you be gone long? I will miss your stuttering company. I do confess, your maleness provides welcome relief from so many women about me."

Haworth was already scarlet from the heat of the waters, but his cheeks flushed nearly purple at this. "I—find I too would like a respite from the women about you."

Dashiell gave him a long look. "From any one of them in particular?"

"I don't need to tell you," was the hoarse reply. "You've guessed, of course. I suppose everyone has. This is precisely why I need to go away for a time."

"Mm. I see. Haworth, even if Charmaine were not engaged to me, do you honestly think she would be a good match for you? You can barely string together two coherent words in her presence."

"Of course you find it humorous," said Haworth stiffly. "I have not had my entire life to grow accustomed—nay—*indifferent*—to such beauty and charm."

"Point taken. But my...feelings for Charmaine aside, I ask you again: do you think you could manage her? She is clever and willful and, I fear, not always the angelic creature she appears—"

"You malign her, Dash!" cried Haworth, striking the surface of the water.

"I hope I do," he answered equably. "And I mean no slight upon your own mettle, my good man. I sometimes think Charmaine will be more than I can manage either. But I am obligated to make the attempt."

Haworth fell silent again, ruminating over these injuries to his adored one's image.

The matron with the air bubble in her shift now had the misfortune of overturning her chocolate, her cup sliding into the bath and sending a murky swirl through the green-gray depths. Dashiell retrieved it when it bobbed up and restored it to the flustered bather.

"I say," Haworth ventured again, when the embarrassed woman waded away, "I know you have never been one to wear your heart on your sleeve, but—if it be not too intimate a question—do you suppose Miss Blakely feels confident of your affections? It—strikes me that a little stuttering and oafishness on your part in her presence would not go entirely amiss."

To Haworth's surprise, his friend's countenance darkened. "You are right. I have been an indifferent lover. Perhaps not always, but—I will confess to you that, in the time we were away, I began to suspect she and I were not as well-suited for each other as two engaged people might hope to be."

"I see," returned Haworth. He could not help the hopeful lift in his voice. "And now that you are together again?"

"Now I am quite certain of it." There was no need to say outright that he and Charmaine did not seem to love each other at all, beyond a mild, cousinly attachment. "But Haworth—it makes no difference. She and I will be wed in any case."

"But—but—"

"Unless Charmaine chooses to end our engagement, we will be married in the spring," Dashiell went on. "We will be neither the first couple nor the last to marry for reasons other than violent love. In fact, we will be, I suppose, as fond of each other as many a husband and wife."

Crestfallen, Haworth slumped lower in the water, not even caring that his empty sleeve came untucked and floated to the surface.

Dashiell considered him ruefully. "Believe me when I say that, if Charmaine ever decided she did not want to marry me, I would bear you no grudge if you made the attempt to win her, Charles. It would not impair our friendship."

"Thank you," said Haworth with glum dignity. "I don't suppose it likely she would break it off, you being rich and handsome and two-armed and so on, but I can't help feeling she deserves more than mere fondness. I would *adore* her."

Dashiell was certain he would. At least, for a time.

Two hours later, when they had finished with bathing and their daily rub-down and were returning up Union Street, some devil prompted him to open the subject again. "I think a man might find a more peaceful life with such a wife as Miss Hapgood will make, despite her uncle. She is pretty enough, and there is a winning frankness to her. She hasn't any fortune, but you have enough, Haworth. Why do you not transfer your affections to her?"

"You say it as if I were capable of giving my heart at my convenience," protested Haworth. "That is not the case, I assure you. *You* might be able to transfer your affections to Miss Hapgood, since you feel only the most inexplicable, wishy-washy emotions toward the divine one, but I could never—it will be very long before I care for another woman as I do Miss Blakely. Very long, indeed."

It was just as well, Dashiell thought, as they passed the hospital. For he had no sooner made the proposal than he wished it unsaid. While Dashiell could not settle for himself once and for all whether Miss Hapgood was just another ambitious young lady like countless others, he was not indifferent to her. And should Haworth ever choose to pursue her, Dashiell might then have to resent his loyal friend, even as he found himself (to his bewilderment) resenting the elderly baronet.

Because, it seemed, Haworth was right. It would require no great effort on Dashiell's part to "transfer his affections" to Miss Hapgood, whether it ought to be done or not.

Or, at least, it had required no effort Dashiell was aware of.

Somehow, some way, he feared it was already done.

Therefore, the second colloquy of note before the card party: "What do you say, Charmaine, to a stroll along the gravel walk?"

For such a self-possessed young lady, she failed to hide her surprise. "Why—do you mean now, Dashiell?"

"At your convenience." He had interrupted her practice at the pianoforte, having waited for an opportunity to find her alone.

Curiosity sparked in her eyes. "I'll get my cloak and meet you by the door."

Two minutes later they were skirting Queens Square, Charmaine trying to adjust her eager pace to his slower one and scowling at his cane as if it offended her. Probably it did.

It was a bitter day, cold and gray and damp. Dashiell felt an answering ache in his leg, but he ignored it, determined to have his say with this girl he knew too well and too little.

They entered the walk, thronged despite the chill, and Charmaine turned to him teasingly. "Well? To what do I owe the honor, my almost-lord-and-master?"

"Do you consider walking with a cripple like me an honor?"

"Not the crippled part, especially, but you know very well you haven't sought my company alone even once in all the time Mama and I have been here. So either you must mean to communicate something very exciting or something very dreadful."

"How dreadful can it be, if you sound so delighted?"

She tucked her arm through his, only to untuck it a few steps later because his gait lurched more than she liked. "Go on, then. What is it?"

He had thought *ad infinitum* how to approach the subject, so he was prepared. "Haworth means to go away in a few days. He has business in Bradford and does not know when he will return."

"I was wrong, then. For that news is neither very exciting nor very dreadful."

"Is it not? Won't you miss him any?"

She cast him a sidewise glance, measuring. "Of course I will. He is a likeable young man, despite being so tongue-tied."

"He speaks fluently enough when you are not about," rejoined Dashiell. "Nor can it be news to you that he is quite taken with you. I rather thought you enjoyed it."

She pouted at this. "Well? Who does not enjoy a little flattery?"

"Then you feel no more than general liking for him? And a pleasure in being flattered?"

"How vain you make me sound! I do not know why you press me in this manner. How could I have feelings for Mr. Haworth beyond liking and friendship, Dashiell, when I am engaged to you?"

He paused to let a maid laden with shopping pass in front of them. That, and the pace his companion set taxed him, but his pride would not permit him to mention it. A thousand thoughts crowded him. The same thoughts which kept him awake the previous night.

"Our engagement is of very long standing, Charmaine," he resumed finally. "If you did like Haworth more than you felt you ought, it would not be astonishing. I suppose one cannot help having feelings beyond liking and friendship, whether they are appropriate or not. You have not had the opportunity to meet many other people, while living at Chardis."

Charmaine tucked her mittened hands in the pockets of her cloak, her gaze fixed on Barton Fields. "Not so very many, no."

Behind her abstracted look, she was thinking very hard. Her betrothed could have only one of three reasons for raising such a sensitive topic in this manner: (1) he was jealous of her affections;

or, (2) he took issue with her flirtations out of male pride; or, (3) he wanted to be released from their engagement but, as a man of honor, knew that she must end it.

The first possibility seemed ruled out by his careless attitude toward her—unless that attitude hid tumultuous feelings, which she doubted. Did the man truly care about anything?

The second possibility was also unlikely—Dashiell seemed altogether indifferent to her popularity with men at the balls, to her frustration. His male pride could only suffer if he thought himself wanting in her eyes, but he never seemed a bit bothered by what she thought.

That left only the third possibility. He wanted to be free.

Fleetingly she contemplated the idea of release from her engagement. Why, it meant she might dance and flirt to her heart's content and not have to watch the gentlemen slink away when they learned she could not be won. It meant she might experience the joy of making men violently in love with her and hearing who-knew-what impassioned speeches and proposals! Suppose one of them were to say he would die of love for her, as they did in novels? It would be too delicious. How unfair that she had been hobbled from the start by this engagement, before she could even enter the world!

But the cooler hand of reason soon reined in these galloping visions. For, to gain such freedom, she would give up a husband so eligible that most girls would eat their hearts to have him. Even Margaret admitted she would choose Dashiell over Sir Dodkins—that any young woman would. And, while the envy of those around him might not feed Dashiell, Charmaine thrived on it.

By the time they reached Church Street, she made up her mind.

No, she did not prefer to release him. If she must marry someone, he would serve admirably. But she meant, insofar as possible this winter, to both have her cake and eat it. She would have men violently in love with her *and* she would keep her enviable lover.

Her choice being made, she then had space for other realizations, chief of which was to wonder why he offered her the alternative in the first place. Did *he* long to be released? Did *he* have inappropriate feelings for someone else? Her thoughts flew to the night of the play, when she caught him looking at Margaret, before Charmaine even knew who Margaret was. Margaret was the only other young lady of his current acquaintance, but, if that was as violent a love as Dashiell could muster—a look here and there, or collapsing beside the girl to have a cup of tea—Margaret was welcome to it. Charmaine would not begrudge her such meager interest, and nothing could come of it in any event.

It was infuriating, however, that he should even think of relinquishing her, Charmaine, so cavalierly, for whatever reasons!

She turned to him with a bewitching smile. "Tell me, Dashiell—what need do I have of meeting other people?"

"You seem to enjoy those you have met in Bath," he said warily, noting the smile. "Even the ones you originally objected to."

"You are right. You're always right. While I can't say I am especially drawn to Mr. Arbuthnot or Mrs. Hapgood, I am excessively fond of Margaret. But then, she is an endearing creature, is she not?"

His hesitation was so slight only the eagle-eyed Charmaine could have noted it. "Miss Hapgood seems an amiable young lady."

"Ah, then you approve of my friendship with her?"

Another pause. "Whatever our original objections to the family, Miss Hapgood herself seems respectable enough."

This made Charmaine grin inwardly, thinking of Margaret's pleas for money and dreams of pawn-brokers. But she was satisfied by his lackluster praise of the girl—Dashiell might absent-mindedly think her worth looking at or chatting with if she presented herself, but clearly he had conceived no Grand Passion.

She returned, therefore, to the matter at hand. "Very well, that tribute must suffice for my friend. But as to your earlier remark, just because I enjoy meeting new people, does it necessarily follow that I am no longer content with relationships of longer standing?"

"It does not," he admitted.

They reached the Crescent and stopped to take in the view. Once more, Dashiell steeled himself. "I only mean to say that, because you were so young when we were engaged, you might have found such a commitment restrictive, especially in the last two years when I was absent. You had no chance to have your fun, as it were."

For a moment, Charmaine almost doubted herself. To hear him speak what she had just been thinking—what she had so often thought! Was there some consideration, mixed in with his cavalier treatment? Was his crime lack of passion, rather than indifference? Perhaps his nature was simply too phlegmatic to please her, but he cared as much as he was able. It was worth pondering.

If he truly wanted to marry her, was he offering to release her for her own sake? That is, he did not want to marry her at the cost of her happiness? Because, if such were the case, she would not need to punish him. She would only need to train him better in how to show his love. Not in these stiff, honorable, dull ways.

To test her new theory, she tucked her arm once more in his, saying, "If the two years were long without you, you have more than made up for them. I could not be happier with our engagement. In fact, Dashiell, I hope all our married life will be so pleasant as these last few weeks."

The trap baited, she stole a glance at him, and therefore she did not miss the fleeting shadow in his eyes. The indrawn breath. The infinitesimal halt in his step.

Ah.

So he did not, in fact, want to marry her.

A surge of indignation overpowered her then. She whipped her gaze away and withdrew her arm, pretending an interest in the arc of homes enclosing one side of their path, the luminosity of their Bath stone quenched by the overcast sky.

Without consulting him, she marched ahead, struggling to master herself, and she was some ways down the row before she could even unclench her fists. More than one passerby along the walk turned to admire the beautiful girl, only to shrink back from the hard glitter of her eyes and set of her jaw. Charmaine, for once, didn't notice them.

Curse him!

Curse him for a horrible, heartless, indifferent, soulless, stupid, blind, lame, ungrateful *lump* of a man! He didn't want to marry her? Why, she might marry anyone she pleased, with a snap of her fingers! And, instead, she had put up with his stupid desire to join the army and his long absence and his boring letters and his completely unnecessary crippling of himself and his inability to dance and his lifeless courtship! *This* was the man the world found so eligible? Ha! A rock made a better lover than he! Why, she would break it off with him this very afternoon, only she wouldn't give him the satisfaction.

Her angry steps took her as far as Number 4, where she clutched the black railing with mittened hands and wished she could kick the door in.

Only when a plan for revenge formed did her expression soften and her smile return.

It was simple, really. She had once told Margaret she intended to love Dashiell in precisely the same proportion that he loved her, but now she decided this ratio would not do at all. No—he must love her *desperately*, and, in return, she would be cool and distant and heartless until the debt was paid. How, exactly, she could make him love her desperately remained to be seen, since the usual techniques left him unmoved, but she would think of something.

Just see if she wouldn't.

Charmaine was nearly a third of the way along the Crescent before Dashiell roused himself and set off after her, more aware now of the disappointment scything through him than his injured leg.

That was that, then.

He had not had much hope Charmaine would decide to end their engagement of her own accord, and now he had none at all. Short of her falling madly in love with another man—and Dashiell thought the odds better that she would be struck by lightning—they would be married in the spring.

They would leave Bath, they would marry, and he would never see Margaret Hapgood again.

CHAPTER TWENTY-ONE

**How now, my Lord! What! throw up your Cards before
you have lost the Game?**
—Colley Cibber, *The Careless Husband* (1705)

Margaret's newfound optimism survived the days before the baronet's card party, though tried at times by having no one to confide in and by her mother's querulousness. Mrs. Hapgood caught one of her imaginary colds and was confined to bed, insisting Margaret and Alwyn read to her and dictating fretful letters to other family members. Whenever they were released from these duties, Margaret and her uncle played cards or backgammon or went for walks. Once they stole out to watch Mr. Longshanks ride in Sydney Gardens, and another time she escaped to Princes Street to practice the Gluck piece, where she was both relieved and disappointed not to see Mr. Waite.

To no one's surprise, Mrs. Hapgood declined attending the card party; nor did Margaret or Alwyn try very hard to persuade her. As Margaret noted, her mother's presence would make nine, compelling at least one of the tables to play a round game, and Mrs. Hapgood had not much head for cards. Alwyn only thought that, after their days of confinement, he and Margaret might stay as long as they pleased if Augusta remained behind.

After a half-hearted suggestion to Margaret that they hire chairs, which his penny-pinching niece rejected, Alwyn resigned himself to a brisk walk through the winter chill and hoped his nose wouldn't get too red. He was spared this, however, when a note arrived from the baronet, begging that he might send his carriage for them.

"Another compliment to you, my dear," observed Alwyn, scribbling a hasty acceptance.

And Margaret did indeed feel very grand to be handed into the barouche again, the wraps tucked about her, and the horses left to do all the work as they made their way up Broad Street, past the Fountain Buildings and Oxford Row and Belmont, before turning into the lane which led to the Weston Road and St. James Square. Her uncle pointed out various sights, but she was distracted by what lay ahead.

Now that it came to it, she was not certain she would have a moment alone with the baronet. How could she, when they were each pinned to a card table with at least two other players? But she must find an opportunity—she *must*.

When they arrived at Sir Dodkins', it was not the cold alone that brought color to Margaret's face or a tremble to her hands.

There was the Waite party just being admitted when the barouche clattered up, and Margaret didn't know which was harder to bear: Charmaine's arch look or Mr. Waite's unreadable one.

She need not have worried about her mother making a ninth at cards, for Sir Dodkins had invited a handful of other guests. Margaret recognized the man from Molland's and the turbaned woman from the ball, but their names and connections ran out of her head. (When Charmaine embraced her, she hissed, "Imagine what lively gatherings you will have at Hargate Hall with these fashionable sprigs. But beware Madame Turban does not steal him from under your ungrateful nose!")

The setting made a deeper impression. The house was brilliant with light and a great fire roared in the drawing room. Margaret tried not to stare at the richness of the thick carpets and painted ceilings and Louis Quinze furniture. Square marquetry tables were set with candles at the corners, fresh packs of cards and ivory fish, but first Sir Dodkins plied them with tea and coffee and biscuits, playing the good host while servants circled.

As she stood at the tea table, cup in hand, Margaret's eyes followed him anxiously about the room. She was right in thinking that holding private conversation at a small party would be more difficult than at a ball. Here not a word could be said that would not be heard by others, if they chose to listen. Mrs. Blakely, for instance, complimented the baronet on the cunning cabaret tables, with their curved legs and black lacquer, and he launched into an explanation of the Chinese scenes painted on the trays, with the Molland's gentleman interjecting comments about his own collection. Charmaine was teasing Uncle Alwyn about a scene in *St. Irvyne* that she found ridiculous but which he defended as dramatic, while Haworth sputtered occasional contributions. A ruddy, heavy, older man quizzed Mr. Waite about whether Napoleon would withdraw more troops from Spain, while the latter attended politely.

Margaret stood woodenly by as Mrs. Waite and the others canvassed the usual topics, and she thought Madame Turban frowned at her. (Though surely "Madame Turban" could not be her real name.) She wondered what to say if the baronet approached her, but it was Mr. Waite who came to have his cup refilled.

His proximity drove Margaret's task clean from her mind. Having not seen him since the fancy ball, she did not think, with all her worries, that she could bear it if he scowled at her again. But when she finally glanced up, she found no sign of anger. He actually smiled at her, his narrow eyes crinkling in that way that made her insides turn over. Whatever caused his bad mood had passed. Or perhaps it had nothing to do with her in the first place.

"From my observations in the Upper Rooms, I would swear you prefer tea to coffee, Miss Hapgood, only you do not appear to be drinking either beverage." He nodded toward her full cup.

"Oh. No," she said lamely. Her gaze dropped again, only to notice what nice hands he had, his long fingers curled around his cup. It had been one of those fingers which traced the bite mark on her own hand those weeks ago. She could almost feel the featherlight touch again and thought, *it was well worth being bitten*. Then she blushed hotly and took a hasty, burning sip of her tea.

Dashiell did not notice her confusion, being too wound-up himself. He should not be talking to her, after all. He should not be crossing rooms to come and talk to her, now that he knew the danger. For he would only end in liking her more and more, and what was the use of that?

And yet here he was.

Wishing she would look at him again, he made another attempt to draw her out. "I am having coffee myself, you see," he said encouragingly, "that I might keep my wits."

His effort succeeded, and she gave him a shy smile. "Mr. Waite, I don't suppose you are ever in danger of losing your wits. At least, I have never seen you at a loss."

"Have you not?" he muttered. *Take notice, Miss Hapgood, for this is what it looks like.*

It was that disarming smile of hers—guileless and genuine. The sight of her arriving in the baronet's vehicle had galled him, and he had tried to nurse this resentment, telling himself that, yes, she was just a fortune-hunting, ambitious girl like any other and not worth any heart-rending, but then she smiled and turned everything topsy-turvy, banishing his suspicions.

Of course she was not going to marry that old man for money!—Dashiell slandered her to think it. Whatever the baronet had in mind, it did not then follow that she thought the same. It was not her fault, after all, if others besides himself were drawn to her. There were men who preferred gaudy coquettes like Charmaine, and others who chose the Miss Hapgoods of the world. Allured as he was by her sweet and honest countenance. Her openness. Her candor.

As quickly as that, he absolved her of suspicion.

The space between them dwindled—he did not think he moved, but he might have. He might have inclined toward her because the knob of his cane dug into his palm, a warning. It went unheeded.

She smelled faintly of lily-of-the-valley. And warmth. Heady, heady.

Her eyes, wondering and tentative, lifted again to his. *Just tell her*, he thought. *Charmaine be damned. Throw everything to the winds.*

But then came a burst of laughter, a clinking of cups, and they both reacted as if someone had dashed them with cold water. Dashiell straightened abruptly, wincing when his leg protested the sudden movement. Great God, what was the matter with him?

Why did the realization that he—cared for her—make him more reckless, instead of more cautious?

Striving for nonchalance, he retreated a step, glancing about the room as if to say, *This is no* tête-à- tête. *Anyone is welcome to join us.* And when he did speak, his voice was nearly normal (only a half-shade too hearty): "I always drink coffee when I play cards. For I don't know the stakes and have no wish to lose vast quantities of money."

Vast quantities of money!

That brought Margaret back to earth with a bump. She set her own tea down hastily. What was she about, letting this man fascinate her? If anyone needed to keep her wits about her, it was she. She might be an excellent card player, but she had too much on her mind this evening to play her best. Heaven forbid she lose and deepen the hole her family was in!

"Do you suppose we will play for high stakes?" she asked, trying to hide her alarm. "In my family, we are wont to play for pins."

She shook her head at a passing footman who proffered a tray of biscuits, and he moved on.

"I am very interested in these Bramleigh ways," Mr. Waite said, now sounding more himself. "I suppose that, just as you danced with your sisters, you also partnered each other in whist. Well, then—at the end of an evening, who would have the largest pile of pins?"

"It could be anyone," she murmured. "We all play like fiends."

"Ah. I had better be careful around you, then."

Margaret heartily seconded this opinion. Indeed, she had better not be at Mr. Waite's table at all. He would only distract her, and she did not want his sharp eyes on her when she stole away to make her proposal to Sir Dodkins.

When the baronet gestured for the servants to remove the refreshments, Margaret removed to her uncle's side and was rewarded with a table made up of Sir Dodkins, Alwyn, Mrs. Waite, and herself. Better yet, both Mr. Waite and Charmaine were seated at the farthest table, so she would not have to reckon with either one.

"What stakes will we have?" Sir Dodkins asked them. "A guinea a fish?"

Margaret just managed not to gasp, but it was a near thing. Her uncle remained bland and blank, though whether that was due to confidence or his usual indifference to money worries she couldn't guess. Thankfully, Mrs. Waite replied, "Oh, Sir Dodkins, I could not bear if my play proved costly to anyone. What would you say to a shilling a fish?"

In comparison to guineas, shillings were a reprieve, but Margaret had hoped for pennies.

They cut the cards, and the draw paired her with Alwyn. He was not the cleverest whist partner, but he knew enough and had played enough at Bramleigh to follow her lead.

As the rubber progressed, however, Margaret found she had not counted on how Mrs. Waite's presence would influence his play. In the first place, it made him inattentive, and Margaret several times had to remind him of his turn, or which suit had led, or which was trump. In the second place, she twice caught him playing a kinder card than he ought, to help Mrs. Waite take the trick. Margaret was preoccupied herself, tracking their winnings and losses. When they lost a handful of fish in one game, she paled at the calculation: half-sovereign, two bob. The next was not much better, and they were in for more than a pound.

All the while she must attend the conversation, as if she were not every minute agonizing that the fifty pounds she must beg would balloon to sixty by the evening's end, and when, oh when, could she ask him?

Before an hour was gone, she almost hated everyone in the room for their easy amusement, their easy chatter. For no one else was an evening's pastime so fateful. Charmaine's and Mr. Waite's table in particular seemed the center of all things delightful, with even Mrs. Blakely smiling because Charmaine teased and laughed and flirted and shed happiness all about her. Margaret need not have feared that Charmaine or Mr. Waite would do anything to discompose her because they seemed to have forgotten her altogether. There was Charmaine slapping down her cards triumphantly and wagging a finger at her betrothed, which he playfully knocked away, and Margaret wished irrationally that she were placed with them after all. It would not be so very bad to lose to *him*.

"Miss Hapgood, all your attention is on your cards," Sir Dodkins remarked. "You must not be so serious. Do you not enjoy whist? We could choose another game when we finish the rubber."

"I adore whist," she answered truthfully. "Forgive me if I have been quiet."

"Maggie's counting cards, I suppose," put in Alwyn. "She and her sisters all do. Quite the sharp ones."

Sir Dodkins and Mrs. Waite laughed pleasantly, but Margaret flung him the briefest look and said, "Uncle Alwyn is just complaining because he often loses to us. If he ever finesses, it is more often by accident than design, especially when he does not pay attention to what has been played."

"Too true, too true," admitted her uncle, winking at her. "My partner is saying I have been too chatty and not holding up my end. Am I right, Mags?"

"It is fortunate, perhaps, that you are not a professional gambler, sir."

Play resumed, and Margaret was relieved to see Alwyn settle down and make a greater effort. Now he returned her leads, and when he ignored them it was because he had the hand to do so, not because he was comparing notes on Sydney Gardens versus Vauxhall or asking the baronet where he purchased his tea.

By the end of the rubber, Margaret and Alwyn had reduced their losses to a crown, so nearly a tie that, when Sir Dodkins asked if they would like to play another, they eagerly agreed.

Meanwhile, the other two tables finished their rubbers and decided to combine in a round game, but Margaret paid no attention to this, determined as she was to come out ahead.

The first game, luck was against them, and they played poor hands to a demoralizing defeat. *One pound three*, Margaret calculated silently. But the second saw both a change in their fortune and a greater rapport growing between uncle and niece. Margaret led through the honours, and the third game ended with a shut-out of Sir Dodkins and Mrs. Waite.

"Bravo!" cried the baronet, as if he and his partner were the victors. "Well played, Miss Hapgood, Mr. Arbuthnot. Very well played. Let me tally the score—I fear Mrs. Waite and I are in your debt."

"Yes," said Margaret, too quickly, "for two pounds and two shillings."

Sir Dodkins blinked in surprise, and Alwyn hastened to say, "Isn't it marvelous, how Maggie can calculate figures in her head? Heh, heh. She can't help it. But she's a good girl, for all that. Do you check it, Sir Dodkins, and make certain she reckoned correctly."

It took the gentleman some minutes, and Margaret tried not to fidget in impatience, but at last he looked up and said, "Why, yes indeed. Two pounds, two shillings."

"How perfectly convenient," said Mrs. Waite, drawing out her reticule. "That's one guinea from me and one from you, Sir Dodkins."

"Indeed," he agreed, "and I always pay my debts promptly. I will also call for some wine and music, if you will excuse me." With difficulty, he rose, surreptitiously stretching his stiffened limbs, and stalked away.

Alwyn and Mrs. Waite turned to smile upon each other, but before they could say a word, Margaret was on her feet. "Please don't let me disturb you," she urged, before Alwyn even thought of rising. "I think—I will ask Sir Dodkins if he might call his carriage for us."

"What's the hurry, Mags?" protested her uncle. "You heard him. There's going to be wine and music."

"No hurry—I just mean for later. Excuse me. Please excuse me."

The passage was empty, apart from a startled footman trimming the light. "May I help you, miss?"

"I—need to ask Sir Dodkins something," she stammered, going all over scarlet.

Judging from the man's expression, young ladies going alone in search of the host was *not done*, but Margaret was too desperate to care about that. She raised her chin and assumed the loftiest tone possible under the circumstances. "Where has he gone, please?"

The footman gestured at another door along the passage, and Margaret scurried away.

This must be Sir Dodkins' library, for it was floor to ceiling books, with a large walnut desk anchoring the room and two leather armchairs placed before the fireplace. The baronet had his back to her and was removing a flat box from the drawer of a Pembroke table.

"Sir Dodkins?" said Margaret, in little more than a squeak.

He straightened up in surprise. "Miss Hapgood? Is something amiss?"

Certainly her high color and enormous hazel eyes did nothing to reassure him, and Margaret felt herself trembling.

Just ask! What is the worst that could happen? He could refuse and avoid you in future. But he is too much a gentleman to shout it all over town.

"Did you not trust me to hand over your winnings, my dear?" he teased.

"May we—would you be so kind—it was such a pleasure to be driven here," fumbled Margaret, cursing herself.

"I will certainly order the carriage to take you home again," he answered, "but I hope you are not thinking of leaving so soon?"

"Thank you, sir. That is—no. We are happy to stay longer. Such a—lovely evening."

He waited another moment, but Margaret's throat seemed to have fused shut.

"You are sure you are well?" he asked.

She nodded, her panic rising. And then she screwed her eyes shut and clenched her hands in fists and blurted, "Sir Dodkins, might I ask a favor of you?"

Leaving the box, he came around the desk to take her by her elbow and lead her to one of the armchairs. "Of course you may! Of course.

Please, sit. I am sorry there is no fire lit here. What favor may I do you, Miss Hapgood?"

She truly felt dizzy now, and hot, despite the empty fireplace. He must think she had lost her senses.

"S-Sir Dodkins, I have not known you long, but you have been all kindness. And I am sorry to trespass on that kindness by asking—"

When she did not go on, he prompted, "—By asking...?"

"By asking if I might borrow fifty pounds!" she uttered, throwing pride and caution aside. "I would certainly repay you—over time—over a fair amount of time."

He sat back in the chair opposite her, speechless. Whatever favor he thought she might ask, this was not it.

Mortified, she could raise her eyes no higher than his hands, and some detached part of her noted how frail they were. Pale, not tanned like Mr. Waite's. What if her astonishing request caused Sir Dodkins to have a spell, like her papa? She had not thought of that. What if catarrh weakened the heart, and Margaret inadvertently killed him?

But he sounded quite steady when he finally said, "Are these gaming debts?"

"Gaming debts?" cried Margaret, surprised into staring at him. "No! No—never! I am no gambler, sir. I only ever played cards with my family, before this." There was no mistaking her honest indignation.

"Are they your *uncle's* gaming debts, then?" he pressed.

"No, Sir Dodkins. I assure you. The fifty pounds is for jewelry. I am afraid my papa did not give us quite enough—pin money, and we have overstretched ourselves. The Bath shops are so...enticing. I—cannot ask Papa to send more because he isn't well, you see. He has a heart condition. I can't bear to trouble him with this. I don't dare."

With no difficulty at all, she burst into tears, and then she found his arm about her while he patted her shoulder comfortingly, murmuring, "There, there. Poor girl. You mustn't fret yourself this way." A handkerchief was pressed upon her, and Margaret, with no dignity left to her, blew her nose loudly in it.

And then the baronet rose and went to the table again, where he opened the heavy box and counted out some notes. "Take these, my dear, and dry your tears."

Margaret gaped at the windfall in her lap: fifty pounds in notes of several denominations, drawn on Hoares Bank. And atop the little heap, one golden guinea. "Sir?"

"Take it, with my blessing," he sighed. Closing the box, he replaced it in the drawer.

"Oh, Sir Dodkins!" she cried, scrambling up and sending the money spilling to the floor. She lurched across the room and fell on her knees, grasping his hand. "Thank you so much. I will repay you—I will. I promise you. Thank you."

"Shhhh..." he soothed, freeing himself from her grip. "I must return to my guests now and will make some excuse for you until you feel well enough to return. We cannot talk about this at present, but you may trust I will call on your family later in the week."

"My—family?" She puzzled. But then she realized the baronet was likely not in the habit of making loans with only the security of a young lady's word. He must require a promissory note of some kind, and of course Alwyn would know all about such things, given his past carryings-on.

"Yes, of course," Margaret said more firmly, smiling to show she understood. "Thank you again, sir." She dashed the remaining tears from her cheeks and stood, backing away, that he might go. "I am so grateful for your kindness and friendship."

He made her a courteous bow, and then he was gone, closing the door quietly behind him.

Margaret required some minutes to calm herself. She could hardly believe he had given her the money, though she held it in her hands. It was too, too wonderful! She would go the very next morning and pay the jeweler. No longer would the Sword of Damocles hang over their family. And then—then she would take every opportunity to show Sir Dodkins her deep, deep gratitude for his unexampled goodness.

Chapter Twenty-Two

True Friendship in two breasts requires
The same Aversions, and Desires.
—Jonathan Swift, *The Life and Character of Dr. Swift*
(1733)

The following morning found Margaret in the Union Passage shop of Chauncey Vale, Master Jeweler, while Tilly waited outside. The small proprietor greeted her appearance with wariness, especially when she held his bill out to him.

"Yes, miss? I suppose you have come to argue terms with me, but I am afraid they are standard and not negotiable," he declared, taking hold of the counter with both hands, as if he expected Margaret to push it over.

Braver now, with the ready money in her reticule, she drew herself up. "I am not here to do any such thing, sir. I am here to pay the bill in full."

The jeweler stared and doubted. He reached up to straighten his wig, though it was already straight, and his mouth worked, torn between questions and conciliation. But when he saw Margaret draw out her purse and the sheaf of banknotes, he blossomed anew with smiles and servility.

"Well, well, I knew it would work out. Thank you, miss. I am glad to be on good terms with your family again, and I hope they are enjoying the pieces. We would appreciate your further custom—"

"Yes," Margaret cut him off. Any further custom from her family would be over her dead body, but she pinned a smile on her face while he wrote out the receipt and nodded her thanks before rejoining Tilly.

Once outside, she smiled in earnest. It was done! She would have to figure out how to repay Sir Dodkins, of course, but at least he would not send bill collectors or threaten to arrest Uncle Alwyn for debt.

From Union Passage, it was a short stroll to the Pump Room, where she had been entreated by Charmaine to meet her. While the frosty day made Tilly walk faster, Margaret looked forward to being indoors.

She found her friend at the pump, grimacing as she sipped from her glass. "Oh—ugh—how horrible it tastes. One would almost rather be ill. But I wanted something warm while I waited for you. Tilly, you may go. I will get Miss Margaret home somehow."

After the maid slumped away, Charmaine thrust the water at her. "Here. You finish it. If you were truly unwell and faint last night, as Sir Dodkins claimed, it will do you good."

Still buoyant with success and relief, Margaret felt ready for anything. She choked down a swallow of the mineral water and then took Charmaine's arm and pulled her away from the crowd. "You are right—I wasn't ill, though I felt faint enough with nerves. Because what do you think? I asked the baronet for the fifty pounds, and he lent it to me, and I have just come from paying the jeweler."

"You—did—*what*?" Charmaine could not have looked more thunderstruck if Bonaparte himself had appeared and asked her to dance. She positively goggled at Margaret, her mouth open until she remembered herself and popped it shut. "Say all that again!"

Margaret complied, adding hurriedly, "That is why I stole from the room last night. Sir Dodkins had gone to fetch the guinea he owed me for losing at cards, and I followed him. It took me a minute to screw my courage up, but I did it."

"No, no, no," frowned Charmaine. "This is no way to tell a story, and this is no place to tell it. We must walk abroad, where we won't be overheard, and you will tell me from the very beginning, without omitting a single detail."

Margaret's protests that it was too cold out were ignored, and the next minute they were rushing through the churchyard toward Orange Grove and the North Parade. There were few walkers braving the weather, so the girls were free to crunch across the frozen grass of the Bowling Green, clutching each other's hands and giggling.

Beginning again from the moment the party divided into separate card tables, Margaret told her story with as many details as she could remember, Charmaine listening in silence. Even after Margaret finished with "and then he left me to return to the guests and told you all I felt unwell," Charmaine still held her peace.

"Well?" asked Margaret, impatient. "Have you nothing to say? I have succeeded!"

Then Charmaine crossed her arms and gave Margaret a long, long look. Rocking on the heels of her boots, she said simply, "Why, I congratulate you, Margaret. You have succeeded. You are engaged."

"W-what?" sputtered Margaret. "What are you talking about? Were you listening to me?"

"Intently."

"Then why do you say I am engaged, when I said nothing of any engagement?"

"You stupid girl, why would he give you the money, otherwise?"

"Why—to help me! Because he is kind and I begged!"

Charmaine rolled her eyes with eloquence. "What a fool you are. A man might give a beggar a copper because he is kind, but he does not give a pretty young lady *fifty pounds* out of sheer kindness. Trust me. You are engaged. He considers you engaged. Why do you think he is going to call on your uncle?"

Nausea roiled through Margaret. "Because—I thought he wanted a promissory note of some sort. As a guarantee."

"Oh, he wants a guarantee, all right." She gave Margaret's arm a shake. "Come now. Don't look like that. Your methods may be unorthodox, but they are effective. Perhaps I ought to go around asking eligible gentlemen for fifty pounds, just to see what happens."

But Margaret looked positively green.

Charmaine prodded her again. "Honestly. What sort of bargain did you suppose was being struck?"

"I thought he liked me like a daughter. Like his lost daughter," Margaret replied faintly. "I thought he gave me the money because he was fond of me in that way. And, in return, I was willing enough to be his temporary daughter, while we were in Bath."

"Good Lord," groaned Charmaine. "No wonder your family is always courting scandal. You are the most shocking innocent I have ever met."

"I will get the money back from the jeweler," declared Margaret, straightening. "I will get it back and ask him to write out the bill again. And then I will write to Sir Dodkins saying I do not need the fifty pounds after all, thanking him all the same, and I will wrap the banknotes inside and deliver it all myself to St. James Square."

Charmaine shrugged. "You may as well leave it with the jeweler."

"But why?"

"In the first place, Margaret, I highly doubt you could get the money back, even if you begged. It would look so very suspicious! And the jeweler would guess, rightly, that if he relinquished the notes, he might never see the debt cleared. He might even call the constable to have you dragged away."

Margaret groaned and covered her face with her hands, but Charmaine continued inexorably. "In the second place, even if you had the fifty pounds in your purse again, I also doubt Sir Dodkins would take the money back and behave as if nothing had happened. Therefore, let the poor jeweler be paid."

"What do you mean? Do you not think I could make Sir Dodkins understand I was truly only asking for a loan?" Margaret asked. "After all, whoever heard of a young lady proposing to a gentleman? Even I know that isn't done!"

Charmaine only shook her head slowly and patted Margaret on the arm.

"But—if I can't return the money right off, I can still refuse him when he comes. Yes. I will do that. Refuse his proposal *and* promise to return the money when I am able *and* apologize all 'round for the terrible misunderstanding."

Turning suddenly, Charmaine took both Margaret's hands in her own. "Listen to me, Margaret. I don't know what sort of place Bramleigh is, but you cannot treat a gentleman—a baronet, no less—in such a manner. You cannot make a fool of him, however much of a fool *you* have been."

"What do you mean, make a fool of him? I don't mean to make a fool of him! I just don't want to marry him!" she wailed.

Charmaine made an impatient sound. "Apart from being quite old, what is wrong with him, pray? He has even got over his dreadful cough that made him wheeze like a pair of bellows. I rather like the man, myself. Wouldn't you like to be Lady Hargate? You will triumph over your sisters. Not one of them is a 'Lady.' Though perhaps I will always call you Margaret Hargate."

But Margaret was in no mood for jokes. "Charmaine, *you* might be quite comfortable marrying a man you do not love, but I cannot say the same."

"For pity's sake—I suppose Sir Dodkins will be as loveable as any other husband, as husbands go," said Charmaine. "I thought you too practical to insist on a love match."

"I don't insist on a love match!" cried Margaret. "I don't insist on any match! I did not come to Bath to get married! And, if you were my friend, you wouldn't taunt me. You would help me think what to do."

"I *am* helping you, you infant. I am helping you see reason. I am helping you understand the way the world works. I am helping you by telling you to make the best of a bad situation. Nay—not even a 'bad' situation, considering most young ladies would rejoice in your place. Look—there is a tiny chance I am wrong, and the baronet did hand over fifty pounds just because he pitied you. In that case, I will happily admit it, for your sake. But, if I am not wrong, Margaret, you must promise me that you won't try to give back the money—money which you no longer have—and you won't try to say it was all a big misunderstanding. Because, if you do, you will make him hate you. He will still marry you, but he will hate you for humiliating him, and you will be miserable until the day he dies, which, thankfully, will not be terribly far in the future, but it will likely seem long to you."

By the end of this speech Margaret was limp with defeat, and Charmaine took this as a promising sign. She threaded her arm through Margaret's and got her moving again around the green.

"Imagine the blow to his pride and dignity if you reveal that you think him too old and decrepit for love, and you only wanted to charm his money from him!"

If only to stop the flow of words, Margaret said, "I see. I understand." All she really wished to do by this point was march straight home, climb in bed, and be utterly alone.

Charmaine had other ideas, however. She tugged on Margaret's arm again. "I'm getting cold. Let's go back indoors. Have you been in the Lower Rooms?"

Margaret had not, but she could not in her present mood properly appreciate the pleasant ballroom, with its expansive views of the parade grounds, river and hills, and Charmaine had to drag her around like an automaton.

"I do hope Dashiell and Mr. Haworth don't come here for a late breakfast after their daily bath," Charmaine murmured. "If we see them, we will steal back out."

"Very well."

"Cheer up, you! At least Sir D says he will be gone for some days. You have this lovely reprieve from both him and your money troubles."

"I would welcome the money troubles now," said Margaret, "if it meant I might give the fifty pounds back without consequence."

"Well, you can't. It is now the *jeweler's* money, and you will never see it again, I assure you. Therefore you may as well enjoy being free of the debt."

Charmaine was growing tired of the subject. She had her own news to share and had waited long enough. Leading the way to one of the vast mullioned windows, she turned her back on the view with an excited little clap. "Here now—I know you are preoccupied and even angry with me for telling you the truth, but now you may have your revenge. For it is my turn to take my medicine."

"What can you mean?"

"I mean I would like your advice."

"My advice? Whatever for? You have just got done calling me stupid and a fool," Margaret grumbled.

"You *are* stupid and a fool—with Sir Dodkins at least. But I well know you think me stupid and a fool in turn, because you've told me a hundred times I do not appreciate Dashiell enough."

This was nothing but the truth, but she held her tongue.

"I have decided," Charmaine announced, her face alight with mischief, "contrary to what I said before, that I would like Dashiell to be very much more in love with me than he is now. I would like to charm him entirely."

In spite of Margaret's crisis, Charmaine had chosen the one subject which could make all else fall away, and she had Margaret's full attention.

"What has brought about this change of heart?"

Charmaine shrugged. There was no need to reveal her humiliating time in the Crescent. "Say just that I cannot bear his insulting indifference any longer. If he has a heart in him, I should prefer it be devoted to me."

In Charmaine's position, Margaret would prefer the same thing, but she was still puzzled. "How could I possibly advise you?"

"Hmm. This may surprise you, Margaret, but I ask your opinion because Dashiell has taken a liking to you."

"I don't know what you mean."

"Do not deny it! He seeks you out in company. It did not escape my notice at Sir Dodkins' party, and that was not the only occasion. I suppose he will seek you out again when you all come for supper."

"I have never asked him to," Margaret whispered, too aware of the pleasure flooding her at Charmaine's words. Then it was not her imagination—Mr. Waite liked her! Or, at least, did not mind her. Apart from the one time at the fancy ball where he glared at her, her company did not appear to disgust him.

"I know you have not asked him to seek you out, you goose," Charmaine said with a wave of her hand. "I am not *accusing* you of anything; I am making an observation. Tell me: what does he talk to you about?"

Margaret racked her brain. What *did* they talk about? Nothing vital. And yet she treasured their conversations. "I don't know, really. Coffee? Cards? Dancing. Your necklace and where I got it. Families."

Charmaine's brows rose. "That's all? No more?"

It did sound commonplace, when Margaret summed it up. And yet not a moment felt so, when it was taking place. When they spoke, it was not merely words. There was connection. There was even *intimacy*. He was a friend to her, she felt.

"Perhaps," ventured Margaret, "it is not the subjects so much. You are very beautiful and intimidating, Charmaine. You certainly overawe Mr. Haworth. Maybe if Mr. Waite does not mind talking to me occasionally, it is because—it doesn't mean anything. I want nothing; I require nothing; I expect nothing. Nothing can come of our acquaintance. Such a person will always be easy to talk to." She sighed a little in confessing it.

"There is *one* danger attached to your acquaintance," Charmaine rejoined. "His friendliness might be misinterpreted as approval of a match between Mr. Arbuthnot and my aunt Eliza. Though I suppose we've been very clear on that—"

"He has never once mentioned them to me," said Margaret. Her heart lifted a little at this realization. Was it he because he liked her more than he feared the danger?

But, tapping her chin with a thoughtful finger, Charmaine dismissed this soon enough. "Or perhaps he talks to you in order to keep an eye on your uncle. Or it began that way, and then..." Another shrug. "In any event, it is a good point, Margaret—and one I had not thought of—that he talks to you because you put him at ease. You want nothing from him, and he wants nothing from you because he already has me. You are perfectly safe to talk to. Safe and harmless."

"Yes," agreed Margaret softly. "So, I thank you for your courtesy, but you see I have no advice to offer. Our situations are entirely different."

Charmaine pouted. "I persist in thinking, however, that, though Dashiell may not be violently in love with you, he nevertheless *likes* you better than he likes me."

Margaret lost her patience in turn. "Perhaps if you were more inviting, then. If he thought you welcomed his attention."

"Who says I don't welcome it?" demanded Charmaine. "Have I not always complained of how little he loves me?"

"Yes, you have. To me. Have you ever...told him how you feel?"

But Charmaine's eyes glittered at this. "I am the lady. It is not my responsibility to woo."

"I did not say woo him!" argued Margaret. "I am just saying, if he felt surer of your love, you might feel more sure of his."

At this, Charmaine stalked away, leaving Margaret in awkward solitude at the window. But she waited, pretending serenity and interest in their fellow promenaders. After another minute, Charmaine swept back to her side.

"So wise," jeered Charmaine. "Even on subjects you know nothing about. I hope the baronet will not be surprised to find how unsympathetic you can be, behind that innocent face."

"And I hope Mr. Waite shares your delight in quarreling," retorted Margaret. "If he does, your marriage will be a blissful one."

Once again, Charmaine's quicksilver moods shifted, and she burst out in a laugh. "Oh, I do like you! Even when you exasperate me. It is so tiresome when people do not make any show of resistance. It makes me want to bully them."

"You don't say," said Margaret dryly. "All the more reason for you to favor Mr. Waite. He does not seem easily bullied."

"No," Charmaine replied, her brow thoughtful. "Here: I will take your advice and be nicer to Dashiell. But before I make him more sure of my love, I must be more sure of his. What do you say, Margaret—when you come to Princes Street and Dashiell seeks you out, suppose you got him to talk about me? Instead of coffee, cards, and dancing, I mean."

Margaret felt her color rising again. "I don't know that he will seek me out."

"Stop already with the modesty! Let us say, then, *if* he seeks you out, I want you to ferret his feelings from him and discover what would make him love me more."

"No," said Margaret.

"Yes," said Charmaine. "*Please!*"

"It is none of my business, and he would think me most inquisitive and interfering."

"He won't. He has already formed his opinion of you, and he likes you. Therefore, he would indulge you. I am asking you as my friend."

"I think what you are asking is beyond what can be expected of a friend."

"And I think you are wrong. I would certainly do as much for you, if you wanted to know how deeply Ods Bodkins loved you. Please, please, please!" she wheedled.

This went on for some minutes. Ultimately, it was the wheedling which wore Margaret down. That and the uncharacteristic vulnerability in Charmaine's eyes. Margaret was too used to managing matters to resist a genuine cry for help.

"Oh, very well," she relented. "*If* he seeks me out."

"Darling!" cried Charmaine, embracing her. "See if I don't do you a good turn for it. Why, I will do you a good turn now. I will walk you back to Henrietta Street and buy you a trinket to wear tonight.

I saw just the thing when I was last on Pulteney Bridge. A bracelet to match the necklace I've lent you. No, no—don't fuss at me. I insist upon it. Now, come."

Chapter Twenty-Three

A Friend is he that loves, and he that is beloved.
—Thomas Hobbes, *Aristotle's Brief Arte Rhetorique*
(1637)

For a young lady with much on her mind and most of it distressing, Margaret looked remarkably well the evening of the Waites' supper. She wore again the nut-brown silk Elfie and Frederick had given her, adorned by Charmaine's necklace and the new matching bracelet. Though it was not expensive, even by Margaret's standards, she had argued against its purchase. But Charmaine wouldn't hear of it, only giving her hand a final squeeze before she climbed into her sedan chair. "Wear it as a reminder of your obligation. I depend upon you."

It took much bundling to make Mrs. Hapgood comfortable for the walk to Princes Street, but the exertion of pushing her chair in turns sufficed to keep both uncle and niece warm, and at least it did not rain.

When the Waites' servant realized they came on foot, he took their wrappings with a disdainful grimace mirrored by Mrs. Blakely, but otherwise their welcome was warm. A crackling fire blazed in the drawing room, which Mrs. Waite kindly placed them nearest, while her son oversaw the footmen lugging Mrs. Hapgood's chair up the steps and indoors, so she could tumble back into it.

"I wish I might have practiced a few more times," Margaret whispered to Charmaine under cover of general conversation.

"Never mind. You may run through it again after supper, and I will sing loudly over any blunders," Charmaine whispered back. "You have far more important tasks tonight, and I intend you will not lack opportunities."

Charmaine's meaning was soon clear, for, when Mrs. Waite led the way to the dining room, Margaret found herself placed at Mr. Waite's right hand, across from Alwyn, and as far from Charmaine as she could possibly be. While they were only eight people altogether, the table was wide and long enough for fourteen, so the distances were considerable. She had to admire Charmaine's planning, for Mrs. Waite at the foot of the table could only speak to Alwyn if she raised her voice and the entire party overheard.

Mr. Waite wore a black coat this evening, paired with a pearl-grey waistcoat the very shade of his unsettling eyes. She might have bore his gaze calmly, except, when he held her chair out and gestured for her to be seated (the footmen again occupied with Mrs. Hapgood), she was standing nearer than he thought, and his fingertips just swept her bare forearm. They both startled at the contact, he murmuring an apology and Margaret whipping her arm away as if he had clawed her. She then had to disguise her movement by pretending to arrange a wayward curl. *Oh, dear.*

Such a beginning made her mind unhelpfully blank. She could not think of one single thing to say and was grateful again for Alwyn's presence.

"Very pleasant situation you have here," her uncle began, as the soup was served. "I do love a good blaze, and our lodgings in Henrietta Street have rather cramped little fireplaces that put out as much smoke as heat."

"We are glad to make you comfortable," said Mr. Waite. He sounded no more at ease than Margaret, who was staring at her soup.

It was natural to talk about the last time they had gathered, at the baronet's card party, and Alwyn introduced the subject, Charmaine and Mrs. Waite and Mr. Haworth helping him along. It seemed Mr. Haworth and Mr. Waite had quite trounced Charmaine and her mother at whist.

"Mama and I are penniless now," Charmaine explained to the table at large. "We were utterly at their mercy."

"Only—it's only because Dash and I—we spent so much time playing cards—army life," returned Haworth apologetically.

"La, sir," Charmaine laughed. "No excuse is necessary. You won 'fair and square,' as they say. To imply otherwise would be reckless." She waved her fork playfully at her betrothed. "Is it not true,

Dashiell? Did not gentlemen in the army shoot each other, if one accused another of cheating at cards?"

"They tried to. We saw it more than once. But you may fling any accusations you like, for they most certainly did not shoot young ladies."

"I should have liked to see the baronet's home," Mrs. Hapgood sighed, as one of the footmen helped her to the vegetables. "My brother tells me it was quite elegant."

A discussion of Sir Dodkins' establishment followed, and Mrs. Blakely had much to say regarding French furnishings, which drew Charmaine to tease her and then Mrs. Waite to defend her and Alwyn to tease Mrs. Waite and so on. In the middle of this, Margaret heard Mr. Waite's voice, low enough that it only reached her ears: "I hope you are feeling better, Miss Hapgood. Sir Dodkins did say you were unwell at the card party. First to be stricken by homesickness, and then by general *malaise*! Perhaps Bath harms as many people as it cures."

If anything was calculated to tie her tongue further, this was it. He did not sound as if he believed in her purported ailments any more than Charmaine had.

"Yes, thank you. Much better." *Little said, soon mended* must be her guiding proverb.

They attended the general talk again, Margaret pinching herself under the table and spinning her new bracelet around her wrist. She must do better than this. She must stop being an awkward lump just because he sat beside her. But honestly—how was it that she was always aware when his gaze chanced to rest on her? Not that it did very often or for very long, but she felt it each time. Felt it and felt her own response.

Come now! she commanded herself, gripping the bracelet so it bit into her. *You promised Charmaine.*

Charmaine made some jest at the far end of the table that was met with laughter, and Margaret turned desperately to Mr. Waite, blurting, "How witty she is!"

He blinked at her but then said, "Yes."

"I've—grown fond of her in the past several weeks. I can only imagine how—fond of her you must be after so many years."

There was the slightest pause. But then he nodded and took a sip of his wine.

"So lovely and charming and clever," Margaret rattled on, her voice rising in pitch. She wished she could just drown herself in the ragout if she was going to be this inane. She was supposed to be eliciting *his* praise of Charmaine, not supplying it herself!

His narrow gaze narrowed further, and Margaret saw it flick toward his betrothed and then return to her. "Does this admiration mean you have overcome your tendency to quarrel with her?"

"Dear me, no," admitted Margaret, surprised into honesty. "That is—our bickering does not prevent me from acknowledging her virtues. And now that I know her better, I understand she sometimes provokes simply to amuse herself."

"Charming indeed."

"Yes," she agreed, glad he at least said one thing she could report to Charmaine, even if she suspected he was being sarcastic. She would leave out the sarcasm. "Utterly charming," she repeated. "In so many ways. Countless ways."

"Tell me—what brought on this encomium to her merits?"

"Oh—nothing, nothing," answered Margaret lamely. "I should—love her very much, if I were going to marry her."

His face crinkled in its engaging grin. "Should you? I do not know what reply to make to that. Should I express pity for you, that you cannot, in fact, marry her? Or relief, that I need not then compete with you? Should I be flattered, that you envy me my beloved, or outraged, and challenge you to a duel?"

He called Charmaine his beloved! Even as it made her own smile falter, she stored it away as another piece of evidence for her friend. How could it not make Charmaine's heart soar, to be called charming and beloved by such a man? Now, if she could only encourage him to show more affection, she would have fulfilled her duty.

"You said a few minutes ago that gentlemen did not duel young ladies," she reminded him daringly. "But—if I were a man, I am certain I could win Charmaine from you."

"Indeed? Why so?"

"You—are so...nonchalant with her, Mr. Waite. So seemingly uninterested. I know you are not truly uninterested; only sometimes you *seem* so, to your peril."

Without removing his eyes from her, he held up two fingers to refuse another serving of the ragout. "Ah. And you feel, Miss Hapgood, that you know a more successful way to win my lady love?"

Margaret thought, judging by her own erratic pulse and heat-flooded countenance, that Mr. Waite needed advice from no man living on how to win his *lady love*. But—well—Charmaine felt otherwise.

She must soldier on.

"Yes," she declared. "You see, I would shower her with attention and tell her how dear she was to me every day, if not even more frequently. I would beg her to name the date for our marriage and tell her that—that, if she could not be mine, I would surely *die*."

There was another pause. Margaret suspected she might be at risk of dying herself, if this went on much longer. At least she had been right to accept the bracelet from Charmaine as a bribe—she could not do this again for all the jewels in the royal treasury.

"It is fortunate, then, that I am not competing with you," he said lightly. "Though, in my defense, I would say she and I have already chosen a *season* for our marriage, if not a specific date, and she has already declared herself mine, rendering any dying on my part unnecessary at this stage, if not downright impeditive."

"There it is, you see," Margaret said earnestly, her voice very soft. She looked full at him. "You make a joke of it, Mr. Waite."

"I...do. I admit."

"Yes. Therefore, I should win her from you. Because I would give her—I would give her my sincere, almost painful love, which only grew, no matter whether it was fed or starved, confessed or unspoken, welcomed or rejected. I would love her because I could not help myself. She would be—no matter the consequences—my all in all."

He regarded her a long moment—it might have been five seconds or five hours—the intensity such that she held her breath. Indeed, had the ceiling collapsed on her head, Margaret would not have been able to stir.

Then, shortly, tearing his eyes away:

"I yield." His voice was rough. "She would be yours indeed."

They said no more. Margaret did not think she could manage another word to him—her throat had closed, and she felt the prick of tears, though it could not be tears. And he—he turned to Alwyn as if nothing had passed, demanding of him in a hearty voice whether he preferred a ruby or a tawny port wine.

When the ladies left the gentlemen to their bottle of Warre's, Charmaine hurried Margaret to the pianoforte, both that Margaret could run through the Gluck again and that she might share what she had learned.

"He says that you are charming, and he called you his 'beloved' and his 'lady love,'" Margaret reported, happy to have the sheet music to look at.

Charmaine raised wondering brows but scooted closer on the bench. "Start over from the beginning," she said aloud, as if she were referring to the music. Not that the older women were paying any attention. Mrs. Waite and Mrs. Blakely were helping Mrs. Hapgood back to her chair and positioning her the most comfortable distance from the fire.

"I primed the pump, as it were," said Margaret, hammering on the keys, "saying how much I liked you, and he agreed that you were charming."

"Mm. And the 'beloved lady love' bit? Was that also just in agreement with you?"

"No, indeed. He referred to you as that with no prompting from me. That is, I said, if I were a man, I should be very much in love with you, and he asked if I envied him his 'beloved.' So you see? He might as easily have called you his 'intended' or asked if I envied him his good fortune, but he chose 'beloved.' And the 'lady love' part was when I encouraged him to be more demonstrative. He asked if I thought *I* could be more successful in wooing his lady love."

"My, my. You certainly did get beyond coffee, cards and dancing," mocked Charmaine. "But I thank you for wasting no time in attacking the matter."

"Yes, I knew you would bother me until I did so," Margaret said as her friend turned the page for her. "So I have been faithful in my commission. It is up to him now to act upon my hints."

Charmaine made a face. "Why does that not reassure me? I cannot say that one 'charming' (spoken in agreement) and two endearments are much. He might say the same of his dog. Won't you ask him what he likes best about me, when you next get a chance?" she cajoled, nudging her. "Shhhh...don't fuss. I'm sure you will manage. Now, see, here they come."

After their audience disposed themselves around the room and were all attention (though Margaret saw her mother hide a yawn), she launched into the opening bars, saying a prayer and keeping her eyes trained on the music. She really was the most musical of the not-particularly-musical Hapgood daughters—none of her sisters would dare play a piece in front of near-strangers that they had only practiced a dozen times through—but Margaret was by no means a prodigy. Charmaine kept her promise, however, and sang beautifully over her accompanist's shortcomings, and the two girls were greeted with sincere applause.

"*Bravissime*! Encore!" cried Alwyn, heartily seconded by a stammering Haworth and Mrs. Waite and Mrs. Blakely.

"You had better just play yours now," Margaret told Charmaine, half rising from the bench, but then Mrs. Hapgood said, "Oh, go on, Margaret. Give it to us again." And, more importantly, Mr. Waite said, "Miss Hapgood, Charmaine, if you would indulge us? It would be a delight to hear it once more." And there was his unsettling gaze moving from Charmaine to her, and there went all the sheet music, dropping from her flustered hands.

Charmaine gave her a wry look, replacing the pages on the instrument, and the whole matter was got through a second time. Then Margaret was glad to escape to the chair nearest her mother, that she might enjoy her part being done. But no sooner did she sit than Mrs. Hapgood complained, "I am too hot now, Margaret. Wheel me well back and fan me, or I will faint."

A small hullaballoo followed, with several of those present helping to wheel the chair and rearrange furniture and clear a path, over Margaret's insistence that she could manage it herself. Charmaine looked on with amusement, smiling to herself when it happened that Margaret and her mother ended up on the far side of the drawing room, where Mr. Waite happened to sit.

Margaret saw the smile as she fanned her mother but thought Charmaine could hardly expect much, with Mrs. Hapgood between herself and Mr. Waite. But more to the point, even were they unobstructed, how could Margaret possibly address him, when she still felt raw and exposed from their talk at supper?

But Charmaine was determined to make something happen because she announced that they must all prepare themselves for a longer repertoire, lest all her diligent practice go to waste.

By the second time through "Love in Her Eyes Sits Playing," Mrs. Hapgood dozed off, and when the fair performer transitioned into another song, Mrs. Hapgood's head lolled to her chest. Margaret pretended not to notice, but her fanning slowed considerably.

She felt, rather than saw, Mr. Waite's glance, and it spurred her to say, "You must pardon Mama for dropping off. This is late for her."

Mr. Waite straightened his lamed leg, rubbing it absently. "You had better save your apologies for Charmaine. I was not the performer who bored her to sleep."

In spite of herself, she smiled.

Thank heavens. He was not going to refer to their earlier conversation, the good, good man! Call it self-absorption or call it youth, Margaret could not help but feel that, on pretense of helping Charmaine earlier, she laid bare her own feelings for him. She must have! It was so obvious (to Margaret) that, when she spoke of how she would love Charmaine, were she in his place, what she truly meant was that she would love *him* so dearly, were she in Charmaine's place. Nay—that she loved him dearly already, without the legitimacy of Charmaine's place!

But here was a mercy.

Because he was a kind man, he would act as if it never happened. As if nothing had been confessed. As if they spoke only of Charmaine all along. Because he was kind, he would sweep Margaret's mortifying revelation neatly under the rug.

Her gratitude was very great, as was her eagerness to prove she was perfectly at ease and could converse as carelessly as any heart-whole young lady. "Mama was not bored," she explained, "but at home she would have been long abed." This brought on a wince, as she suspected young ladies should not mention beds in company. "Beds" being surely another taboo word. Beds, legs—legs such as Mr. Waite's, in their snug breeches. Breeches. Oh, dear.

But Mr. Waite ignored this slip as well, and he continued to watch Charmaine. Margaret closed her eyes in relief, but then heard him say quietly, "I welcome this opportunity to continue our earlier conversation, Miss Hapgood."

What? Margaret clutched her mother's fan so tightly she heard a snapping sound, and she hastily folded it. He *did* want to continue it, then?

Well, she did not. Absolutely did not.

Why should he want to, after all? Had he no pity for her painful revelation?

She made no response, only spreading the fan in her lap to inspect the damage.

"You do not ask me why," he continued in a grave voice.

No. Nor would she. She tried to straighten the wooden piece she had cracked and ended in breaking it altogether.

"I was...curious, you see," he persisted, "whether, when you described how Charmaine would best be wooed and won, you expressed her preferences or your own?"

"Hers, of course," said Margaret, unable to avoid answering a direct question. But hope lifted its head. Perhaps he was giving her a chance to declare that she had not been speaking of herself? Yes. He wanted her to have the comfort of confirming it. She nodded at this. "We discussed Charmaine."

"Yes. You spoke of her desire for attention. And for professions of love."

"That's right. You—ought to tell her what you like about her."

"I see. I just wondered, Miss Hapgood—would you say her expectations are typical of your sex? Would *you* prefer to be won in such a fashion?"

"What—I? I have nothing to do with the matter!" Never mind that he had won her without so much as lifting his little finger.

"Forgive me," he said, somewhat abashed. "I overstep. I have no right to press you, of course."

He didn't. Have any right.

She tried to fold the fan again, but the broken slat left the silk bulging out untidily.

No, he had no right to press her, but she felt herself yielding nonetheless. Was this part of love? That he could elicit confessions from her without effort? That she could not resist the temptation to be known by him?

"I suppose any woman who loved would...treasure attention from her beloved," she said softly, "and I suppose any woman who loved would never tire of hearing how he loved her. There, she and I are the same. But—unlike Charmaine, perhaps—I should not care for attention from someone I did not care for myself." Sir Dodkins was in her thoughts when she added this. "In that case, he had better not be prompted."

Charmaine's piece concluded in several rousing chords, followed by her listeners' applause, which Margaret joined in automatically. Mrs. Hapgood snapped to consciousness, clapping her hands as if she had caught every note. Then people stood and moved about, and talk swelled the room again as the footmen entered with the tea, but Margaret found herself still in her seat.

She must get up. Congratulate Charmaine on her performance. See to her mother and decide how much longer they would stay. Chat with the hostess and thank her.

But she could not do any of those things quite yet.

Mr. Waite had left his seat as soon as the music ended. He even now stood beside Charmaine, complimenting her, Margaret supposed, though she could not hear what he was saying.

No. She heard nothing. In fact, the only words filling her mind were the ones he spoke just before rising.

He had not looked at her; his mouth had scarcely moved. And yet she heard him. Unless she had imagined it.

Imagined him saying: "If any man loved you, Miss Hapgood, he would require no prompting."

Chapter Twenty-Four

As for my love yt doth never relente,
For of you I do dreame.
—Thomas Engelend, *Disobedient Child* (1560)

Dashiell and Haworth made one final visit together to the King's Bath before Haworth left.

It rained, a heavy and settled rain that made the men curse as they followed Monmouth Street down to Westgate. Between managing his cane and his umbrella, Dashiell lost his footing, his good leg sliding and his bad one unable to plant and stop him; Haworth, whose only hand held his own umbrella, could do nothing to prevent his friend's fall.

"Blast! That was a bad one, Dash. Can you stand?"

For his concern, he received only muttered blasphemies, but he took these agreeably. "Indignity aside, Dash, look how you've improved. When Miss Hapgood sent you sprawling in the colonnade, you could hardly spring up again in this fashion."

His companion only growled, dabbing mud from his greatcoat, and they walked on. Dashiell dreaded Haworth leaving. He dreaded having no buffer from Charmaine; he dreaded being a lone man among women—no, that wasn't entirely true. If two of the women in his house had not been Charmaine and her mother, he might have resigned himself easily enough.

And if one of the women were Miss Hapgood, I might never even notice Haworth's absence.

The thought stung, a twist of pain that had nothing to do with his damned leg or the fall he had taken. A strange little stab mixed inexplicably with something like...joy.

Because he loved her. Miss Hapgood.

He knew that now. Or admitted it now.

He did not simply like Miss Hapgood. He did not wish only to be a friend to her. His feelings were not so mild that they could be dismissed as interest. Or fondness.

He was in love with her.

Dashiell knew he was being a fool, but his idiocy harmed only himself. He had lain awake half the night, running over their conversation in his mind, hearing again her tremulous tone when she described the love she was capable of. A love so generous and passionate that Charmaine could no more aspire to it than she could forget what she looked like.

Right there at the supper table, Miss Hapgood's words woke something in him, as startling as it was intense. Because he wanted that love she spoke of. Wholly for himself, that he might return it in kind.

He had thought and thought, going in circles. Suppose he confessed to Charmaine that he loved another? She would release him out of affronted pride alone. Uproar in the family would follow, a division of his mother from her brother. Dashiell would be cut from his uncle's will and from his uncle's plans, not that he was terribly attached to either Uncle Matthew or Chardis.

But how could he be justified now in making such a confession to Charmaine, when he had already offered her the possibility of release, and she had refused it? Refused it decidedly.

He could not.

He could not, and, therefore, he would not.

He had come to the same conclusion a thousand times already, so why did he need to remind himself of it, over and over?

As Dashiell and Haworth sank once more into the mineral-green depths of the King's Bath, the ease it gave his limbs rallied his spirits. Why, what a self-absorbed ass he was! Haworth was a dear friend, and here they were, soon to be parted for an indeterminate period, and Dashiell could barely tear his thoughts from his own woes.

"Tell me, Charles," he said with an effort, "what do you expect to find in Bradford?"

Haworth plucked at his sleeve where he had pinned it. "Oh, nothing much. A brace of ancient servants. Old-fashioned furnishings in shut-up rooms with frightening paper-hangings. A mountain of correspondence. Some meetings with my aunt's steward and calls upon the neighbors. In my rush to settle in Bath, I left much undone, and I will be greeted as quite the prodigal."

"Shall you be lonely?"

"Probably. But, if I recall, the vicar has a bevy of unmarried daughters. Perhaps I will snatch at the prettiest of them."

"Ah. Then the next time I see you, you might be a married man."

Haworth sighed, shifting on the stone bench. "I don't think I could manage it, Dash. Not quite yet. It might require me seeing you and Miss Blakely married first. If I knew past doubt she was beyond my reach, perhaps then."

"Well, if you cannot marry the vicar's daughter until my day of reckoning, I hope you will return anyway," Dashiell said.

Haworth's ginger brows flew together. "Confound it, Dashiell! I object thoroughly to you speaking of Miss Blakely as if she were some dread sentence laid upon you. Ungrateful dog! When I think how, for such a treasure, any other man would give his—would give his—"

"Would give his left arm?" supplied Dashiell.

With a roar that made heads turn, Haworth smashed his remaining fist on the surface of the water, sending drops pelting in all directions and swamping his companion in a murky wave. But before their fellow bathers could do more than gasp and wonder if the two gentlemen would come to blows, they were gripping each other by the shoulder, doubled over with laughter.

"Cursed fool!"

"Blasted plaguey cripple!"

"At least I still have four limbs to my name."

"At least I can walk across town without collapsing from my own clumsiness."

No doubt Mrs. Waite would have reproved them for this unseemly display of soldiers' humor, especially when they were surrounded by the ailing and invalid, but fortunately she would never know about it.

"Listen to me," Dashiell said, when they settled down again. "Let's get breakfast in the Lower Rooms before you go. My treat."

"Fine with me. It may be the last good meal I eat. My aunt employed the most execrable cook, whom I had not the heart to dismiss."

An hour or more later, as they sat at their coffee and bath buns, Dashiell said, "I have an idea for you, Haworth. You have accused me more than once of not appreciating Charmaine properly, so it would only be just that you should have your chance."

"What can you possibly mean?" choked his friend.

"Precisely what it sounds like. Look, Charles: you and Charmaine and even Miss Hapgood are all of one mind. You all believe I have been the most unsatisfactory lover—"

"*Miss Hapgood* thinks so?" demanded Haworth. "How do you know that?"

Dashiell waved this away. "She told me last night at supper. I believe Charmaine put her to it, frankly. In any case, she sang Charmaine's praises, as you are wont to do, and then told me I must do a better job of showing my affection."

"Exactly!" Haworth thumped his hand on the table. "Have I not said as much?"

"You have, and I have just said that you have said as much," Dashiell said impatiently. "Therefore, my idea for you: if you would like to try for Charmaine, I give you my permission."

"But—but—how—I," Haworth sputtered, as badly as if the young lady were herself present, "Whoever heard of such a proposal? And how can I, even if I ought? I will be at Bradford."

"You may use your absence to your advantage," argued Dashiell. "God knows you don't seem capable of putting your best leg first when the lady is around. You must see what you can do, when not under her basilisk stare."

"Oh, you're one to talk about best legs," jeered Haworth, but his thoughts quickly ran ahead. "Leaving her 'basilisk stare' aside—another unworthy aspersion—what do you mean I can use my absence to my advantage?"

"Precisely what I say. You stumble all over yourself when she is about; you cannot remember your own name when you try to speak to her, nor even gather your thoughts, much less express them. If you are in Bradford, you have a much better chance of making yourself agreeable."

"Do you mean because absence makes the heart grow fonder?"

"Perhaps. But more to the point, I mean that you may then put your thoughts in a letter to her. You must tell her how you feel. Fluently and persuasively. And then see what happens. If she comes to prefer you, I will bear you no grudge."

"Oh! Oh!" Haworth began to tear his bath bun to fragments as he pondered this. "Dash, I don't mind telling you, that even the thought of taking pen to paper to address Miss Blakely fills me with terror. Suppose she finds my sentiments laughable?"

"She well may, being Charmaine," Dashiell answered ruthlessly, "but you will be in Bradford and never know of it. I am certain she could control her mirth long enough to answer you."

"Confound you for a heartless bastard."

Dashiell only shrugged. "In my heartless, bastard way, I *am* trying to help you, my friend."

Now Haworth proceeded to roll the bath bun fragments back and forth between his nerveless fingertips. "But—what should I say? Charming, heartless fellows like you, upon whom women naturally fawn, may say little or nothing and still succeed, but I—"

"Good Lord, Haworth. Just put down some of the drivel you have subjected me to! That she is divine, beautiful, charming, deserving of more than mere fondness, and so on. Use your imagination."

This adjuration only made matters worse. Haworth was turning rather pale and trembly. He signaled a passing waiter, gasping, "Pen, ink and paper, my good man. Quickly." In answer to Dashiell's skeptical look, Haworth added, "I must do it now, or my courage will fail me."

While Dashiell stared out the windows at the lashing rain, Haworth hunched over his draft, pinning one end of the paper with his coffee cup and alternately scribbling, scratching out, or throwing the pen down to clutch his hair or pull his whiskers. All the while he mumbled to himself and several times had to stop altogether and mop his brow with his napkin.

"All right," he announced at last. "Here it is. Tell me what you think. 'My dear Miss Blakely, I think you have already guessed why I had to go away. I think you are divine and beautiful and charming, and I love you and have Dash's permission to address you. Charles Haworth.'"

Dashiell considered. "Well, Haworth, it has sincerity in its favor, and it is more than I have ever said to her, at any rate. I think you'd better leave out that bit about having my permission—she would only think the less of us for it. You, for needing permission, and me, for granting it."

Obediently, Haworth lined through the offending passage.

"And why not boast about yourself some? You have much to offer a young lady, after all."

"You mean the money and the estate in Bradford?"

"Yes, those, by all means. But you must also say more about your love. Why it would be superior to mine, for instance."

"Superior to yours," Haworth muttered. "Why it would be superior to yours."

"Have you not been telling me so, over and over?"

"Yes." The way Haworth said it was almost a question. Grimacing, he took up the pen again, plunged it in the ink, and resumed his scribbling and hair-clutching. Dashiell ordered a second coffee and bun.

"Here now," Haworth said, sitting back and looking haggard. He thrust the sheet across the table at his friend.

"'My dear Miss B...think you already guessed...divine and beautiful...'" read Dashiell aloud, skimming the passages that were unchanged, "'I love you a great deal and can offer you my fortune and a comfortable home. If you could ever return my feelings, I would be grateful. Yours sincerely, etc. etc.'"

"Well?" prompted Haworth anxiously. "I haven't any gift with words, you see. At least I'm not stuttering like a fool."

"Though all the blots on the page have something of the same effect," mused Dashiell. He tapped the paper thoughtfully, his gaze wandering again to the mullioned windows and the raindrops streaking down the panes.

"Tell me, Haworth—do you feel this does justice to your feelings?"

"No," Haworth groaned. "Not by a mile." He cleared his throat and added manfully, "I say, Dash—you're better at this sort of thing, I suppose. At least, you never seem at a loss for words, even if you never say nice things to her. Can't you have a go at fixing it? I'd be in your everlasting debt."

There was a pause. Haworth flushed, thinking he'd overstepped the bounds of friendship, asking a fellow to make love on his behalf to the fellow's own girl. But, before he could take it back, Dashiell plucked the pen from the table, dipped it fastidiously in the ink and bent over the page. He wrote quickly, fluidly, his color coming and going. Then he flung down the pen and shoved the paper back to Haworth.

The latter seized it as if it held his fate—perhaps it did. He read to himself what Dashiell had written, his lips moving soundlessly. Swallowing, he glanced up at the other, but Dashiell was staring at the rain again. Haworth read the passage again. Looked at Dashiell again.

"I say…I don't know how you did it, but—this is it, Dash. This is exactly how I feel."

"Then you had better make a fair copy when you get to Bradford and mail it when you think you can stand to."

"Yes," he agreed. "And—if she refuses to hear me and tells me to take myself off, at least I will know I have said my piece. And said it with astounding eloquence. My only fear (besides her rejection) is that she will guess I had help."

Dashiell shrugged. "I have told her that you speak fluently enough when she is not around. She will merely suppose this is what you have been prevented from expressing."

"Perhaps. Although—are you certain you are willing for me to write this? However Miss Blakely might feel toward me now, after receiving such a letter, she might *fall* in love with me, on the spot! Not that I mean to give you an inflated opinion of yourself."

"I deserve no credit," Dashiell replied shortly. "I heard something like it somewhere."

Haworth's face fell. "You mean in a play or a book? What if she recognizes it?"

"She will not. She was nowhere about and—only I know of it."

Studying the paper again, Haworth set his shoulders. "Very well. I will send it to her. Exactly as you have it here. And you must take the consequences."

"I have been warned."

As he and Haworth made their way back through the churchyard, Dashiell felt a flicker of hope. It threatened to grow into a blaze, and he had to tamp it down with effort. But suppose, only suppose, Charmaine was won over by Haworth's letter? Only suppose she were to consider the man in a new light. And suppose she were then to come to Dashiell and ask to be released from their engagement?

He shouldn't dwell on the possibility, or the inevitable disappointment would be that much more bitter. In fact, he must put it altogether from his mind.

And yet, had not *she* said such words would surely win Charmaine? And Haworth agreed with her, it seemed.

Certainly they had worked on Dashiell.

For, tucked safely away in the pocket of Haworth's greatcoat, in Dashiell's elegant script could be read:

I would give you my sincere, almost painful love, which only grows, no matter whether it be fed or starved, confessed or unspoken, welcomed or rejected. I love you because I cannot help myself. You are—no matter the consequences—my all in all.

CHAPTER TWENTY-FIVE

These are so many advices which it is easy to give, but difficult to follow.
—Edward Gibbon, *Miscellaneous Works* (1796)

A wave of illness swept the occupants of Henrietta Street after the musical evening. Mrs. Hapgood had all the gratification and inconvenience of a genuine fever, but for once there was no one to make much of her because Margaret and Alwyn were also laid low.

"Your mum asks again if a doctor may be called," Tilly reported lumpenly on the fourth day, setting down a tray of tea and unappetizing gruel.

"How ill does she look?" asked Margaret. She raised herself slowly and gave a weak smile when she realized the room no longer spun.

"No worse than ye, miss, and a touch better than your uncle, who still complains of aches and a bursting head."

"No doctor, then," decided Margaret. "Tell her I will check on her myself. Perhaps later, after another nap. Would you open the shutters, Tilly? I should like to see if it still rains."

"It does," Tilly said shortly. "All wet and miserable for days like Noah and the flood."

"At least I haven't missed much. It's no weather for walking."

"Hasn't stopped others from coming out."

Margaret's spoonful of gruel paused. "What do you mean? Have you seen many people on Pulteney Street?"

"What would I be doing on Pulteney Street, miss? I've been here, tending on you folks. I only mean that you've had some messages and callers and well-wishers." Pulling the pocket of her apron out, she set several notes and cards on the side table. "And there's some flowers and treats, which I'll fetch, now you're awake."

Gruel forgotten, Margaret struggled up and reached for the offerings. The room was dim and her eyes still watery, but a quick sorting through revealed two notes from Charmaine; a letter from Edith; a calling card from "Mrs. Humphrey Waite," with "Mrs. Matthew Blakely" handwritten beneath it; another card from a "Mrs. Lincoln Turner," whoever that might be; and—oh, heavens!—an engraved card from Sir Dodkins Hargate.

So the baronet had returned. Returned and wasted no time in calling. Margaret shut her eyes in relief that she had been too unwell to receive visitors. He could not be put off forever, of course, but every day that she might continue free seemed precious to her.

Charmaine's first note was a hasty scrawl, dated the day after they dined in Princes Street: "I have much to discuss with you. Can you walk in Sydney Gardens later? Send word."

The second was from the following day: "If you are going to lie abed, I am too. I fear I have caught the same cold. Do come visit, however, if you recover before me."

Tilly came trooping back, bearing a vase of hothouse flowers in one arm and a basket of oranges in another. Plopping her burdens unceremoniously on the desk, she plucked out the fresh candles she had jammed in the vase, lit them in the fire and replaced the spent ones in the sconces.

"Thank you, Tilly. What lovely flowers and fruit! Who are they from?"

Tilly pointed at the vase. "The Waites." Then at the oranges. "Sir Dodkins Hargate."

"Oh." What must a basket of oranges have cost? Ever so much! On the one hand she was impressed. But on the other, she wondered why she should have to marry the baronet over fifty pounds, when it was clear the expense had not much encumbered him.

"Tilly, can you please take half those oranges and deliver them to the Waites in Princes Street?" It would be a nice thank-you and would cheer Charmaine, as well as relieve Margaret of some of the guilt of receiving them.

She waved the next card. "And did you see this Mrs. Lincoln Turner? I do not recall the name. What did she look like?"

"Older lady wearing a big turban."

Mrs. Lincoln Turner was Madame Turban? Why ever should she call on Margaret? "How odd. What did she want?"

"Just to wish you well and to say she would call again later."

Margaret shrugged and laid the card aside, not interested enough to ponder further. She did not dare ask questions about Sir Dodkins' call, however. Frankly, she didn't want to know.

"Thank you, Tilly. You may go."

"If anyone else calls, are you home, miss?"

Margaret shuddered and huddled deeper in the bedcoverings. "No. No, not today."

When the door closed behind the maid, Margaret opened Edith's letter. It was two pages, crossed, and written in such a rush that Margaret had difficulty making it out.

> *Margaret!*
> *How* could *you keep such a secret from us? Papa only just received the letter from your suitor, announcing his intention to call, and then the baronet arrived the very next day! Baronet!!!*
>
> *At first I could hardly understand why such a person begged to make Papa's acquaintance, but Papa guessed it soon enough and said, "He wants Margaret, I'll be bound. The sly minx! With all her talk of not wanting any husbands. Well, so long as she has not allowed her mother and uncle to run wild in Bath or forgotten why I sent her in the first place, I'll have no objection." Then*

he was off in a flash to hunt up a copy of the barone-tage and read about this Sir Dodkins Hargate. You will know without my telling you that, once he learned of the baronet's estate in Dorset, Papa was all smiles and approval, though he wondered you "couldn't catch anyone younger," until he decided there was likely "no one in Bath under the age of eighty to be had for love or money."

I spent a dreadful day preparing the house to receive such an august person and begged for Rosemary to come advise because, as you might guess, Button was fit to be tied and threatening to turn in her notice over such a to-do, and Dorcas was in tears, and Hal hiding and no use at all. I wanted to cry and hide myself.

But Bramleigh looked as well as it could the next morning when Sir Dodkins arrived in his barouche. I thought Papa should have a fatal episode, he was so terribly excited. I confess, I was prepared to meet some-one very ancient, and he is indeed quite old, but rather handsomer than I expected and very well-mannered. Papa took him into the library, but I had slipped a knot of paper into the catch earlier, to prevent the door shutting all the way. Then I pressed my ear to the crack and found it quite a simple matter to eavesdrop, since I did not have to fight to take turns with you! In short,

Sir Dodkins gave a little speech to the effect that he had made your acquaintance in Bath, had danced with you and called upon you and taken you driving and hosted a card party in his home which you attended—all of which I was astonished to hear because you said no more of him in your letters than that he was an old man with a cough, whose feelings you had hurt. He praised you as "a kind and lovely young lady" and a "credit to your family," and Papa in his turn boasted that you were wondrous capable and that Bramleigh had never been better managed than under you. (I repeat this to you faithfully and not to further swell your pride.) Sir Dodkins then told Papa of his family's long roots in Dorset and how he had the misfortune to lose both wife and children years ago. I quite pitied him! Though, when he asked Papa's permission to pay his addresses to you (and Papa eagerly agreed), I could not help but doubt his success. You said you have no desire to marry and have given me no reason to suppose your feelings have changed, so why would you marry this old man and run his house, when you already run Bramleigh and may do what you please? You would be rich, I suppose, but you take such delight in being thrifty that I am not certain you could wring from wealth the joy which other young ladies can.

I tried to say as much to Papa after Sir Dodkins was

gone, but he hardly heard me. He was capering about and urging me to write to you and say that he <u>fully approved the match</u>, especially since the baronet neglected to inquire into Papa's finances and even said at one point that he "had no need of an heiress." I dread to think how disappointed Papa will be when you refuse Sir Dodkins, but surely you will refuse, won't you?

Write to me very, very, very soon.

Your loving sister,
Edith

Margaret read this several times through, slumping lower each time until she finally rolled to her side and curled in a ball.

Ugh. So that was where Sir Dodkins had taken himself off to! He must have decided he would need her father's consent more than her uncle's, and he lost no time in getting it. Had he only said as much when she begged him for the fifty pounds, Margaret would have understood his intentions immediately and would have made some excuse for not needing the money after all. Or would it even then be too late? Charmaine thought so. She thought it too late for Margaret to retreat from the moment Sir Dodkins handed her the banknotes.

"Well, Papa will be happy," she muttered to the bed hangings. "Because I must accept Sir Dodkins." Burying her face in the pillows, she stifled a groan. One day she would explain herself to Edie. Explain the jewelry debt she had shamefully failed to prevent and explain how her request for a loan was interpreted by the baronet as a plea for him to hurry up and offer for her, already.

"At least it will make Papa happy. And Edie said he was kind and well-mannered, which he is. And generous. There are worse husbands." But in spite of all these truths, Margaret still cried herself back to sleep.

Another dreary, rainy day passed, bringing another little stack of cards, including a second from Mrs. Lincoln Turner and a thank-you note from Mrs. Waite for the oranges. Even Mr. Longshanks left a message: "Sorry not to have seen you at the last two balls. Anxious to show you my new saddle when you are feeling more the thing."

When the sun finally reappeared, Margaret's spirits lifted accordingly. She was well again and could not bear to keep to her room another moment, even if resuming the business of life entailed receiving the baronet.

She did not expect to find her mother up, knowing a genuine cold would fell Mrs. Hapgood twice as long as an imaginary one, but Margaret was pleased to find Alwyn at breakfast.

"Good morning, Uncle!" she greeted him, as she filled her plate. "How glad I am to see you recovered."

"You as well, Mags. And look at this sunshine! What do you say to a walk in the Gardens this morning? Should be cold but glorious."

"I should love it above all things!"

"Then eat up and fetch your cloak and bonnet."

An hour later they were leaning on the balustrade of the Chinese bridge, overlooking the canal, and Margaret had told him about the baronet's visit to Bramleigh.

"So you see, Uncle Alwyn, I expect he will call shortly and put the question to me."

"What a triumph for you, Maggie, even when you refuse him."

"Oh, but I shan't refuse."

"Not refuse him? I know he's rich and all that, but I hardly thought you the sort who would marry for money alone, though you do seem to worry about it more than most your age. I rather thought you preferred Mr. Waite, if you preferred anyone."

Horrified to have her secret referred to so matter-of-factly, Margaret just managed to stop herself from clapping hands to his mouth to silence him. "Shhhhh! How *can* you say such a thing? In Sydney Gardens, for all to hear? Never say it, ever again."

"Very well," he said meekly, "though I don't see the harm in it. He's a handsome chap, for all he's a cripple, and it's not as if anything can come of it, he being engaged and all."

"Yes, Uncle, *I know*. Therefore, please do not mention it again." She was grateful for the brisk air, which made her flushed cheeks less suspect. "To return to Sir Dodkins, I plan to accept him and would not be surprised if he considers us engaged already."

Taking a deep breath, she told him of her desperate request to Sir Dodkins at the card party, his compliance, her visit to the jeweler, and Charmaine's opinion.

"And now I see she was right," Margaret concluded. "For Sir Dodkins lost no time in asking Papa's permission. He sees us as engaged in all but name, and I imagine we will be engaged in fact, as soon as he can next speak with me."

Alwyn was frowning and pulling his moustache, deep in thought. "Still and all, though, Mags, you don't want to marry the old chap, do you?"

"I don't see that I have much choice."

"There is always a choice," he declared. "For heaven's sake. What a mess you have rushed into, and all for fifty pounds. Did I not say the money would come from somewhere, when it was needed?"

Her eyes flashed. "Uncle Alwyn, you expect the money to come from Papa, but he doesn't have it, especially after paying for our time here, and it would risk his health to demand it of him! Besides, it doesn't matter now. As Charmaine says, returning the baronet's money would only humiliate him."

"Oh, I don't know," said Alwyn. "Occasional humiliation builds character. If I had to choose myself, I'm sure I would prefer one short, sharp blow of humiliation to lifelong degradation."

"Whatever can you mean? Why would marrying me be degrading?"

"Not marrying you in particular, my dear. Rather, marrying someone who did not care for one and who married one because she could see no way out of it."

"I don't *not* care for him," Margaret protested. "I mean, I am not in love with him, but I do respect him as a kind and worthy man. And I feel grateful to him. Well—grateful and resentful both, but more grateful than resentful."

"An endorsement to warm any man's heart," said Alwyn dryly.

"No, I have been thinking about this. You remember in *Sense and Sensibility*? Marianne learned to love Colonel Brandon, even though he was old and even though she began by loving someone else."

"So you *are* in love with someone else!"

"Stop! I only mean to say that I will try very hard to love Sir Dodkins when we are married."

"Look, Margaret. I know your papa and probably you and your sisters think I'm a hopeless rogue, but I haven't lived this long without learning a few things. And I say you shouldn't marry this old fellow if you don't want to, no matter what he or anything else thinks. Better to have everyone call you a jilt than to be stuck with someone you don't want and have to learn to love."

Margaret only shook her head. Nothing was serious to Alwyn Arbuthnot. *Nothing*. "But I don't want to be called a jilt!"

"Now, now," he soothed. "Remember when Alice got herself in such a pickle because she was dressing up as a boy, and Joseph had to marry her?"

"Ye-e-es...but—"

"And remember when Elfie eloped with her Frederick and set the world on its ears?"

"Yes...but—"

"But everything turned out fine! People will sneer and gossip, as they will at any nine days' wonder, but the nine days pass and you find you have got what you wanted. I say you tell Ods Bodkins that you are very, very sorry, but you cannot bring yourself to marry him, and that you will have the fifty pounds back to him as soon as you are able. Then let him kick up whatever fuss he may. I'll warrant a man like that will want to keep it quiet."

This was difficult counsel for Margaret to hear, and she mistrusted her own willingness to believe him. Was it possible she could yet escape? Could the baronet be trusted to say nothing, even if he were angry and humiliated by her refusal? And where, again, would the fifty pounds come from? Would Sir Dodkins, in his resentment, turn the screw even more forcefully than the jeweler?

It was ridiculous to take advice from Uncle Alwyn, she told herself as they walked home. After all, the only reason she found herself in this mess was because Alwyn and Margaret's mother were so little able to advise themselves! Indeed, was not the fact that she found her uncle's counsel tempting proof enough that it was wrong?

But what, then, should she do?

Suppose the baronet called that very afternoon? Or—worse—was even now waiting for them in Henrietta Street?

It was not Sir Dodkins whom Margaret and Alwyn returned to find in the drawing room, however, and, when she saw their visitor was alone, Margaret's heart settled back in her chest where it belonged.

"Why, welcome, Mrs. Turner," she said, seeing Alwyn had no memory of the turbaned woman. "What a pleasant surprise."

Chapter Twenty-Six

I am a woe woman this heavy day.
—Henry Brooke, *The Female Officer* (1778)

"Mr. Arbuthnot, Miss Hapgood. I was sorry to hear of your recent ill health," Mrs. Turner said, resuming her seat. The pale sunlight streaming through the windows emphasized her wan complexion and the drabness of her clothing and head covering.

Alwyn and Margaret might wonder at her concern, but they thanked her for it and made polite conversation for the requisite quarter hour, not much enlightened during that time. When it was passed, she rose again.

"Miss Hapgood, I know you have just come from walking and may be tired, but the day is so fine. I would welcome a companion while I take a turn."

Suspecting she would learn the real reason for Mrs. Turner's visit, and not sorry for an excuse to avoid Sir Dodkins longer, Margaret agreed, and they set out. Such a day was made for window-gazing and admiring views, but Mrs. Turner showed no interest in dawdling, merely casting glances as they went, as if eager to avoid her acquaintance.

"Have you known Sir Dodkins long, Mrs. Turner?" Margaret asked, when they reached the bridge.

The woman threw her a sharp look. But, finding only polite inquiry in Margaret's face, she answered, "A very long time. I am his neighbor in Dorset."

"How nice. I have never been to Dorset, but my family hails from Somerset near Taunton."

"Yes, I have heard tell of your family."

That silenced Margaret. Were they truly so infamous? Perhaps Uncle Alwyn was right—if the Hapgoods (and presumably her scapegrace Arbuthnot uncles) were notorious in the larger world, what harm would one more black mark on the family name be? She would just become "Miss Margaret Hapgood, the jilt," and the world would spin on.

"I am the baronet's neighbor," Mrs. Turner repeated, not noticing Margaret's discomfiture. "And Lady Hargate was my dearest friend. Marcia and I attended school together and thought it our great good fortune that we married men whose estates lay so close together. When she was dying, she asked me to be a mother to her young daughter, also called Marcia, and I was. Faithfully. With no children of my own, Marcia was dear to me as a daughter could be.

Mr. Turner and I frequently had her to stay with us for weeks at a time, though Sir Dodkins hated to part with her. And when I lost Mr. Turner, Marcia was my only solace."

"I am so sorry," murmured Margaret, knowing the younger Marcia Hargate's sad fate all too well. But she had an inkling now why Mrs. Turner was seeking her out. If Sir Dodkins hoped to find a surrogate daughter in Margaret (before Margaret cornered him into marriage), did Mrs. Turner share those hopes? Did she, too, wish Margaret might replace lost Marcia?

"You are somewhat like her," Mrs. Turner went on, as they turned down the High Street past the Guildhall Market. "Not physically—Marcia had golden hair and blue eyes. But there is something in your demeanor, how you carry yourself. The expression about the eyes. I cannot put my finger on it precisely, but I know Sir Dodkins recognizes it as well."

It must be confessed, the prospect of being wife to an aged baronet and surrogate daughter-in-law to his equally aged neighbor did not flood Margaret with delight. She could sympathize with them but still wish it were otherwise.

"You must wonder why I sought you out," Mrs. Turner said. "Why I tell you these things. We had not spoken much before."

"We had not," admitted Margaret.

Mrs. Turner paused, pretending to inspect a display of carrots and turnips. "It is this: Sir Dodkins and I have been neighbors, friends, and even parents of a child, in a way, for a good many years. Marcia used to say many times after my Mr. Turner died that she wished her father and I might marry. 'You are my mama,' she used to say. 'It would make my heart glad to know you had each other. I hate to think of either of you alone.' And—before the baronet made your acquaintance, he seemed content enough to know me."

"Ah," said Margaret, and her eyes, reflected in the plate glass shop window, were very wide. So *that* was it! Mrs. Turner did not seek her as a potential daughter; she warned her off as a rival! Perhaps Charmaine was right, in calling Margaret stupid and a fool. For how could she so misinterpret these situations?

In the same shop window, her companion studied her response.

"That would be lovely for you both, to be together," Margaret said honestly. "Did Marcia ever mention her wish to her father?"

Mrs. Turner sniffed and drew herself up. "I do not know. Sir Dodkins and I have never discussed it."

Margaret could only suppose that, if Marcia had ever expressed it to her father, he felt no inclination to act upon it. After all, she had been gone for several years now.

She turned to address Mrs. Turner directly. "Why do you tell me this now?"

For the first time that morning, color flooded Mrs. Turner's pale cheeks. She began to walk onward, but slowly, and Margaret followed.

"You seem a kind girl," Mrs. Turner said. "Not like that Miss Blakely."

"Mrs. Turner! Miss Blakely is my good friend."

"She's a cold one, for all that. A sharp one and a cold one. Flashy enough."

"Please—say no more about Miss Blakely," Margaret entreated. "I assure you, she has warmth enough."

Mrs. Turner looked skeptical. "I don't mean to offend you. The reverse, in fact. I mean to say that I am glad Sir Dodkins has not turned his attention to such a one. She would have led him a merry dance, begging your pardon. But you seem modest enough. Please—I pray you will speak plainly with me."

"What can you wish to know?" Margaret asked with trepidation.

"Only this: are you and Sir Dodkins engaged?"

"Madam!"

"You must forgive the effrontery of the question."

"But—if you are such old friends with Sir Dodkins, why do you not ask him?"

"I will answer that, if I must, but first I beg you to tell me. *Are* you engaged?"

Poor Margaret floundered a moment. "We are not—yet."

Mrs. Turner's took a long breath. "Not...yet? But you hope to be?"

Margaret hoped nothing of the kind, but how could she explain herself to this woman? "We are not. But I must tell you, he has asked my papa's permission to pay his addresses."

Here Mrs. Turner gasped, one hand flying to her midsection. "Yes. I am not surprised. He can be decisive when he has made up his mind. And, if you say you are not engaged yet, that means you plan to accept him?"

Margaret's lips parted, to say the fatal word, but no sound emerged. Somehow, telling Mrs. Turner that she planned to accept the baronet felt irrevocable as telling the baronet himself.

"He is very eligible, of course," Mrs. Turner sighed. "Despite the May-December nature of the match, there is nothing astonishing in your wanting to marry him."

"But I *don't* want to marry him!" protested Margaret unthinkingly. "That is—Mrs. Turner, it isn't what you suppose. It isn't what the wide world supposes! I am not the least bit interested in his title or his wealth or his estate or anything!"

"Indeed? You will understand if I find that remarkable."

"But it's true," insisted Margaret. As the two women passed through the Abbey yard, they instinctively kept close to the building to avoid any acquaintances emerging from the Pump Room. "I did not come to Bath to find a husband. We are here for my mother's health and—and my uncle. I never sought out Sir Dodkins, much less tried to attach him."

Mrs. Turner reached for the façade of the church for support. "Are you telling me you intend on refusing him?"

Oh, how delighted Margaret would have been to give Mrs. Turner such an assurance! As delighted as Mrs. Turner would have been to hear it. But it could not be. Margaret gazed upward at the carved angels climbing Jacob's ladder, wishing she could likewise escape this uncomfortable situation.

Finally, she answered quietly. "Mrs. Turner, it does not seem appropriate that I should give you my answer before I give it to Sir

Dodkins himself. I can only say that, if it were possible you should win him instead of me, I would be glad of it."

Several emotions passed in waves over Mrs. Turner's pallid face: indignation, unbelief, sorrow. "He will ask you, and you will accept him, ungrateful as you are. If it were not so, you would have told me. And, though I was wrong, perhaps, to pry into your affairs, I hoped swallowing my pride and taking you into my confidence would have spared me your taunts."

"My *taunts*?" exclaimed Margaret. "Madam, believe me, I have said nothing to taunt you, and, if you took my words that way, it was not my intention."

"How can it be otherwise?" demanded Mrs. Turner. "You, a pretty young lady who has captured Sir Dodkins' eye—and I, an old friend who has never excited more than gratitude and friendship—you say you would be glad for me to win him? If you value him as little as you claim, why not declare that you will refuse him?" To Margaret's dismay, tears sprang to the older woman's eyes. "Is it not painful enough I have revealed my heart to you, but then I must see how dismissively you consider him? You, who are unworthy of him? For you are unworthy, if you cannot value him and if you throw it so cruelly in my face that he would never be mine."

"What? I beg you, Mrs. Turner—you misunderstand me completely!"

But the woman shook her head and hurried away. For a minute, Margaret debated: should she throw up her hands in defeat and return home, or should she follow and attempt to make herself understood?

Perhaps it was because she was weary of not saying exactly what she would like, weary of being constrained by social conventions and social judgments, but Margaret thought she would be *shot* if she would let Mrs. Turner dart off, thinking her nothing but a heartless coquette who collected gentlemen like beads on a string and disdained those less admired!

Gathering up her cloak, she dashed after her, dodging other promenaders and calling the woman's name after she spied her turban some ways ahead. If anything, Mrs. Turner walked even faster, not looking back, but Margaret had the advantages of youth and height and, just past the Lower Rooms, caught her sleeve to halt her.

"Mrs. Turner, I insist you hear me," Margaret panted.

"What more is there to say?" returned the other, stonily.

"Much. But not here. Let us go over to the Walk."

Neither spoke another word until they reached the end of the Terrace Walk's stone railing. And there, before her courage could fail her, Margaret told her all. Her family's financial and health difficulties; the debt incurred by her mother and uncle; the impossibility of paying the jeweler without a loan; how she had thought Sir Dodkins looked upon her as another Marcia; and Sir Dodkins' misinterpretation of Margaret's actions.

"I did not realize he would feel he had to marry me," she explained, "not until my friend Charmaine—Miss Blakely—told me so. I would never have accepted the money if that were the case! I would have robbed a bank first. And it is not that I am ungrateful or that I disdain Sir Dodkins as an eligible gentleman. He is entirely worthy of esteem, and I do esteem him, but I would rather not have to marry him. But I *must* accept him, Mrs. Turner, for the sake of his pride and as a sign of respect, but can you understand now how I would far rather he loved you?"

Mrs. Turner listened intently throughout, skepticism warring with belief. Margaret could see that she still could not comprehend how any woman could resist the baronet, and it was fortunate the older lady never overheard any of Margaret and Charmaine's impertinent discussions of him.

Very well. There was yet one more card to play, and Margaret the gambler laid it down. "Mrs. Turner, I will make one more confession to you, but you must promise me never to speak of it to anyone."

As no one in the history of confidences had ever been able to resist this line, Mrs. Turner nodded, hypnotized.

Margaret cast glances all around, but seeing no one she dreaded, she leaned closer. "It is this: if I have been unappreciative of the honor Sir Dodkins does me, it is because I have already given my heart to someone. He doesn't know it. He can never know it. And he can never be mine, but it is done."

As she hoped, all Mrs. Turner's doubts and hostility crumbled away, undone by both the earnest confession and Margaret's pleading eyes.

"Why can the gentleman never be yours?" Mrs. Turner asked in a softened tone.

"He is engaged to another."

The older woman covered Margaret's hand with her own as it rested on the balustrade. "Thank you, child, for telling me this," she said at last. "I see now why you can neither care for Sir Dodkins nor refuse him."

"You...agree then?" Margaret asked despondently. "That I cannot refuse him?"

"I think he might have proposed to you, my dear Miss Hapgood, even without this matter of the loan. He is fond of you."

Margaret sighed. "Perhaps. But I can't help but feel his fondness is a mixture of nostalgia and pity and a desire to rescue me from my troubles. If only—" she broke off, regarding her companion thoughtfully.

"Yes?"

"If only he knew of Marcia's wishes and your own."

"You would not tell him!" cried Mrs. Turner, releasing Margaret's hand to clutch herself.

"You have nothing to lose but a little pride," Margaret urged. "He is such a gentleman—if he knew of your feelings and did not return them, no one in the world would ever know but the two of you. Please! Tell him. Take this chance, for your own sake, if not for mine."

"He has only ever been a kind friend and neighbor, Margaret," Mrs. Turner protested, forgetting to be formal in her distress. "And he has known me for years."

"Do you love him?" Margaret persisted. "You asked me earlier a question you said you had no right to ask, and now I return the favor. Do you love him?"

Mrs. Turner covered her face with her hands and did not reply, but slowly, painfully, she nodded.

"Then you must take the chance. You will never forgive yourself if you do not."

Straightening, Mrs. Turner dropped her hands and fixed Margaret with a challenging stare. "And you? I could say the same to you. Have you told your gentleman your feelings for him?"

"It isn't the same thing at all!" Margaret objected. "I told you he is engaged. It would not be right. It would do no good and would only hurt a dear friend."

"Gracious," breathed Mrs. Turner. "You mean you are in love with Miss Blakely's Mr. Waite?"

For the second time that day, Margaret fought an urge to clap a hand over someone's mouth. At this rate, all Bath would know before nightfall!

"Good heavens, Mrs. Turner, hush! You mustn't shout things from the rooftops."

"Oh, my dear girl. I can't help but feel you would be a better match for him than that cold creature—"

"Shhh…I already said, you must not say such things of my friend."

"Well, if he knew your feelings, he would surely choose you, and then there would be no question of you marrying Sir Dodkins."

"Well, he *can't* know my feelings, and you *promised me* you would say nothing. Nor can he choose me because he's already engaged to her, so we must think instead how you can tell Sir Dodkins your feelings. And it must be done right away, so that I don't have to put him off or jilt him. It is our only chance, Mrs. Turner."

Mrs. Turner put a faltering hand to her head covering. "I don't see what can be done. It is too late. I cannot simply thrust myself between the two of you and ask him to marry me, even for Marcia's sake."

But Margaret had no more patience for misgivings when so much was at stake. They must make one more play before they admitted defeat.

"Come back with me to Henrietta Street, Mrs. Turner. I have a plan."

Chapter Twenty-Seven

Before I take any man in hand, I will knowe whether hee be a thorne or a nettle.
—Joseph Hall, *Meditations and Vowes Divine and Morall* (1605)

It was not an out and out lie, Margaret told herself. For when the baronet next called, Hudgins told him Miss Hapgood was resting, gathering her strength after her cold, that she might attend that night's ball. But while it was entirely true she was still recovering, Margaret had no intention whatsoever of attending the ball.

"You will not go, but you want me to attend?" asked Alwyn doubtfully. After so many weeks of his niece's tight rein, he was leery of this sudden slackening.

"Yes, please," Margaret said. She was sewing a dress for Alice's baby and held it up to inspect her progress.

"My dear, I know you want to avoid Sir Dodkins and the Moment of Truth, as it were, but you can hardly skulk at home for the remainder of our time here."

"I know it. I don't intend to. I only need a little longer, to see if something else won't come up." She opened her workbasket to search for yellow ribbon. "You go and dance with Mrs. Waite. Perhaps tonight will be the night she agrees to elope with you. And make my apologies to Charmaine. I have only one request: that you keep an eye on Sir Dodkins and Mrs. Turner and report back what you see."

"Want to make sure your unwelcome lover doesn't turn his attentions elsewhere?"

"Precisely the opposite, Uncle. I would be delighted if he turned his attentions elsewhere, but I hardly dare hope."

After so many dull days at home, Alwyn was not one to look a gift horse in the mouth, and off he went as requested.

The next morning Margaret paced impatiently in the breakfast room. Hudgins backed in with the chafing dish, whistling to himself, and he nearly dropped it when she greeted him.

"Miss! You're up early. I will build up the fire. Will you be receiving callers today?"

"No callers," Margaret said quickly. "That is—only female callers."

"No Sir Dodkins, you mean?" he clarified, earning himself a frown.

"No gentlemen callers," Margaret said. She inspected the contents of the chafing dish to avoid the servant's knowing look. "Thank you, Hudgins."

Some while later, Tilly poked her head in. "It's Miss Blakely, miss. Shall I admit her here?"

Eagerly, Margaret pushed away her plate. "Send her up to my chamber, please, so that we are not disturbed. Is the fire still lit?"

"Margaret!" cried Charmaine, sweeping in. "It's been ages." The girls embraced, and then Charmaine held her away and pulled her nearer the window. "My, how hale and hearty you look, considering you've been languishing in bed the past week. I believe you stayed ill so long because you didn't want to visit my own sickbed."

Charmaine did look paler than usual, and Margaret was happy to fuss over her now, seating her nearest the fire, calling for tea, and pulling the coverlet off the bed to tuck about her. "If I could not sit by your bedside, you will now have the pleasure of telling me your pains. I am quite used to it, for Mama frequently demands my sympathy."

"Oh, never mind that. I am well enough now and have far more interesting things to share."

"About the ball? I have heard nothing yet because my uncle has not yet risen."

"Indeed. I suspect he had a busy night," Charmaine replied archly. "But I will come to that presently. First I must tell you the most pressing news: someone took advantage of your absence to prey upon Sir Dodkins!"

Margaret only smiled. "How dramatic you are. I have told you more than once that the other ladies are welcome to him."

"You are not yet engaged, then? I thought I would have heard something, even sick as I was, if you were."

"We are not yet engaged. To be honest, I have not been receiving many callers."

Charmaine laughed. "Very well. All is fair in love and war."

"But who preyed upon him?"

Tilly entered at that moment, and the girls had to wait for the tea tray to be placed, but when the door closed again, Charmaine threw the blanket aside and moved closer to Margaret on the settee.

"Everyone in the ballroom turned to look at her when she appeared. I did not recognize her at first: an older woman in a striking dark blue gown, with beautifully dressed hair of silvery white."

"Oh, honestly, Charmaine," Margaret scoffed. "Whoever heard of silvery white hair?"

"You must ask your uncle, if you don't believe me. Her hair was silvery white, and we all stared, and then, what would you imagine? Mr. King was moving toward her to ask her name when your own Sir Dodkins stole a march on him! He intervened and said, 'Anna, is that you?'"

"Well?" said Margaret, removing the tea strainer from the pot and setting it in its dish. "What did this Anna say?"

Charmaine waved her hands impatiently. "I don't know. Something like, 'Yes, it is I, Dodkins.' That isn't important. What is important is who this Anna was, Margaret! Here—stop with the tea things for a moment and pay attention to me. Margaret, this Anna was *Madame Turban*!"

Margaret affected surprise. "Madame Turban without her turban?"

"Yes. Madame Turban has, underneath her turban, silvery white hair. Like—moonlight! And Madame Turban, when she doesn't cover her moonlight hair or wear colors that blend with sodden skies and muddy pavement, is rather lovely, for her age. For any age, really. I could tell Sir Dodkins was all astonishment. He looked as if he had never seen her before. They danced together twice and spent much of the rest of the time talking. That other fellow from the card party—the one with the moustache—he hovered about as well."

"Most interesting," said Margaret.

"Margaret!" groaned Charmaine. "I know you don't want to marry him, but it's rather humiliating to have some woman twice your age snatch him up. My aunt Eliza said to Mama, 'I had thought Sir Dodkins was making up to Miss Hapgood, but now I am not so certain.' And Mama said, 'I fear it is always that way with gentlemen—out of sight, out of mind.'"

"I'm sure your mama is right," agreed Margaret. "At least, I hope so. It would prove a great relief to me if Sir Dodkins forgot me altogether."

Charmaine only shook her head, accepting her cup of tea. "What a Margaret you are. And I suppose you will not feel a jot different when I tell you that, when the ball ended, I saw Sir Dodkins handing Mrs. Turner into her chair, and when he did, she *passed him some-*

thing. Something small and white and folded. Something very like a note."

"A *billet-doux*, no doubt." Margaret gave a mysterious little smile of her own.

She expected Charmaine to hound her for some time about Sir Dodkins' perfidy and girded herself to defend Mrs. Turner's secret, but instead Charmaine rose abruptly, crossing the room and making a show of rearranging the flowers sent by the Waites.

"These are lovely. Did the baronet send them, before he forgot you?"

"No, you goose. Did you not know? Tilly said they were from the Waites."

"From Aunt Eliza?"

"I don't know. I suppose so. Tilly just said, 'the Waites.'"

Charmaine glowered. "If that isn't the final nail in the coffin," she muttered.

"If what isn't the final nail in the coffin?"

"These are Dashiell's idea," said Charmaine, slapping now at the flowers. "I'm certain of it. When *I* am bedridden for days, he merely tells my mother—on day three!—that he hopes I feel better soon. When *you* are bedridden for days, he sends flowers! It is unendurable. I *hate* the man."

"Charmaine Blakely!"

"What? I want to be loved! He knows that. You told him so. You told him to pay me more attention and to speak his love, and he has done neither."

"But Charmaine, you have been sick and confined to your room—"

"Margaret, I *live under the same roof as the man!*" Charmaine snapped. "If he can think to send you flowers, he could have made more effort with me. I do not know why you're defending him."

Margaret could hardly say why, except that she loved Mr. Waite and could not bear to have him spoken ill of. That, and her guilty conscience weighed upon her. "He is a good man," she said weakly.

"Oh, such a good man," jeered her friend. "You are always telling me how fortunate I am to have him. Do you know what I think, Margaret? I think you would be glad to marry him yourself."

"I have already said so," Margaret said through gritted teeth. "If the choice were between Sir Dodkins and Mr. Waite."

"What if the choice were between Dashiell and Mr. Haworth?"

"Wh-what?" Margaret blinked up at Charmaine. "What has Mr. Haworth to do with anything?"

Before Charmaine could answer, they heard a voice in the passage. "Mags! Knock, knock." This was followed by an actual knock and Alwyn Arbuthnot's entrance. "Why, good morning, Miss Blakely. I did not know you were here."

"Charmaine has been telling me about the ball."

"Ah, yes, the ball. I would give you a full report, Maggie, but just now I am headed out." He reached up to touch his pomaded hair. "A visit to the barber, you know. What would you think if I had him shave off my moustache?"

"Oh! I have never known you without one."

"It would be quite fashionable, Mr. Arbuthnot," put in Charmaine. "I think you ought to try it. You will be as unrecognizable as Mrs. Turner was at the ball."

"Was Mrs. Turner at the ball?" he asked.

"Uncle!" exclaimed Margaret. "Charmaine tells me that every eye was upon her and that, underneath that turban of hers, she has hair of moonlight silver. How could you not notice?" And, more importantly, how could he not remember she had expressly asked him to keep an eye on Mrs. Turner and Sir Dodkins? Impossible man!

"Mm," he shrugged. "Truth be told, I spent a great deal of last night in the card room." With a careless salute, he bowed and slipped away, leaving Margaret shaking her head in exasperation.

"Yes, I'm afraid, with Mr. Haworth gone, we hardly arrived at the ball before Dashiell seized upon Mr. Arbuthnot and carried him away to the card room," Charmaine explained. "I think he has been quite starved for male company. That and, seeing Mr. Arbuthnot unaccompanied, Dashiell probably thought he better keep an eye on him. Mr. Arbuthnot did not return to the ballroom until the dancing was nearly ended, and then it was only to scurry over and claim my aunt Eliza. So perhaps Dashiell's efforts were not altogether successful."

"Shall Mr. Haworth return anytime soon?" asked Margaret absently, still distracted by her uncle's utter unreliability. She began stacking the teacups and saucers for Tilly to remove.

"That depends."

"On what?"

"On my response to him."

When Margaret gave Charmaine a questioning look, the latter grinned and removed an envelope from the pocket in her green silk spencer. "This is what I have wanted to tell you, above all things. I have been bursting with the information for two days now and would have broken into your house and forced the confidence on you today, even had you been on your deathbed! See? Mr. Haworth has written me a letter!" She waved it gleefully. "Yes, you are surprised. Believe me, I was as well. Especially when I recovered enough to sit up and read it for the first time. I thought I should faint away! Dashiell told me that Mr. Haworth speaks fluently enough when I am not nearby, but the eloquence of his writing utterly amazed me."

Margaret was staring at her. "Mr. Haworth has written you a *love* letter?" Not that he should be writing her any sort of letter, given Charmaine's engagement to his own friend!

"He has." She could not prevent a glow and a smile.

But Margaret was rendered almost speechless by this betrayal, as if Haworth's usual stuttering and stammering had left him to infect her. "But—but—how could he? He is Mr. Waite's dear friend! They—have been through war and—hospital together! He—how can he—how does he *dare* to make love to you when you belong to—how could he prove so very false?"

"Do you call it false? I call it daring," Charmaine declared, quite pleased by Margaret's stupefaction. "I call it passion and violent love! Love that cannot be denied or suppressed. Love that does not send lukewarm wishes for the beloved's health via the beloved's mother."

This additional hit at Mr. Waite hardly registered, but Charmaine's high-flying praise of Mr. Haworth's letter succeeded in distracting Margaret from her outrage, and she could not prevent a skeptical look. "Charmaine, surely you exaggerate to call it 'passion' and 'violent love.' He may not stumble over his words when he sets pen to paper, but is Mr. Haworth truly capable of lyric flights as you describe? You simply want to think ill of Mr. Waite."

Charmaine tapped the letter against her other hand. "It is true I want to think ill of Dashiell—that I *do* think ill of Dashiell. But you wrong me if you believe I think favorably of Mr. Haworth's letter simply out of spite. If you were to read it, you would understand what I mean. You would understand why I find myself seeing Mr. Haworth in a whole new light."

Mr. Haworth had so plunged in Margaret's estimation, however, that she had no desire to read his treacherous professions of love. She was more interested in what Charmaine intended to do.

"What new light would that be, Charmaine? Surely you don't intend to throw Mr. Waite over for Mr. Haworth."

"Why shouldn't I?" demanded Charmaine, rising to stride about the room. "Why shouldn't I prefer someone who loves me to someone who would hardly notice if I lived or died?"

"You exaggerate again."

"A little, but you understand me. Admit it: Mr. Waite does not love me."

"He does not express it as you would wish," Margaret said, choosing her words carefully.

Charmaine stamped her foot. "For pity's sake! Would you say he expressed his love as *anyone* would wish? If you were engaged to him, and he behaved thus, would you marry him?"

Would she? Margaret had a sinking suspicion she would. And yet, he did *not* behave toward her as he did to Charmaine. To her he was kind. He was intent. He sent flowers. When she unintentionally bared her heart at the supper, he gave her the chance to excuse herself.

"You would," accused Charmaine.

"At least Mr. Waite isn't a traitor to his friends," Margaret evaded her.

Charmaine dismissed this. "As I said, all's fair in love and war." She resumed her seat with an unladylike *flump*. "Even supposing Mr. Haworth were traitorous—which I do not grant you, but, even if I did, I would find it rather dashing—he has other superior qualities. He is rich. He is not bad-looking." She ticked these off on her fingers. "He has an estate of his own very near Bath, which would be more interesting than living at Chardis for the rest of my life, as I would with Dashiell because that is what Papa wants."

She waited for Margaret to comment, but Margaret said nothing.

"He hasn't that left arm, to be sure, but as Dashiell cannot dance either, there they are even." Charmaine frowned at her. "Say something, Margaret. Would you marry Mr. Haworth if he loved you dearly and the—other one—did not?"

"I don't know what to say," answered Margaret. "I think it far more important you know your own heart. All the money and homes and looks and arms in the world would not matter a jot if you didn't care for him. If you don't love him—"

"I might love him!" vowed Charmaine. "I can't help thinking of all the other things, too. Like how lovely it would be to jilt Dashiell, when he has been so heartless to me."

"Oh, Charmaine. I don't think revenge ought to play a part at all. It would be cold comfort if you had to marry someone you don't want and spend the rest of your life with him."

"Who says I don't want him?" Charmaine retorted. "I am just saying revenge would be nice. I didn't say it would be *all*."

"Do you love Mr. Haworth?" demanded Margaret again.

Charmaine squirmed. "I might. Is it so bad to think you might love someone simply because he loves you first? Especially if he is a worthy gentleman who writes letters that make your heart thrill?"

Rolling her eyes, Margaret said, "I must take that on faith."

"No, you will not take it on faith," declared Charmaine. "I will make you a believer. Here—" Scrabbling at the letter with unsteady fingers, she managed to unfold it. "He says much nonsense, of course, about my hair and my eyes and my voice and so on. I won't trouble you with that. But listen, Margaret, to this part: 'I would give you my sincere, almost painful love, which only grows, no matter whether it be fed or starved, confessed or unspoken, welcomed or rejected. I love you because I cannot help myself...'"

But Margaret was backing away, horror-struck, her hand upheld. "Stop—oh, stop."

"What is it? What is wrong with you? You are pale."

"You—say Mr. Haworth wrote you that?"

"Of course. Who else have we been talking of? What ails you, Margaret?"

"It's—too private to share with me."

"Don't be ridiculous."

"I will—never be loved like that. Therefore, I had better not hear it."

"Well, if that isn't the silliest reason I ever heard! You take all the fun out of it. And why did you ask if Mr. Haworth wrote it?" Charmaine persisted. "Do you think it unlike him?"

"I don't know him well enough to judge."

"But did you mean you thought he...read it somewhere? Or heard it, in a play? I did wonder at first, but I could not think of anything."

"No. Nothing like that."

"Then, do you think he is not sincere?"

Here Margaret felt on safer ground and she replied, "I have no doubt Mr. Haworth means what he writes. It was obvious from the first he was taken with you. It just...surprised me to hear him express it thus. It was so very...so extremely...personal."

"Yes," agreed Charmaine, reassured by her friend's earnestness. Giving her another long look, she sighed and folded up the letter, replacing it in her pocket. "Well, I won't read you anymore, since it disturbs you so, my modest mouse. But you see my dilemma. I always thought it would be delicious, to be addressed in such terms, but I discover it is more than delicious. It is *irresistible*! Why, Mr. Haworth might have *both* his arms shot off or—or—or hair and whiskers three times as red, and I think I would begin to love him all the same. That is all I wanted to say. But if I throw Dashiell over—oh! What will Papa say?"

Rising, she embraced Margaret and gave her cheek a kiss. "What a darling you are. Never mind that no one has loved you like this. Perhaps your second husband will, after the baronet has kicked the bucket."

On that incorrigible note, and to Margaret's very great relief, she took her leave.

Chapter Twenty-Eight

He that covereth a transgression seeketh love; but he that repeateth a matter separateth very friends.
—Proverbs 17:9, *The Authorized Version* (1611)

He had betrayed her.

No, that was melodramatic.

But he certainly made a fool of her. Margaret could picture it: Mr. Waite and Mr. Haworth laughing and joking together with that "soldiers' humor" which Mrs. Waite disapproved. Perhaps Mr. Waite teased Mr. Haworth for being so sentimental about Charmaine. Perhaps he said, "Speaking of sentimental, you will scarcely credit what Miss Hapgood said to me at supper the other night..." In Margaret's imagining, he could hardly repeat her words for laughing, and Mr. Haworth roared in turn and clapped him on the shoulder, congratulating him on his pitiful conquest. And then, later, when Mr. Haworth sat alone at Bradford, his mind on Charmaine, he thought, "Why not? Perhaps all girls like such effusions, such vows and hair-tearing."

How else could it have come about? How else could Mr. Haworth possibly come to repeat *word for word* what Margaret said to Mr. Waite?

She had the very small satisfaction of learning she was right. She told Mr. Waite such words could win Charmaine's heart, and so they had. But what was that tiny satisfaction, compared to the very great humiliation of having her confidences repeated, the whispers of her bared soul trumpeted to the world?

Oh, she could never meet his eyes again! Nor speak with him in her former trusting manner. If he had not so wounded her, Charmaine's news that she might prefer Mr. Haworth would have filled Margaret with sunlit hope! She would gladly have hidden from Sir Dodkins the rest of her time in Bath, if necessary, claiming illness after illness to avoid him, so that she might plot instead how to charm Mr. Waite. She would have joined the little gang of thieves in Sidney Gardens and picked pockets and cut purses until she had the fifty pounds to repay her debt, and then she would have tied the baronet and Mrs. Turner up in a boat and set them adrift until they were forced to marry each other.

But none of these outrageous schemes would be necessary, it appeared. Not only did Mr. Waite *not* like her, after all, and *not* consider her a friend (for who would treat a friend so?), he could not even be said to respect her!

She had been badly, badly fooled. And now she wanted only to return to Bramleigh to lick her wounds. To take up her duties and forget everyone she ever met in Bath.

As it was, she could only march over to the side table, yank Mr. Waite's flowers from the vase, and pitch them in the fire. She would not cry about it, she told herself. There had been too much crying already.

By the afternoon Margaret found she could no longer bear to remain within doors, nursing her unhappiness. She must get out. If she kept to the walks, she could avoid the baronet's barouche, and surely a limping Mr. Waite could be dodged, even if Margaret were pushing her mother's chair.

"Mama, it's another beautiful day. What would you say to a walk? We can return the books to Bath Street and choose new ones."

"Oh, I would rather wait for Alwyn to return. I cannot think what is taking him so long!"

"But you know how he dallies. And besides the books, I want to buy a Christmas present for little Freddy and some plums for the pudding."

The mere thought of shopping, and authorized shopping at that, overcame Mrs. Hapgood's resistance, and they were soon in Bath Street, poring over the catalogue. They had selected Mrs. Edgeworth's *Leonora* and were debating whether Alwyn would prefer Mr. Lewis's *The Bravo of Venice* or an old favorite like *The Castle of Otranto* when someone addressed them.

"Mrs. Hapgood, Miss Hapgood, good day."

Margaret stiffened. He must have entered after them—she had peered so carefully through the window and seen only the usual aged and enfeebled subscribers inside.

"Oh, Mr. Waite, how nice to see you. Do you patronize this library as well?" Mrs. Hapgood asked, when Margaret merely made her curtsey and then stared at a point beyond his shoulder.

"I do not," he admitted. His smile was tentative, but Margaret didn't see it. "I saw you crossing Stall Street and thought I would step across to say how pleased I am to see you both well again."

"Thank you," uttered Margaret, when her mother nudged her. "And please thank Mrs. Waite again for the flowers she sent."

He had a brief memory of his mother receiving a basket of oranges, reading the accompanying card, and saying, "Miss Hapgood thanks us for the flowers we sent? I wish I had been so thoughtful, but it must have been you, Dashiell!"

He bowed again. "We are so glad you enjoyed them." With the slightest emphasis on the *we*. He found his initial joy in meeting her checked by this uncharacteristic coolness. She was never cold to him. Shy sometimes, or uncertain, or troubled, but never cold.

Had he somehow offended her?

It was an easy leap to suppose the offense must be the final words he spoke, when he last saw her at the supper. His hint that any lover of hers would require no prompting to show affection. It had slipped out. Honesty, not flirtation. But she clearly disliked it, thinking it disloyal to Charmaine (fair enough). Or she disdained being courted behind her friend's back. Or both.

Before he could think how to remedy matters, she had bid him farewell and turned back to the clerk.

He was dismissed.

An hour after this shock, Margaret faced the second person she wanted to avoid. Wheeling Mrs. Hapgood through the Orange Grove toward the Terrace Walk, she saw an older couple strolling arm in arm ahead. Older people in Bath were nothing unusual, but when they passed the Lower Rooms and paused to look over the grounds, the lady turned toward the gentleman, and Margaret gasped.

"What? What is it?" asked Mrs. Hapgood, perking up and looking about.

"Nothing," hissed her daughter, turning the chair sharply to steal away down Lilliput Alley.

But it was the very suddenness of movement that made the lady glance over, and when she saw the Hapgoods, she gave a marked start, dropping the gentleman's arm. Then her companion must also turn to look, and his surprise exceeded the lady's. He flushed and made a hasty bow.

"Miss Hapgood, Mrs. Hapgood, what a pleasure to find you recovered at last," said Sir Dodkins Hargate.

"Yes, yes," replied Margaret, equally discomfited. "I see you are on foot today, sir."

"I am. Yes. On foot."

As the only composed member of the group, it was Mrs. Hapgood who said, "Margaret and I were shopping. After a week's confinement, it is delightful to be out of doors."

"Indeed, indeed," said the baronet. "Er—Mrs. Hapgood, while I know Miss Hapgood has met my neighbor at various balls and in my home, I believe you have not been introduced to Mrs. Lincoln Turner?"

The two ladies murmured greetings, smiled.

"Thank you for the basket of oranges you sent," Margaret managed, after another moment. "We were sorry we were not well enough to receive you."

If possible, he colored even more deeply. "Yes. Well. If it is agreeable to you, perhaps I might call tomorrow morning?"

Feeling as if she were signing her own death sentence, Margaret nodded once. Her eye caught Mrs. Turner's, and the trepidation in the latter's eyes did not reassure her.

"Your bonnet is very becoming, Mrs. Turner," spoke up Mrs. Hapgood again. "The blue and silver lining quite complements your eyes and hair."

"Thank you, madam. It is quite new," Mrs. Turner replied, with another look at Margaret.

Another awkward silence fell, and then the Hapgoods excused themselves, having to maintain the pretense of heading down Lilliput Alley.

"How odd!" Mrs. Hapgood said as they passed Sally Lunn's. "Sir Dodkins seemed very ill at ease. Alwyn told me he was an urbane gentleman, for all that he was blushing like a schoolboy today. And that Mrs. Turner was not much better. She has rather pretty hair, even though it is almost white." She patted the ends of her own locks, still only barely streaked with silver.

"Yes, she was looking well," Margaret answered with a rueful smile.

"We were not the only ones to think so," her mother continued, eyeing the shop windows they passed. "Oh! Do look at those gilded sconces, Margaret! Wouldn't they be just the thing for the drawing room at Bramleigh? Slow down! You didn't even look over."

"We already have sconces at Bramleigh."

"Not like those ones. Oh, very well," she sighed, settling back and clutching their purchases resignedly. "I meant to say that, before I knew that was Sir Dodkins, I thought, *those two people are standing quite close together*, and when they turned and one of them was the baronet, you could have knocked me down with a feather!"

"Why is it so surprising, Mama? They are neighbors in Dorset."

"It's so surprising because Alwyn told me the baronet was sweet on you!"

Margaret's steps faltered, but she pushed on. Thank God her uncle said no more than that! "I don't know about 'sweet on.' He had a daughter once. I think I remind him of her."

"That's not nothing, my dear. Remember how that Colonel Brandon liked Marianne Dashwood because she reminded him of the poor girl who was ruined? I wanted Marianne to marry Willoughby, but I suppose it all turned right in the end. The colonel was too old to carry her around, but at least he didn't make a habit of seducing young ladies."

"Just so," said Margaret. And then she was relieved to have her mother distracted again by the wares in a bow window.

When they returned to Henrietta Street, Alwyn met them, utterly transformed by the shaving of his moustache.

"Alwyn!" cried his sister, even rising from her chair to marvel at him. "How handsome you look! I declare—you are ten years younger."

"You don't say?" He preened before the looking glass. "Well, it never hurts to look one's best. And if I am to be surrounded by such pretty women in Bath"—here he kissed his sister and his niece on the cheek— "I must try to hold my own."

"It certainly was the longest shave," Margaret observed. "You were gone half the day."

"Was I? Well, we have been home so many days I could not resist a long walk."

"Neither could we!" exclaimed Mrs. Hapgood, although she had not walked a step. "We bought plums for a Christmas pudding and a toy for Freddie."

"Did *you* make any purchases, Uncle Alwyn?" Margaret asked, rather suspicious of his long, solitary walk.

"Oh, now," he frowned playfully at her, "have no fear, Maggie mine. I bought no more than a coffee and a bun. Perhaps two. Two coffees and two buns. Now what new books have you selected? I say we start one of them after supper."

Despite everything, Margaret slept the sleep of exhaustion and youth, waking the next morning to rain and the clinking of pattens and Tilly building up her fire.

"Hudgins asks what you say today, miss. Gentlemen callers or no gentlemen callers?"

Margaret rolled to the edge of her bed and let her head hang off. "Yes. Yes to gentlemen callers today."

"Then I'd better curl your hair," said the maid.

Precisely at eleven the barouche was heard, and Margaret fled to her chamber, calling back, "You must speak to him first, Uncle Alwyn."

"Will it be yea or nay, Maggie?" he called after her, but she didn't have an answer for him.

After five or ten minutes of staring at the smoky streets, ears strained for the murmur of voices, she was summoned below.

"Good morning, my dear Miss Hapgood," said the baronet, turning from the window. "I hope the rest of your shopping was successful yesterday."

"Yes, thank you. And you? Did you and Mrs. Turner enjoy your walk?"

He seemed prepared for this question, giving a quiet affirmative as she seated herself.

"Miss Hapgood, I will not beat about the bush. You must know why I am here today."

"Yes. You are here because you feel you must be," Margaret answered. She fixed him with imploring eyes. "Because I borrowed the fifty pounds from you." She had decided she would be as honest as she could be, and as frank, without injuring his pride. "As I explained to you, I did need the money very much, and I am so grateful to you, both for your generosity and for not telling my papa when you called at Bramleigh. I did not mean to put you in a corner, Sir Dodkins. I did not mean to prey upon your honor and noble character! That is, I did not mean to force you to offer for me, when I begged the loan from you. Please believe me when I say that! It was my stupidity and—naïveté, and you should not have to pay for my shortcomings more than you already have."

He sat back, unable to hide his surprise. "Miss Hapgood, I did not expect this."

"I am sure you did not. This is what I mean—I can't seem to understand or follow all the social niceties. But why should you have to offer for me, therefore?"

Something in his countenance softened, and he leaned forward to pat her hand. "I see. Miss Hapgood, you are a good, good girl. Thank you for telling me this. It may be unconventional, but I am not sorry to hear it."

Margaret felt the stir of hope. "You are not sorry to hear it? Oh, sir! How glad you make me. You have been so kind to me—I only want you to be utterly free to do what you would like and marry whom you choose, left to yourself."

Looking away from her, he stared at the rain-streaked windows for a moment, a rueful twist to his thin mouth. Margaret observed him closely. Did he, in spite of dancing with Mrs. Turner at the ball and walking happily with her yesterday, not care for the woman? It had only been two days, of course, since Mrs. Turner and Margaret put their plan into action, but the results already appeared so fruitful! Not only had he seemed to see Mrs. Turner for the first time as more than a drab neighbor, a piece of the furniture, but he had sought her company. If it was nothing more than his native kindness and manners, poor Mrs. Turner would be heart-stricken. Though she still might win him in time, if only he continued single.

Sir Dodkins suppressed a sigh and turned to her again. "Thank you for your generosity, my dear. But you must trust that I am here of my own free will. I have asked your father for his permission to address you, and your uncle for good measure. We may not have chosen the timing and circumstances, my dear Miss Hapgood, but I pray you will still do me the very great honor of becoming my wife."

No words came. Her breathing went shallow and all she could hear over the sound of it was the ticking of the mantel clock. How could this still be happening?

After a pause he went on. "This cannot be a surprise to you. Your father said he would write at once. Perhaps it is my clumsiness in asking. It has been long—very long—since I made such an attempt. I imagine I should give you my reasons." He gave her a questioning look, but Margaret was too occupied in trying to remain conscious to answer him. He continued. "From our earliest acquaintance I have felt a fondness for you, Miss Hapgood. You reminded me—if you will forgive me—of my beloved daughter Marcia, whom I lost a few years ago. Dear Marcia. It is something about your demeanor, the expression of your eyes. Your kindness. She was like that. I enjoyed your company—found myself seeking it. Repeatedly. And when you approached me at the card party—well—" he broke off, swallowing sharply. Then he cleared his throat. "Well—I could not rescue my Marcia from her fate, but I could rescue you."

"Ah," breathed Margaret, fighting a lump in her own throat. She thought, one day, when all this was ancient history, she would tell

Charmaine she had been right after all. Sir Dodkins *did* see her in a daughterly light.

Not that it mattered.

"Sir—you did rescue me from the debt," Margaret assured him, "and, again, I thank you. And I thank you for the honor you do me. Believe me when I say it *is* an honor to receive your addresses. But please, *please*, do not sacrifice yourself and marry me against your wishes."

Another hesitation. Then: "It is not against my wishes, Miss Hapgood."

"But you don't love me!" cried Margaret, desperate. "Not as a husband should love a wife! Not as a wife would wish to be loved. You are being honorable. Which is not nothing, but honor is not love."

"We will, I trust, come to love each other."

She heard the decision in his voice and knew he had wrestled and made up his mind. If she could not convince him otherwise, they were lost. That meant the only two plays left to her were the same she had used on Mrs. Turner.

She sighed, but it must be risked.

"It is not me you love," Margaret said again, rising to gather her courage. "I think you might prefer Mrs. Turner."

The baronet had been rising to his own feet in politeness, but here he nearly tumbled back down. "Mrs. Turner?" he gasped.

"I am sorry to be so bald about it, but I know you and she are good friends. Old friends. I would hate to come between you."

"Miss Hapgood, Anna and I are indeed old friends. So much so that, after we encountered you and your mother in the Terrace Walk, I told her of our situation. I explained my obligation to you, how I had given you to understand that I would offer, and how I had spoken to your family. She agreed that it would go against my character to shirk the consequences of my actions."

Margaret stared, fighting an urge to slap the mantel and stamp her foot in a most Squire-Hapgood-like (and probably un-Marcia-like) fashion. Did he mean to say that, after she tutored Mrs. Turner in what to wear to the ball, how to dress her hair more becomingly, and even what she might declare in a little note to Sir Dodkins, that woman repaid her efforts by *agreeing* that he should propose to Margaret? What was to be done with such people?

"Do you love Mrs. Turner?" she demanded, abandoning subtlety in her frustration.

He flushed a mottled scarlet. "Miss Hapgood, I am trying to tell you that whatever past relationship I had with Mrs. Turner is neither here nor there. I am determined to make you a good husband, if you will have me—"

"I'm afraid I can't have you," Margaret interrupted. Clearly, the last card must be played. At this point she might as well have hand-bills posted throughout Bath! "I am sorry to say that, while I am grateful to you and honored by your proposal—I cannot accept it, sir. In fact, I cannot accept any gentleman because I—have already given my heart to someone else."

"Someone else?" he echoed, dumbfounded.

"Yes," said Margaret. "This is why it was absolutely unpardonable of me to ask you for money and make you feel you must rescue me. I can only say again that I acted in utter ignorance of what it would entail. But, that being said, you must let *me* bear the consequences. It is no reflection on you, Sir Dodkins. None at all. I am sure I would be tempted to accept you, were I not already—attached to this other person."

"But who is this person, whom you could neither ask for help nor hope to marry?"

"Nobody. Please do not ask. He doesn't know about it, and he is already engaged to another."

"Is it your friend Mr. Waite, then, the man engaged to Miss Blakely?"

Margaret groaned, sinking back onto the settee and covering her eyes. Was it so obvious? Never mind posting handbills—everyone (including the man himself) already seemed to know her most deathly secret!

"Forgive me," he said at once. "That was a most presumptuous question."

"It is all right," she mumbled. "Only please do not mention it again."

She heard him pace back and forth for a time, but at last he resumed his seat.

"Miss Hapgood, of course I will not press you to marry me when your heart is elsewhere, but I grieve to think you might never know happiness."

"Oh, I will be fine, after a time," she said contrarily, raising her head. "Even if he were free, I—will probably never marry." That is, even if he were free, she doubted he would ever return her feelings, given that he had made fun of her to Mr. Haworth. "I will go home to Bramleigh and manage things and take care of my parents."

"Yes. Your father said you excelled at that."

"Moreover, I will repay you, eventually," Margaret assured him. She reached for his hand then. "I can promise you that. And I will never forget your goodness."

He covered her hand with his own. "You may call upon me at any time."

They stood, Margaret wanting to hug him with relief. Possibly something similar occurred to her erstwhile suitor, for Sir Dodkins said, "My dear, now that we understand each other, I wonder if we might still be friends?" A smile curved his lips, and Margaret thought it really became him. "That is, would you greatly object to favoring Mrs. Turner and me with your continuing company?"

"Sir Dodkins, it would be a pleasure," Margaret smiled back. The role of surrogate daughter had never appeared more welcome. "In fact, my family would be most honored if you both would join us for a little Christmas dinner. We are going to have roast pork and plum pudding."

He raised her hand to his lips. "I may overreach in answering for Mrs. Turner, but I am sure we would be delighted. And may we invite you all in turn to breakfast with us tomorrow in Sydney Gardens?"

"Oh, we would love that!" Margaret beamed. "Or at least Uncle Alwyn and I would, and my mother, if she is well enough."

"We will see you there, then, Miss Hapgood."

"Yes. And, please, Sir Dodkins, won't you call me Margaret?"

CHAPTER TWENTY-NINE

A faint sun emerged for their breakfast with the baronet and Mrs. Turner the following day, and Mrs. Hapgood agreed to join them.

"I told you there was something between Sir Dodkins and that woman," Mrs. Hapgood said as they made their way down Pulteney Street, "whatever Alwyn said about the baronet and you."

"Yes. But things are far better this way."

It was not hard to persuade Mrs. Hapgood, but Margaret had less success composing a letter Edie could read to the squire, because he would surely explode after the first sentence and not stay to hear the reasons for her refusal. If only there were good news of Alwyn's progress to soften the blow! But there was nothing. (She put the letter aside for later.)

Mrs. Turner stepped forward first, as they emerged into the Gardens, her gloved hands outstretched to take Margaret's. "Sir Dodkins and I have claimed the best table for our breakfast. It is fully in the sun, and we might even be warm, once we have a little tea and coffee inside us." In Margaret's ear she whispered, "My dearest girl, he has told me how things stand. You brave, honest child!"

They were a merry party. Alwyn at his most charming, Mrs. Hapgood having nothing to complain of, and the baronet and Mrs. Turner almost competing to draw Margaret out and make much of her. The music played; the food and drink were the better for being provided by their hosts; and it was great fun to watch people from the shelter and comfort of their sunlit nook.

Margaret nearly forgot her other troubles in her enjoyment, until she heard her mother say, "Oh, do look. There are the Waites and the Blakelys! Yoo hoo! Good morning to you. We are just finishing our breakfast."

Mrs. Turner drew a sharp breath, and she and Sir Dodkins exchanged concerned glances, which made Margaret want to crawl under the table. Instead, she must stand to greet the newcomers, her eyes carefully avoiding Mr. Waite, who stood back, leaning upon his cane. Charmaine skimmed to Margaret's side, taking her by the elbow. "Sir Dodkins and Mrs. Turner, so lovely to see you, but you must not think to monopolize Margaret," she teased. "If you are indeed finished, won't you walk with us?"

Sir Dodkins gave a little bow and turned to the young lady in question. "Well, Margaret? You will decide. What would you like to do?"

"Oh. I suppose walking would be nice if you all like," Margaret answered, trying unobtrusively to fling off Charmaine, for when Sir Dodkins called Margaret by her Christian name, Charmaine gave her a pinch.

With some fussing and arranging, the enlarged party set out down the wide main pathway. Margaret began by wheeling her mother's chair, but when the baronet relieved her of her duties, Charmaine took hold again, pulling on her to draw her out of earshot.

"How perfectly convenient," Charmaine hissed, striking onto a side path and taking Margaret with her. Mrs. Blakely called after them to wait, but her daughter pretended not to hear. "They are all so very slow and infirm that I will have a good minute with you to myself. Tell me at once: are you and the baronet engaged yet?"

"No—he—"

"Well, you will be very shortly, if he already calls you 'Margaret,'" Charmaine interrupted. "You will still write to me, will you not, when you are lofty Margaret Hargaret?"

"Charmaine, I will never—"

"Watch out, here they come. No—don't look back at Mama. Everyone is in a black mood because of Dashiell relenting."

"What do you mean 'relenting'?"

Charmaine stared and actually halted. "Don't tell me you don't know!"

"Know what?" Margaret cried.

"Shhhh! Come along." She tugged on her again. "Know that Dashiell gave Aunt Eliza permission to marry your shiftless uncle."

Now it was Margaret who stopped as if turned to stone. "He *has*?"

"Yes, yes! Come on. He has, and the banns will be read in St. Swithin's this Sunday, if nothing can prevent it. We are in uproar! Mama is furious and not speaking to Dashiell at all and just barely to Aunt Eliza, and she has written Papa, and he is about to descend on us like a vengeance!"

Margaret could not at first spare any concern for the inhabitants of 4 Princes Street; her thoughts were all for those of 12 Henrietta Street. Uncle Alwyn to marry Mrs. Waite after all? With the *blessing* of her son? How could it be possible? And why had Alwyn not told them?

Craning her neck to look behind her as Charmaine hustled her onward, her gaze caught that of Mr. Waite. In fact, he was watching them rather intently and made no pretense of looking away. She felt that familiar, treacherous flutter in her midsection, but she ignored it and turned away.

"Your papa will try to prevent the marriage?" she asked.

"Of course he will. He will come and rate Dashiell and Aunt Eliza soundly and make himself generally disagreeable, and I doubt I will be allowed to see any of you again. He will drag me and Mama back to Chardis, and Aunt Eliza, if he can prevail with her. I cannot bear it! I cannot! These past several weeks have been so very delightful, and I counted on at least a few more."

But Margaret could not pay Charmaine's fate the attention it deserved. "Charmaine, do you think your father will succeed in breaking up my uncle's engagement?"

Charmaine frowned at her, and her green eyes shot sparks. "Well, what if he does? Margaret, I have been very clear with you that my family unanimously disapproves and opposes the match. I don't know what has got into Dashiell that he should change his mind and bring all this down upon our heads, but I am very displeased! I am not speaking to him and have been careful to take up a book or sewing whenever he enters the room. But never mind all that—have you nothing to say about never seeing me again?"

"I should be very sorry for it," Margaret amended hastily. "Very sorry indeed. I hope it will not come to that."

"Well, it will," Charmaine answered with grim certainty. "But never fear—we can write to each other. I rather like secret correspondences."

Secret correspondences! Margaret had been so caught up in the other revelations that she had forgotten to ask if Charmaine answered Mr. Haworth's letter. But before she could form the question, Mrs. Blakely called to them: "Charmaine! Stop! Have you forgotten our appointment at the milliner's? We had better head back now, and, Eliza, I do urge you to accompany us. There was a cap in particular I wanted to show you."

Charmaine heaved a sigh. "You see how it is?" she whispered. "The walls are closing in." Grimacing, she took Margaret by the hand and returned to the others.

"We are sorry to excuse ourselves so abruptly," Mrs. Waite was saying. "The milliner is in Pulteney Street, so we thought we would stroll in the Gardens beforehand, but we hope to see you again soon."

"Always a pleasure," said Alwyn with a bow. He and Mrs. Waite just glanced at each other, but now that Margaret knew their secret, it seemed the softness in their look must be patent to all. "And you, Mr. Waite?" added Alwyn. "Do you accompany the ladies?"

"I had better," Mr. Waite replied, also throwing a look at his mother.

Margaret knew what it meant: he would not abandon her to be run down by her disapproving relations. Good and loyal son! But if he was a good and loyal son, why had he decided to let her marry someone his family (and he, presumably) thought disreputable? And if he was a good and loyal son, how could he not then be a good and loyal person? How could the same man be both kind and unkind?

"Let us go, then," insisted Mrs. Blakely. "I detest being late." She hooked one arm through her daughter's and the other through her sister-in-law's and hauled them away as if they were under arrest.

"Dashiell will not be able to keep up," protested Mrs. Waite.

"I will be there," he said to their retreating backs. He made to follow, and Margaret felt his gaze touch on her again. Not that she was looking at him. She was fiddling with her glove, pretending great interest in it.

"Shall we go as far the labyrinth?" asked Sir Dodkins. "Margaret found her way through, have you not, my dear?"

"I have," she murmured. Mr. Waite was prying a pebble from his boot heel.

Her elders discussed whether it would be too cold in the hedged maze, and if they ought to explore a grotto or the arbors instead. In the distance, the band on their balcony resumed playing, the scrape of violins just audible. A cold breeze whipped Margaret's cloak against her ankles.

Why was he dawdling? Why didn't he just go?

If they were still friends, she would have asked him why he changed his mind about Alwyn. But they were not still friends. She felt his gaze again but kept her eyes lowered.

Finally, there was a crunch of gravel, and Mr. Waite limped away.

"Margaret will cast the deciding vote," Mrs. Turner was saying. "Shall it be the grotto, or have you had enough for one morning? You are looking somewhat peaked."

"Perhaps the grotto and then home to rest," answered Margaret, not caring. She only knew they could not head home now, or they would overtake Mr. Waite again.

Thus another half hour was consumed in exploring the grotto before they could thank them again for breakfast and prepare to go.

"We will see you again for Christmas dinner I hear," Mrs. Turner smiled, "if not at church. Where will you attend service?"

"Laura Chapel. And you?"

"Sir Dodkins and I will attend St. Swithin's in the upper town. It is very near the Paragon, where I live."

Margaret favored Alwyn with a speaking look. "Ah, yes. St. Swithin's. I myself have never been there, but perhaps one day."

She waited for Sir Dodkins and Mrs. Turner to be out of earshot before turning on him. "Uncle Alwyn, I had but a moment with Charmaine, but she had very interesting news."

He grinned at her. "Did she? What news was that?"

"You know very well what news! Why did you not tell us that you and Mrs. Waite are engaged?"

"Engaged?" echoed Mrs. Hapgood, gawping at him.

"Is that where you were, when you were gone so long, getting your moustache shaved?" Margaret demanded.

"Now, now," he laughed, releasing the chair to hold up both hands in defense. "If I did not tell you, it is because she had not yet told her own family. That is, apart from Mr. Waite, who knew, of course."

"What can you possibly mean? Charmaine said something about Mr. Waite 'relenting' and giving his permission, though the rest of the family still opposes the match. How did this come about?"

Another breeze whipped her cloak and Mrs. Hapgood's shawls, and Alwyn resumed pushing the chair. "Very well, since the cat is out of the bag, it seems, I will reveal all. You see, I had no idea myself that my luck was going to change, which just goes to show you, Maggie, that I was right when I told you something always turns up."

"*Please*, Uncle Alwyn," she begged, "tell your story. I am eaten up with impatience."

After a few more teasing remarks, he at last began. "It was the night of the last ball, you know. You refused to come, Mags, because you were still afraid Sir D would corner you and force a promise from you. Well, I no sooner arrived, than Mr. Waite—I suppose I may call him Dashiell now, as he is to be my stepson—ludicrous idea—the man looks at one as if he would as soon shoot you as greet you—" ("Uncle, *please!*" from Margaret.) "—So, *Dashiell* approaches and asks to speak with me and takes me aside to the card room. We sit at a table, and he rudely runs off a few other people who think they might join us for a hand. He even looks thunderous at Mr. King, who put his tail right between his legs and fled—All right, all right, Maggie, no need to poke me! I say, 'To what do I owe the honor of this private audience?' and he says, 'Sir, it has not escaped my observation that you have feelings for my mother.' And I say, 'That I do; I won't deny it.'

"'May I ask what your intentions are toward her?' he asks.

"'They are nil,' I say, 'because I am not permitted to have any.'

"'And if you were permitted?' He leans toward me with those gunpowder eyes."

("Really, Alwyn, you ought to write novels!" exclaimed his sister, only to be shushed by her daughter.)

"'Then my intentions would be and have always been entirely honest,' I say. 'I care very much for your mother and prize her happiness, but she will not make a peep without your say-so.'

"He thinks a minute, and then he says, 'Mr. Arbuthnot, am I wrong in supposing you have no fortune of your own?' Just as cool as you please, as if he had any right to ask, but as I said there's something implacable about the fellow, and everyone must yield to him willy-nilly, for all that Margaret is so fond of him."

"Uncle!" she screeched, horrified. They were to Laura Place by this point, and she gave him a push to hurry him.

"I don't see the harm," her mother said far too loudly. "He is very handsome. When you read that book to us, I always imagined him as Mr. Willoughby and Sir Dodkins as Colonel Brandon. It is too bad he is to marry Miss Blakely, not that she isn't a pretty thing."

"Yes, Mama. Mr. Waite is indeed handsome, and I am quite aware nothing can come of it." She knew it was easier to agree than to protest. "Please go on, Uncle Alwyn."

Being so near home, however, he put her off. And then there was all the business of getting the chair back inside, asking Hudgins to build up the fire in the drawing room, resolving some question of the Christmas menu with Flint, and ensuring Mrs. Hapgood was comfortable. Margaret simmered with impatience. But at last the door shut behind the footman and Alwyn picked up his story again.

"As I was saying, he asked me what fortune I had, cool as you please, so I answered, cool as you please, that I had none to speak of, only a small income from my late mother and a stipend from my brother-in-law. 'My fortune,' I said, 'must lie rather in my ancient family name and excellent connections, as well as my dedication to the happiness of my beloved.'

"For the first time, he looks like he isn't sure what to say next, and then he says, 'Yes—as for these excellent connections, I suppose you mean your Hapgood relations?' I thought he was going to beleaguer me about Alice dressing as a boy or Elfie eloping or your papa's cousin compromising that governess—all quite old scandals, you know, and I meant to tell him life is too short to mount so many dead horses, but he didn't mention any of those things. He said, 'Do you see them often?'"

"Perhaps, knowing about the scandals, as he already must, he simply wanted to know how much his mother would be burdened by these...irregular connections," Margaret suggested.

Alwyn shrugged. "It may be. I told him I was at Bramleigh perhaps four weeks of every year and saw Alice and Elfie in Buckinghamshire or in town perhaps twice a year. And he frowns and rubs his chin and says, 'You still see the older sisters, though they are married?'"

"Such a good uncle," murmured Mrs. Hapgood.

Margaret fired up, as she had with Charmaine. "And why shouldn't you? Did you tell him Elfie and Alice are quite respectable and that Joseph is a clergyman and Frederick the heir to both his father and his baronet uncle?"

"Of course I began all that, Mags. What do you take me for? The man may be intimidating, but I am perfectly capable of defending myself. Besides, I thought that, once he was done with your sisters, he would begin on all my past peccadilloes, and what a bore that would be! But it all turned out to be a lot of worry for nothing because I no sooner launched into all that business than he sat back and said, 'Mr. Arbuthnot, you may pay your addresses to my mother, if you wish. I only ask that you wait until tomorrow, that I may speak with her first.'"

"But *why*?" Margaret wondered. "Why do you think he changed his mind?"

"Isn't it obvious?" Mrs. Hapgood beamed. "Once he got to know Alwyn, my brother's kindness and charm and gentility won him over, and he knew he shouldn't have listened to gossip when his mother's happiness was at stake."

Margaret seriously doubted this, but she would not waste breath debating.

"I don't know, frankly," Alwyn replied, putting his hand to his upper lip, only to realize he no longer had a moustache to rub. "I asked Eliza—when I *asked*, you know, and when she said yes, to my everlasting joy—and she said much what you did, Augusta. But I must say, he does not seem won over by my virtues; nor does it appear he consulted his relations on the matter."

"Charmaine says the Blakelys are up in arms," Margaret put in. "And her papa will be arriving shortly, presumably to knock heads together."

"Indeed?" Alwyn's brow furrowed. "Well, the man can hardly object when the banns are read. Eliza is certainly of age, and he has no legal power over her. And surely she will persevere if she has her son's support."

"But suppose this Matthew Blakely wears down Mr. Waite until he retracts his consent?"

"Hmm...yes. I see what you mean." He tapped his fingers on the fireplace mantel. "I had better send her a note. See how firmly she is set on our union. Blakely will not be here terribly soon, surely. Eliza says Chardis is near the Sussex border, somewhere outside Petersford. No direct coach from there. The soonest he could arrive would be two days from now, if he set off the instant he heard from his wife."

"Two days from now will be Christmas, Uncle."

"Right. Right you are. Well, my girls, I am afraid I will not be joining you in Laura Chapel, then. I had better attend St. Swithin's that day and make sure nothing happens to my bride."

Mrs. Hapgood protested this change in plans, but he strode over to kiss her cheek. "I'll be back for the supper, Augusta, unless the man runs me through with his sword. We must make some little sacrifices here and there because, don't you see, if we get around this Matthew Blakely, we have every chance to capture the prize for which we came to Bath—my wealthy and beautiful bride!"

CHAPTER THIRTY

**Promises and Pye-Crusts, they say,
are made to be broken.
—Swift, *A Treatise on Polite Conversation* (1738)**

"Welcome, Sir Dodkins, Mrs. Turner," Margaret greeted them warmly. "Happy Christmas! Did my uncle not return with you in the barouche?"

Mrs. Turner embraced her and curtseyed to Mrs. Hapgood before replying. "My dear, we intended to invite him—it being so cold and foggy out—but we thought he must have attended Laura Chapel after all."

"Alwyn was not at St. Swithin's?" Mrs. Hapgood asked, alarmed.

"He was not, madam," answered Sir Dodkins.

"But he said he would attend there," she insisted, as if this would alter matters.

"To meet Mrs. Waite," Margaret explained.

The baronet and Mrs. Turner looked at each other, and he deferred to her. "My dear Hapgoods, I am afraid we did not see Mrs. Waite there either. In fact, we did not see any of the Waites or Blakelys."

"How odd," said Margaret. "Perhaps they chose to remain home and wait for Mr. Matthew Blakely's arrival." She gave a little shrug. "I am sure there is some ready explanation. My uncle is not always as particular about details as one would like. He can tell us what happened when he returns."

Mrs. Hapgood knew this to be true about Alwyn, and for another half hour she lay aside her concern and made conversation with their guests. But when supper was announced and he still had not appeared, her agitation burst out anew.

"Oh, Sir Dodkins, where can he be? Do you suppose he was waylaid by thieves? It is so dark and smoky out."

The baronet was all consideration. "Madam, I see you will not be easy until he returns. Shall I call my carriage, and Mrs. Turner and I go in search?"

"We could not ask that of you," fretted Margaret. "What about supper? You will be hungry."

"You will not be easy unless we go," pointed out Mrs. Turner kindly. "We will gulp down a little tea to tide us over and then return triumphantly with your uncle to feast." Nor would she hear of Margaret accompanying them. "My dear, who will keep your mother calm, if you do not stay?"

Mrs. Hapgood thought it only natural that their guests be as anxious for Alwyn as she was, but Margaret saw them to the door with many apologies and hot bricks to keep them warm.

The streets were quiet and empty. Sir Dodkins had attached bells to his horses' bridles, however, and Margaret could hear the festive jingling long after the driver turned them toward Laura Place and the bridge.

An hour passed, bringing a wave of tears and faints and vapors from Mrs. Hapgood, and Margaret had all she could do to get her mother upstairs to bed with Tilly's assistance. Then she was left to pace the drawing room while the roast pork dried out and the plum pudding congealed. Her own worry alternated with annoyance, then grew into anger, before revolving once more to fear.

At last, at last, she heard the sound of a carriage drawing up outside, and not stopping to wonder why she did not hear bells, Margaret flew to the door to throw it open.

It was not the baronet's barouche, however, but a landau, and it was not Sir Dodkins and Mrs. Turner who descended from it, but rather Mr. Waite, Mrs. Blakely, and another man Margaret could only suppose was Mr. Matthew Blakely. He had dark hair and green eyes like his daughter, and one could see he must have been quite handsome in his youth.

Margaret stared at these unexpected apparitions and didn't hear a word of Mr. Waite's introductions, only making an automatic curtsey and stepping back dumbly to allow them entrance.

"You cannot be surprised to see us, Miss Hapgood," said Mrs. Blakely in a cool voice, after Hudgins saw to their wrappings and they were seated in the drawing room.

It seemed rude to begin by contradicting her, so Margaret made a noncommittal sound in her throat.

"Where is your mother?" was Mrs. Blakely's next question.

"She has retired," Margaret murmured. "She was not feeling well. Have you—had a happy Christmas?"

Mr. Blakely threw her a sharp look. "Are you making fun of us, young lady?"

"What? No!" Margaret exclaimed, astonished. Helplessly she looked to Mr. Waite for assistance. What was happening here?

To her further amazement, she found him regarding her with some complacence. "Aunt. Uncle. I think it pretty clear Miss Hapgood has no idea why we've come. I said she would not."

Mrs. Blakely's mouth disappeared in a thin line, and she looked to her husband.

"Come now, young lady," said Mr. Blakely.

"Come now, what, sir?" demanded Margaret, feeling her temper rise. "Mr. Waite is correct. I cannot guess the reason for your visit. Which comes at an unusual time. We might even now have been in the middle of our supper with guests."

"And yet you are not," Mrs. Blakely observed.

There she had her off balance, and Margaret could only stammer, "Oh—but—we would be, except—"

"Except your uncle is missing."

"Oh! How did you know? Sir Dodkins and Mrs. Turner are even now driving through town, looking for him."

"They won't find him in town," growled Mr. Blakely. "They would do better to follow the Bath Road. They are likely halfway to London already."

Margaret merely blinked at him. "I don't understand."

Mr. Waite's eyes gleamed. "We believe my mother and your uncle chose not to wait for the banns to be read, Miss Hapgood. In brief, they have eloped. The post coach will have them at the White Horse in Fetter Lane by the early hours of the morning, and from there they may run for Scotland or marry at their leisure."

If Margaret were not already seated, this news would have chopped her legs from beneath her. "But—why?"

Even as the words escaped her, she knew the answer. She was *looking at* the answer. Alwyn and Mrs. Waite had not wanted to run the risk of their match being thwarted by Matthew Blakely's arrival. They made their plans the day before, when Alwyn sent Mrs. Waite his note. There had been several notes and replies altogether, and this was the result!

"Precisely," said Mr. Waite, who had followed the shifting thoughts and realizations on her face.

"I knew nothing of this," she breathed. "But why are you here? Do you hope to catch them?"

Matthew Blakely waved his hand in dismissal, as if his sister's elopement were a fly buzzing around his luncheon. "If Eliza has lost her senses, she has lost her senses. Nothing can be done for it now."

"Though you did assure me she promised not to elope," Mrs. Blakely accused her nephew.

"And so she did," he agreed in his mildest tone. "But, dear Aunt Celia, I'm afraid I absolved her of that promise."

Both Mr. and Mrs. Blakely were unable to repress a start on hearing this, and Margaret suspected that, if she herself were not present, they would have had much to say about it. But she *was* present, and they must perforce content themselves with glaring at their unaccountable nephew.

"Miss Hapgood," resumed Mr. Blakely, after another pause, "as I was saying, we are *not* here to discover my wayward sister or your uncle. We are here to seek out my daughter."

"Charmaine? Whatever can you mean?"

Mrs. Blakely sniffed. "Miss Hapgood, please do not play the innocent."

"I beg your pardon!"

"This cannot be a surprise to you," Mrs. Blakely insisted. "You know where she has gone."

"If Charmaine is not in Princes Street with her family, I have no idea where else she may be," declared Margaret. But, again, just as she spoke, a disturbing possibility streaked into her head.

She could not have. She *would* not have.

But, being Charmaine, she very well may have.

The sudden color which accompanied this thought did not go unnoticed by her visitors, and Mrs. Blakely sprang from her seat. For an instant, Margaret thought the woman would lunge at her, and Mr. Blakely and Mr. Waite must have thought the same thing, for suddenly all of them were on their feet, Mr. Blakely grasping his wife's arm and Mr. Waite standing, arm outstretched protectively, before where Margaret shrank back in her chair.

"Take this!" shrieked Mrs. Blakely, pulling something from her pocket and flinging it at Margaret. "I got it off her worthless maid, whom we have dismissed! And I would not have brought it to you, you low, conniving girl, but Dashiell insisted."

"Madam," Mr. Waite's voice was sharp. "Remember yourself."

It was a folded note addressed to "M.H." With shaking fingers, Margaret retrieved it and removed closer to the fire, where the sconces flanking the mantel gave stronger light and where she could turn her back on the Blakelys. Lifting the seal, she hardly knew if hope or dread weighed heavier on her heart.

Dearest of Margarets—

By the time you read this, I will be far away, beyond the reach of Papa's influence or that cursed engagement which has so long confined me to loveless and lifeless tedium. You, who know all, must surely have suspected what measures I would take to be free!

I have gone to join the one who loves me passionately, and I trust you will appreciate the irony, remembering how I criticized your sister for eloping and am now eloping myself. May I one day hope to regain respectability as you have so often assured me she has. Ha ha!

You will frown because I did not tell you beforehand, and indeed I meant to in Sydney Gardens, only Mama pulled me away before I could. And now at least you may proclaim your entire innocence in the matter, though you are a clever girl and may have suspected I would take such a step after you read my darling's letter.

May we meet again soon, dearest Margaret, Lady Hargaret. (For surely the baronet has proposed by now.) I am sure Mama and Papa will be angry longer than Dashiell (who might possibly not mind at all), but as I am their only daughter, I trust they will forgive in time. Not that it matters. Charles and I will have you and Sir Ods Bodkins to Bradford in the New Year.

Happy Christmas and farewell for now.

Your devoted friend, the soon-to-be
Charmaine Haworth

"What does she say?" demanded Mrs. Blakely, when Margaret at last looked up. "Where has she gone?"

Margaret bit her lip, but it was Mr. Waite's eyes she sought first. "I'm afraid—she has—eloped. With Mr. Haworth."

In a creditable imitation of Mrs. Hapgood, Mrs. Blakely shrieked and flung a hand to her forehead, falling back against her husband.

He merely deposited her on the settee, however, to stalk over to Margaret.

"May I see that note?" he asked, extending a peremptory hand.

Margaret clutched it to herself. "It is addressed to me, sir. I had rather not share it."

"Then I assume it contains something incriminating."

"I object to that word, Mr. Blakely. I have committed no crime."

Matthew Blakely snapped his fingers with impatience. "Come now. I did not mean to imply you committed a crime. Though, if you will not show me the note, how can I help but think you have been her confidante—perhaps even her advisor—in this rash action? If she has indeed eloped with this Haworth person, she has broken solemn promises made to her mother and me, as well as to her cousin."

Again Margaret shook her head, holding the note behind her. "I did not advise her to take this step, sir. Nor did she consult me." Her voice only shook a little. She swallowed. "But if anyone should be angry, it is Mr. Waite here, who has the greatest right, he being the most wronged."

"And yet how calmly he takes it all!" Mrs. Blakely scolded. "Dashiell, if you had shown my girl greater affection, this would never have happened! She would never have been tempted by this—this one-armed man!"

"It is not Mr. Waite's fault Charmaine preferred Mr. Haworth!" Margaret rushed to defend him, forgetting that she had herself faulted Mr. Waite for the same reason. "He cannot help that he does not feel things strongly," she explained, "and that Charmaine chose someone who did. It is simply a case of mismatch. No one is to blame. Except perhaps Mr. Haworth," she added, "who I think ought not to have wooed her, when she was already engaged." She then shook her head at Mrs. Blakely reproachfully. "But even so, if they are soon to be married, you will have to forgive Mr. Haworth for that, just as you will have to forgive him for losing an arm."

Mrs. Blakely only burst into noisy tears, burying her face in the furniture and hurling epithets at Margaret and the world in general that Margaret affected not to hear. Mr. Blakely huffed out a sigh and then plopped down beside his wife to pat her shoulder absently. "There, there, Celia. It is terrible, but, at this stage, we could hardly fetch her back without greater scandal."

Margaret found Mr. Waite next to her. "Might I read the note?" he asked *sotto voce*.

She hesitated, reviewing the contents in her memory. He would find some insults to himself, some tasteless jokes at Margaret's and Sir Dodkins' expense, and—and he would learn that Margaret had read Mr. Haworth's letter.

Well, what of it? Charmaine did not say what her lover's letter contained, so Mr. Waite would still be ignorant of his offense against her.

"I have told you the essence of it," she whispered.

"She was more courteous to you than to me," he answered. "I was left entirely in the dark."

With another glance at Charmaine's distressed parents, Margaret surrendered it.

He read it quickly, and not by the twitch of a muscle did she detect any emotion one might expect. There was no rage, no jealousy, no heartbreak, no desperation.

It was exactly as she told his family: he did not feel things strongly.

"Thank you." He returned it to her, making no comment on its contents. "Would you be so kind as to call your footman back, Miss Hapgood?" Then he crossed to his aunt and uncle and urged them to command themselves. "We should not trespass on Miss Hapgood's patience any longer. There is no more to be learned here. You must return to Princes Street and await further news."

The Blakelys donned their outer garments once more and prepared to depart, Mrs. Blakely still leaning upon her husband and moaning, but Mr. Waite appeared inclined to wait them out.

"Won't you be joining them in the carriage?" whispered Margaret.

"It's a lovely evening for a stroll," he said, even as Hudgins opened the door on the chill and fog.

Shivering, and not only from cold, Margaret returned to the drawing room, her empty stomach giving a growl of protest. He followed after, standing at the other end of the mantel where Margaret warmed herself.

"I am sorry for that," he said after a moment. "For their rudeness and suspicion."

She gathered her shawl more closely. What did she care for the Blakelys' rudeness? And why should he apologize for it? Out loud she only said, "I understand they are upset."

"And I am not, of course," he went on lightly, "because, as you remarked, I do not feel things strongly."

There was a note of provocation in his voice, but this was dangerous ground, and she hastened to change the subject. "While I have this opportunity, Mr. Waite, I do wonder—why did you change your mind and tell Mrs. Waite she might marry my uncle?"

His eyes flicked to her face an instant and then away. "Perhaps I realized they care for each other and will be happier together."

"Yes," she agreed, "but what of your—original objections? Uncle Alwyn still does not have any money, nor a great deal of money sense, I am sorry to say—"

"The point is moot now, Miss Hapgood. Are you saying *you* have changed your mind?"

"No. Of course not." He had not answered her question, she noticed. "I fear the rest of your family is not very happy with you."

"I suspect not. But Charmaine's elopement provides plenty of distraction."

Margaret shook her head. Even if he did not love Charmaine, how *could* he be so calm about it? And why did he linger now?

Had she given him any encouragement at all, all would have been made plain. It was hope that held him there—Charmaine was gone—would her coolness toward him remain?

It was Charmaine's farewell note that did it. It meant she *knew*. If Miss Hapgood had read Haworth's letter, then she knew that Dashiell remembered her words from the supper party. Because Haworth would have used them. He said he would. Did it make no difference, then? None at all?

He moved toward her, prepared to say and do God-knew-what, when the door flung open and the footman coughed. "Miss Hapgood, will Sir Dodkins return soon? Flint asks if she should warm the food again."

"Yes, please, Hudgins." She roused herself and raised her eyes to Mr. Waite's. "Sir Dodkins and Mrs. Turner were kind enough to go in search of my uncle," she explained, "but we know they will not find him."

"No, they will not," he muttered, straightening, thinking that Miss Hapgood might never see that confounded Sir Dodkins again either, if Dashiell saw him first.

All right, then, he would not speak tonight. But he would have his say, however she might feel toward him and whoever she might already be engaged to.

At the door, her arms about herself for warmth, she uttered impulsively: "I wonder if I will ever see you again."

The hint of a grin came and went. "Oh, that you may depend on."

"I may?"

The cold wind lifted and tossed the ends of his greatcoat. "Of course," he answered, starting down the steps. "For we are related now. Or will be, in a matter of days."

Chapter Thirty-One

The greatest wonder lasteth but nyne dayes.
—John Lyly, *Euphues* (1578)

The double elopement was the talk of Bath.

The servants must have leaked the scandal, Margaret decided, for all other parties had a vested interest in keeping things quiet. She herself had only spoken to Sir Dodkins and Mrs. Turner, who returned later that Christmas evening, and they assured her it would go no further.

At first Margaret was unaware of the furor, occupied as she was in tending to her mother, who alternated between transports of joy and grief that her remaining brother was no longer at her side. There was also the tentatively triumphant letter to write to her family, now that she could counterbalance the news of refusing Sir Dodkins. She hoped nothing happened to prevent the marriage. Suppose Alwyn told Mrs. Waite of the fifty-pound debt, and she changed her mind? But she was compromised now and must marry him. But what if Mr. Waite called Alwyn out and shot him, or Alwyn shot Mr. Waite?

She posted the letter nevertheless, and, as the days passed and she heard no dreadful news from either her uncle or from Princes Street, she began to hope all might truly be well.

Without Alwyn's chaperonage, balls were out of the question, and Margaret could not convince her mother to go for a walk in the wet and foggy weather, but at last the sun reappeared, and Sir Dodkins and Mrs. Turner persuaded them to drive to Prior Park.

"Forgive my vulgar curiosity, Margaret," Mrs. Turner said, as the barouche climbed Ralph Allen's road, "but have you heard from either your uncle or Miss Blakely?"

"Neither. We remain in suspense," she confessed. "I hoped you might have news for me, if you saw the Blakelys or Mr. Waite around town."

"I did see Mr. Waite outside the King's Bath yesterday morning," Sir Dodkins put in, "but when I asked after his family's health, he said he had yet to hear from his mother and that he knew nothing of his aunt and uncle's health because they had returned home to Hampshire."

"You mean to say that poor man is all alone in that house?" asked Mrs. Hapgood. "Oh, I pity him! That Miss Blakely was a pretty thing, but she has used him very badly. Very badly indeed. As did his friend Mr. Haworth! Only one arm to the man, but he managed to snatch away Miss Blakely all the same. What is the world coming to?

Why, Margaret, we should invite Mr. Waite to supper. We are family now."

Margaret flinched at the idea. "Oh, Mama, I had rather not. We have no host, remember. It would be strange."

Mrs. Turner intervened. "Madam, perhaps it would be better at present to keep your distance. There has been some...talk."

"What talk?" cried Margaret.

"You must not let it trouble you, my dear," Sir Dodkins soothed. "People will do anything for amusement. But there have been some handbills, some illustrations of a lampooning nature. Elopements and jiltings and runaway brides and such. It will pass."

"It is already passing," agreed Mrs. Turner.

Whether that was truly the case or whether her friends only tried to lift her spirits, Margaret's enjoyment of the outing was ruined. She walked the lovely grounds; she admired the Palladian bridge; she asked questions about Ralph Allen and Bath stone, but all the while she felt everyone they encountered stared at the Hapgoods and whispered behind their hands.

It was a great relief to return home.

"Margaret!" shouted a familiar and well-loved voice as they entered. "Margaret! Mama!"

It was Edith, running to welcome them, with the squire behind her! All was forgotten in the joyful reunion, her papa clapping her on the back and shouting, "You've done it, my girl! You've well and truly done it!"

"But Papa," gasped Margaret, when they had their fill of hugging and kissing and hopping up and down, "I only *hope* Uncle Alwyn and Mrs. Waite are married. They should be, by now, but I have no way of knowing."

"They're married all right!" crowed Edith. "For we had a visitor while you were out."

"That woman's son," supplied the squire, beaming. "He called to say he heard from his mother, the new Mrs. Arbuthnot."

"Mr. Waite called?" asked Margaret.

"The wealthy Mrs. Arbuthnot." Her father sighed in deep satisfaction. "Your uncle is now entirely hers to deal with. Too late to cry off now. Not like your old beau there. Was that the baronet I saw drive off?"

Margaret would have liked to enjoy her father's approbation a little longer, but perhaps his delight in Alwyn's marriage would be enough. "Oh, Papa, he is a very good man, but he only felt fatherly toward me after all, and now I think he will soon marry the lady who was with him, a longtime friend closer in age."

To her amazement, her father waved all this away. "Very well, very well. I suppose he was rather old for a girl like you."

"Oh, Papa!" She came and threw her arms around him again. "Then you don't much mind if I return to Bramleigh and take up my duties again? Have you come to take Mama and me home?"

"What? No. You're not going anywhere. When you said Alwyn was vanished but going to be married, I decided we must have a little celebration. Edie and I have come to spend the rest of the lease."

Edith leapt up to grab Margaret by the hands. "Isn't it wonderful! You must show us everything, Margaret. And Papa says we may have ten pounds apiece for pin money! May we go to the Gardens now? Or the art auction?"

"You and I will go to the Gardens," the squire responded, "along with your mother, but Margaret will stay here."

"But why, Papa? I would like to go with you."

"Because that Mr. Waite said he had a particular message he must deliver to you, and he will return soon," answered her father shortly. He was already ringing the bell, which immediately brought Hudgins, as he and Tilly and Flint had been listening outside the door.

Mr. Waite must have word of Charmaine, Margaret realized. She forgot Sydney Gardens at the thought of seeing him again. It had been days. Days of silence and isolation. How had he fared, facing the town gossip and handbills and lampoons alone? (And thanks be to God her father did not seem to know about all that.) If Sir Dodkins had met Mr. Waite outside the King's Bath, he must not have hidden at home, as the Hapgoods did.

She was not left long to wonder.

No sooner had her family set out than Tilly appeared, announcing his arrival.

"Miss Hapgood." He wore his dark blue frock coat and pearl waistcoat and breeches today, colors reflected in his eyes. He was somewhat pale but looked otherwise well. Not like a man heartbroken or hounded about town by gossipmongers, she was glad to see.

Margaret made her curtsey and then said, after a hesitation, "I understand we are truly cousins now."

His grin broke out. "We are, and you sadly cannot decline the connection, though I am become notorious in Bath."

She found herself smiling in response. "I might say the same to you. I hear our families are the talk of the town." Joking with him made her feel lighter already. Perhaps Uncle Alwyn was right: being a nine days' wonder was not so dreadful.

"Sir Dodkins tells me the Blakelys have gone," Margaret went on. "I hope it was not the scandal that drove them to leave."

"Hm? Oh, no. I rather think it was the utter collapse of all their hopes," replied Mr. Waite amiably. "How that Sir Dodkins spreads sunshine wherever he goes. Have I told you he is one of my favorite people?"

Margaret thought he was almost laughing, and she wondered at his high spirits.

When they had taken their seats she said, "My father tells me you called earlier with the news. We do thank you—my uncle is not the most reliable correspondent."

"Then you will reap your first benefit of the match, for my mother is an excellent one. She is likely even now penning a letter to you Hapgoods and encouraging him to add a line in his own hand."

Remembering Mr. Waite's own metaphorical hand in Mr. Haworth's letter, her smile faltered. Oh, right. While Mr. Waite gave every indication of wishing to continue their supposed friendship, in the intervening days, Margaret had come to the opposite decision. She must distance herself from him, she had resolved, because she loved him in spite of all. She must distance herself for her own sake. From his jokes and his false kindness and interest.

"How lovely," she said now. "My papa will be glad to hear it."

Mr. Waite settled back in his chair, crossing his ankles and absently rubbing his weaker limb. "I enjoyed making your father's acquaintance, Miss Hapgood, and I suspect that was your younger sister peering through the window-curtain, though she did not appear
in the drawing room to receive me. After hearing so much about the
Hapgoods of Bramleigh, I look forward eagerly to knowing them
better."

"Yes," said Margaret. "Speaking of Papa, he said you had a particular message for me?"

"Mm." He sat up straighter. Uncrossed his ankles. Ran a distracted hand through his dark hair which altogether rumpled it.

"Was it...from Charmaine?"

"I'm afraid not."

"You have not heard from her, then?"

"No." He made as if to stand, but seeing Margaret still seated, he
only hunched forward, his elbows on his knees. "I did hear from
Haworth, however. They are married as well."

"Mr. Haworth wrote you?" uttered Margaret. "I am astonished
that he dared!"

"Well, of course he dared," Mr. Waite frowned at her. "He is one
of my dearest friends."

Now she was on her feet. "One of your dearest friends?
The—man who wooed away the woman you were engaged to, right
under your nose? He stole her from you!"

He looked relieved to rise himself and thought of coming closer
to her but considered her clenched fists and paused. "Haworth did

woo Charmaine under my nose," he conceded, "but it was with my permission. My express permission."

"*What?*" she nearly shrieked. "Why ever would you grant him permission?"

"Because I didn't love her, and he did," said Mr. Waite simply, holding his palms up. "Charmaine didn't love me either—I'm sure she must have mentioned it to you once or twice—but she was set on marrying me anyway, for all the world's usual reasons. And I was willing to marry her, for all the world's usual reasons, until—until I wasn't."

Margaret felt suddenly light-headed, and she drifted over to the escritoire, that she might put a hand on it for support.

"Haworth did me a very great service, taking her off my hands," he mused. "I'm not sure what I would have done, else. I had crazy thoughts."

He didn't love Charmaine? This was hardly news, to be sure—given Charmaine's constant complaints—but she liked to hear it all the same. *But he doesn't love* anyone, she reminded herself firmly. *It is his lukewarm nature that is the very root of the problem! Only see how he jests about such serious matters. Just as he laughed at you.*

Having buttressed her failing resolve, she raised her chin, prepared to take him to task for his callous treatment of her friend. But she was stopped dead by the look in his eyes. It was the slicing one, and it had its usual effects on her.

"Don't look at me like that," she blurted, holding up an accusing finger.

He came a step closer. "Like what?"

"Like you are trying to slice me in half."

Another step. "My dear Miss Hapgood—or Cousin Margaret, I should say. Why ever would I try to slice you in half?"

"I—don't know," she answered, shaking her finger again. "But you must stop."

He took just one more step.

"I can't," he said.

Then he caught the trembling, upraised finger and pressed the lightest of kisses to its very tip.

Margaret nearly collapsed.

Suddenly she was in his arms, and he was pressing his lips to hers and whispering unintelligibly, urgently, and she was kissing him back, her own arms wrapped around his neck. This went on for some amount of time until Mr. Waite's impaired leg gave out under their combined weight and they tumbled to the floor.

Only then, when he clutched the weakened limb, muttering curses, and she was struggling to clamber from atop him without crippling him further, did Margaret come to her senses. "Good heavens, Mr. Waite! What are we about? Are you all right?"

"No," he said through gritted teeth, "this has ever been your effect on me. But you can help me. Give me your arm."

She obeyed, setting her feet so that she might assist him to stand and holding out her hand. He took it promptly, gave a jerk, and pulled her back on top of him. "Kiss me, Cousin Margaret."

"No—Dashiell—no—stop a moment!" She was panting by this point, her golden-brown hair tumbling loose about them and her lace tucker dangling half out. She scooted away from him and slapped at him when he reached for her again. "You must explain."

He groaned, but he rolled up on his elbow and grinned at her. "Must I? Can't it wait? No—don't pin your hair back up quite yet."

"I must!" said Margaret. "Suppose Tilly or Hudgins were to come in! Suppose my father were to return? He might shoot you."

"That would be rank injustice, then," Dashiell laughed, "for he gave me his permission to speak to you not an hour ago. Said he could hardly keep up with all the gentlemen offering for you."

"You call this offering for me?" Margaret retorted, but she was smiling. She couldn't help but smile. Her heart was bursting—singing!

"Well, I was about to offer for you, only you lunged at me and took my breath clean from me. I haven't faced an attack like that since Salamanca."

"*I* lunged for *you*?" she protested, smacking his wandering hand again. "You had better beware, or I will maim your other leg—I mean limb."

"Never fear, my darling. You have already delivered a fatal wound." He made a fist and thumped it against his chest. "Right through the heart."

"Oh, Dashiell. Do you really love me?"

"Really and truly."

"Then why did you repeat what I said to you at the supper?" she demanded. "You cannot deny it because I know Mr. Haworth used those very words—*my* words—in writing to Charmaine. She showed me his letter! I was so humiliated, so hurt, that you would break my confidence that way."

"Break your confidence?" He sat up and pulled her to him. "Foolish girl—I was desperate. When you spoke those words to me, I knew I loved you. And I knew I was doomed unless I could somehow get rid of Charmaine. Haworth was more than willing to make the attempt to win her, but he knew not how to go about it. So I helped him. If I gave him your words, it was only because they were already burned on my heart. How else could I have repeated them verbatim? I could only give him those words and hope they operated on Charmaine with a fraction the devastation they had on me."

Margaret could voice no response to this because of the lump that had risen in her throat, but she turned loving eyes to him, and Dashiell understandably chose to press his advantage.

It was some time later, when they were seated together on the settee, his arm still about her, that she said, "I have a confession to make, too."

"And what would that be?" he murmured against her hair.

"We came to Bath to find a rich wife for Uncle Alwyn. My family was depending on me. We did not know your mother would be here, but even before we discovered her, my uncle told us he loved her and wanted to marry only her. Therefore, I set out to throw them together." She told him about overhearing Charmaine and Mrs. Blakely at the Sydney Hotel. "That was why we appeared at the theatre that night."

"I am glad you did. But I see my aunt was right to call you conniving."

"She was! At first, at least. But Dashiell, I later felt badly for trying to entrap Mrs. Waite," Margaret persisted, "because I liked you and admired you. I decided I would do no more for Uncle Alwyn, and he must sink or swim on his own."

"Then I too have a confession," he said, drawing a finger along the line of her jaw and over her lips. "I cannot blame you for trying to force a match between them because my mother would never have consented to marry your uncle if I had not encouraged her."

"Yes, Dashiell—you did, and you would not tell me why you changed your mind."

"Wasn't it obvious? I changed my mind because I thought you were going to marry that Sir Dodkins, and I thought I would have to marry Charmaine. I couldn't bear to think we might never see each other again. If my mother married your uncle, I would always have you in my life, to some degree. I asked Alwyn, and he confirmed that he saw all of you Hapgoods at various times throughout the year. So however long and empty my marriage to Charmaine proved, I would at least have perhaps a week every year in your company." He took her chin in his hand and lifted it to look her in the eye. "Now you must be frank with me, Margaret. I know you refused Sir Dodkins—he told me so yesterday—probably terrified by the murderous look I gave him—Did you ever think you might like to marry him? He has money and a good name, to be sure."

"Never, never! I will tell you the whole sorry tale, and you will understand how it came to appear that I was encouraging him." And she did, beginning with the night of the concert, when her mother and Alwyn appeared with their new jewelry, and ending with the baronet's loan. "Charmaine told me Sir Dodkins would feel obliged to offer for me—which he did—and she told me that I must accept him. I could see no way out of it, but Mrs. Turner's longstanding attachment to the baronet proved my salvation at the eleventh hour. While you were matchmaking between Charmaine and Mr. Haworth, I did my best between Sir Dodkins and Mrs. Turner. Thank heavens he admitted he only felt fatherly obligation to me!"

She sighed. "Such a to-do, and all for fifty pounds, not that fifty pounds is nothing."

"Well," said Dashiell, "your story does explain something." Reaching into his waistcoat pocket, he retrieved a folded note, which turned out to be a draft on the Waites' banker. "My mother enclosed this for you in her letter. She said you are to regard it as a wedding present. And, since you have refused to marry Sir Dodkins, she must refer to our own wedding, my dear."

"Dashiell!" Her eyes glowed to see the cheque. "I will thank her right away, my new aunt! Sir Dodkins did not press me for repayment, but I should like to all the same. It will be my wedding present to them." Giving her intended a kiss on the cheek, she made to rise, but he caught her again.

"Come here, my matchless Margaret. You may not move even a foot from me until you name the day we will be married. Unless you prefer to elope. It's quite fashionable, I hear."

Laughing, she poked him. "I think there's been quite enough of that, and if our families are already infamous, a third elopement might lead Mr. King to drive us from Bath."

"When, then?"

"Papa and Edie will be staying for the rest of our lease, so why do we not publish the banns and be married in a month's time? We will need every minute of it to think how to announce it to the Blakelys and Charmaine!"

"Whatever you wish. Though I quake with fear, when I imagine Charmaine's wrath," he grinned. "Uncle Matthew and Aunt Celia are nothing in comparison. When Charmaine hears, the heavens will rain fire and destruction, you know."

"I know," agreed Margaret more soberly. "But I find she likes it better when I stand up to her. I will remind her that, firstly, she chose Mr. Haworth (who adores her); and, secondly, that she is still rich and will now have two estates; and, thirdly—"

"Thirdly?" he prompted.

"Thirdly," blushed Margaret, "that she could never, never, never ever love you like I do."

"I see," he said, gathering her to him again. "Very persuasive, that last reason."

"Do you have a better one?" she whispered.

"I do," he said. "This."

The adventures of the Hapgood family continue with Edith's story in *The Purloined Portrait*.

THE HAPGOODS OF BRAMLEIGH

The Naturalist
A Very Plain Young Man
School for Love
Matchless Margaret
The Purloined Portrait
A Fickle Fortune

THE ELLSWORTH ASSORTMENT

Tempted by Folly
The Belle of Winchester
Minta in Spite of Herself
A Scholarly Pursuit
Miranda at Heart
A Capital Arrangement

PRIDE AND PRESTON LIN

www.christinadudley.com

www.ingramcontent.com/pod-product-compliance
Lightning Source LLC
Chambersburg PA
CBHW031829310726
48972CB00005B/1223

9781963408034